T0387331

Acclaim for

THE HYBRID SERIES

"Readers, start your engines! Candace Kade's final installment of her Hybrid Series does not let off the gas until you're left breathless and cheering at the end. My heart raced as I flew through page after page of this cyberpunk world on the brink of civil war. As stakes grew higher and hope hinged on a hairpin turn, I burned through *Augmented*, crashing headfirst into the Lee Urban fan club—no regrets."

—LYNDSEY LEWELLEN, author of *The Chaos Grid* and *The Crier Stone*

"Kade has done it again with this thrilling ending to The Hybrid Series! *Augmented* left me catching my breath at times and warmed to my core at others. For anyone who struggles with feeling caught between worlds or wrestles to rediscover your true identity, you will find a friend in Urban and her team. Sacrifice, friendship, and the willingness to risk everything for something greater abound in this satisfying ending to the trilogy that had me cheering all the way."

—BRADLEY CAFFEE, author of The Chase Runner Series, *Sides*, and *Captive*

"Race through a futuristic, high-stakes world of alliances and misfits in the conclusion to The Hybrid Series. Fast-paced action scenes will keep you reading late, while deeper questions of destiny and belonging linger long after the final page."

—KATHERINE BRIGGS, author of *The Eternity Gate* and *The Immortal Abyss*

"Unlike anything I've ever read."

—JILL WILLIAMSON, Christy Award-winning author of *By Darkness Hid*

"Don't miss this gripping addition to the [Hybrid] series for an unforgettable adventure!"

—TRICIA GOYER, *USA Today* best-selling author of 90 books

"A must-read for fans of young adult literature and science fiction!"

—LORI LANGDON, author of the Disney Happily Never After Series

"A dystopian world unlike any other I've seen. *Enhanced* has it all—high stakes, mysterious threats, college freshman awkwardness, and a plot that accelerates almost as fast as Urban's motorcycle. This book kept me looking over my shoulder while I turned pages faster than I could read."

—NADINE BRANDES, best-selling author of *The Nightmare Virus, Romanov,* and the Out of Time series

"Pulse-pounding and unique, *Enhanced* is a stunning urban sci-fi debut you won't be able to put down."

—KARA SWANSON, award-winning author of *Dust* and *Shadow* and co-founder of The Author Conservatory

"Author Candace Kade gives us an intriguing premise, complete with an action-packed plot that challenges all of us to consider who we really are. Are we the popularity scores the world gives us, or are we something more? And what will a life of striving for approval cost us? Fans of dystopian and science fiction writing will appreciate Kade's worldbuilding, and anyone looking for heart in the midst of a wild ride will enjoy the read."

—SHANNON DITTEMORE, author of *Winter, White and Wicked* and *Rebel, Brave and Brutal*

"Kade spins an imaginative and futuristic tale of mystery, DNA and danger—don't miss out!"

—NOVA MCBEE, award-winning author of the Calculated series

"Slick and intelligent! Imaginative worldbuilding lays the groundwork for pulse-pounding action . . . A riveting, incredible read. Hop on for this thrill ride!"

—RONIE KENDIG, award-winning author of The Droseran Saga

AUGMENTED

AUGMENTED

THE HYBRID SERIES | BOOK 3

CANDACE KADE

Augmented
Copyright © 2025 by Candace Kade

Published by Enclave Publishing, an imprint of Oasis Family Media, LLC

Carol Stream, Illinois, USA.
www.enclavepublishing.com

All rights reserved. No part of this publication may be reproduced, digitally stored, or transmitted in any form without written permission from Oasis Family Media, LLC.

This is a work of fiction. Names, characters, places, and incidents are products of the author's imagination or are used fictitiously. Any similarity to actual people, organizations, and/or events is purely coincidental.

ISBN: 979-8-88605-222-0 (printed hardcover)
ISBN: 979-8-88605-223-7 (printed softcover)
ISBN: 979-8-88605-225-1 (ebook)

Cover design by Kirk DouPonce, www.DogEaredDesign.com
Typesetting by Jamie Foley, www.JamieFoley.com

Printed in the United States of America.

For Pris.
The future looks good.

01

SHARK ATTACK

I'M THE HYBRID.

Bright sunlight filtered through the waves to where Urban sat under water. Cold ocean brushed up against her skin.

She had been with Lucas on the pleasure cruise ship three weeks, and the truth of who and what she was still hadn't sunk in. Under the full-body wetsuit, Urban shivered at the cold unfamiliarity of her own body. She no longer recognized it.

A Shark Attack Race certainly didn't feel like the most appropriate time or place to experiment with her new Aqua genetics.

Her brother, however, disagreed.

A tremor in the water had Urban whipping her head around. Razored teeth glinted as a shark shot toward the crowd. Urban back-pedaled, trying to put as much of the ocean between her and the approaching beast as possible. Aquas around her screamed and scattered like a panicked school of fish.

At the last second, the great white swerved and headed back toward the racecourse. Urban's heart stopped pounding as Lucas flashed a devious grin before crouching lower on the shark he was riding, urging it to swim faster.

"Go, Lucas!" an Aqua girl next to her cheered, voice slightly garbled underwater.

Beside Urban, Aquas sported a variety of green and blue suits, each shade representing their favorite shark racer. Some even had squid bombs they released, filling the water with vivid colors. Urban found the whole experience of the Shark Attack Race both horrifying and intriguing.

"First race?" the Aqua beside her asked.

Urban nodded.

The Aqua girl, wearing Lucas's mochi green color, pointed. "Look over there. The race course starts on the sandy underwater dunes, and weaves through the obstacles in the giant coral reefs and floating rings, then makes its way toward the surface where the ship is."

Bubbles flew out of the girl's mouth as she spoke.

Urban stared curiously. With her newfound Aqua abilities, she could now communicate, breathe, and smell underwater. Fresh seaweed, and something oddly reminiscent of clam chowder, kept distracting her.

Twelve shark riders rounded out of sight behind the giant cruise ship. The spectators swam to the top of the boat to catch the last part of the race. Urban's fingers hovered near the strap of her stun shield as she followed.

Escaping the experimental lab hadn't erased the pain of what had happened. The bruises on her wrists had faded, and other physical changes weren't visible, but something in her chest remained raw. At least her weapon brought a small level of comfort.

The past few weeks on the pleasure cruise with Lucas seemed to stretch an eternity, and yet they still had one more day before heading back to the Asian Federation. Urban had sent pings to her family and friends, but the pleasure cruise blocked all outside communication until they reached the harbor.

Urban was desperate to let everyone know she was alive and to see to them again. She wondered what being reunited with her family would look like. She'd left on rocky terms. Lillian hadn't spoken with her after Urban had gone against her wishes to seek out their bio parents. Would she still be mad?

And what about Everest? Would he continue to put the cause first?

Urban shoved the thoughts aside as she followed the mass of Aquas onto the ship's top deck.

She wrinkled her nose at the salty brine lacing the surface air. Somehow, the smell was always more potent out in the open. Water splashed under her feet from all the dripping Aquas, but she remained steady against a sandpaper-like textured walkway. With hair still dripping, she followed the masses up to the sunny deck where the Shark Attack Race finished on the surface. The ocean stretched in all directions, encircling the ship's platform.

Her brother had caught up to the other racers and was now in third place.

"How do they train the sharks?" Urban asked, turning back to the girl.

"They are a special breed genetically engineered for the purpose of racing," she explained. "The sharks are bigger than normal great whites and have brain enhancements that make them docile for riding. Genius, right?"

Urban nodded as she refocused on the race.

Lucas rode with one foot on each pectoral fin, his Aqua grip boots keeping him steady. His hands clung to the tip of the shark's dorsal fin as it split out of the water. The other riders did likewise, their heads breaking the surface followed by the tip of their shark's fins as they zigzagged their way around floating barrels, a robotic octopus with flailing tentacles, and jellyfish the size of Extended Reality Domes.

The cheering grew louder.

A jumbotron at the center of the cruise ship projected each racer's position in real time. Several patrons nervously downed fruity florescent drinks and eyed the holo gambling boards, no doubt checking their "investments."

It was unbelievable the number of illegal activities that took place on the cruise ship. Urban had seen more than she wanted of performance enhancers, gambling of every possible variety, and false identities. The faces around her ranged from mild kitties, to humans with exotic facial features, to fierce predators—all of them holo projections.

To keep safe, Urban had also accepted a false identity from Lucas. She still cringed when her brother introduced her. Even the name he'd booked her room under, Gasair Minnie, was designed to inflict maximum humiliation.

Catching her reflection in a mirror, Urban sighed. She had long eyelashes that tangled in her hair. Her face was eclipsed by a giant nose and eyes which protruded like that of a bulldog, a look only amplified by her heavy-handed eyeliner. It was altogether mortifying—exactly what Lucas was going for. But Urban refused to give him the satisfaction of letting him see her embarrassment. At least no one on the ship gave her a second glance.

Lucas had, fortunately, spared a few extra crypto points to buy new clothes, so she didn't have to wear the ridiculous cat costume he'd given her. She didn't dare access her own account for fear of alerting Supers Against Soups or any of the other organizations hunting for her whereabouts.

Ever since escaping the underwater prison, she'd been more vigilant. At least, that's what she told herself as she remained wide awake in bed each night, unable to sleep.

She'd also purchased a few of the illegal ink bombs that were in abundant supply on the ship. Just in case. They'd proven an excellent distraction when Lucas had rescued her.

Urban still couldn't believe everything that had happened the past few months.

She was glad to be free, of course. But a small voice at the back of her head whispered that she wasn't much better off. That her life would never be the same again.

She longed to be on dry land again—away from all the Aquas and the constant reminder of her new Hybrid genetics and the weighty burden that came with it.

Surviving capture had made her stronger, but it came with a price. Something deep within Urban had shattered.

It was in the way she studied people, each encounter cloaked in suspicion. The way her eyes darted, constantly alert to her surroundings. Her perspective of the world had shifted, turning reality into a string of dangerous uncertainties.

The only thing that was clear to Urban was the need to get off the ship—away from the underwater research lab.

I'm not safe until I'm far, far away from all forms of water.

There was a shout as the racers came back into view.

Lucas launched an ink bomb, devouring the racer in front of him in a cloud of black. The racer crashed into a barrel and Lucas slipped past him into second place.

The giant projected scoreboard updated amid cheers and curses.

The racers drew near the end, speeding toward a pulsing red line projected over the water. With the surface obstacles out of the way, Lucas and the other racer darted back under the waves to gain speed. Their figures became nothing more than shadows streaking toward the finish line.

It looked like Lucas was gaining on the first rider, but it was hard to tell as blackness swallowed them. Urban thought Lucas had activated another ink bomb but then noticed a strange dark shadow moving with them.

An Aqua looked up and screamed. Another shrieked and stumbled into Urban, scrambling to get away. Urban also looked up.

Above, a creature the size of a killer whale swept through the sky. Its head and chest were that of a lion, but it had two large wings that stemmed from its back and converged into a spiked tail. Its sandy mane blew in the wind as it lifted its head and pierced the air with an animalistic roar. Fire streaked across the sky.

Pandemonium broke out as the creature touched down on the ship's wet deck. The Aquas knocked each other over in their haste to escape. The beast ignored the chaos as it advanced—straight toward Urban.

02

GAMELYON

URBAN STARED AT THE CREATURE AND A MEMORY returned. Back in the Western Federation, when she was competing in the arena against the Scorpions, her suit deflated around her, the crossbow aimed at her heart, ready for the kill shot. A giant beast with kind golden eyes had swooped down. Then she was safe.

Tiana! Urban's eyes widened. *It's the Gamelyon!*

The majestic creature stopped directly in front of her. Pawing the ground, it snorted and shook its mane. Then it stared, watching her with attentiveness. Its massive scaled tail thumped behind it.

Was it . . . wagging?

It had to be the same one that saved Urban in the AI Games. Then again, were there any other Gamelyons? Genetically modified creatures typically weren't allowed in the wild for fear of destroying existing ecosystems. They were only designed for the games. *So, what is it doing so far from the stadium?*

Urban blinked. *And how does it recognize me with this identity scrambler?*

The creature stepped closer, lowering its head. Its huge, glossy body shimmered in the light of the sun, layers of thick fur tumbling down its neck, stopping at its tail. Warm breath huffed toward her from its long snout.

Urban tentatively pressed her hand to the Gamelyon's wet muzzle. The creature looked up with understanding and intelligence in its golden eyes. She stroked it across the head, fingers raking through its coarse fur. She breathed in the familiar scent of damp animal and charred wood.

Everyone around her was screaming and running for cover—the Shark Races and associated winnings all but forgotten. Urban felt distant from the chaos and ignored the other Aquas. Soon, only she and the powerful creature remained.

"What are you doing here?" she mused.

As if in answer, the Gamelyon extended one of its dragon-like talons where a hand-written note was tied. Urban read it aloud. "A gift for Lee, Urban." The five words were scrawled in messy and smudged handwriting. There was no signature at the bottom or any indication of who had sent it.

"A gift? What does that mean?" Urban asked, but the creature only shook its mane. It pawed at the ground again, and Urban got the impression it was waiting for her to do something. She took a step back in surprise. "You want me to climb on, don't you?"

The Gamelyon's massive tail thumped the deck, sending a tremor through it.

Urban thought back to the last time she'd ridden the creature in the stadium. She'd won the games for her team. Being on the back of such a powerful creature made her feel invincible, powerful, and alive.

She'd been desperate for a way off the ship, and here it was, staring her in the face. *If I flew home, I could be reunited with my family immediately.* Not to mention, she would be safe in the air—away from water and her attackers.

Something at the back of her mind questioned who the gift was from and whether it was safe to accept, but she ignored it.

Urban stepped cautiously forward, fingers stroking the creature's muscled back. Halfway down, it changed from fur to worn scales. Part lion. Part dragon. An engineering marvel.

"Urban?"

Her head snapped up. Lucas stood on the deck, dripping wet, his dark eyes full of worry.

"What are you doing?" Her brother crept cautiously toward her.

Urban couldn't help but be surprised. Lucas had pretty much ignored, despised, and made fun of her for most of their lives. How strange it was to have him suddenly concerned for her safety. Their newfound understanding had changed some things but not everything.

"I'm leaving," Urban told him.

The Gamelyon bared its teeth and Lucas froze. "On that? Right now?"

"I have things to do." Her answer sounded weak, but it was true.

But Lucas was surveying Urban closely. "You're running away."

"And you wouldn't know anything about that." Urban was suddenly defensive, though she didn't know why. Her brother always knew how to get under her skin.

"Oh, I'm an expert at running away from problems," Lucas admitted. "Which is why I'm pretty good at recognizing it," he added pointedly.

Urban swung her leg over the Gamelyon. "I'm not running away from anything. Just going back home the faster and safer route."

Lucas shot her a knowing look. "Keep telling yourself that."

03

JINGCHA

URBAN DUG HER HEELS INTO THE SCALES of the creature's side, hoping it would understand her command.

The Gamelyon responded immediately and ran down the deck away from Lucas, leaping over the railing of the ship. Urban's stomach dropped as they plummeted toward the ocean. With a jolt, the creature unfurled its wings, and they soared above the sparkling blue water. Its talons grazed the ocean, shooting plumes of water around them, then they launched upward toward the clouds.

Soaring far above, she looked down at the boat fading in the distance. Guilt pricked her. Maybe she shouldn't have left her brother, especially after he'd made a genuine attempt to repair their relationship. Not to mention, if it weren't for him, she would have been recaptured by the underwater research lab . . . or worse.

But she had enough on her mind with being the hybrid and returning to the Asian Federation from the dead. At lcast, that's what the news was sure to think, and maybe even the rest of her family.

Lillian. Mother. Father.

It had been so long since she'd seen them. Months. And during that time, she'd traveled the world with the Dragons, competed in the AI games and won, been targeted multiple times and nearly killed, then betrayed by Coral and trapped in an underwater prison and experimented on. So much had changed.

As they climbed upward, the water glittered far below, beautiful, bright, and blinding.

Urban left her worries behind and closed her eyes, breathing in the fresh air. This high above the ocean, only a hint of salty sea spray remained. The wind whipped her hair behind and caressed her cheeks. Beneath her, the warm, muscled body of the Gamelyon moved rhythmically.

A sense of freedom soared through her as they flew over the endless waves.

She wasn't sure how much time passed. Eventually, the sun set and the sky darkened around them. The air grew chilly, and wispy clouds hid the emerging moon from sight. Land appeared, and with it, Urban's thoughts went to what awaited her there.

Danger.

She'd thought she'd be safe once she was back on solid ground, but now that she drew nearer to it, she was reminded of all the attacks on her life that had happened there too. From Blossom and the Deadly Five, to SAS bugging the Lees' house and trying to trap her, to purple zones, Coral's hacking, and betrayals.

"Is anywhere safe?" Urban asked the Gamelyon.

The creature didn't respond.

At least on land, she would have her family and guard back. At the thought, she checked her retina display. A jolt of excitement zipped through her as she blinked back online again for the first time in months.

Without the cruise ship blocking outside contact, she was free to message her family and Everest. She couldn't believe she hadn't thought of that until now. She could let them know she was alive and on her way to New Shanghai. They would probably arrive about the same time she would and could take her to safety. After that . . . well, she could figure out a plan later.

But she knew she wouldn't be able to escape it much longer. Decisions would need to be made about what being the hybrid meant for her body, her family, Advancements in Enhancements—the world.

Decisions she didn't want to think about.

Urban accessed the local news network to see what she'd missed. None of the headlines were good.

[New Shanghai Riots Break Out
After Natural is Murdered by SAS]

[Protests Shut Down by Local *Jingcha*
After Two Enhanced Politicians "Die in Sleep"]

[Violence. . . The New Norm?]

[Will the Asian Federation Take After
the Western Federation's Civil War?]

Urban stared at the last headline.

Civil War?

Surely the news was exaggerating. She thought back to one of the last times she'd seen Everest. They were in the Western Federation and he told her about the challenges the local AiE members faced. He mentioned civil war as a potential outcome if Naturals and Enhanced couldn't reconcile soon, but she hadn't seriously considered the possibility.

Now, it looked like things in the Asian Federation had escalated as well.

How have things gotten bad so quickly? And what will they do if they know the hybrid exists? Her stomach knotted. *Will it help or make things worse?*

Urban's head was still spinning with the possibilities as New Shanghai sparkled to life in the distance. Its skyscrapers shimmered with neon lights and festive colors.

She had forgotten what time of year it was. The last time she'd been in the Asian Federation, it had been Lunar New Year. But now, instead of the buildings displaying festive crimson, it was replaced by green, white, yellow and russet, the lucky colors of the upcoming Dragon Boat Festival.

What else had she missed since she'd been gone? It seemed like ages since she'd been in the Asian Federation.

As the holo projected ads and characters came into view, Urban realized it was time to steer clear of the city and head for border control. She guided the creature toward the structure, but the Gamelyon paid her no heed.

"Hey!" Urban pulled tight against its furry mane, attempting to turn it, but again with no success.

All enhanced animals had to go through a special division of border control before entering or exiting the Federations. A couple years ago, someone had smuggled in a mutant animal and nearly destroyed the New Fujian ecosystem. Breaking this law was serious.

Urban made several more forceful attempts to change course, but the Gamelyon flew on nonetheless.

Where are we headed?

Using her AI map's routing prediction feature, a pulsing green arrow overlaid on reality. It showed them headed toward a park at the Metropolis' edge. It had a low sosh and probably wasn't in use anymore.

Why is the Gamelyon taking me there? This seemed like a bad idea.

Suddenly, Urban's retina display pinged a warning.

<Citizen, disembark your illegal animal and report to city officials immediately.>

Urban blinked the message away and quickly scanned the ground beneath her. Sure enough, trailing them was a red and black vehicle with the gold hammer and sickle. A military Flyer aimed something up at her.

Another warning appeared.

<Citizen, this is your last warning. Turn in your illegal animal and report immediately to local immigration authorities.>

They must not know who I am because my illegal identity scrambler is still on. I should take it off.

She hesitated.

If she did, she still wouldn't be able to control the Gamelyon, and then they'd know exactly who was breaking the law. She would be reported, and the news would blow up. She couldn't handle that attention right now. Perhaps there was a chance she could get the Gamelyon under control and avoid this whole mess.

Urban was still weighing her options when another ping arrived.

<Citizen, a warrant for your capture and arrest has been issued.>

"Whaaaaa—"

Before she could think, a bright flash lit up the sky.

Instinctively, the Gamelyon dove. Above them, a neutral-beam injector zipped past where they'd just been.

Soldiers. Weapons. Capture.

Urban's mind grew hazy with panic. It was like being back in the underwater prison.

No. I won't be captured again.

She tightened her grip on the matted fur of the Gamelyon.

"Go!" she screamed.

The creature needed no encouragement as it winged its way toward the darkened park. Wind whistled in her ears, the only sound in the eerie silence that engulfed them.

Until an electrical power up noise emanated from the ground below.

The Gamelyon dipped sharply and out of range of the next NBI attack. At a flurry of *pops*, the creature spun and twisted, dodging each one. Urban's stomach began to grow queasy.

The trees beneath them came into sharp focus as they neared

the ground. But there was something else there too. Flashing gold lights.

Urban groaned.

A whole fleet of autonomous *Jingcha* vehicles crashed through brush and flew over rocks, chasing her.

"Citizen, land immediately and turn yourself in to local authorities," a robotic voice ordered over a voice enhancer.

Urban guided the Gamelyon away from the main road and over the thicker part of the forest. The flashing lights slowed but didn't stop their pursuit.

The Gamelyon's muscled and scaly sides grew slick with sweat from exertion, and Urban's arms burned from holding on. She sensed they couldn't go on like this much longer.

A small, inky lake surrounded by thick foliage came into view. A worn-down pagoda stood alone on a small island at the center of the water. The moon broke free from behind the clouds and bathed the clearing in gentle white light. All around the lake, decrepit hover coasters, aerial carousels, solar raceways, and other rides sagged under the weight of age and rust.

As they flew over the water, a new sound came from behind them. It wasn't the powering up of the missiles but an electric hum. Urban turned to look just as there was a *swish*.

A giant arrow shot through the sky and struck the Gamelyon in its hindquarters. The beast roared. She gasped as electricity zipped up her spine and blue tendrils jerked across the creature's body.

The Gamelyon suddenly seized up, its wings stopping their beating.

They fell from the sky.

Urban peered down.

The lake was a long way down. She braced herself as the water rushed up to meet them.

At the last second, Urban leaped off the Gamelyon, straightened her limbs, and pinched her nose shut.

The jolt of the warm water shuddered through her stronger

than a NBI blast. And then she was sinking.

For a moment, the terror of being underwater clawed at her. But then she opened her eyes and inhaled slowly. Fresh lake water filled her lungs, so different from the salty brine she'd grown used to in the ocean.

I'm an Aqua now.

She steadied her breathing before searching the water for the Gamelyon and spotted the beast thrashing at the top of the lake. From her vantage point below, it looked like a mythical sea creature surrounded by a halo of moonlight.

She felt an odd sense of protectiveness for it, but there wasn't anything she could do. *It's not mine and it's not going to drown. That's what matters.*

Forcing herself to turn away, she focused on her more pressing concern. Escape.

The lake was murky and dark this time of night. She wondered if there was anything else alive in the water around her and shuddered.

She touched down at the base, bare feet squelching in the cold mud—she'd forgotten her shoes on the ship. Slowly, she waded on the bottom of the lake toward what she hoped was land. Between the mud and the water weighing her movements down, it was slow going.

Brilliant light exploded above her.

Urban shielded her eyes against the spotlight.

She lifted her feet and began swimming quickly, heading away from the light.

Gradually, the lake sloped upward, and she sloshed her way onto land. She could see the Gamelyon had been subdued. Flyers hovered over the water's surface with spotlights swaying from side to side.

"Unknown citizen," the robotic voice intoned. "Come out and report to local authorities immediately."

Urban crept toward the forest, grateful the moon was once again hidden behind the clouds. Mud squeezed between her toes.

"Freeze!" a female voice ordered.

Urban's eyes widened as she noticed the *Jingcha* several meters away. The Flyer unfurled her giant wings and flew toward Urban. *No chance of outrunning her on land.*

Urban's pulse pounded erratically. Without thinking, she darted back toward the water, but before she could make it, the Flyer slammed into her, lifting her off her feet.

She landed hard on her back, the wind knocked out of her. Urban stared up at the darkened sky, disoriented.

She shook her head to try and clear it. And instantly, her jiu-jitsu training kicked in. Her mind raced through options. However, with so many *Jingcha* crawling all over the place, her best shot was to get away as fast as possible and hide.

"Over here!" the Flyer shouted at the other *Jingcha*. "We found her!"

Urban kicked out at the Flyer, catching her in the chin. The woman grunted in pain and Urban used the space to roll away.

Leaping to her feet, she darted across a road.

A Super stepped out from the trees, stun gun extended, blocking her path.

Urban didn't have time to react before pain exploded in her shoulder. She cried out, but there was no sound.

I can't move.

Her body seized and she fell to the ground, rigid.

The Super was already by her side and yanked her into his chest. The other hand pressed a weapon to her cheek. "Don't move."

As if she could.

"We got her," he yelled.

Urban breathed heavily, mind whirling with possibilities. None of them good.

Soon, *Jingcha* swarmed the space. Lights blinded her, weapons snapped with electricity, and the air buzzed with talking.

Someone shoved Urban to the ground, the Zeolite-coated road cutting into her face. Nano cords bit into her wrists as her hands were bound behind her back.

Panic overwhelmed her senses.

Captured.

She breathed shallowly.

I must get free.

She was barely aware her captors were talking again.

"Who is it?" one of the *Jingcha* asked.

"Let's find out."

Someone ripped off the tiny chip on her forehead. Instantly, the projected image of Gasair Minnie disappeared, replaced by Urban's real face.

There was a moment of silence while the *Jingcha* scanned Urban using their retina display. Then a whistle. "Looks like we caught a ghost."

04

无家

PRISON

PRISON IN NEW SHANGHAI WASN'T AT ALL what Urban expected. The cell reminded her more of a party lounge.

She gingerly touched her sore shoulder and examined her surroundings for what felt like the tenth time that day.

The door to her cell was metal, with a large reinforced window imbedded in it. Urban peered through it several times, but all she could see was a brightly lit and empty corridor beyond. Above the window, a projected room number displayed "KOL CELL 3112".

Is there really a wing of prison just for Key Opinion Leaders? That would explain the décor.

The walls surrounding her were black with flecks of paint that sparkled like stars on a dark night. A flaming pink, bedazzled loveseat sat against a corner, with an accompanying hover footstool. There was a metal coffee table and a queen bed overflowing with soft comforters and fluffy pillows.

Urban opened a mini fridge that hummed quietly near the door. It was stocked with glasses of water and health bars made of crickets. She made a face. She wasn't *that* hungry.

The room was decorated with projections of virtual flickering candles, a painting, even a full tea set and tray. Urban was sorely disappointed to find the latter not real. *I could use a good cup of tea about now.*

Despite having prior experience with escaping unwanted prison cells, Urban couldn't even begin to think of a way to get out.

With her identity being found out, she'd eventually be tracked down again anyway. She'd have to stay on the run. That is, unless she wanted to remain a fugitive of the law forever—which she didn't.

She thought about her options for leaving legally. Wasn't she allowed to ping a family member or see a lawyer or something? At least, that's how it always worked in the vids. So why had she been left alone in her cell all day?

She wondered if the *Jingcha* knew about her status as the hybrid. And if that was why no one had come.

This is all a big misunderstanding.

She kicked at a cabinet and nearly lost her balance, realizing too late it was just a holo decoration.

How is it I went from being a good sosh-abiding citizen to captured and thrown in a cell twice within the year? Coral's betrayal hadn't been her fault. But this . . .

"Stupid, stupid, stupid," she muttered. "What was I thinking?"

"You weren't."

Urban's head jerked up. A visitor peered at her through the window at the door. She'd thought her cell was soundproof, but his voice came through crisp and clear.

"You weren't thinking," he clarified. The man shifted, revealing the two security-bots next to him. "Allow me to introduce myself. I'm Mako, President of Croix."

Urban blinked.

Croix was her biggest sponsor. *Was* being the key word.

Disappearing for months on end at the bottom of the ocean without responding had a tendency to end contracts like that. Urban assumed they'd forgotten about her long ago. What was the president of the company doing here at her prison cell?

The man before her was short and skinny for an Enhanced.

But his eyes sparked with embers of passion. He looked around late forties but had his hair cut into the latest trend and wore holo projected glasses. His distressed black jeans and tailored smart top fit him perfectly. He certainly looked the part of the rebel brand leader.

Urban tucked a strand of hair behind her ears and smoothed her prison suit, suddenly self-conscious of her appearance.

"May I come in?" Mako asked.

"Uh . . . sure."

With a hiss, the locking mechanism released and the door slid away. The security-bots entered first, with Mako following. There was a commanding and calming presence about him that made Urban immediately offer him the best seat in the room.

Mako waved her offer away then turned to one of the security-bots. "Tea?"

The bot's abdomen popped open revealing a teapot and several cups inside the storage compartment.

Urban gaped. *If I'd known a month ago I'd be having tea with the president of Croix in a prison cell . . .*

"Here you are, sir," the bot said.

Mako reached in and retrieved the teapot to set it on the table, along with two porcelain cups, and poured them each a drink. He took a seat, the hover stool dipping slightly, before he motioned Urban toward the loveseat.

Urban hesitantly sat and then reached for the tea. The warmth of the cup instantly seeped into her hands, lending her a sense of calm.

Urban waited for the president of Croix to speak.

He took his time, sipping his drink and studying her. "I have to admit, we weren't sure we'd ever see you again. So, when an informant told me you were in this holding cell, I hardly believed it. I had to come see for myself."

Urban remained silent. *Is this some sort of trap? He shouldn't have found me here. Unless maybe the news covered it?* She tried not to think about that possibility. *What else does he know? More importantly, what does he want?*

"I imagine you're wondering how I knew you were here?"

Is he an Inceptor? That was silly. Anyone would ask that question. But she tried to pull up Gene-IQ to scan his enhancements anyway, forgetting her retina display was deactivated in the cell.

"I have my sources," Mako went on. "I've been keeping an eye out, should you choose to return to society again. Though, I wasn't expecting such a spectacular entrance."

Urban grimaced. "Would you believe it if I told you I wasn't either?"

Mako threw his head back and laughed a long, genuine laugh, during which Urban shifted uncomfortably in her seat.

When he spoke again, a smile played at the corner of his lips. "I like you." He took a long sip of his tea then set it down. "Which brings me to why I'm here. I'd like to offer you a new contract with Croix. As I'm sure you're aware, your last contract was voided after you disappeared and failed to perform your KOL duties."

Mako held up his hand as if to ward off any excuses Urban might offer. "I don't need to know your reasons. But I am here to personally extend a renewed contract."

Urban stared at him in surprise.

Finally, she found her voice. "Why do you want to sponsor me?" She opted for directness. "I'm in prison. Doesn't that mean I'm in trouble?"

Mako chuckled. "Oh, you certainly are in trouble. Big trouble."

Urban swallowed.

"That's why we're so interested in continuing your sponsorship."

Urban nearly choked.

"As you know, Croix is a brand for rebels. Athletes. World changers. Within the span of a few months, you have managed to single-handedly destroy PKU's AI in the tryouts, win the games against the Scorpions, disappear, then return from the dead riding a Gamelyon. Can you see how this aligns with our brand?" He leaned back as if resting his case. "You're perfect."

Urban remained silent a moment, considering.

"If it helps with your decision," Mako said, "we're prepared to offer you the lead sponsorship role, which means double the pay."

Urban's jaw dropped, and she hastily closed it.

"Should you choose to accept, we'd also like you to compete in Race to the Clouds."

Urban blanched. Her father had competed in RTC back in his day, and it was still one of the most dangerous races in the world. Not to mention that most contestants trained for years before trying out. And she wasn't a race car driver. She didn't stand a chance.

"We've already put in your application and qualified your vehicle," Mako continued. "Though you can, of course, select a different vehicle to compete in. And you don't need to win, or even qualify. In fact, you don't have to participate at all, if you don't want to. Just trying out alone will garner the media attention and PR we'd like and result in a bonus for you."

Urban blinked. This was a lot to take in. A darker thought crossed her mind.

"What about—what about Vance?" she asked, remembering she wasn't the only KOL Croix supported. Vance, the Scorpion's lead, tried to kill her on multiple occasions. He was involved with the organization that kidnapped and experimented on her. She shuddered at the thought.

"We cut his contract." Mako frowned. "Due to confidentiality agreements, I can't discuss the details, but he no longer works with us."

Urban took a sip of tea to collect herself. Then she put her cup down. "I appreciate your generous offer. Can I take some time to think about it?"

"Of course, of course." Mako rose to his feet. "I've occupied enough of your time. I'll let you go. I just wanted to get a word in before your next visitors arrive."

Her pulse quickened. "Next visitors?"

"A Mr. Lee Byronne and Mrs. Zhou Flora?"

Urban inwardly grimaced but forced a smile. "Thanks."

Mako dipped his head then left.

No sooner was he out the door, when a woman shoved her way past the security-bots and into the room. Even visiting a prison, she was impeccably dressed in a gold smart suit, heels, jewels covering her wrists, and with silky black hair pulled up into her signature tight bun. Not a wisp of hair escaped.

Her lips thinned as she saw Urban, and she stilled.

"Mother?" Urban whispered.

To Urban's surprise, instead of a lecture, her mother moved quickly forward and soon held Urban in a tight hug.

Gratefully, she hugged her mother in return. Mother's body was like a warm cocoon of safety.

An unexpected surge of tears began to stream down Urban's cheeks. The emotions she'd kept pent up since she'd escaped the research lab all came rushing in. Regret. Anger. Guilt. Pain. And that unfamiliar, ever-present brokenness.

"I'm sorry, Mother. I'm so sorry," Urban repeated over and over, now completely sobbing. "I never should have left."

Mother gently stroked Urban's hair. "It's okay. You're safe now." Her normally overpowering Bulgarian rose perfume now carried a comforting presence.

Why did I ever think leaving my family was the answer to my problems? Urban pressed her wet cheek against her mother's soft smart suit.

"Did I miss the party?" a voice boomed.

Urban and her mother separated in time for Father to barrel toward them. He stopped when he was directly in front of Urban, as if suddenly unsure of himself. He extended a hand.

Urban took it and they shook.

"It's good to see you, Urban." His voice held a faint touch of emotion.

"You too, Father."

Urban's eyes latched on a figure lurking in the corner, hesitating. *Lillian.*

Urban's breath caught. She hadn't seen her sister since leaving for the Western Federation, a decision Lillian had made very clear she disapproved of. Urban had received the silent treatment since then.

Lillian's wide brown eyes stared at Urban, as if unbelieving she was really there. Her perfectly proportioned black eyebrows pinched together, and water filled her eyes. Then she was running and crushing Urban in a vise-like hug, a muffled sob escaping her. Urban had rarely seen her older sister cry. Not when they were bullied in the orphanage. Not when they were adopted. Not even when Lillian's migraines rendered her bedridden.

They cried together.

Lillian gradually released Urban. "You're—you're alive." Her face crumpled and then she was pulling Urban back into her embrace. "We all thought you were dead."

Finally, Lillian eased away, inhaling a deep, steadying breath.

"Lillian. I've missed you so much," Urban gulped.

Her sister lifted her gaze and smiled.

"We want to hear everything that happened." Mother eyed the room suspiciously. "But somewhere . . . else. We've alerted the staff at our New Shanghai summer condo we'll be arriving soon for a short stay."

"Let's see about bailing you out of here." Father turned to one of the security-bots.

Urban smiled.

"Don't think this means you're not in trouble," Mother added, wiping the smile right off Urban's face.

They made their way toward check out, but the security-bot waved them on. "Lee Urban, your stay has already been taken care of."

Father frowned and exchanged a glance with Mother.

Urban's legs grew shaky. *Who else knows I was here?*

With thoughts still spinning, Urban found herself leaving the prison facilities sitting in a Wasp G6, accompanied by two

Supers, a security-bot, and her family.

Urban snapped to the present. She spoke the question that had been plaguing her. "Everest, is he . . ."

"He's fine," Mother said. "No one suspects he's a Natural. He's been doing quite well for himself, actually."

Urban let out a sigh of relief. Then another thought crossed her mind. "About Everest and our dating charade—"

"Don't worry about that."

"No . . ." Urban hesitated. "I was going to tell you. . . it wasn't always a charade. We dated for real before Lunar New Year."

"I know."

"You—you knew?" Urban stammered.

Mother's lips twitched. "Do you really think you could hide something like that from your own mother? I knew the second you started whistling around the house something had changed. With a little investigating, it was easy enough to figure out."

Urban blushed.

"I'm still displeased you thought it wise to deceive me." Mother gave Urban a sharp look before continuing. "But I knew all along. He's a good one, that Everest."

Everest. The thought had Urban jolt upright. *I can finally reach him!* She sent Everest a ping letting him know she was safe.

The response was almost immediate. A location request.

Urban glanced at her family before rejecting it and sending Everest a ping instead.

[Urban: Can't talk right now. Long story. Meet soon when I'm back in New Beijing?]

[Everest: YOU'RE OK. I've been searching all over the world for you. Let's meet ASAP once we're both back in New Beijing. How about here?]

A map location in the Outskirts dropped, and Urban accepted it.

Warmth filled Urban's heart, and she found herself smiling giddily at the device.

[Urban: Sounds good. Can't wait to see you!]

[Everest: You have no idea . . .]

[Everest: You better not be late.]

[Everest: I'll keep blowing up your pings until you arrive or your AI advisory-bot runs out of capacity to sort all my messages. ;)]

Urban sent him a laughing response and blinked out of dual reality mode, even as more pings from Everest came in.

The thought of seeing him again filled her with delight. But then it evaporated at the thought of what she would have to tell him.

What will he think once he finds out I'm the hybrid?

She swallowed hard.

This changes everything.

05

无家

FAMILY

THE AUTONOMOUS VEHICLE SCREECHED to a stop in the middle of a street. Shiny buildings surrounded them, and up above, drones and Flyers zipped in an orderly line, navigating the Metropolis skies with ease.

But on the ground, a group of Naturals with face shields and identity scramblers obscuring their faces charged across a crowded road. Vehicles slammed to a stop or swerved to avoid hitting them. The pedestrians held holo signs with varying messages and images declaring freedom and showing grotesque images of Enhanced dying. Some shook their fists at the Flyers up above.

Urban stared slack-jawed. "What's going on?"

Mother tucked a wisp of escaped hair from her immaculate bun. "Things have become . . . complicated since you've been gone. Naturals want equality and are taking drastic measures to get it."

"Is AiE making any progress?"

"Not fast enough. Some people are turning to violence, and like the West, a fissure is splitting even the Advancements in Enhancements." Her brow wrinkled. "I worry for the unity of its members."

Everest told Urban one of the key topics at the AiE Summit

in the West was how to keep participants without succumbing to violence. More and more of its members were joining rogue sects that used gruesome measures to attract the attention, and change, they wanted.

And look where it had gotten them.

Civil war.

If the Asian Federation was headed down the same path . . .

Their vehicle accelerated again. The downtown Metropolis of New Shanghai glowed with iridescent light. Familiar luxury stores, holo ads, and hoverdrones flew by. Urban thought its downtown felt similar to New Beijing, only more humid and with additional foreign shops.

Soon, they arrived at the Financial and Trade Zone luxury condos. A rose gold metallic building shot into the sky. Large pillars lined the entrance, and several Supers clad in shiny smart armor stood at attention. After scanning Father's tatt, the guards waved them inside.

Their party rode an elevator to the 121st floor and exited into an empty marble hallway with a large doorway at the end of it. Father scanned his tatt again, and the family made their way past several waiting maids holding warm towelettes. Urban accepted one and tried to pat herself down, aware she hadn't showered since she'd left the cruise ship.

This house was slightly smaller than their home in New Beijing but still spacious by Metropolis standards. The living room boasted three-story reinforced glass that covered the entire side of one wall. Beyond the window, the ocean raged against the shoreline. Its endless battle was peaceful in the setting sun's soft rays.

Urban caught the scent of oolong and seaweed as they entered. Mother's heels clicked sharply across the marble floors as she made her way to a large curved couch. Lucas came wandering into the room crunching seaweed and sipping tea.

How did he get here so fast? Was I really in prison that long?

"Finally." He set the plate down on the table.

"Lucas!" Mother stood. "How was your semester abroad?"

Urban locked eyes with her brother. She had found out his "semester abroad" was little more than a party trip on the pleasure cruise. Thankfully for her, his stint on the ship ended up saving her life.

While she didn't agree with many of Lucas's decisions, Urban wasn't going to rat him out. She tried not to laugh at the panic in her brother's eyes.

Lucas offered his most charming smile aimed at Mother and Father. "Delightful." His gaze shifted back to Urban. "Good to see you again, Sis." He offered her a hug, which she gratefully accepted, awkward as it was.

Lucas sniffed the air. "You smell like a swamp."

"And there's the Lucas we all know and love." Lillian plopped onto the couch. "I was starting to worry."

Urban had forgotten what being with her family was like. They weren't perfect, but neither was she. And they meant all the more to her now.

Pain and regret ached in her chest. *There's nothing I can do to change the past. But there's still much to fix in the present.*

Something soft brushed against Urban's waist. Looking down, she saw nothing at first. Then, slowly, a huge white cat with bright purple spots shimmered into view.

"Baozi!" Urban tried to scoop up her cat, but it squirmed away to rub against Lucas's legs, most likely due to the snack he was now eating.

Lucas pushed Baozi away. "What is Urban's annoying cat doing here?"

"Is Jiaozi here too?" Lillian searched the room hopefully.

"Your cat is back in New Beijing," Mother said. "We thought it would be a nice welcome home gift for Urban to have her pet."

Steaming cups of jasmine pearls were placed before them on a handcrafted rosewood table by a maidbot. They settled on the couch while Father slumped with exhaustion into a seat. Lucas sipped his tea deliberately, no doubt hoping not to get questioned further about his semester abroad. Mother's immaculate fingernails tapped the table.

Urban swallowed, bracing herself for the questions and the lecture to come.

"You did a foolish thing, throwing yourself into danger by going to the Western Federation and then returning and running away from the local authorities," Mother said. "But what's done is done."

Urban stared in surprise. *That's it? No verbal lashing? No reinstallation of that abominable safe child app?*

Mother eyed her sharply. "You're eighteen now. You have to learn sooner or later to live with the consequences of your actions. Now"–she settled back–"tell us what happened."

Urban hesitated.

I'm the hybrid. What if they reject me? I'm not one of them. But they're my family. Besides, I've never shared their genes.

She had to tell them. With a sense of relief, she spent the next few hours explaining everything. Since she'd been out of contact since leaving the Asian Federation, she started there. Finding her fake bio dad, being thrown into the games, their Hypersonic aircraft breaking down, one of the Deadly Five showing up, and Coral's betrayal. How she escaped using her new Aqua abilities and got onto a passing cruise ship–but she left out any mention of Lucas being on said ship.

Urban tugged at the sleeves covering her scarred wrists as she described the underwater research lab, but Mother's sharp eyes caught the movement.

"They put me in a trial. One that only an Aqua could succeed at and that anyone else would not survive." She took a deep breath. "I succeeded."

Her family fell into stunned silence, and Urban suddenly felt exposed and self-conscious.

"Does that mean you're–you're the hybrid?" Lillian barely breathed.

Urban nodded, gazing at her tea, unable to look them in the eyes.

"I don't believe it." Father's voice was hoarse.

Mother stared at Urban with a strange, unfamiliar expression.

"I can show you if you like," Urban whispered. "I already tested it. I'm definitely an Aqua."

A bot hovered toward them, and silence filled the room as it poured each a fresh cup of tea. Urban shifted uncomfortably, wanting to stop the quiet from stretching but feeling at a total loss as to how.

Lucas, who had already heard the whole story, took a loud slurp of tea and grimaced. "This stuff is terrible." He glanced down at his cup. "You all really need to invest in your own tea garden."

Mother blinked out of her stupor. "I'm . . . shocked. This is a lot to take in." She reached out and laid a hand on Urban's arm. "I'm so glad you're alright, Urban," she said. "I can't believe everything you went through. And we had no choice."

Father's expression was grave as he cleared his throat. "You mentioned one of the Deadly Five attacked you?"

"The Deadly Fifth," Urban clarified.

"And you say his daughter is the Giver Gene Pool lead for the Dragons?"

She nodded. "I think that's who was working to kill me in the games last semester."

Frowning, Father leaned forward. "Once the world finds out the hybrid is real, you'll have worse to deal with."

Urban blanched. "What could possibly be worse?"

"*All* of the Deadly Five coming after you," Father said bluntly. "Which they will."

Mother gave Urban's arm a reassuring squeeze. "Don't worry, AiE has a plan for protecting the hybrid. We just . . . never imagined it would be you."

"They have a plan? What?"

Urban's parents exchanged glances, doing nothing to alleviate

Urban's fears.

"The AiE leadership, or a representative, will want to meet with you first," Mother said evasively. "They'll gather intel, but mostly," she hesitated, "set up their political campaign for securing the public's vote."

"This is all about political power?" The words had a bad taste in Urban's mouth. "Are they going to try and make me their pawn?"

"Figurehead, more likely," her father corrected. "You wouldn't be directly involved in any of the politics. You'd just be the face of change."

Urban wasn't sure she liked what she was hearing.

"And that face of change comes with many dangers," Mother added. "Hence the additional security."

"But that's only half the hybrid's role," Father went on. "The other half is providing them with your hybrid DNA so that they can prove to the world you are the hybrid, giving them information on how to share your hybrid genetics with others."

Urban rubbed her arm. The bruises from all the blood samples were finally fading but still visible. "Will they run experiments?"

"Yes," Father replied, almost reluctantly. "But only what you feel comfortable with. We will make sure they don't overstep."

Urban wanted to believe him but doubt crept in.

Can we really do that? We're backed into a corner with little leverage. AiE knows we won't last long without their protection and are in no place to make demands.

"Urban," Mother said gently, "it's your choice whether you help their cause or not. You can say no. Your Father and I will support your decision, no matter what."

Urban felt a sudden rush of gratitude. Somehow, she'd just assumed her parents would force her into whatever plans AiE had for her. Given they were founding members, it made sense. But now they were supporting her, even if it meant coming at the cost of AiE's plans.

"If we commit to AiE, there's no going back," Father warned. "Either we need to send you somewhere far away that will be safer from attacks, or you need AiE's protection. The longer you stay with us, the more danger you will be exposed to. So, we need to decide right now what our course of action will be."

Urban stopped breathing. *This is all happening so fast.*

"What do you want to do?" Father pressed.

She wanted to scream.

So many decisions. Could she really turn down the only politically active organization willing to help her? Supers Against Soups were out for blood. So were the Deadly Five, and who knew what other nefarious organizations. And what would happen to Naturals all around the globe if she didn't join forces with AiE? If she were to choose self-preservation over the greater good?

Can I really go back to having my body experimented on? Her skin crawled at the thought. *But without AiE's protection, can I stay alive?*

She may have escaped the underwater prison, but Urban felt more trapped than ever.

"Dear, why don't you get some sleep and think it over tomorrow? You have a lot on your mind," Mother suggested, giving a pointed look at Father.

Father moved his teacup aside, then stood. "We'll delay the decision as much as possible, but I'm afraid that still won't buy you much time. We need to act quickly."

"How much time do I have?" Urban tried to keep her voice from quavering.

"Tomorrow we'll take the earliest ride to New Beijing. When we arrive, you need to have a decision made."

06

无家

NEW BEIJING

GOLD FLORESCENT LIGHTS FLICKERED TO LIFE as Urban set foot in the room. A K-pop band played, and the air fresheners clicked on to diffuse the scent of jasmine—her favorite smell. At least it had been back when she was dating Everest.

The settings were all the same from her last stay at the house. When had that been? It felt like a lifetime ago.

Since then, as the hybrid, everything had changed.

Urban stormed toward the smart mirror and swiped furiously at the controls until all the settings were cleared and returned to default mode.

She sank low onto the bed as emotions warred within her.

A headache began to pound against her skull, and she massaged her temple.

Right now, I just need sleep.

She approached a paneled wall that automatically slid open, revealing sets of silk sleepwear. Changing into one, she popped a painkiller before slipping under the airy blankets, her head sinking deep into the plush pillow.

Despite being dead tired, she couldn't shut off her thoughts.

Urban searched for a sleep headset but found their summer home lacking in this department. Instead, she lay on her spacious bed, staring up at the white ceiling. One moment she was too hot, the next too cold. In her retina display controls, she adjusted the room's temperature, darkness, and ambient noise.

Nothing worked.

Her thoughts spun around and around like a fish trapped in a whirlpool, despair encasing her. Seeing Everest soon, now that she was the hybrid. Apprehension over her pending decision with AiE. But mostly, about what being the hybrid meant for her and her family's future.

A heaviness descended on her chest and tears pricked at her eyes.

It's up to me to change the world. I just don't know if I can do it.

The New Shanghai Metropolis blurred past Urban as the maglev shot forward. Warm morning light bathed the city in brilliant colors through the transporter's clear ceiling and walls. Outside, the tall, domed buildings changed to lush greenery as they sped toward New Beijing.

Urban yawned. Her family reclined in their private compartment on the pristine white couches next to marbled tables. Baozi curled in a giant ball, occupying one of the seats, white fur blending in with the chair so it looked like the leather had purple spots.

They reached a bridge spanning a wide river and crossed over it, sparkling water beneath them a glare of light and prisms of blues.

Soon, a maidbot approached. "Would you like a beverage?"

"One latte please," Urban said.

From the bot's metal sternum came the sound of frothing milk. A moment later, a panel opened and a latte extended from within the cavity of its chest.

Urban gratefully accepted the porcelain mug. Taking a sip of foam, she cupped her drink and stared back out the window. Purple flashed in her vision as Baozi leaped onto her lap.

"*Ai ya!*" Urban cried in surprise. Her mug flew out of her hands and onto the floor, shattering and spilling coffee everywhere.

Urban swatted her cat away.

"I told you Baozi is annoying." Lucas smirked.

Urban ground her teeth, watching as a maidbot cleaned up the mess.

"It's okay," Lillian said softly.

"No. It's not." Urban stared at the cup now in a hundred pieces on the floor. Tears suddenly threatened to spill over, but she held them back.

It's just a cup.

But she couldn't shake the sense that something was wrong with the situation.

With the world.

With her.

I thought being Enhanced would fix things. So why do I feel so broken?

The landscape blurred around them. She blinked back the reappearing tears to check the time. They'd be arriving in New Beijing any minute, and she still hadn't made a decision.

I want to help Naturals around the world, but being AiE's figurehead is dangerous. Then again, I'm already a target. How much worse could it get? What will joining cost me and my family?

Then there was allowing them to sample her genetics. What exactly would they need to replicate her special hybrid DNA? If it was anything like the painful injections and tests at the underwater research lab, she wasn't sure she could go through with it.

"I know whatever you decide will be the right choice," Lillian said, interrupting Urban's thoughts. She'd forgotten her sister was there beside her.

Urban swallowed. "I don't feel like there is a right choice. Help the world but lose a piece of myself, or selfishly keep m—" she stopped before continuing in a whisper, "my hybrid enhancements to myself? If I join AiE, I might not survive the continued attacks and experimentation. But if I don't help, I'll never be able to live with myself."

"This time will be different," Lillian said. "I don't know what it was like being trapped in the underwater research lab, but this isn't the same. You would have advocates—me, Mom, Dad, others within AiE—and they wouldn't be doing anything against your will. You wouldn't be trapped."

Urban pulled her legs up to her chest and hugged them. "I just wish none of this had happened. I wish I weren't the hybrid."

"I wish this hadn't happened too," Lillian said soberly. "But I believe in you. You've been given this gift for a reason."

"Gift?"

"You're an Aqua now. You have the ability to have any enhancement you want. Isn't that what you always dreamed of?"

It had been.

Back when she was a Natural, living in the Metropolis, going to uni, and wanting nothing more than to belong with the Enhanced. She'd risked everything for that life. But somewhere along the way of blood samples, lab tests, anesthesia, hospital gowns, injections, and experiments, that dream had died a long, slow death.

Now, she just wanted to be a Natural.

And as much as she tried, she couldn't shake the cloud of fear that trailed her like a looming rainstorm.

"Now arriving at our final destination, New Beijing," a robotic voice said.

A familiar landscape came into view as the maglev slowed to a gradual stop at the center of the Metropolis. Below the platform, autonomous cars crawled slowly across the streets in the constant traffic. Pedestrians crowded the sidewalks in a hurry. A few people rode hoverboards or walked exotic pets.

Urban and her family disembarked and climbed into several waiting vehicles before joining the flow of traffic. Thirty-three minutes later, they stopped in front of an industrial-looking building and climbed out. After making their way past multiple security checkpoints, they arrived at a lobby.

The entrance to AiE's headquarters was even more intimidating than Urban had expected. She wasn't sure what she had envisioned, but certainly not this.

She stood in the spacious circular lobby with a waterfall that dropped from the ceiling into a large black basin. The room was completely silent except for the water splashing down and the sound of their shoes crossing the marble floor. It smelled of chlorine—like the underwater research lab.

Urban stopped in her tracks. A sudden memory triggered at the smell of chlorinated water.

She shook her head to try and clear it but her breaths came quick. Shallow. Her fingers stretched toward her stun shield, eyes shifting to note the exits in her surroundings. Two. She counted the guards at the other end of the hall. Six. Each had MagTouch M600s clearly visible in their holsters, and the two Flyer guards had poleaxes as well.

I'm safe, she repeated to herself.

Urban forced herself to move again and caught up to her family.

One of the guards, a Super, scanned Father's tatt then moved aside. "Those two stay behind." The guard motioned at Urban's brother and sister.

Lillian stepped forward in protest, but Father gave her a look, and she backed down.

The behemoth of a door slid open, and the rest of the guards stood aside. Urban followed her parents, heart racing.

She still hadn't come to a decision, and now she was about to meet the Regional Precepts for AiE.

Urban entered a large room with a 360 view of the Metropolis.

They were high enough to be in the Fly zone, and there was a special doorway just for Flyers. Delivery drones and people with a wide range of wings passed by the windows on all sides. A single AiE Precept sat among several empty chairs around a mahogany table.

The woman had sea-foam blue eyes and silver hair. Her youthful features contrasted with the look of sadness and wisdom in her eyes. It was the kind of depth that only came with time. "Welcome." She gestured at them to sit. "Thank you for coming on such short notice."

Urban's retina display picked up her identity as private, and the woman made no motion to link with any of them.

"For everyone's safety, it's best if we don't link," the Precept woman explained. "The rest of the council decided it would be more secure if I met with you all first. My name is Sato Winter. Premier of AiE."

A maidbot laid out four teacup sets and filled them.

The Premier wasted no time. "We received an encrypted message informing us you're the missing hybrid?" The statement was more of a question, an invitation—or challenge— to explain.

Urban felt like she was back at PKU's application interview as Sato Winter regarded her carefully. Urban assumed they'd accept her word, but now, as she thought about it, that seemed silly. What would happen if the council didn't believe her? That would certainly make her decision easier.

Urban swallowed then recounted her story.

When she was finished, Sato Winter leaned back, slender fingers clasped. "Would you happen to have access to your retina recordings?"

"No." Urban clenched her teacup. "They were deactivated when I was kidnapped. I don't have anything after the under-water pod."

"That is unfortunate." Sato Winter viewed her through slitted eyes.

Urban flushed. "I'd be happy to give you a demonstration of my Aqua abilities."

"Thank you." Sato Winter took a sip of tea. "I think the question the rest of the council will have is, how do we know you weren't an Aqua all along?"

"I have her medical genome record that dates back to when she was four years old," Mother responded. "She's always been a Natural, until the microneedle patch activated her dormant genes."

"Very well. We will have the lab analyze those," the woman said. "However, we'd also like for our expert in residence to work with you going forward, to test your capabilities. According to our intel, you've already met her. A Ms. Li Blossom?"

Urban almost fell out of her chair.

Blossom? My roommate? Urban remembered the SAS badge she'd found in their dorm room. She thought it belonged to Blossom, but if that were true . . . then did that mean that the badge belonged to someone else? Or could she, like Coral, be working with multiple organizations and playing them all?

"Blossom is a member of the World Enhancement Organization but has informally partnered with us," Winter continued.

"Blossom?" Urban finally managed to speak. "But she's just a first year in uni."

"A prodigy's age doesn't matter," Sato Winter informed Urban. "She was, of course, enhanced from birth, but she's naturally talented. She's leading the way in reverse engineering the hybrid genetics and is paving the way for the work that needs to be done."

Was Blossom really working with WEO? Urban thought back to the first time they met.

Urban had been impressed by how her roommate had secured "genetic engineering" as one of her top keywords. It was an extremely competitive one to get, and Urban had wondered how she'd managed it. If she were leading the way in the scientific community, it would make sense. But why hadn't Urban found anything in QuanNao about it?

"If you are indeed proven to be the hybrid," the Premier said, "this will have huge ramifications for the Nonproliferation Treaty for Deadly Enhancements. If people can receive hybrid genetics, then they can get lethal enhancements at any point in their lives. What's to stop them from breaking the treaty?"

Urban stilled, never having considered this. Next to her, Mother shifted in her seat.

"There will be many people resistant, even afraid of your genetics." Winter paused and took a sip of her tea, eyes studying Urban. "Which is why we want to use the Gamelyon as the symbol of positive change. People will associate it with your victory in the games. With power. But also, with a new era of enhancements. And thanks to your little stunt arriving back home yesterday, you and your Gamelyon are already all over the news. But we wanted to make sure no one found out about your time in prison, hence bailing you out quietly."

Urban's heart sank. She was already in AiE's *guanxi* debt.

"We've purchased the Gamelyon from port authorities and managed to secure a permit. You may ride it in designated areas."

Urban's eyes rounded. "I can keep it?" she asked incredulously.

Sato Winter smiled for the first time, a real smile that made her frosty eyes twinkle. "It most likely won't fit in your apartment, so we have a facility for it, but yes. You are welcome to visit and ride it at any time.

"Now," she continued, ignoring Urban's attempt to thank her, "the next step in our plan is to tip off several of our media connections about your hybrid genetics. Once the news circulates, we'll start pressuring our political allies to pass the Natural Rights Act."

"What's that?" Urban asked.

Winter hesitated for a fraction of a second. "The Natural Rights Act is a highly secretive bill we've been working on for some time. It states that rather than allow genetic enhancements be something purchased, everyone will be given hybrid genetics instead. When they're of age, they will take an aptitude test, which includes their preference for a certain gene pool, and then, based on that test, will be given genetic enhancements."

Urban suddenly remembered a conversation she'd had with Everest what felt like a lifetime ago. He'd mentioned this bill. It was AiE's number one priority, but without media coverage, it wouldn't get passed. The augmented-free campaigns were a way for those in power to prevent any news about the hybrid from escaping out to the public.

"But what makes you think the media will cover my story? Haven't they shut down all previous attempts of anything having to do with the hybrid?"

"You are aware of our dilemma." Sato Winter regarded her carefully. "That is the problem we've encountered thus far. We're hopeful since you're already a loved KOL, it will air. If not, we'll have to find a new angle. In the meantime, we will put everything in motion to get the right politicians to vote in favor of our bill. Having popular opinion on our side by having you as our representative will help make the process smoother."

Sato Winter set her teacup down delicately. "Once we've confirmed your hybrid genetics, we'd like to extend an offer to be our figurehead." She raised her hand as if to ward off any questions or objections. "You need not make an immediate decision. Just consider our proposal. We will await your response."

07

LAB RAT

THE LAB WAS STERILE AND BRIGHT. NOT THE sort of place Urban would voluntarily spend the weekend.

As she followed a medbot through the halls, she thought back to her conversation with the AiE council. *Can they really bring equality to Naturals? Change the world? If they're so powerful, why do they need me? Why can't someone else be their figurehead? If I accept, will Croix rescind their offer? What will it cost me?*

She'd been over the questions a thousand times in the hours following the meeting but was no closer to any answers.

Despite the pending offer, AiE had insisted on assigning Urban a new security detail. Armored guards followed close behind her. Two of them were Camos, trailing invisibly, but Urban could see their presence in her augmented maps. She recognized Trig's familiar triangle, but there was a new blue circle for a Flyer Camo.

Urban's other two security guards were Supers who hemmed her in on either side. AiE had foregone subtlety since Urban was a widely recognized KOL now.

Lucas also stood protectively close to her, bolstering her courage.

As they followed a bot to a private room, Urban's throat

itched, and she wondered if her asthma was acting up again. It had been awhile since her last flare-up. She had the urge to cough but restrained herself out of habit.

In the past, she had to hide her asthma. It was one of the many giveaways that she was a Natural. Now . . . well, now she wasn't sure if that mattered. Would her DNA still show up as Natural? Or Enhanced? Or something else entirely?

She was led into a spotless white room with florescent lighting, a hovering examination bed, and several pieces of shiny equipment.

Pressure built in her chest. Even though she didn't recognize most of the devices, it reminded her too much of the underwater research lab. Her breath came quickly, in shallow, panicked gasps.

She tentatively took a seat on thin, crinkly paper lining the examination table. A bot approached and, with her permission, swiped her tatt. Urban's display informed her that all her medical records, plus current resting heart rate, body temperature, blood pressure, respiratory rate, glucose levels, and other stats from her tatt's body tracking abilities, were being transferred.

The bot reached for a syringe.

Urban's brain turned fuzzy with panic.

No. No! NO!

The bot hovered toward her.

Scrambling, Urban backed up on the examination table until her spine pressed against the wall.

Lucas leaped in between them. "Back!" He swiped a jar of cotton balls and brandished it at the bot. "Stay away from my sister."

The bot tried to circumvent him.

"I'm warning you!" Lucas opened the jar and tossed the cotton balls. They fell harmlessly between them. Any other time, Urban would have laughed. Any other time.

At that moment, a man in a white lab coat entered the room.

"Lee, Urban?" The man looked confused as he took in the scene. The bot was still trying to get around Lucas, and Urban remained scrunched up atop the examination table.

"Yes?" she managed.

"I'm Dr. Watanabe. Here to conduct your biometric screening?"

Urban tried to force her body to move but remained pressed against the wall. "Is there any chance we could continue without the, uh, syringe?" She motioned at the medbot, which hovered uncertainly on the other side of Lucas.

"Ah." Dr. Watanabe's face cleared. He turned to the bot. "Leave us."

The bot dipped its head and whirred away.

Instantly, the pressure in Urban's chest lightened, and she slowly climbed down from the table. Lucas set down the empty jar as the doctor spoke.

"We can start with X-rays, MRIs, and the genome sequencer. At some point I am going to need to take a blood sample, but we don't have to do that today, if you'd prefer not."

Urban wrapped her arms around herself. "Would you mind waiting until the end of the visit?"

"Not at all." The doctor stood. "Let's start with those X-rays. But first . . ." He indicated a little adjacent room.

There, Urban changed into a head-to-toe immersion suit that monitored all her vitals. Upon her return, the doctor proceeded with the X-rays. The machine took images of every part of Urban's interior body, leaving her feeling awkwardly exposed.

Then came the MRI, followed by fMRI machines, both taking all sorts of brain scans.

It would be awful if her very thoughts were on display.

She knew the machines couldn't read her mind but wondered what they might find. As the hybrid, would her body, brain— everything—be visible to the world?

She tried not to think about it. All she had to do was get through the next scan. And then . . . the next.

"Now, for the DNA sequencing." Dr. Watanabe pulled on a pair of gloves then handed Urban a swab. "Rub the inside of your cheek with this."

Urban reluctantly did as she was told, then the doctor took the swab and placed it in a collection vial. "We'll have this sequenced within the hour, but mapping it and identifying variants will take longer. I'll have my team of bioinformaticians working on it make it their top priority. Still, it could take a while."

They moved onto the EKGs, then so many machines, Urban lost track of their names and functions. With each test, she felt like a piece of herself was slipping away.

At the end, Urban's heart had stopped racing enough to give the blood sample another go.

"Very well," Dr. Watanabe said. "I'll be in the other room analyzing your results. I'll return once you're done." He turned on his heels.

"Are you sure you're up for this?" Lucas asked as soon as the door shut. "You know you can wait until later."

"I want to get it over with and not have to come back." Urban sat in a chair while the bot dabbed a mesh substance covered in cleaning solution on her forearm. She turned her head away so as to avoid seeing the sharp needle.

"In that case," Lucas projected a vid on the wall, "here's something to distract you."

A vid began playing of a close-up of Lucas's face. He made a shushing motion and then clicked on an identity scrambler. Instantly, his face changed into a terrifying gorilla with blood dripping down its teeth. It didn't really seem appropriate at the moment.

"What is this?" Urban asked.

Lucas grinned. "Just watch."

In the vid, Lucas tiptoed into a room and hid inside an XR pod.

"I am now disabling the XR vacancy feature," Lucas's voice in the vid explained. "Now the pod will appear empty."

Sure enough, the pod's red "occupied" light switched to green.

With a prick, the bot gently slid the needle into Urban's vein. She inhaled a sharp breath. Lightheaded, she focused her attention on the vid.

Lucas fast-forwarded until the time stamp showed an hour had passed. It slowed to normal speed again as a man made his way toward the pod. He scanned his tatt and the door slid open. The man started to climb in when Lucas jumped out, hooting and growling like a deranged animal.

The man stumbled backward, falling down before scrambling to his feet and running away.

In the doctor's office, Lucas grinned broadly. "Wasn't that awesome?"

"You could get in big trouble for that," Urban pointed out. "Identity scramblers are illegal."

"So worth it."

"You wasted an hour of your life too."

Lucas wiggled his eyebrows. "Not wasted. I spent the time premeditating my next epic prank. Which . . . here it comes!" He gestured at the vid.

Urban glanced at the tubes pumping her blood away and felt queasy. She quickly directed her attention back to the vid.

They were halfway through Lucas's prank highlights when the bot withdrew the needle. Urban let out a shaky breath of relief.

The bot whirred away, and Dr. Watanabe stepped back into the room. "It's confirmed," he said to Urban. "You are indeed an Aqua." He tapped several virtual displays filled with graphs and charts. "You've somehow retained your original Natural DNA while also integrating the genetic material of an Aqua. This phenomenon is groundbreaking."

Urban forced a smile. "Does that mean we're done here?"

Dr. Watanabe looked up, surprised. "Why, of course. I'll draw up a full report and send it to headquarters." He turned and left, and as Urban watched him go, she couldn't stop the sinking feeling.

My DNA will never again be my own.

08

AI FACTORIES

AI FACTORIES LOOMED, SLABS OF GREY AGAINST a sky of putrid green. They were just as dark and oppressive as Urban remembered. Her retina display flashed a warning as she skidded through a turn on her motorcycle.

<Entering yellow zone. Exercise CAUTION>

Her guards remained close but just far enough to give her the illusion of privacy. Urban hardly noticed them as her eyes darted frantically across the deserted factory. They stopped on a figure leaned against a wall. Everest had switched out of his Metropolis tech and wore rugged Natural gear, along with an outdated headset, but she'd recognize him anywhere.

Every nerve ending within her buzzed with energy as she rode slowly through the debris toward him. She parked, and, with trembling fingers, removed her helmet, turning to Everest.

Piercing, starry black eyes met hers. Everest strode purposefully toward her, and without hesitation, he took her hands in his calloused ones.

They gazed at each other for a long moment.

Crash!

Urban jumped, and quickly pulled out one of her ink bombs. A rat scampered past them, and she blushed.

Everest observed the scene with a furrowed brow. "Let's go inside."

He led the way around the abandoned building, stopping at a tall, eerily desolate entrance. Urban followed Everest and, recognizing where they were, gasped.

It was the AI factory she'd worked at a year ago. Only, now it was empty and joining the ranks of abandoned buildings.

"The jobs ran out here," Everest explained. "The AI startups no longer need human supervision."

Urban stared at the once-familiar walls now covered in graffiti.

"More and more Naturals are without work," Everest told her. "I'm having a hard time keeping the violence down in the Outskirts. People are afraid. They don't know how they're going to provide for their families."

Urban couldn't shake the icy tendrils curling around her heart as she scanned the deserted factory. She'd seen firsthand how hard life as a Natural was at the AI factories. She'd lived it. For a short period, anyway. But it had been long enough to solidify her resolve to never end up in the Outskirts.

Maybe the hybrid DNA can help Naturals. Maybe it can fix this.

Her gaze jumped back to Everest. "Are there any other types of jobs Naturals could do instead? Something other than the AI training roles?"

Everest's lips tightened. Without saying another word, he led her inside the structure.

The factory, once full of human chatter, now lay in silence. Everest swiped at spider webs, continuing onward past what used to be the main lobby and toward the rows of Extended Reality Domes. They were all gone—smashed or missing.

"People took them for living shelters," Everest explained. "Better than sleeping in the elements. Not to mention, some of them still have working filtration devices attached."

People were living in those? Every minute she'd spent working in one had been claustrophobic agony. She couldn't imagine how terrible it must be to make that home.

No one should have to live like that.

Their feet crunched over broken bits of the ash-gray dome as

Everest picked his way toward a ladder leading up to the empty XRD floors.

Urban's hands gripped the cold steel bars as she pulled herself up. A sense of deja vu washed over her. The last time she'd climbed up this same ladder was to finish her AI internship. Angel Qing, or Coral, had hacked into her system that day and warned her.

At the thought of Coral, Urban's stomach tightened. Her ex-roommate had warned and protected her many times. All to gain her trust so she could betray her.

That betrayal still stung.

Everest's feet clunked against the metallic walkway as he stepped off the ladder. The cavernous blackness swallowed them until he activated a feature on his pulse shield. Light flooded the space, exposing once-gleaming floors and walls. Now, they wore signs of neglect, the light casting shadows on the broken and grimy remains of a few domes that hadn't been taken.

Urban raised an eyebrow at the pulse shield. "You really should stop stealing Inventor tech."

"Why?" Everest lowered himself onto the walkway, feet dangling over the edge. She joined him. "There's no reason Inventors should be the only ones to benefit from their tech. For example." Everest withdrew what looked like a silver ball. "This lock hacker works on most doors and has been incredibly handy."

"Just please don't get caught with a Magtouch."

"Don't worry about me." Everest smiled, but then his expression turned serious. "You, on the other hand . . ."

Urban glanced up at him. Did he suspect she was the hybrid? The sooner she got this over with the better. "Everest, there's something . . ." She broke off, and Everest looked at her questioningly. Inhaling a deep breath, she launched into the story recounting Coral's betrayal, her time in the underwater prison, and then her escape.

Everest had gotten to his feet halfway through her tale, restless. When she finished, his normally expressionless face had grown taut.

"*Wozi*," Everest swore. "If I ever find the scientist who did this to you—" His face flushed.

She had never seen him this upset before, and it unnerved her. He blinked, as if startled. "Sorry." He sat next to her once more and exhaled a long breath. "I should have been there."

"It's not your fault," Urban was quick to assure him. "You weren't allowed to travel with the team. None of us could have guessed Coral would betray us like that."

Everest nodded. Then suddenly his expression changed. It was as if their whole conversion had caught up to him. "You said *you're* the—hybrid?"

"Yes." Urban rubbed at the scar on her arm.

Everest's eyes roamed over her as if looking for physical signs of such a change.

"An Aqua, actually," Urban added.

Everest's eyes nearly bulged out of his head. "What?"

Her voice faltered. "They enhanced me. That's how I was able to escape. I can breathe underwater now."

Everest regarded her for a long moment. "Well, this certainly explains a lot."

"Like what?" An uncomfortable prickling sensation crept up her spine.

Everest hesitated. "How much do you know about the *heiwang*?"

"The dark web?" Urban remembered a student in her Mixed Media Arts class last semester using it to cheat on an assignment. That was the only time she'd actually seen someone engage with it. "Not much."

"There's a bounty on the *heiwang* for the hybrid. If users find out you're what they're looking for . . . it would not go well."

Urban bit her lip. "But the *Jingcha* will shut that down, right?"

"If the *Jingcha* had that kind of power, the *heiwang* wouldn't exist to begin with. As it is, it's impossible to keep the anon users accountable."

"But surely there are ways around anonymity?" Urban asked. "Obviously, it has to be Dawn or Vance who did this." *Or one of the many other people who want me captured or dead.*

"It's not that simple." Everest met her eyes. "Urban, I need you to promise me something. If AiE offers you protection, take it. No one with a bounty on them in the *heiwang* lasts long."

Urban stiffened.

"With AiE's protection, you'd be safe," Everest stressed.

She motioned where her guards stood down below at the entrance to the building. "They've already given me extra security."

Everest shook his head. "That's not enough."

"They did promise me additional protection," Urban told him, "but it's in exchange for being their figurehead. And how will that make me any safer? If I accept, I'll become a bigger target, not just in the *heiwang*, but in real life."

"You're already a target in real life," Everest pointed out. "The question is whether you'll have the security you need." His voice softened. "Why don't you want to be their figurehead?"

She shifted uncomfortably on the ledge. "I can't do it. I've always kept under the radar—a Natural hiding in plain sight. I've mastered the art of blending in, not attracting attention."

"Is that what you call crashing PKU's stadium and becoming the top trending KOL overnight?"

"That was different. A mistake."

Everest raised an eyebrow, trying to hide a smile.

"Hey," Urban said. "I'm serious."

Everest's expression sobered. "Me too. You're not a Natural hiding anymore. You're a KOL. Even if you don't accept the position for AiE, you can never go back to obscurity."

Never go back.

There was a sudden pressure in her chest and a sharp sting in her eyes.

Don't cry.

She looked up into the blackness of the facility, blinking rapidly.

Everest scooted closer and wrapped his arm around her shoulder. "Hey, I know this is a lot to take in. You've gone from Natural, to Enhanced, to Hybrid. That's more than anyone else in this world. But you're also stronger than everyone I know. If anyone can do this, it's you."

At least one of us thinks so.

As if reading her thoughts, Everest said, "Urban, you've been doing this your whole life. Who else has straddled both worlds of Enhanced and Naturals? No Enhanced would understand Naturals the way you do. And no Natural would have a clue what it feels like to live among the Enhanced. I've been trying for the past few months, and it's a nightmare. I'm exhausted. I can't believe you've been doing this most of your life. You navigate the world of the Enhanced with ease."

Urban shook her head. "I've spent time in both worlds, but I've never fully belonged in either. With the Enhanced, I was always hiding a part of my self. A fraud. And among the Naturals, I may have genetically matched, but I never lived in the Outskirts. Most of that way of life I only know from dating you."

"Urban, look at me."

She lifted her eyes to him.

"I can't speak for all the Enhanced, but as a Natural, I can tell you that you belong."

Urban considered his words. Could they be true?

Everest leaned in so close she could smell the familiar scent of jasmine and smoke. Then his lips brushed up against her own.

Happiness ballooned in Urban, spreading its warmth. She never wanted to take moments like these for granted again.

Everything else fell away. The fears, expectations, all burdens temporarily removed while she enjoyed this one little slice of happiness.

All too soon, the moment ended and Everest was pulling away. He smiled down at her. It was one of his rare smiles, one that filled his entire face.

A hundred memories flashed between them in an instant.

The last time she'd seen that smile had been over Mooncake Festival. She'd met his parents and spent the evening enjoying their home-cooked food and gazing at the night sky on the rooftop together. It was a simple memory, full of joy.

Urban wondered how many moments like that they'd get, now that she was the hybrid. Now that so many lives depended upon her.

Nothing seemed simple anymore.

Everest gently brushed back a strand of hair that had fallen into her eyes. "If you weren't the hybrid—if you could do anything—what would you do?"

She thought for a moment. There were wisps of a dream that would come and go in snippets over the years. But it had been long buried. It took a while to recall the details again. "I think I'd like to open up an art school for Naturals."

He cocked his head. "Why?"

This time Urban didn't second-guess herself and the words flowed. "It would be a mid-way school. One in which Naturals could learn from the best instructors and practice their craft. Then, when they got close to graduation, I'd use my KOL connections to get them internships at the biggest art studios. Eventually, it would help more Naturals integrate with the Enhanced."

She waited for Everest to laugh or tell her it was impossible. The Enhanced would never mix with Naturals. Instead, he nodded. "Like a bridge between the Outskirts and the Metropolis?"

"I never thought of it that way before . . . but yes."

"That's a beautiful dream." His tone was uncharacteristically emotional, and Urban turned to look at him.

"What's your dream?" she blurted. After being apart for so long, it almost felt like they were starting all over again.

Everest smiled and his gaze took on a far-off expression. "Similar to yours, actually. I never thought of an art school as the means for it, but that's brilliant. I've always wanted to create a space halfway between the Metropolis and the Outskirts, where both the Enhanced and Naturals can meet. A place with clean air, safety, and learning opportunities for the Naturals and a chance for Enhanced to mentor Naturals but also get a glimpse into their lives. An exchange program, if you will."

"What's stopping you from doing it now?" she asked.

"Well, a lot of my time is currently going to this beautiful girl who needs a big strong man to protect her."

Urban punched him in the shoulder.

"Ah, there's the martial arts coming out again." He laughed then leaned back. "In all honesty, my focus right now is helping AiE get the legislation passed that will bring equality. Without that, there's no point in an exchange program. Like you said, change won't last."

Urban stared at her feet. The light had disappeared into blackness below. Musty air brushed against their skin.

"So, you've already met with AiE?" Everest asked.

"Yes." Urban recounted her meeting with them and their plan to continue hacking the news networks.

Everest's eyebrows went up. "That's their plan? We've been trying that for nearly a year now with no luck. We're running out of time, and that strategy has already proved ineffective. Every single time, we get shut down by an augmented-free campaign."

A little dismayed, Urban asked, "So what would you suggest?"

"We have to try something different," he mused. "Some other angle the news will be forced to cover." He looked at her. "You're a KOL. Can you think of any big event that would guarantee coverage?"

Her conversation with her potential sponsor, Croix came back to mind. She could think of something, alright. Something so huge that every media outlet would be covering it for weeks.

It also happened to be the deadliest event of the year.

09

DEADLY PROPOSITION

PURPLE MIST SNAKED THROUGH THE DARKENED room and brushed against Urban's skin, reminding her all too much of the purple zones that could kill. Though she was grateful this was only a trick of the lights in the banquet hall, it was still unsettling.

"A toast." Sato Winter lifted her shot glass. She sat at the head of the table of AiE leaders in the seat of honor. Now that Urban's hybrid genetics had been confirmed, the rest of the AiE regional leaders were willing to meet with her.

Urban, with her mother and her father, had been seated on the opposite end of the table from Sato Winter, as far away as was possible. Not that she expected anything different. Still, it was a visual reminder she had little power, even among her allies.

The other AiE Prefects raised their glasses as one, the light dancing over their tailored suits and fine silks. Urban's own dress rustled as she followed their lead and lifted her glass. She felt some measure of comfort knowing her alcohol dehydrogenase pill had already dissolved in her rice wine.

"To equality among Naturals and Enhanced." Sato Winter tipped her head in Urban's direction. *"Gan bei!"*

"Gan bei!" Everyone echoed, then downed their shots.

Urban studied each AiE Prefect as they returned to their conversations.

The woman next to Sato Winter had introduced herself as Cao Lotus, Premier of Research and Development. She was a Natural.

The man with a mouthful of food next to her was a Super in military attire. His combat boots and a buzz cut were exactly as Urban remembered them. This was the man Everest reported to, Sung Ray, Premier of Operations.

The next man, a Flyer with beautiful crimson wings, had introduced himself as Kimora Glacier, Premier of Communication. If the bags under his eyes were any indicator, it seemed all the augmented-free campaigns had been taking a toll on him.

The last woman identified herself as Nik Violet, Premier of Strategic Initiatives. By the way her eyes bore into Urban, she knew instantly that Violet was an Inceptor. Urban shifted to avoid the woman's gaze and tried to focus on the food instead.

Dishes spun automatically on the lazy Susan in front of them. It was laden with foods ranging from squirrel fish in sweet and sour sauce, to crunchy walnut shrimp, sautéed scallops and asparagus, crisp, pan-fried turnip cakes with dry shrimp and sausage, and glazed lamb chops.

If Urban hadn't been so nervous, she would have devoured it all. Instead, she picked at a steamed pork bun. She sensed Father and Mother equally on edge next to her. Even though Urban knew the restaurant had top-notch security and a private, noise cancelling banquet room, the thought of discussing dangerous matters made her uncomfortable.

Black-lacquered chopsticks, inlaid with mother of pearl, tapped plates and scraped against porcelain bowls. Overhead, the stringy notes of the zither strummed a somber tune.

Sato Winter's lips thinned, eyes engrossed in QuanNao. After a minute, she silenced the chatter to draw their attention and pulled up several news titles and displayed them over the table. "We have a problem. As you can see, Urban's return to the Asian Federation on the Gamelyon was covered in depth. Our piece about the truth behind her genetics and the discovery of the hybrid?" She flicked up QuanNao.

"Nothing."

Several people frowned.

"But what about our sources?" Glacier demanded. "I reached out to every loyalist we still have in the media industry. They all covered the piece."

Sato Winter pulled up a new image. "The article went live for about an hour. Started trending, then nothing."

"Another augmented-free week?"

"More than that. It was completely scrubbed in four out of six Federations. You can't find a trace of it."

"So, the news won't touch her?" Ray asked.

"Worse," Sato Winter stated. "She made the list."

Glacier sat upright.

"What's that?" Urban ventured to ask.

Winter's expression was grim. "Anything that's considered fake news or dangerous to the general population goes on a banned list. Media outlets can't cover it, brands won't support it, publicly traded companies can't endorse it without receiving a serious sosh infringement. Basically, many things in augmented reality are blocked regarding that person."

Urban abruptly set her chopsticks down. "But why am I on that list?"

Sato Winter pulled up images of the Western Federation. "See this violence? This is the growing divide between Naturals and Enhanced. You're the only one who can bridge that gap. But in the process, things could get worse. No Federation wants a revolution on their hands. They'll do whatever it takes to keep the peace—including suppressing information pertaining to the hybrid."

"So, what's our next play?" Glacier asked, ruffling his wings in displeasure.

"Continue your work hacking the media and trying backdoor networks to post our stories," was the reply. "The Natural Rights Act won't be up for another three months. We still have time. We'll also build a grassroots plan for getting the word out. If Urban accepts the role, we will begin scheduling large, in-person gatherings for her to speak at."

Urban bit her lip. She'd researched her idea until late last night and knew her pitch but nerves still chewed at her insides. If this meeting was any indicator, AiE viewed her as more of a poster child and not a member with valuable opinions to contribute. She got the impression she was only invited to this meeting because she had yet to announce her decision.

"What if it doesn't work?" Urban spoke tentatively.

Sato Winter blinked at her. "What do you mean?"

Urban resisted the urge to squirm under the Premier's firm gaze. "That strategy has been tried for over a year. But each time access is gained, another augmented-free challenge is issued, rendering the campaign useless."

Sato Winter regarded her coldly. "And you have a proposition to fix this?"

"More like a work-around." Urban felt emboldened having everyone's attention. "What about the Race to the Clouds?"

The leader's blue eyes narrowed.

"What if we used the RTC to garner the attention we need?" Urban suggested, ignoring the warning glances from Father. "Race to the Clouds is the perfect opportunity."

She switched the table to a 3D projection of a mountain road cut dangerously around sharp corners, jagged peaks, and lethal obstacles. Vehicles raced up it, and at the very top, blasted off into the air toward the clouds and the finish line.

"It attracts an annual viewership of 600 million and has international coverage." Urban gained confidence as everyone continued to listen. "The media is forced to cover all contestants, so *if* I decide to accept the position of figurehead, and *if* I compete in the race, they will have to cover me or risk losing their viewership."

"An interesting proposition," Sato Winter remarked.

"What about section 5.11 in the Race to the Clouds handbooks? It states all competitors must have a sponsor in order to compete. If you're on a banned list, no sponsor will touch you."

At her father's cool voice, Urban was taken aback. She hadn't counted on Father, the one person who knew more about this race than anyone in the room, opposing her.

Her mind momentarily blanked before remembered she had an answer to this too. "Actually, it was my brand sponsor who suggested it. Croix offered me a position as their sponsored lead and I've accepted. They've already put in my application months ago for Race to the Clouds. Their plan was to have me attend and potentially try out, nothing more. But I could compete." She double checked her messages to make sure Croix hadn't changed its mind now that she was on the list.

Nothing. She was safe. For now.

Sato Winter interlocked her fingers and leaned forward. "And why would your sponsor continue your contract? If you don't get coverage, they gain nothing by having you as a KOL. If they weren't planning on having you actually compete, why have you attend at all?"

"I don't know how they expect to get any coverage," Urban had to admit. "But they did say I fit their rebel brand image."

"I don't like it." Sato Winter shook her head. "Your sponsor has to have some ulterior motive for keeping you on board."

"Maybe, but what other alternatives do we have?" Glacier challenged. "None of the news outlets can afford *not* to cover the event. By the mere act of racing, she'll gain instantaneous coverage. Perhaps that is why her sponsor continues to retain her."

"But she is not a race car driver," Ray scoffed. "What are the odds of her making it past the qualifiers? It takes hard work and years of training to succeed in these types of missions."

"Maybe she's not a race car driver, but she's close." Violet spoke for the first time. She turned to Urban. "I had security run a background check before suggesting we extend to you the role of figure head. They said you've competed in underground motorcycle races. Is this true?"

Urban's gaze flicked to her parents. "It was just one race, but yes."

"One underground race isn't going to win her the most prestigious race in the world," Ray growled. "Besides, motorcycle racing isn't a transferable skill set to car racing."

"She doesn't need to be able to drive a car," Lotus said tapping a piece of her tech. "This year they're bringing back the motorcycle division."

Urban was pleased to see the AiE member falling right into her plan.

"But that's the most dangerous division of all," Father said soberly, and Urban's spirits sank again. "Remember, they removed it after too many casualties."

"I agree." Sato Winter placed her hands on the table. "We cannot risk Urban's life."

"There's no way she will be able to qualify to compete anyway," Ray doubled down. "Most racers have been training for years and are genetically engineered exclusively for this race. She doesn't stand a chance."

Urban knew she was losing control. The one plan that actually had a shot at succeeding in helping Naturals was slowly slipping away. She had to convince them.

Urban leaned forward. "What good are my hybrid genetics if the laws aren't in place for us to use them? The only way to get the media's attention is for me to try out."

There was a collective silence.

"I think if we can find a trainer for Urban, it's a possibility we should seriously consider," Glacier finally said. "I'm having a hard time with my communication leads. More and more are getting weeded out or disappearing. My hackers are having to exploit harder loopholes to get through backdoors. A backup plan would be wise."

"No coach will train her with this short of notice or go near her now that she's on the list," Ray argued.

But Urban could think of someone who wasn't engineered for the races and had won. Someone who didn't care at all that she was on the banned list. The last person in the world she wanted to be her coach.

Father.

10

KINTSUGI

"ABSOLUTELY NOT." FATHER TOOK A LONG SIP of wine. "You're not racing and I'm not training you."

Urban sat in the living room of their house with Mother, Lucas, and Lillian. The rest of her family was quiet.

"But it's the only way," Urban protested.

"Do you have any idea how deadly the race is?" Father stopped and looked around the room nervously, as if the bugs they'd swept might still be there and someone could be listening in on their conversation.

"I know it's dangerous," Urban responded. "Some people even die. But some people defeat impossible odds. They win. Like you did."

"*You* are not some people." Father finished his wine and motioned a bot to bring over another drink, a shot glass this time.

Urban closed her eyes. *I need a coach who actually knows how to win this. He's my only option.*

"Please."

"No."

She hated to have to pull this card, but it appeared there was no other option. "Father," Urban began evenly, "I'm racing whether you like it or not. Even if I don't have your support or AiE's, I'm going. The only say you have is whether you'll help me."

It was a bluff.

AiE reluctantly agreed to support Urban's decision on the condition she found a coach to train her. To be honest, she wasn't sure if she would accept AiE's offer at all, but she was leaning in that direction. She just hoped her father didn't call her on it.

He was silent so long, Urban thought he might not respond at all. Then he threw back his head to down his drink and slammed the glass on the table. "Then you're going to die."

He stood abruptly and left.

Mother rose with her elegant grace. "I'll talk to him." Her voice was edged.

"Don't worry, sis." Lucas said as he patted Urban on the back. "I'll help you train. What other Aqua is going to take a chance on a loser like you?"

"Oh, great. Thanks."

Lucas winked then left the room.

Lillian had been checking her pings and now also stood. "Sorry, Urban. AiE needs me. See you soon?"

Urban nodded, and Lillian offered a sympathetic smile as she departed. Urban was staring blindly, contemplating her options when, to her surprise, Father returned. His face was ashen, his posture changed.

"I'll be your coach," he said stiffly.

Urban jumped to her feet.

"On one condition." He lifted a finger. "You have to place in the top five RTC qualifiers. If you succeed, I will be your coach all the way through. If you fail, I will discontinue coaching you. Though I can't force you, I'd encourage you to forfeit the race should that happen."

Urban froze, uncertain if she heard right. But his expression was deadly serious.

The RTC was highly competitive. She'd be lucky to qualify at all, let alone place in the top five. But this was her only chance.

Her stomach twisted. *It's impossible. But what other option do I have?*

She lifted her chin. "I accept."

Father merely grunted and was gone.

His change of heart was bewildering. *I'm sure I have Mother to thank.*

With a shaky sigh of relief, Urban retreated to her old room, passing Mother's studio on the way. The door was closed, per usual. It had been left opened only once—when their house had been bugged. The last time Urban managed to sneak in, Mother's paintings of Naturals all quickly disappeared to reveal holo projections of Enhanced.

Urban still found it odd her mother painted Naturals but tried to hide that she did. There were so many things about her mother she found baffling.

She trudged past the studio and into her own room, with its floor-to-ceiling window displaying a riot of colors from New Beijing's skyline. Her art supplies—expensive brushes, ink sticks, and rice paper—were still arranged haphazardly across her desk.

When had been the last time she made something beautiful? It seemed like such a luxury.

Exhausted, she snuggled up under her warm comforters. A huge cat plopped on top of her and Urban groaned. "Baozi! Not now!"

Despite her protests, the cat made no effort to move. Sleepily, Urban stroked the flaming purple spots. The warmth of the bed and the gentle purring lulled her to sleep.

Urban set foot in the bright studio where she was to meet her Artisan mentor. As soon as Dr. Yukio found out about her reappearance in New Beijing, he reached out to schedule a mentoring session. It seemed a trivial thing to spend time on, given everything currently going on in Urban's life, but then again, so did most things. Besides, she missed making art and could use a distraction.

The studio was adorned with traditional minimalist furniture, lots of natural lighting, and a few tasteful paintings and plants. Three large wooden work tables clustered together at the center of the room. Two were covered in various teapots and pottery, the third one was empty.

Urban wandered toward the teapots. Some were broken, others were cracked then pieced back together with what looked like golden glue, and still others remained intact.

A shuffled gait reached her ears a few seconds before Dr. Yukio appeared. He wore his long cloak, but today, the hood was pulled back, revealing his scarred face and mechanical eye. Urban was surprised not to see the holo projection he used in classes to speak.

"Why are you here?" Dr. Yukio asked, a gravelly voice coming from the tech imbedded in his body. His one good eye studied her carefully, vivid blue tracking her movements. "That's the question you're asking yourself."

Urban blinked. She'd forgotten how observant her mentor was.

"Humans are strange," he continued. "When they face the biggest trials in life, they often forget the most important things." He gazed pointedly at her. "I'm here to help you remember, to focus your mind."

She inclined her head. "Dr. Yukio, I'm grateful for your willingness to help in that way, but right now, I have other . . . priorities. I need to prepare for the Race to the Clouds, which I might be competing in." She hesitated, debating how much to tell her mentor. "It's really important that I win."

Dr. Yukio regarded her a moment. "I understand. Might I suggest this is the single most important thing you can do to train? Half of the RTC is a mind game. If you're not in the right mental space, victory won't be an option. I'm here to help you get in that headspace."

"But I'm most likely leaving for the Western Federation soon." His mechanical eye blinked off. "Haven't you heard? I'm taking a sabbatical this semester. I'd be glad to join you, so as to continue your lessons. I'd like to aid in fostering a winning mentality."

Urban tried to hide her surprise. She glanced doubtfully around the studio. "By making art?"

Dr. Yukio offered a slight smile. "You'll see."

Urban studied her a mentor a moment. "Why are you helping me?"

"Do you remember the application process for the program?"

Urban blinked. This was not the answer she was expecting. She thought back to her previous semester, to what seemed like a lifetime ago, when she sat in a classroom like a normal student. Her heart felt a pang.

"I believe it was nomination based?" Her answer came out more of a question.

"Do you know who nominated you?"

Urban had wondered but never found the answer. "No, I don't."

"I did," Dr. Yukio said simply.

Her confusion must have shown, because he went on to explain. "You truly displayed an uncommon artistic ability and drive. There was something different about you than the other Artisans I'd encountered."

"You mean after one class period, you decided all of that and nominated me?"

Her mentor didn't hesitate. "Yes."

"But I don't quite understand. Why are you helping me even now? Don't you realize I'm"—Urban hesitated—"I'm on the banned list?"

Dr. Yukio was unfazed. "Most great artists of history would have made that list. In fact, if you weren't on the list, I'd be worried I picked the wrong person," he said with a smile.

"True innovation, original creativity, and breakthrough art, doesn't come from following mainstream trends or pleasing stakeholders."

Urban considered this. Unsure how to respond, she simply nodded.

"Now, shall we begin?" Dr. Yukio motioned at the teaware, and Urban approached the table.

She picked up a teapot. She didn't realize how clammy her hands were, and she lost her grip. It crashed to the ground, shattering.

"I—I'm so sorry." Inwardly, Urban berated herself as she scrambled to pick up the pieces.

"Perfect," Dr. Yukio declared.

Urban paused, unsure if he was joking.

"We were just about to break one. Though I had a different teapot picked out for you." Dr. Yukio squinted at the pieces. "Hmm . . . yes, I see this is actually the better choice for you."

Urban tried to form thoughts.

"My dear, did I forget to mention you'll be learning kintsugi?"

She stared at him blankly. "Kin what?"

"Kintsugi. The art of mending. Starting with this one." Dr. Yukio picked a portion of the teapot's broken handle from the floor.

"Oh. Alright. But why kintsugi?" Urban asked.

"Because that is where we all must begin," Dr. Yukio explained. "We must be broken in order to be remade."

"But I don't want to be broken."

Dr. Yukio smiled. "No one wants to break. But at some point, we all do. The question becomes what will we do with the shattered pieces of our lives."

Urban's throat constricted as she stared at the former teapot. Surely, most people didn't have to be broken as spectacularly as she already had been. Most people seemed to live relatively simple lives—pain-free, break-free.

Dr. Yukio stooped to the ground. "Come, let's pick up these pieces and begin."

11

INFINI-FIT

URBAN SLAMMED ON THE BRAKES OF HER BIKE, barely avoiding running through a red light.

Ever since leaving the session with her mentor, she'd been distracted. This was the third light she'd almost blown through.

A large hover bus rumbled past, shaking the ground. If she didn't pull herself together, it wouldn't be the race that killed her. Taking a deep breath, she willed herself to focus.

The light turned green, and she shot forward again.

Upon arriving at her destination, she set foot on the ground and gazed up at the towering structure before her, its neon letters glowing: Infini-Fit.

It had been ages since the last time she'd worked out, and Urban didn't feel a bit motivated. But if she stood a chance at all in Race to the Clouds, she needed to start training now.

Her guards dismounted their bikes or touched down from the sky, wings sending gusts of wind her way.

Urban didn't wait for them before charging inside the colossal structure. The sound of hip-hop thumped loudly in the air. She scanned her tatt at the entrance and was walking forward when an alarm blared, stopping her in her tracks.

The patrons inside the gym all stared at her, and she felt her face heating. A moment later, a familiar willowy figure approached.

"Why hello, Urban, dear."

She was just as annoying as Urban remembered from when they'd met at her graduation party. The woman owned the gym, but what was her name again? Thankfully, Urban's retina display came to her aid.

"Hello again, Thistle." Urban forced a smile. "I'm not sure why the alarm went off. Is it broken?"

Thistle studied Urban in a way only Inceptors could. "Oh no, the alarm is working just fine. It seems you've set it off." Thistle shut off the blaring noise, and the gym music picked back up.

Urban tried to keep her expression even. "What does that mean?"

Thistle's eyes darted in QuanNao before focusing back on Urban. "It seems you are now on some sort of list . . ."

Urban's heart sank.

The banned list. Why hadn't she thought this through before coming? She had no idea what being on that list could mean.

"Our gym only admits citizens of good standing," Thistle continued. "Which you no longer are." Thistle gave Urban a patronizing smile. "Sorry, dear. Rules are rules."

Urban's throat tightened. If she kept standing there, she'd start crying. "Right, of course," she managed to say, and turned and left as quickly as she could.

Outside, she paused a moment to collect her thoughts and swallow down the burning in her throat.

She conducted a quick search in QuanNao on the banned list to try and get answers. There were several forums with users bemoaning their situation but no official documents or anything particularly helpful. It seemed it was up to individual businesses and entities to decide how to enforce the banned status.

But I'm a KOL. My sosh is 96. How is it possible I can't get into my gym?

"It will be okay," an accented voice spoke behind Urban, and she whirled around.

Trig shimmered into view, and Urban nearly hugged him.

"That was unfortunate." He motioned at the gym. "But not to worry, I have a gym I train at that will take you. Would you like to go there instead?"

She smiled at him gratefully.

"Very good. I just sent you the address," Trig said and then disappeared again.

With a lighter heart, she found that Trig's gym was only ten minutes away. While not as fancy as Infini-Fit, it was still an impressively large space. She had to leave the guards, all but Trig, outside as she entered.

Urban held her breath while scanning her tatt.

A robotic voice rang out, "Welcome, Lee Urban, guest of Trig Dlamini. Enjoy your workout!"

Urban exhaled the breath she'd been holding.

Inside, fit-looking Enhanced put the workout machines and specialized rooms to use. A muscular, stylish Flyer was already in the main lobby waiting.

"Ash!" Urban exclaimed, delighted.

Ash wrapped her in a hug. "You've really got to stop scaring me. Every time I turn my back, you're in trouble again."

Urban choked out a laugh.

"Where on earth have you been?" Ash released her, taking in her appearance. "What happened? I have so many questions. Like why are we meeting at this low-class gym?"

Where to even start?

As they made their way further inside the workout facility, Urban glanced around before explaining everything that had taken place, stopping short of her recent lab results.

Ash's face contorted with anger. "I can't believe that happened to you."

The urge for Urban to cry was overwhelming, for more reasons than one.

"Hey, you're safe now." Ash laid a reassuring hand on her shoulder.

Urban nodded with a shaky smile and turned to survey the

gym. A giant wind tunnel to her right caught her eye. Inside it, two Flyers hovered above ground, spinning and twisting gracefully up and down, pulse weapons flashing.

Urban's eyes went wide as she watched them spar in midair. Noticing her gaze, Ash poked her. "Pretty cool, huh? Want to try it?"

Urban shook her head. "I think I'll leave the aerial fighting to you. Right now, my focus should be on racing."

"Racing?"

Urban fingered the scars on her wrists. "Well, long story, but I might actually be competing in Race to the Clouds."

"Never a dull moment with you," Ash remarked with a raised brow.

She put her face in her hands. "How did my life become like this?"

"I don't know, but I'm coming."

Urban looked up in surprise. "Don't you have summer plans?"

"Nope. Wingman at your service. Besides, every time I turn around, you need rescuing again."

"Very true." Urban smiled a real smile. "I'd love to have you there."

"Done." Ash paused. "Any chance Lillian will be going?"

Urban quirked a smile. "She has to finish her internship first. But yes."

Ash brightened. "Speaking of . . ."

Lillian strode toward them.

"Hey sis!" Lillian greeted Urban with a huge hug. Upon noticing Ash, she stiffened.

Ash offered a dazzling smile. "Lillian! It's good to see you again."

Lillian grabbed a suit and threw it at him. "Put this on so I don't hurt you."

"Hurt me?"

"We're sparring," she replied crisply.

Ash raised his brow but obeyed and made his way toward the changing room.

"You invited him?" Lillian hissed as she headed to the women's locker room.

"Yes. I haven't seen him in ages, and he wanted to train with me. Not to mention . . . he wanted to see you."

Lillian shot a glance at Urban who shrugged innocently.

They reconvened a few minutes later, all wearing their fight suits. Each suit had a similar look and feel as the ones used in the arena. Once activated, it formed a hardened exoskeleton around the body.

Lillian led the way to a fighting ring large enough to hold Supers and Flyers in combat. Synthetic turf lined the ground, and the walls were padded on all sides. A series of hovering bleachers overlooked the mini arena, thankfully empty.

Before entering the ring, they paused by a wall covered from floor to ceiling in weapons. Ash selected a polearm from among them, while Urban stuck with her familiar stun shield, though she did check out a pulse knife, as well. Lillian opted for her own inventions and bypassed the wall altogether.

"Are you sure this is safe?" Urban asked nervously.

"I've done this a million times. These suits are manufactured from the same source as the ones in the PKU games. You're safe."

Urban wanted to point out that wasn't exactly reassuring. Those suits had failed her twice and nearly cost her life.

But before she could voice her concern, Lillian was jogging across the bouncy turf, in a series of warm-ups. Urban and Ash followed her example.

When Lillian stopped, she retrieved three helmets and handed them to Urban and Ash before donning her own.

"Alright." Lillian turned to Ash, sizing him up. "Let's see if the Flyer version of martial arts can keep up in a real fight. Your suit is activated, yes?"

Ash answered with a wink.

Lillian crouched into fight stance. "Then let's see what you're made of."

Ash adjusted his helmet, then froze. "Wait. You want me to attack you? I don't fight girls—"

Lillian charged, cutting his words short. Ash threw up his polearm just in time to block the attack.

Lillian retreated and began circling again.

"Please, I don't fight girls." Ash seemed genuinely distressed.

"Yes, you've made that point already." She darted toward Ash again, kicking hard, and sending him reeling backward.

"What was that?" Lillian demanded. "You're not even trying!"

Ash sheepishly picked himself up, and Lillian huffed with annoyance.

"I have an idea," Urban said. "How about we have a three-way battle? If Ash manages to win, you have to go on a date with him."

Ash perked up at this.

Lillian flashed a look at Urban before turning back to Ash. "And if he loses?"

"He won't ever ask you out again," Urban stated.

"Whaaaa—" Ash protested but was cut off.

"Done." Lillian activated a small device clipped to her suit. "Too bad for you."

"Battle starts . . ." Urban withdrew her stun shield. "Now!"

Lillian and Urban both charged Ash. Reluctantly, he crouched into a fight stance, with polearm extended.

Urban chucked her stun shield then ran at him with her pulse knife.

Ash caught the stun shield easily but had no time to block her strike. Urban's blade hit the barrier of his protective suit and slowed. An electric current zipped through him, and he yelped.

Meanwhile, Lillian threw a flurry of well-aimed punches. Ash managed to dodge and weave most, but one caught him in the jaw, sending him stumbling back. Still, he refused to retaliate.

Urban, having recovered her stun shield, turned on her sister this time.

"Hey! Whose team are you on?" Lillian demanded.

Urban lunged. "My own."

Lillian activated metal spikes on the back of her suit and angled them toward her. Urban sidestepped to avoid impaling herself on one.

Before she could recover, Lillian trapped her with a force field.

Urban beat her fists in frustration against the pulsing blue. She couldn't break out.

Lillian turned back to Ash, now hovering in the air above them. Activating a laser cannon, she aimed, then fired.

Ash thrust his wings, propelling him away from the streaks of light. He dove and spiraled out of the way as each pulse ripped through the air.

Lillian's laser cannon began smoking and her next shot went wide. Tossing her weapon to the ground, Lillian removed two drones instead.

The force field around Urban weakened, and she finally broke out, immediately charging her sister.

"Peppa, Dede, initialize facial recognition sequence for target." Lillian pointed at Urban.

The drones flew toward her. They hovered around Urban's head, making a loud buzzing noise.

One attempted to stab her with an odd weapon, but Urban dove out of the way. The other bot shot a webbed net at her feet, tripping her.

Urban landed hard on the ground but managed to slice herself free with her stun shield. Lillian was already on top of her, knocking her weapons away. They scrambled, trying to get the better position, jiujitsu training kicking in.

Lillian gained the upper hand as Urban's strength began to wane.

Suddenly, something stabbed Urban in the thigh, and her body seized up.

"Good work, Peppa." Lillian gave her drone an approving nod before turning to find Ash.

He flew above them, taking in the whole scene, still refusing to attack.

Lillian guided her drones toward him. The one with the odd device that froze Urban hovered around and tried to stab him, but Ash used his polearm to knock it away.

Lillian stepped over Urban's still prone form and collected her stun shield. "Play time is over," she announced.

The drones converged on Ash, and at the same moment, Lillian flung the stun shield into the air.

Ash batted the stun shield away with his polearm and managed to dodge another round of webbing from the other drone. But he was too distracted to avoid the other bot and let out a sharp cry of pain.

His body seized up and he crashed to the ground.

Lillian strode over triumphantly and looked down at his immobile body. "Keep dreaming about that date."

She turned to leave, when Ash sprung up from the training mat. Lillian was too surprised to react before he had her wrapped in a choke from behind, one arm holding her neck firmly while the other locked behind her head.

"W–what?" Lillian gasped.

"Surrender?" Ash asked playfully.

Lillian hesitated before reluctantly tapping for Ash to release her. Immediately, he relented and stepped back.

Lillian glowered at him. "You're supposed to be paralyzed right now."

Ash's expression was smug. "That's if I were stung by your bot."

Lillian's mouth fell open, but she quickly closed it. "Yes, well. Good practice."

"See you tomorrow night," Ash said, turning to leave. "2100 at Lin's Fusion Bar," he called over his shoulder. "Don't be late."

Lips pressed, Lillian made her way toward her water container.

As the effects of the drone's paralyzing neurotoxin wore off and Urban slowly stood, a ping arrived in her retina display.

[Ash: Your sister loves me.]

Urban barely held in a laughing snort.

[Urban: I don't know about that, but I'd say you impressed her.]

[Ash: Really??]

Urban studied Lillian.

[Urban: Definitely. She's attracted to brains AND brawn.]

[Ash: Any tips for our hot date? Should I gift her one of those NFT bouquets? I hear they're all the rage these days.]

[Urban: Lillian doesn't like that sort of thing. She loves intellectually stimulating conversations. Go into dinner with a few controversial topics researched. Or theories on the impact on society of some upcoming invention. She'll be smitten.]

[Ash: I owe you.]

[Urban: Not really, given how many times you've saved my life. But you're welcome.]

She joined Lillian sitting against a wall, both quenching their thirst.

Lillian put her container down. "I have news. Some good and some . . . bad."

Urban tensed. "What?"

"Have you checked the news feeds recently?"

"No, why?"

"RTC has been relocated."

"Relocated?" Urban repeated. "What does that mean?"

"Well, that's the bad news. Here, see for yourself." Lillian flicked on a holo and they were instantly immersed in a news feed.

A reporter stood on a mountain surveying the surroundings. "This is Pike's Peak, the host to the annual Race to the Clouds. We've spent the last few years honing the race course's AI. It's like one giant arena with animals, obstacles, and other race-day surprises all hidden within the mountain."

Images of various obstacles ranging from purple water falls, decrepit roads, and mutated giant lions filled the mountain.

"But for the first time in over two hundred years, the race won't be held on Pike's Peak."

The announcer's statement sparked Urban's interest. Her suit cooled to mimic the temperature of the high altitude. Lush green forests covered the mountain and mist shrouded the air. A close-up showed mountain goats chewing grass lazily next to a trail where tourists hiked.

"After searching across the globe's most challenging mountains and peaks, it was difficult to find a good substitute for the race."

A globe spun around Urban in a dizzying whirl, slowing over mountains ranging from rusty browns, to snowcapped icons like Mount Fuji, and finally stopping over the Asian Federation.

"An acceptable location has been agreed upon." The reporter paused dramatically. "For the first time ever, this year's Race to the Clouds will be hosted by New Chengdu on Mount Emei."

"Emei Shan?" Urban breathed. She'd visited the iconic mountain as a child to watch one of her Father's races. It was a stunning peak but with incredibly dangerous switchback roads.

The news reporter continued. "The Emei races have been one of the biggest feeders into the RTC. It hosts its own annual race, with top competitors frequently moving on to participate in RTC. However, the change in location poses a unique set of challenges and opportunities for this year's racers. For one thing, this new mountain is not embedded with AI obstacles."

Urban's hopes jumped at this. Not having to compete in one of the deadliest race courses while also facing off with terrifying creatures and obstacles would certainly make her life easier.

"However, the PKU Dragons have volunteered to help supply RTC officials with the obstacles needed from their own arena storehouse."

Urban's spirits plummeted.

"Game-day officials will be hard pressed to outfit Mount Emei with all its surprises before the race day, but with the help of volunteers at PKU, they are hopeful the task can be done in time for the big event."

Urban glanced at Lillian. She hadn't seen anyone from the PKU Dragons since the Western Federation. She wasn't sure how she felt about their involvement in the games. Especially since she now knew two of them had tried to kill her.

"Mount Emei is approximately five thousand feet shorter than the classic fourteener, Pike's Peak. This means racers will spend less time on the ground and more time in the sky, meaning a complete shift in the design of this year's vehicles.

"Not to mention, previous year champions no longer have the advantage of being familiar with the terrain and race course. Except for the racers who've competed on Emei before, the terrain will be new to everyone. They will be starting on the same page as the rookies, giving this year's newcomers their best shot at winning."

Hope blossomed in Urban. "That's good right?"

"Keep watching."

"This major change is necessary, though. As the civil war in the Western Federation escalates, race officials have deemed it no longer safe to hold the famous race here."

The feed shifted to riots in New Denver.

Urban gasped as what looked like the entire city went up in flames. Hyper sonic missiles zigged their way through space to land on a nearby town, decimating it.

"Due to the civil war, and uprisings in multiple countries, New Chengdu has been deemed one of the safest locations for the race. Hopefully it stays that way."

The vid ended.

Heavy thoughts pressed in on Urban. The Race to the Clouds was the only way to bring equality to Naturals. But would it be too late? The Western Federation was in the middle of civil war and the Asian Federation wasn't far behind.

The stoop-shouldered employees working grueling shifts at the AI factories came to her mind. With factory work drying up, Naturals were left even more vulnerable—and desperate.

This is bigger than I imagined. The violence has to be stopped from spreading.

Civil war couldn't be the answer. Everything didn't need to be burned to the ground to force change. They needed to outsmart the system. *Something I've been doing my whole life.*

But the uncomfortable pressure remained.

How much will joining the race cost me? Is it worth the price?

12

HUTONGS

SMOKE PUNCTURED THE GRAY SKY WITHIN
the dome.

<Entering yellow zone. Exercise CAUTION.>

Urban's retina display sent her a warning, but she blinked it
away. Leaving the pristine Metropolis air behind, she stepped
into the hot, dry, polluted Hutongs and weaved her way through
the open market. Her guards remained close behind, filtration
masks strapped to their faces.

She was grateful the barrier between the Metropolis and the
Hutongs allowed her through. Now that she was on the banned
list, she had no idea what she was permitted to do. Waves of
anxiety spilled over with each place she went. Would an alarm
go off again? Would she be publicly shamed? Would her family
and friends be penalized too?

Everest had recently achieved the sosh he needed to pass
as a believable Enhanced living in the Metropolis. He couldn't
afford a sosh infringement.

Urban set aside thoughts of Everest and her family and
focused on her surroundings. What she needed right now was a
break. Some quiet time alone with New Beijing's best noodles.

On the road before her, an elderly man squatted to examine
fish splashing in cheap plastic basins. The uneven concrete

around him was filled with puddles. Natural kids chased each other in a game of tag while adults bartered over asymmetrical vegetables and scrawny animals. Chickens clucked placidly from within wire cages. All of it so different from the perfectly prepared foods the drones delivered within the Metropolis.

Life in the Hutongs and the Outskirts was messy. Real. In a way the Metropolis could never be. Maybe that was one of the reasons Urban was always drawn to it.

Life here was about more than parties, linking, and social scores. It was about family, tradition, and simplicity. It was a slow and beautiful way of life worth preserving. Even if it also had a darker underbelly Everest seemed constantly entangled with.

I could help create a bridge between the Enhanced and Naturals.

The thought of what it would take to get there, however, made Urban shudder. The last thing she wanted was her body poked and prodded, or to risk her life as AiE's figurehead.

Stop thinking about it, she scolded herself.

Enhanced tourists strolled past, easy to distinguish from the local Naturals. They wore sleek summer XR polos and rompers. The tourists would momentarily stop, no doubt snapping images with their retina displays, which they'd upload to QuanNao later. But for now, everything was blocked in the Hutongs to preserve the old way of life, tech-free.

Picking her way past tourist stores and butchers, Urban spotted a familiar hanging sign: Auntie's Noodle Shop. The scent of garlic and freshly made flour noodles filled the air as she drew closer.

Stepping through the plastic barrier, Urban made her way into the tiny, hole-in-the-wall restaurant, leaving all but one of her guards outside.

It was warmer inside from the kitchen, and Urban's XR suit clicked on to try and cool her. The patrons here were all Naturals. As Urban and her guard, the Super, took seats on plastic stools at an empty table, she noticed Naturals casting quick glances at them.

Urban's guard took one look at the menu and lowered it. "I'll pass."

"But these are the best noodles in town." Urban glanced up at him.

The Super grunted. "Best for getting a stomach ache."

Several patrons, watching their discussion with open interest, shifted and grumbled at this, sending Urban's cheeks aflame.

What was supposed to be a peaceful lunch somewhere she loved was turning into just another day of being an outsider. It felt weird having Naturals eye her with suspicion. Most of her life, it had been the eyes of the Enhanced.

Does the hybrid belong in the Hutongs?

The Super cut into her thoughts. "Don't you get sick after eating food from here?"

Urban shook her head. While most Enhanced stomachs weren't able to process oily food very well, hers was used to it from her time in the orphanage. But she didn't want to have to explain her origin story. And she certainly didn't want to explain her complicated genetics.

A rotund Natural woman appeared wearing a stained apron and carrying an old-school pad of paper and a pen.

"Hello, Auntie," Urban said respectfully.

The woman started, then quickly smiled. "Urban, why hello, dear. I hardly recognized you."

Urban tugged at her sleeve.

Auntie's gaze wandered over Urban's XR suit. "It's been a while."

How much did Auntie know about her life? Surely, they at least had holo projections in their homes. Now that Urban thought about it, she wasn't sure how they got their news, if at all. She envied them.

She smiled at Auntie again. "I've been pretty busy. But it's been too long since I've had New Beijing's best noodles."

Auntie deflected the compliment. "No, no, we don't have the best noodles. But I'm happy to serve you the best I can."

"May I have a bowl of beef *chaomian*?"

"Of course, dear."

Auntie glanced expectantly to the Super, but he just waved her off, and she returned to the kitchen.

The other patrons stopped staring and resumed hungrily tipping bowls of soup noodles to their mouths.

Urban's gaze shifted to the people outside the shop windows. They walked with a slow, easy gait, randomly stopping to chat with one another. It was such a foreign way of life to Urban, she could hardly imagine being known and fitting in somewhere. Not to mention, not having to worry about safety all the time.

Soon, a steaming porcelain bowl of noodles appeared before her.

Urban thanked Auntie and then hungrily dove in. Noodles slid off her chopsticks and plopped back into the bowl more than once as she ate. The homemade fried noodles were slippery and tasted of beef and rich seasoning. The chef-bots in the Metropolis would never be able to rival Auntie's noodles.

When she was done, Urban and the Super stood and made their way back out into the sweltering dry summer heat. Her other guards rejoined them, one on foot, the other two flying or perched somewhere above. She couldn't see them, but knowing they were close by brought her comfort.

Crowds of Naturals and tourists swarmed the narrow alley, but Urban's gaze snagged on an athletic figure cutting a path toward her. His thick black hair was combed neatly to the side, and moss green eyes locked with her own.

Despite his fake-colored retina displays, styled hair, and Metropolis clothes, she instantly recognized him.

"Everest!" Urban called, pushing through the crowd to get to him. As he drew nearer, Everest's face was tight, his stance guarded and alert. His eyes scanned their surroundings, hand lingering near his concealed Magtouch.

Urban squeezed his arm. "Everest?"

His eyes flashed to something above her.

Urban followed his gaze and noticed a large, winged beetle flying through the air. "What's going—"

Everest's eyes widened, and he yanked her to the ground.

BOOM!

Blinding light flashed. A sound like a hundred Aquas roaring at once shattered the air.

A wave of heat slammed into Urban. The scent of something burning assaulted her nostrils. Ringing reverberated in her ears.

Everest kneeled over her with an Inventor's pulse shield extended above. Slabs of brick and debris pelted the shield but didn't hit them. To Urban's horror, the noodle shop was up in flames.

"Auntie!"

The market around them was in total chaos. Vendors darted from their stalls, clutching valuables or pulling injured people to safety. Tourists screamed and ran, while others stood and filmed the whole thing. Debris littered the street as smoke billowed out of the noodle restaurant.

Everest released the stun shield and pulled Urban to her feet. He guided her away from the danger.

Urban balked, twisting toward the flames. "They need help."

"We don't have time," Everest said tersely. "That explosion was meant for you."

As if to prove his point, Urban's two guards drew their weapons and stood on either side of her.

"But Auntie—" Urban's voice cracked. Just a couple minutes ago, Auntie had smiled at her in a room full of frowning people.

Everest's voice and the blaring alarms sounded far away.

"The medbots will be here any minute to help survivors. We have to leave now, or the death toll will rise."

Death toll.

The words jolted Urban from her shock and she forced her feet forward. She followed Everest, her mouth dry, the two guards on foot close behind.

Everest bellowed, "Get down!"

A blast of light shot past them.

The guards sprang into action—one held a stun shield while the other aimed a Magtouch and returned fire.

"Trig, go investigate," Everest commanded.

More blasts answered from an alley, but no response from Trig.

"Trig, can you hear me?" Everest scanned the sky.

"Private com links are disabled here," one of the guards said.

Everest's jaw tensed. "Then help isn't coming. It's just us."

There was movement behind a smoking stall of ruined paper fans. A swarm of figures clad in slick black armor poured out, their illegal face shields preventing identification. Each of their masks was programmed to resemble a yellow serpent wrapped around a bloodied scorpion stinger.

The symbol looked oddly familiar.

The blood drained from Everest's face.

"Who are they?" Urban asked. "What do they want?"

Everest looked directly at her. "You."

Urban froze.

Everest turned to the two guards. "Can you cover for us?"

The Supers surveyed the mass of armored Enhanced approaching. "We'll hold them as long as possible."

"Wait. I can help." Urban came to life and reached for one of the ink bombs at her hip. She wished she had spent more time reading the manual. She didn't know if it could be activated outside of water.

"Get ready to run," she told them.

She swiped her tatt across the ink bomb. Once it vibrated in her hands confirming it had been activated, she flung it at their attackers.

She held her breath.

Nothing.

Then blackness exploded, coating their attackers in slimy residue.

"Go! Go!" Everest pulled her toward a wide residential street, weaving in and out of tourists.

They were half way down the road when a Super stepped out into their path, blocking them.

They skidded to a stop.

Several more Enhanced sprang from the surrounding shops. Before Urban could react, one of the Supers aimed a pulse gun and fired.

A brilliant blue light flashed around her. But instead of hitting her, the pulse seemed to strike thin air, dissipating.

Not thin air. A Camo.

A Flyer shimmered into focus, grabbing at his chest and sinking to the ground.

"Trig!" Urban cried out.

One of her other guards took off into the sky.

Trig propped himself up against a wall. "I'm alright. Go."

An Inventor screamed, swinging Urban's attention away from her guard.

Blasts of light sprayed the ground around the tall Inventor woman as the guard fired at her from the sky. But the woman took cover behind the Super's shield and released a fleet of drones skyward.

The drones converged on what looked like nothing, but then the Flyer guard shimmered into view, one of his wings bleeding. Spinning wildly out of control, he crashed to the ground, wings covered in drone spikes.

"Urban! Go!" Trig urged.

Urban hesitated, but Everest pulled her away.

"You can run," the Inventor shouted, her modulated voice unrecognizable. "But your friends and family can't."

Urban stumbled, but Everest caught her. They sprinted through a stone garden, ducking down an abandoned alley and under drying sausages dangling from windows. The sound of their attackers fell away. Urban's legs burned as they crossed the barrier back into the Metropolis and scrambled into an idling Wasp 8.

Everest's tension seemed to ease a little as their vehicle sped out of the Hutongs, but Urban stared back through the window.

Streaks of black slithered toward the barrier, then having nowhere to go, fanned out and dripped down like poisoned tar. The wail of the *Jingcha*'s sirens haunted the air. Their red and gold flashes reflected off the surrounding buildings' glass and shiny metal sides.

Someone destroyed a piece of the Hutongs because of me.

"Who were they?" she asked.

Everest's jaw tightened. "Did you notice their face shields?"

"The creepy looking snake and stinger?"

"That's the symbol for the Deadly Five."

Urban's stomach clenched. "How did they know I'd be in the Hutongs? Come to think of it," she looked at him, "how did *you* know I'd be there?"

Everest let out an embarrassed cough. "You're still wearing your tracker and everyone on your security team has access to it."

He's part of my security team?

The thought brought a wave of comfort as she fingered the area where a barely visible silver device sat just beneath the skin. Her own mother had implanted the tracker in her arm last semester. Urban had learned the hard way it didn't work underwater. At least today it had saved her life—and for that, she was grateful.

A thought struck her. "If my entire security team has access to my whereabouts, could it be someone from within?"

Everest shook his head. "They wouldn't have had enough time. The plasma imploder was planted ahead of time. The only reason I found out is because remote-accessing a plasma imploder in a dead zone like the Hutongs isn't an easy thing. It tripped one of the security devices Lillian had installed on you."

"But it still doesn't make sense. I didn't tell anyone I was going to the Hutongs. How could someone have known to plant a weapon like that there?"

"My best guess is your AI maps."

Urban wrinkled her brow, confused.

"If someone had access to your location data, they could easily create a heat map of your most visited locations. Then they could plant the imploder somewhere you go often. After that, it's just a matter of using your live location as a trigger for the detonation."

"But the Hutongs are offline." Urban pointed out. "How would they have data on my whereabouts within?"

"They could have supplemented your maps with satellite images of the Hutongs," Everest said. "They would know you often go to that noodle place and could proactively place a plasma imploder there. Then, all they'd need is real-time data to your whereabouts in order to activate it. Since the Hutongs are all offline, the *Jingcha* wouldn't pick up on the weapon's signal."

She blanched. "But I thought my avatar, pings—everything had upgraded security? With my encrypted messages, I'm supposed to be impossible to hack."

"Someone could have stolen your information before the upgrades."

"But if everything in the Hutongs is offline, then how would they be able to activate the plasma imploder?" she protested.

"Remember that flying beetle?" Everest asked, and she nodded.

"That looked like a cybug. Similar to the ones your family invented. Only, I'm guessing, instead of a receiver chip that takes in sound or air quality, this one was designed with a broadcasting device implanted. Once the bug was within close enough proximity to the imploder, it automatically activated. Because it's a bug instead of a drone, it made it past the Hutongs' security wall."

"This is craziness." Urban's brain spun, trying to sift through all the possibilities. "Should I now avoid all my other favorite spots?"

"Most normal plasma imploders have a signal that will ping off nearby hypernet transceivers. So, if the Deadly Five try to set one off in the Metropolis, it would alert the *Jingcha*. But just in case, you might want to have your AI assistant pull up your maps and send you a warning any time you get too close to a location you often frequent."

Urban was almost afraid to ask. "Is it safe for me to go home?"

"I've run background checks on every single person who goes in and out of your family's residence," Everest said. "And with AiE's upgraded drones and privately contracted cyber security team, I think you should be safe."

Should be safe. That wasn't very reassuring. Her thoughts drifted back to the Naturals who had been near the explosion. Like Auntie.

She turned in her seat and flicked on the news.

Everest glanced at her. "Are you sure you want to do that?" he asked gently.

She wasn't sure at all, but she had to know what had happened since they left.

". . . officials have reason to believe the explosion was intentional," a reporter was saying. "But the motive and cause for such a heinous act is still unclear."

The image shifted to show a black and white photo.

"The Hutongs have long been a historical site and held a special place within the heart of New Beijing citizens. Destruction of this treasure is a great loss to our culture and history. And for those who live there, a way of life."

The display switched to show the wreckage of the Hutongs. Medbots pulled bodies out from under rubble.

Urban stiffened in horror.

"So far, there are two confirmed deaths and a dozen in critical care units. Medbots and officials are doing their best to save others—"

Everest shut off the vid and drew her to him.

Tears dripped down her cheeks.

Two people dead. Twelve injured. Maybe more.

She squeezed her eyes shut.

All because of me. It wasn't a distant civil war anymore. It was on their doorstep, and if it continued, it would be much more costly.

Urban straightened. In that moment, she made a decision.

She wiped her eyes and looked into Everest's watchful gaze. "Take me to AiE's headquarters. I have an answer for them."

13

无家

TIME LAPSE

VISIONS OF THE HUTONGS PLAGUED URBAN all the way to and from AiE's headquarters. When she'd arrived, all of the Precepts were otherwise engaged. Urban had ended up leaving them a message before heading home. Somehow, it felt like a failure after the declaration rising within her. She had to do something. Now.

They pulled to a stop in front of her house, and Everest escorted her inside.

The normally peaceful home was laced with an air of danger, like the slightest noise might be an intruder.

Urban wished her family was there. Something about their presence made the place feel warmer. Safer.

At least she had her guards. And Everest. His steadying presence lent her a sense of strength.

Urban made her way into the family parlor where all the decor was white. It was obvious where Jiaozi had sat with his bright purple fur.

Everest lowered himself onto the couch and Urban took a seat next to him as a Natural maid approached. "Tea?"

Everest nodded. "Buckwheat, please."

"And oolong for me," Urban added.

The maid soon returned with a lacquered tray containing

two tiny glazed ceramic teapots and cups. Urban poured Everest a cup before filling her own.

She sipped her hot, earthy tea silently. Everest remained contemplatively quiet.

The bubbly fountain at the center of the room was uncharacteristically dry. *My family must be staying at one of our other houses.* She didn't blame them.

Even now, after removing all the bugs, she couldn't shake the feeling someone was watching her.

Can AiE really keep us safe?

As if reading her thoughts, a prioritized ping appeared. Using the decoder key AiE had given Urban, she opened it.

[Winter: Urban, we received your message and are honored to have you join us as our figurehead. We will be upgrading your security to a level one. This means you will have additional guards, hidden monitoring drones, and two full-time cyber security experts assigned to your avatar, among other precautions. We will be setting all of that up today. Please don't be alarmed by the changes and do let us know if you have any questions.]

Urban glanced over at the house guards. Her thoughts wandered to Trig and her other guards who'd risked their lives for her in the Hutongs. She wasn't sure how she felt about putting more people in danger.

Urban finished reading the rest of the message from Sato Winter.

[Winter: You have also been assigned a personal media and PR specialist, Yu Jasmine. She will help you with any public speeches and press appearances. Please feel free to use her as a resource. We look forward to seeing great things from you, Miss Lee.]

Urban's stomach seized at the thought of all the speeches and public appearances that were expected of her. Then again, those were relatively safe compared to Race to the Clouds.

She looked at Everest. "Do you think I can do it?"

Everest didn't need to ask what she was talking about. He took a sip of tea. "It won't be easy—great things never are." He looked at her, eyes intense. "But if anyone can do it, it's you."

Urban bit her lip.

"Urban, you're the perfect candidate. You have experience in racing. You've been in the AI games twice. And won. As far as rookies go, I can't think of anyone with more relevant experience. You can do this. I believe in you."

Urban let out a sigh and gave him a weak smile. "You know in engineering class when they talk about single points of failure?"

Everest nodded.

"You're not supposed to have them. Everyone knows that. But this plan of AiE's . . ." She gestured wildly around the room. "It all depends on me. I am the single point of failure."

Everest caught her hand. "Urban, whether that's true or not, there's no other way. I'm still researching other options, backdoors, political allies—anything. So far, I've found nothing."

He drew his hand back as another prioritized message, this one from Croix, appeared in Urban's retina display, interrupting their conversation.

[Mako: The Race to the Clouds kick-off party will commence tonight. We secured tickets and would be delighted if you could attend. As your sponsor, one of the contract obligations is making appearances at several of the RTC bashes sporting our gear. If you're able to make it, we'll send over some of our stylists to help you and your plus-one prepare.]

Urban brushed a hand through her coarse hair, suddenly self-conscious. Weeks without a haircut and basic grooming in the underwater prison had left her feeling more than a little shabby.

She sent a quick response to Mako.

[Urban: I'll be there and would appreciate the help of your stylists. Thank you.]

She debated asking Mako right then and there why he was sponsoring her. How much coverage was she really going to get, being on the banned list? But if she brought it up and he didn't know about her status, he might cancel her contract, and then she wouldn't be able to race.

Surely someone with his power would know about her status,

wouldn't he? He seemed to have excellent sources. After all, he'd been the first person to find her in prison.

Then another dark thought crossed her mind. Would being on the list mean she would be denied access to the RTC bash? Surely not. Otherwise, Croix wouldn't be sending her. Right?

Urban conducted a quick search in QuanNao but couldn't find anything about the school's policy on the banned list.

A response arrived back from her sponsor.

[Mako: Expect my team to arrive within the hour.]

Team? How many people was he sending?

Pushing her curiosity and concerns aside, Urban glanced at Everest. "I have an obligatory bash this evening for my sponsor. Want to be my plus-one?"

Everest didn't hesitate. "When and where?"

"It's in a few hours, but the Croix stylist team should be here soon to help us get ready."

Everest raised an eyebrow. "Help us?"

Urban gave a wry smile. "Welcome to the life of the Enhanced."

He rolled his eyes. "Dress up. My favorite."

True to their word, the Croix beauty team arrived in less than an hour. As soon as Urban's guards let them in, the room was flooded with a constant stream of Artisans in bright colors and wearing eclectic clothes.

"Hello, dear," greeted a woman with spiked green hair. She dragged a trundle of levitating beauty supplies behind her. "I'm the head stylist, Luna, and this is my team of beauticians. We'll be conducting you and your plus-one's transformation today."

Everest's eyes shifted back and forth as he scanned all the beauty supplies like a trapped animal.

Luna's team took over the family room, setting up smart mirrors, mixing creams, plugging in diffusers, and filling the space with the scent of eucalyptus. A sound system was set up and techno music reverberated through the walls. One Artisan towed in a portable sink and reclining armchair.

If Urban hadn't known she was sitting in her family's parlor, she would never have been able to recognize the place.

Luna gestured at a hovering seat in front of a smart mirror and Urban gratefully sat, already exhausted. Everest was led to the other side of the room, and she lost sight of him among the bags, trunks, and mirrors. As the Croix team swirled around her debating different hair conditioners and nail styles, she caught her reflection in a mirror.

The girl staring back was markedly different. She'd lost weight and her facial features were sharp. Her hair had grown out to the longest it had ever been, a tangled mess of black that drooped down her back.

But it was the eyes that had changed the most.

Urban was wearing her translucent retina displays which showed her true eye color, a coal black. Since becoming Enhanced, she hadn't felt the need to wear her showy gold ones as often. But the look in them gave her pause. Her expression was fierce—determined.

If Everest believed in her, maybe she had a shot at winning yet.

Two hours later, Urban looked like a new person.

Oils had been applied to her scalp, and her hair was washed, trimmed, and styled. Other team members had cleaned, buffed, and painted her nails, while still others had given her a facial and applied moisturizers and makeup.

Urban had tried to count how many people were buzzing around her, but she'd lost track after fourteen.

"And here you are, darling." Luna spun the chair around so Urban could see her final image in the mirror.

Urban was expecting to see bold, unnatural makeup and hair, but the Croix stylists had opted for a softer look. They'd left her hair long and wavy, her eyes black, and her skin, while made flawless, appeared natural. She was stunning, but in a way that was entirely her own.

Luna handed Urban a lightweight set of clothes wrapped delicately in tissue paper. "Your outfit for tonight, hand-selected by Croix's top stylist."

"Thank you." Urban changed in the adjacent room into a black top with the Gamelyon symbol emblazoned on it. She pulled on distressed pants with intentionally ripped holes. Croix was definitely leaning into the rebel look. Either that, or they were going for broke artist.

Luna's face lit up when Urban returned. "You look perfect, dear!" She clapped her hands. "Alright everyone, time to move out."

Just as quickly as they came, the room emptied, leaving Urban, her guards, and Everest alone in the ringing silence.

Everest tugged uncomfortably at the smart suit clinging to the contours of his body. "Why are the clothes in the Metropolis all so tight?"

Urban pulled him along. "Come on, let's go."

Outside, AiE had sent an upgraded, top-notch security vehicle, more tank-like than car. The ride came complete with force field windows, facial recognition targeting, and neutral-beam injectors mounted above. Urban had only ever seen the vehicle used by the military or high-profile politicians.

Everest let out a low whistle as they climbed in, followed by her guards. Countless new security details followed them from the sky, other vehicles, and even on foot. It was an impressive show of protection, but Urban wasn't sure if she felt reassured or trapped.

They sped away, and all too soon, the Peking University campus stretched before them, familiar and yet intimidating all at once.

Urban let out a deep breath. It seemed like just yesterday and yet ages since she'd last been there.

Each reentry to school was like a time lapse.

Memories flashed before her. Stepping onto campus her

first day for registration with her lone suitcase and a sense of excitement and freedom. The fear she'd experienced when she'd been trapped in a purple zone and almost killed. The motorcycle race she competed in to boost her sosh. Her classes. The KOL parties. Her roommates: Blossom, Hazel, and Coral.

She'd been so naive her first time at uni.

Her second time, she'd joined the Dragons, traveled out of the Asian Federation, competed in the Games and won, been captured, escaped, and discovered she was the hybrid. That time, she'd learned some hard lessons but was still ignorant about what really mattered in life.

Now, she realized how small she was—perhaps a pawn in some invisible game of chess. Or maybe that was the mark of growth, recognizing shortcomings and feeling the burden of just how far there still was left to go.

Everest squeezed her hand reassuringly.

Shoulders held high, Urban set foot onto campus.

PKU BASH

"WELCOME TO THE RACE TO THE CLOUDS kickoff party!" an announcer boomed.

Urban and Everest arrived at their private box seating right as the opening ceremony began. To her relief, she'd had no trouble getting in, despite her banned status. Half of her guards now remained outside while the rest followed them into the lush space Croix had purchased for their private viewing.

The room was circular and dimly lit. An automated drink machine sat in one corner, while several immersive seats filled the space before a smart glass window, allowing a stunning view of the arena below. They were so close, Urban could make out the individual tiles on the stadium's floor.

"I'm Hong, your host for the evening, and do we have a show for you!" The announcer stood atop a hovering dais at the center of the arena wearing a dress of red and green with the RTC logo on it.

The crowd cheered, but Urban shifted uncomfortably at seeing PKU's announcer. The last time she'd seen Hong, Urban was thrown into the arena and had almost died.

"Tonight," Hong continued, "we have the past few years' RTC champions here with us to give a brief display of the caliber of talent exhibited in the race."

Several of the arena tiles flipped over, forming a ramp underground, and a dozen riders zoomed up from the dark. Some drove race cars while others rode motorcycles. The vehicles were stunning works of engineering: sleek designs, brilliant with colors, and powered by the latest advancements to supercharge them.

Around the racers, the space began to change again, tiles flipping over to reveal an impressive course. Glowing fuchsia lights marked out the different tracks. Some portions appeared relatively straightforward, while others dipped underwater or disappeared entirely to form stunning jumps over lava or mini city landscapes.

Then the obstacles appeared. Recreated dinosaurs gnashing their teeth, bots with weapons blocking the road, an enlarged praying mantis swiping its chitin arms, and other terrifying, genetically modified animals blocking the way.

"Are you ready?" Hong asked, and the crowd roared.

Engines revved.

"Samson, activate entertainment mode!"

"Entertainment mode activated," Samson's monotone voice boomed. "Begin racing in three . . . two . . . one. Go!"

The racers shot forward.

The first portion of the course was designed to look like a pathway through a jungle. The main road wove through giant trees dangling with roots and moss and teeming with animals. Other, smaller dirt paths led to shortcuts involving increased danger.

Urban slid into one of the immersive seats and felt the temperature grow to a sweltering humid heat to mimic the climate below. The smell of damp earth and animal fur filled her nose. Wind blew her hair as if she really were on one of the vehicles competing below.

Her chest constricted.

It was just like the last time she'd been in the arena. All of it came rushing back. Hot, dry sand, her suit deflating, Vance's arrow pointed at her heart—

"Urban . . ." Everest sat beside her, leaning close. "Urban, are you alright?"

Urban shook herself. "I'm . . . fine."

It's not real. None of this is real.

And yet, it would be soon. Only, this time, she wouldn't be in the games, but a race. Though hopefully, with a working suit this time. Given her track record, she wouldn't count on it.

Everest was watching her. "Remember, you also have the genetics to win."

Urban glanced up at him, marveling that he knew her so well.

"Not to mention, you'll have the best motorcycle coach around." He winked.

A laugh bubbled up inside her. "Alright, Big Shot."

What would I do without him?

The crowd gasped and Urban's attention swiftly turned to the race.

In the arena, one of the racers veered off the main course and swerved to avoid hitting an enhanced alligator. The creature's skin was a transparent tone, revealing its inner organs.

The racer tried to regain control of his bike but tumbled off and slammed into a tree trunk. He screamed in pain, clutching his arm.

Urban cringed.

The racer zeroed out and the arena's tiles flipped over, taking him to the medbay, and safety, below.

Another racer slowed as he struck a mud pit in the middle of a glowing spiders' nests. He yelled and swatted at the tiny monsters as they climbed all over him, biting and attempting to trap him in their webs. Other racers ran into their own sets of troubles as they bumped over snakes the size of furniture or tried to escape from dog-sized scorpionflies.

Most of the racers emerged from the jungle with their damage counters dropped.

Next, they entered the space portion of the race. This part

was dark, the only lighting coming from stars and planets.

The racer in the lead shot up a ramp then flew into the dark expanse. But he didn't come back down. Instead, he seemed to freeze in zero gravity.

Then, with a flick of his wrist, the vehicle converted into a flying machine, power boosters angling behind him and glowing red before shooting him forward. He landed the jump and gravity reactivated, sending him hurtling down the ramp and into the water portion of the race.

The racer launched an air bubble around his vehicle before disappearing beneath the sparkling cobalt water. He followed an underwater path at the bottom of a lake, the smart glass viewport allowing the audience to track his progress.

Several shapes from the depths of the murky water moved toward him. It took Urban a second to identify them as killer eels, genetically engineered for deep sea-fishing, and each the size of a horse. They were one of the many species of animals that had escaped into the wild and wreaked havoc on entire ecosystems.

The inky black eels undulated with surprising speed toward the first rider as well as the others now entering behind him.

The lead racer didn't have enough time to react before he was knocked off his bike by one of the eels. The others caught up and attacked in a frenzy. His damage counter immediately dropped to zero. The racer, along with his bike, several eels, and a ton of water, disappeared below the arena.

The new rider in first place rode what had to be an Inventor rev cycle. It didn't look like anything Urban had seen on the market. Gadgets and colors filled every available space of the long, armored vehicle.

The racer activated a portion of the cycle, and it glowed. A holo replica of the rider shot out several meters behind him.

Only, the holo was bleeding.

It must have been scent activated too, because the eels streaked toward the image and attacked it with razored teeth.

The real racer escaped the eels just in time to enter a minefield of glowing jellyfish.

He swerved, but his underwater reactions weren't as fast, and he bumped into a few of the jellyfish. Electric blue tentacles struck his helmet and rev cycle before he broke free. His damage counter dropped to 53. He shook his head as if to clear it before rocketing out of the water and toward the next portion of the course.

This part looked like a Flyer's dream.

The racers rode ramps up into the sky, following narrow, hovering roads weaving between obstacles and gravity-defying loops and curves. Holo markers in the form of pulsing circles and arrows highlighted harder routes with bonuses attached. The lead racer kept a steady course, but the third-place rider took a chance and made his way through two back-to-back loops before hitting a pulsing blue holo. The instant power-up created a sizzling blue circle around the bike and sent him ricocheting into second place.

A high-pitched roar shattered the arena.

Scaled onyx wings swept a giant serpentine creature through the air and toward the riders.

It was the same dragon that had attacked Urban when she'd been trapped in the arena. She was glad this time there were several protective barriers between her and the creature.

The racers accelerated, and one flew off the course, zeroing out and disappearing under the arena. Some of the steadier contenders rushed through turns, twists, and loops, managing to stay the course even as they fled from the creature.

The dragon swooped down and snapped at the lead rider, ripping him off his bike. The racer dangled from the dragon's jaws, zeroing out. The creature dropped him into a small pond, and then the tiles flipped and the racer was carried to safety.

The giant creature's head swiveled in search of its next victim. The new lead racer crouched lower to his bike as the finish line appeared, glowing at the end of a large jump. The racer zoomed up the ramp and soared over empty space.

The dragon took the moment of exposure and swooped down again, breathing fire. It reached down with its talons to snatch the lead rider but wasn't fast enough.

With a jolt, the rider landed, drifting across a tight turn, then shot across the finish line. The other racers followed close behind.

Strobe lights danced and music blared as the race finished.

The dragon flew back under the arena, and the other obstacles also retreated.

Despite Everest's earlier words, Urban couldn't stop staring at the racers at the finish line. All were banged up. Then there were the others down below in the medbay getting treatment for injuries their suits hadn't been able to protect them from.

If this race was any indicator, RTC was going to be dangerous.

"What a thrilling race!" Hong announced. "And that concludes our activities for the day. Head over to the Chai Tai Center for the after-party!"

The arena's tiles began flipping back over, and the crowd dispersed.

Everest stood and Urban slowly joined him.

How can I compete and survive?

But then she remembered the underground race she'd signed up for at PKU less than a year ago. She had held her own. And now she was an Aqua—genetically modified with faster spatial awareness and reflexes. Maybe Everest was right about her having a shot at winning.

Then again, she was up against Enhanced who had been racing their whole lives—who were *made* for this particular race. And those obstacles . . . Hopefully the ones she'd be up against in RTC would be easier. But she doubted it.

She followed Everest out of the arena and joined the masses crossing campus. By the pulsing in her augmented display, her guards must be close, but out of sight.

How odd to be back at school but with so many guards at her

side. Fortunately, most people didn't pay her much attention. PKU was full of KOLs, and guards weren't that uncommon.

They walked with the chatting crowds over stone bridges and past ponds with lilies in full bloom. They passed the tall pagoda where Urban had first met the PKU's AI team, the Dragons. Just thinking about all the running the team captain had them do made Urban weary.

A giant skyscraper with a waterfall crashing down from one side of it came into view. Urban stared at it. If she hadn't gone to the Western Federation with the Dragons, she'd probably still be living in those dorms, finishing up school.

How different my life would have been. No one would know I was the hybrid—including me.

They soon reached the Chai Tai Center, and her pulse quickened. As she approached the large entryway, she tugged at the hem of her sleeve and straightened her shoulders.

The heavy thumping of music blasted out as the doors opened.

Going to KOL bashes used to be such a normal occurrence. But now, the music was deafening, the lights glaring, the perfume cloying—an overwhelming assault on the senses. It was as if, after spending so much time in isolation in the underwater prison, she'd lost touch with this side of herself.

Everest gave her an encouraging nod.

Urban took a breath and purposefully strode forward. Together, they passed the security checkpoint and joined the multitude of KOLs.

Settling her nerves, Urban observed her surroundings. Holding her hidden stun shield, she counted each exit and scanned the students for Dawn, Orion, Coral, or Vance. Not spotting any of her enemies, she relaxed a little.

The room she found herself in was slathered in florescent hues of blue and purple. The floors were a shiny material that reflected the paneled walls and ceiling embedded with long strips of colorful light.

Students wearing the most stylish dresses and jumpsuits

packed the space. Every gene pool was represented and, with the help of Gene-IQ, Urban identified many of them as sporting a wide range of enhancements. The students' laughter and animated conversation filled the place with a constant roar of sound.

On the cruise ship, Urban had always managed to skirt the crowds or dart quickly through them. Now, with dismay, she faced the throngs of people Croix wanted her to mingle with. Her stomach twisted in knots.

A spotlight flashed in their direction, blinding her. She squinted, stiffening.

"Who's this?" an announcer boomed.

All eyes in the room turned in her direction.

"Lee Urban, back from the dead?"

Several people gasped.

Urban's heart hammered and she found herself shrinking back. She'd known this would happen. Of course, being a KOL and repping Croix gear, this was what was expected of her. She'd thought she could handle the attention.

But now she wasn't so sure.

Bodies closed in around her, expensive perfumes and colognes hurting her nose. Urban's guards tried to get to her but there were too many people.

The room seemed depleted of oxygen. Urban couldn't get enough air.

She started wheezing.

Can't breathe.

Panic wrestled for control over her mind and it was winning.

But then someone she sensed to be Everest was leading her away from the crowd. The wall of rising panic distorted this fact and made it hard to focus.

He pushed their way down a hallway, away from the noise and light, guiding her gently into a cushioned armchair and out of sight of the throngs.

"Take a deep breath and hold it for five seconds."

Urban did so.

Everest knelt down so he was at her level.

She focused on his black eyes. No, not black, but gold. He was wearing his Metropolis retina displays.

"Again," Everest coached.

Urban breathed in and out slowly, clutching Everest's hand. She gradually became aware of her surroundings. She was in a dim alcove with rustic furniture and only a few people mingling and talking in hushed voices. The thump of the music faded.

"Good." Everest nodded. "Keep going."

Urban inhaled. *One, two, three, four, five.*

"You're going to be okay," he reassured her. His hand brushed a strand of hair out of her face. "Think you can manage for a minute?"

Urban nodded.

"I'll be right back." Everest stood and left.

Urban continued her breathing exercises. She counted forty seconds before he returned with a platter of food.

Urban glanced at the plate and smiled at him. "*Jiaozi!*" She took a bite.

"I heard food helps." Everest took a bite of one as well.

They ate in silence until Urban could breathe normally again. Her body relaxed and she cast a quick glance Everest. "How did you know these are my favorite? I never told you."

"I'm an Inventor. I know things." He grinned.

Urban tried to glare at him but failed.

"Actually, I found out from your avatar profile," Everest confessed. "You have some really interesting facts you posted when you were twelve."

"I forgot about that." Urban eyed him. "Just how many hours did you spend stalking me to find that?"

Everest looked up at the ceiling. "Hard to remember. It was a long time ago."

But then his expression became serious. "Are you feeling better? Do you need another minute?"

"Let's get back in there before they all assume I've died again." Urban straightened. She had just stood to her feet when someone approached.

"Urban!" It was Olive, Urban's former teammate on the Dragons. "Hey. Can we talk?"

The pasty girl's attentive eyes studied Urban. "I'd like to speak to you about the Gamelyon. And . . . recent events." Olive's eyes flickered to Everest, hesitating.

"You can trust him," Urban told her.

The real question is if I can trust you.

Olive studied Everest as if parceling out his thoughts. Then again, with her Inceptor abilities, maybe she was.

After a moment, the girl gave a subtle nod. She leaned in before speaking. "You're the hybrid, aren't you?"

Urban's breath caught.

Olive's blue eyes pierced her own, making her skin crawl. "So it's true," she whispered.

I hate it when they do that.

"Don't hate me." Olive's lips quirked. "You'll have to get better at masking your emotions if you don't want Inceptors to know things."

Urban grit her teeth.

"Back in the Western Fed, I knew when the Gamelyon was released in the arena that something was up," Olive explained. "That's the signal the World Enhancement Organization built in to alert us of someone with hybrid genetics. But I thought it was an error. Then you were captured, and it all makes sense now. What doesn't make sense is why you're back at uni, risking your life with a giant target on your back."

Urban's stomach flipped.

"You don't need to share your plans with me, but I would like to offer you the support and protection of WEO."

Urban questioned whether she needed that on top of AiE's protection, or if it was just a trap to get her to confess her loyalties to AiE.

Urban smoothed her face into an expressionless mask. At least she hoped she did.

"I see you still don't trust me," Olive sighed. "Let me prove that I have your best interest at heart. You're going to compete in RTC to try and reveal your genetics to the world, yes?"

Urban almost gasped.

Olive nodded knowingly. "I won't comment on the legitimacy of the plan. But I will warn you. According to my intel, someone in your division will try and kill you."

Urban hid the jolt she felt inside. "Thank you. We will take your words into consideration."

"Looks like I finally found the party," a voice cut into their conversation.

Dirty-blond hair, confident stance, slight accent. A figure strode toward their group, and with him, dread spiked in Urban's gut.

Olive smiled. "Orion, there you are."

Orion's golden eyes flashed. Those same eyes witnessed Urban being sent to her watery grave.

Thankfully, her hybrid genetics had kicked in, allowing her to survive the maze. Still, she couldn't believe how casually Orion had watched as she nearly died. It was a miracle she'd managed to escape him at all.

And now, only a few weeks later, he'd already tracked her down.

"I've been looking for you," Orion said to them, but his eyes hungrily drank in Urban.

Fight-or-flight kicked in, rendering Urban's brain a useless buzz of activity. She wanted to run and run. Panic clawed its way at her like a wild animal.

Everest rested a hand on her back, taming the panic. His fingers tapped a gentle reminder. Count five seconds, breathe. Count, breathe. It made her thoughts clear again.

Orion offered a smile that seemed so sincere it made her nauseous.

When Urban had been on the Dragons' team, she'd assumed she managed to hide her emotions and thoughts from the Inceptor.

But in the underwater lab, she discovered Orion had known about her Natural status and read her like a book.

Why is he here?

Everest adjusted his stance to stand slightly in front of her. "Orion, is it? I believe we met once at some joker's jiu-jitsu gym."

Orion's smile didn't falter in the slightest. "Ah, that's right. You're the newbie who was trying to learn the basics. I hope my instruction helped and you've learned your lesson since then."

Everest looked at him, expression blank. "I've learned a lot, actually."

"Enough to protect her?" Orion's eyes flicked lazily back to Urban. He chuckled. "You never know when she might need it."

Everest turned to Olive who was watching the interaction with interest. "I'm sorry, but it looks like we have other engagements to attend to."

He steered Urban away, back to the main hall, but Urban couldn't stop from trembling.

Everest wrapped an arm around her. "That Inceptor will never go near you again," he promised in an undertone.

"Do you think Olive was telling the truth?" She changed the subject.

"I don't know," Everest confessed. "I'll reach out to AiE and run the intel past them. Regardless, I doubt they want you working with WEO. They're too divided to be trusted. Half of the organization has gone rogue, like Orion and Coral. And I doubt Olive's offer changes anything."

A tall figure and his entourage was approaching them. Everest straightened, and Urban's retina picked up the newcomer's identity.

<Lung Lennox, head of the board for the Games for Peking University. Sosh 97 . . .>

Lennox's black hair was slicked straight back in thick waves, and he was impeccably dressed. He looked exactly the same as the last time she'd seen him, when he'd paid her family a visit.

"Urban!" Lennox boomed as he stopped in front of them.

"Hello, Lung, Sir."

"It's so good to see you again!"

Urban tried not to show her surprise. The last time she'd seen Lung Lennox was after she'd crashed PKU's AI. As the head Inventor, he had wanted to know the cause. When Urban refused to tell him what her enhancements were, he'd left irate, and her family had reason to believe he was the one who had planted some of the bugs in their house.

"Might I have a word with you?" Lennox motioned toward a wall. With a flick of his wrist, it slid away, and he entered, along with his security detail.

Urban and Everest exchanged glances.

Warily, they followed. Once Urban and Everest stepped foot into the space, the wall slid shut behind them.

She stood in a dimly lit lounge. The scent of whiskey and expensive cologne hinted at power and authority, putting Urban on edge.

"Sit down, sit down." Lennox gestured at several sets of plush leather armchairs. "This is one of my private rooms. It's too noisy out there for these old ears."

Urban took a tentative seat, with Everest next to her. The guards assigned to her remained outside.

A Natural came by with a steaming pot of tea and poured them each a cup. Urban set hers down on a bamboo coffee table to keep her trembling hand from spilling it.

A mechanical whirring sound drew nearer as a woman walked toward them.

Not walking but . . . hovering? Urban wasn't sure what she was looking at exactly.

The woman had legs and arms surrounded by a metallic exoskeleton that seemed to be helping her float forward. Her body was unnaturally thin and still. Gears and knobs attached to her head were the only signs of movement. Translucent tubes snaked their way down her neck and into various other parts of her body. Her skin was ghostly pale and her eyes were vacant—completely devoid of life. Forced open by some sort of stimulant.

It's a corpse.

Urban shuddered. She felt Everest stiffen beside her.

Yet upon closer inspection, there was the tiniest movement in the chest. The woman was breathing.

So why did she look dead?

Urban couldn't tear her eyes away from the abomination.

"Meet my daughter, Odonata," Lennox said.

Bile rose in Urban's throat. She swallowed. "It's nice to meet you."

"I've heard so much about you, Lee Urban."

Urban blinked in surprise.

Though the woman's mouth had remained shut, she had communicated through speakers imbedded in her suit. Her voice sounded like a young girl.

Definitely human.

Lennox nodded approvingly, as if this were all perfectly normal. "Odonata is my right-hand woman when it comes to running the Games. Isn't that right, darling?"

The woman continued staring off into space, unblinking. With a mechanical whir, her head jerked up and down. Her lips spasmed, and a smile forced its way across her face.

Urban felt sick.

"I wanted to have a quick chat with you, Urban, in private," Lennox continued, seemingly ignorant of the effect his daughter was having.

Urban forced her eyes away from the woman.

"A lot has happened since you first enrolled at Peking University. Starting with your tremendous display in the preliminary games, to your victory against the Scorpions, and then your baffling disappearance. Since then, it's come to my attention you've joined a certain . . . how do I put this?" He paused to take a sip of tea, "List. If you know what I mean."

The banned list again.

"I'm aware this is a delicate topic," Lennox remarked. "I'm not here to pass judgment, and excuse me if I come off as offensive, but PKU has a reputation to uphold. It has been decided by the school's board that students of such a nature are to be restricted from attending our prestigious university."

Urban stared at him. "Are you saying I can't come back?"

His eyes sparked. "Of course you can return. You just can't enroll in classes as a student. I'm very sorry. As you know Peking University is . . ."

Urban's thoughts were spinning.

She was banned from the gym, and now uni. What if she lost her KOL status and Croix canceled her sponsorship? *Will I still be able to race?* She had no idea what to do if she couldn't get word out about the hybrid.

So many questions. But one thing was certain. She needed to get away from this awful party and Lennox and his so-called daughter as soon as possible.

Urban set her cup down. "I appreciate your candor on the matter. We'll be leaving now."

She stood up, and Everest did likewise. She avoided looking at Odonata again.

The wall panel slid open, blasting them with sound and light.

Urban stepped back into the raucous main hall, and the door shut behind them. Everest was silent as she stood still a moment, trying to reorient herself and collect her thoughts.

She wasn't welcome here.

Or anywhere. Not only was she the controversial hybrid, she was on the banned list.

Blinking back tears, she took in her surroundings. This would probably be the last time she was welcomed at a KOL bash on campus. Tomorrow, she'd be on her way to New Chengdu to begin training for the race.

Everest's words echoed in her mind. *"You can never go back."*

He was right.

Never go back.

15

NEW CHENGDU

A STORM BREWED OVER NEW CHENGDU. DARK clouds rallied to scatter bolts of lightning down on the Metropolis. Urban's helix pod shook and bounced, her stomach lurching with each sudden drop.

Father slept next to her, oblivious to the weather, most likely drunk. Lucas stared with glazed eyes at something in QuanNao, gripping the arm of the chair. Her guards and Ash sat stiff-backed, attention fixed on the window.

When the pod smoothed out again, Urban continued her research on Race to the Clouds. She'd already read the entire handbook on the flight over and was now researching previous years' winners. She stopped when she came to a familiar name: Lee Byronne.

Her father's image was younger, happier, and carefree. His current worried wrinkle lines and the slight hunch to his posture looked nothing like the old picture. The hair growth stimulants were doing little to help.

Urban opened up the vid of his race.

She had watched her father's victory when she was much younger, but now, she absorbed every detail. The track on his race day was wet and slick. He had started out near the back but had quickly taken the lead, bypassing a terrifying number of obstacles—everything from enhanced giant wolves to augmented reality obstacles like fake landslides and other illusions designed to strike terror in the contenders.

The whole thing was just like the AI games, only worse.

In the vid, another racer tailed Father closely, until they were almost parallel coming up to one of the tight turns. Their vehicles locked together, then slid out of control.

Father jerked free and shot forward, but the other racer didn't have enough time to recover. He tried to veer away from the approaching drop-off but overcorrected.

The racer careened off the side of the mountain, tumbling to a sickening crunch at its base. Smoke poured out of the wreckage.

"The lead racer, Phan Fox, just slid out of control and off the mountain," the commentator said gravely. "I see medbots coming, but this doesn't look good, folks."

The vids zoomed in on the grisly remains of the vehicle. Urban looked away and researched the stats. There was usually at least one casualty per year.

Hopefully, this year would be an exception.

"We will be arriving in five minutes," a robotic voice announced. "Please prepare for landing."

The air grew turbulent again, and Urban blinked out of augmented mode, immersing herself fully into reality. The clouds disappeared, and the twinkling night lights of a Metropolis came into view. New Chengdu was like the city of New Beijing, only it had a brighter glow and sparkled more vibrantly with color.

Their pod descended further and approached a private landing strip.

Soon, Urban was standing outside in the cool, bright night of the Metropolis. Music and karaoke filled the air, warm and inviting.

One of the guards climbed into a waiting vehicle and, after checking it, motioned Urban and the others inside.

As they sped away, Urban took in New Chengdu. Even at this hour, people were out and about, strolling leisurely. Some headed toward local mahjong gambling stations to sip tea, trash talking loudly as they went. Others stumbled drunkenly out of hole-in-the-wall restaurants and bars. The sharp scents of spicy *huajiao* peppers and stinky *mapo dofu* filled their vehicle.

New Chengdu always stuck out to Urban as a more colorful way of life. The residents were laid back compared to the ambitious status climbers of New Beijing. Not that their sosh didn't matter. It just wasn't the single most important thing. Urban wondered if it would be easier for Naturals to live here.

Soon, the Metropolis sounds faded, as they sped across mostly empty roads lined with trees. Despite being out of the city, the air was wet and humid, which struck Urban as odd. Now that she thought about it, she didn't remember New Chengdu having a pollution bubble around it. Maybe with all the surrounding forests, they didn't need one.

After driving for an hour, the forest grew thick with people and activity. Urban sat up in her seat to get a better look, nerves tingling.

Vehicles of every shape and size imaginable lined the road. Trainers, pit crew, and racers lingered near tents, drinking from thermoses. Music blasted through the air, a popular song with autotune precision and an upbeat chorus.

A host of reporters—some bots, others Enhanced—floated, flew, or walked down the streets. Urban's Gene-IQ app picked up specialized enhancements to help with capturing stories.

The woman closest to Urban was a Flyer with curved wings made for maximizing maneuverability and speed, making her nearly impossible to outrun. The man behind her had Iris Illumus, an enhancement which allowed him to see things far away. The next had facial features arranged in a gentle way so as to encourage people to speak freely and without inhibition around her.

Almost like getting someone drunk but with a single look. Urban made a note to avoid that reporter.

As they continued past, sponsor booths, hovering food trucks, and campers all disappeared, giving way to a quiet, one-lane road. Lush green trees crowded together, blocking out the night sky.

Urban's vehicle made its way through two security checkpoints before gliding to a stop. The headlights of their ride illuminated thick forest, but the house was nowhere to be seen.

She stepped out into the chilly air and her XR suit instantly warmed her. It was colder than she had expected for this time of year, but she hadn't accounted for the high altitude.

A humming sound emanated from nearby, and lights clicked on, bringing a house into view. Huge, sharp walls and wooden beams shot into the sky. It was as if the builders had started out constructing a fortress, and midway, pivoted to a log cabin.

Father led the way past a large gap made of rock where an open-air fire pit was surrounded by a circular couch with pillows. The way the furniture disappeared into the rock and the lush forest draped around them like a canopy was unlike anything Urban had seen in the Metropolis of New Beijing.

"Ah, here we go." Father opened a panel attached to the house. He flashed his tatt across a scanner and a set of double glass doors slid open, granting them entry.

Two of the guards went first, lights clicking on as they swept the house.

"All clear," one of them reported.

If the house looked big from the outside, it seemed gargantuan from the inside. A set of wooden stairs led up to a huge receiving room with multiple leather couches. Clustered around the room were pillars supporting a tall, arched ceiling, and balconies on all sides boasting more sitting areas that overlooked the space. A huge hearth took up the opposite wall, an array of preserved goat antelopes, moon bears, and Asian golden cats hanging above it. Despite its earthy, log cabin tones, there was something chic to it, as well.

"I wanted a space large enough to house the rest of the team," Father explained.

Urban looked up in surprise. "Team?"

"You can't win the RTC without a group of experts behind you," Father said. "They'll be arriving soon. We'll have introductions then." Without saying more, he disappeared down a wide corridor.

Lucas rushed in the opposite direction. "Dibs on the best room!"

Urban followed her brother, pondering her father's words. She didn't really care about the rooms, so long as everyone was safe. She settled on a space on the second floor, feeling more protected higher up.

The room had several windows with a view obscured by darkness. Urban could make out the blurred shape of trees set against a backdrop of a starry sky. Despite the windows being shut, the fresh scent of distant smoke and damp earth penetrated the room. In the quiet, the crickets were chirping their lullabies, and a gentle wind was rustling through the wooded forest.

Urban felt herself relax. She had never been a nature person, but maybe that was because she hadn't been around nature like this. Back during her time working at the AI factories, she'd hiked the crumbling portion of the Great Wall a few times, but it had been dry and hot, the land brown and arid. Most of the plants were nothing more than shrubs or unimpressive scraggly trees. The sounds from the nearby Outskirts and Factories were always a constant hum in the background.

Here, it was silent and still. A peaceful respite from the constant noise she had grown accustomed to. But the peace was short lived as the quiet began to weigh on her.

Flipping on the room's holo display, Urban selected a local news network and turned the sound up as a Super with a charming smile appeared on the display. "We are thrilled to meet the contenders in the Race to the Clouds. And this year, we're celebrating our two hundredth anniversary. That's right! In honor of this milestone, we have a couple of surprises for spectators and racers alike. To get the full experience, select the RTC app for live updates, exclusive interviews with the racers, weather updates, freebies, and more."

Urban blinked on her augmented mode and downloaded the app.

<Welcome Lee Urban to the Race to the Clouds. Status: Rookie competitor in the Unlimited Division.>

Text scrolled across her retina display. In the bottom right corner, a weather icon appeared, along with links to the top trending vids, and more.

When Urban looked at herself in a mirror, she saw the app marked racers with an electric blue lining around the eyes. It would be obvious to anyone in reality who met her that she was one of the competitors.

"This group represents the best racers from around the world," the newscaster continued. "With every Federation represented, we have over fifty rookies contending for one of the five available spots."

"That's right, Ming," another reporter chimed in. "This elite group will have five days of qualifying races over the next month. Last year, the winner had a total ground-to-sky time of just under eight minutes. Which means, contenders will need to clock in at under ten minutes to qualify. Though, of course, with the changes in this year's race course, that number will change too."

Urban sank onto a bed next to the window. She was actually going to be competing against the world's most elite racers.

Nervous excitement filled her. Tomorrow, her first day of practice would begin.

16

无家

MOUNT EMEI

"YOU NEED TWO THINGS TO WIN THE RACE TO the Clouds." Father looked at Urban over an empty wine glass early the next morning. "A really fast ride and quick reflexes. If you have one but not the other, you'll lose, or worse, die."

They sat in the prep room with tall mirrored walls, a long table laden with breakfast stretching before them, and behind that, a floor-to-ceiling window. Early morning light danced above the tree line with a clear view of lush green mountains rising majestically in the distance.

So far, it was just Urban and her father. Lucas and Ash were out scoping their surroundings. The rest of the team still hadn't arrived. Only the security detail remained, their constant presence hovering nearby.

"Almost all competitors have a mix of either Inventor or Aqua enhancements," Father said. "The Aqua genetics gives the quick reflexes and spatial awareness for navigating the switchback turns of the mountain road. The Inventor genetics allow contestants to invent the best vehicles to compete."

They still hadn't tested her abilities. Urban knew she could breathe underwater, but what else? She hadn't noticed any other changes. Hopefully, she had these supposed better reflexes.

"Now, you will be racing in the Unlimited Division," Father continued. "That's where all the most exotic vehicles compete. There's less regulation around those vehicles, and thus, the only shot we have at getting your particular motorcycle is there."

Urban shifted.

"This is an extremely dangerous race, and doing it as a hybrid . . ." He picked up his empty wine glass, stared at it, then put it down. "The last-minute change in courses will help level the playing field a bit, but you're still at a disadvantage. The other racers were genetically modified for this and have been training for a long time. You're coming in with less than two months to practice."

"I know."

Father rubbed at his blood-shot eyes. "If we're going to do this, I need your best effort. I need you to trust me. Can you do that?"

Irritation needled at Urban. Here he was asking for her best efforts, when he was already slightly tipsy.

But she ignored her growing anger. She needed Father's help if she was going to have a chance at this. "Can you teach me how to win?"

"I already did."

"You mentioned some genetic alterations I don't have control over. Is there anything else? Something practical I can work on?"

Her father eyed her coolly. "How about we start with the race itself. What do you know about it?"

"Everything in the handbook and in QuanNao."

Father waved his empty glass in the air. "None of that matters."

Maybe it had been a mistake to choose Father as her coach.

"Come here." He stood. "Let me show you the race. We're going for a little road trip."

Urban hesitated. "The handbook states it's against the rules to practice on the course before the designated training days."

"We won't be training," Father said dismissively. "Just taking a ride up the mountain. That's allowed. Come."

Outside, the earlier sunlight had vanished and it was drizzling and chilly. Urban's guards trailed them at a distance, giving them some privacy.

"At three thousand meters, the weather is very unpredictable," Father said. "Which is one of the biggest risks for race day—you have no idea what you'll be competing in. You have to be prepared for everything."

Urban adjusted her smart suit settings for more warmth.

"It's also easy to get dehydrated up here, so be sure to drink more than usual," he advised. They walked up to one of the hoverstops and waited.

Around them, the dark green forest stretched for miles in all directions. Moss-covered ancient stones lined a stair path that disappeared into the forest. Even the bouncy, Zeolite-coated road was empty of vehicles.

In minutes, a slick, silver and black hovercraft glided to a stop before them. The guards swept it, and then Father and Urban climbed on. Urban took a seat at the front where a large window gave her a perfect view of the road ahead.

"The race course starts further back and goes up this road," Father said. "It will end at over four thousand meters, same as the old race course. Only this time, the transition will be even faster, since the last several hundred meters will be reached in a matter of seconds during the flying portion of the race. Altitude sickness is a real thing. Many of the competitors were genetically enhanced to be more resilient in these conditions. But a few of them, like you, will be at a disadvantage in that regard. If you feel yourself getting dizzy, faint, or nauseous, let me know. Most of the time, drinking lots of water does the trick, but every once in a while, it's more serious and requires oxygen tanks or medical treatment."

"I read abstaining from alcohol and caffeine also helps," Urban said.

"Good job." Urban was pretty sure her father was being sarcastic as he lifted a thermos of what she guessed to be another alcoholic beverage to his lips.

The air grew gradually thinner and colder as the hovercraft whirred up the road. A cliff face of white rock speckled with green arose on one side, while the other side dropped away entirely, revealing the mountain plain below. The rain had stopped, but in its place, a thick fog rolled in. Nearby, large animals scattered off the road as the craft glided by.

Urban pointed. "Are those monkeys?"

Father glanced over. "Yes."

"But doesn't that make the road dangerous? If they're lying around . . ."

"What an astute observation. Why yes, yes it does."

Urban's anger boiled over. "Why aren't you taking this seriously?"

Father's face darkened. "I take this deathly serious."

"That's not what it looks like," Urban stated.

"Appearances can be deceiving," was his only comment.

Urban turned away before saying something she'd regret. Their vehicle continued on.

Father gestured around them. "During race day, the whole mountain will be full of obstacles. They change each year, so I can't say what they'll be. The best advice is to stick near the back of the heat until you reach the tunnels."

At Urban's puzzled expression, he said. "A few of the first riders usually get taken out. That's why all racers have to disable augmented mode. Otherwise, their teams would watch the racers in front and give the ones in the back tips on what to expect."

Urban pondered this as their vehicle passed through the tunnel.

"The Race to the Clouds isn't just a race," Father warned. "It's a mind game. You must learn to face your fears and overcome them. All while going hundreds of kilometers an hour."

That was a little fearful in and of itself.

As they emerged back into sunlight, Father pointed ahead. "This is one of the trickiest parts of the race."

Their vehicle banked hard to the left, avoiding the sharp drop-off.

Her pulse quickened at the steepness.

"We call it the Reaper's Bend, for obvious reasons. Navigate it with caution."

As they reached the last stop, Father climbed out and Urban followed. The fog was now so thick, she couldn't see more than a few meters ahead. A cool wind bit at her, whipping her hair around.

Father led her up a steeper, smaller road where a large parking lot came into hazy view. "This is the most challenging part of the entire race." Father's voice sounded distant in the fog.

"Is this the transition lot?" From her research, Urban knew the space was large enough to fit over a dozen vehicles and their crew while they made the necessary modifications for the flight portion of the race.

"Yes. I wish it were a clear day so you could see it better." They kept walking until they were in front of a large, cylindrical slab. He waved his tatt and a door slid away with a hiss. He stepped into the tube and Urban followed.

With a lurching sensation, they shot upward, ears popping. The slab around them disappeared, replaced by a wall of reinforced glass. Urban caught a flash of greenery before the ground vanished, replaced a few seconds later by sky.

Miles of lush forest stretched in all directions beneath her. The sun bathed the clouds in tufts of persimmon, terracotta, and streaks of goji berry red, infusing the atmosphere with brilliant color.

It took Urban's breath away, the beauty of it awakening something long dormant within her. It took her a moment to place it.

Inspiration.

For the first time since Urban could remember, she wanted to paint. To create. To capture this piece of beauty in a world that seemed dark and out of control.

The tube slowed then stopped, and Urban and her father stepped out. They were in a luxurious empty lobby with more windows and a view of clouds below them.

Father brought her over to the window. "This is where the judges will be on the day of the race."

"Where's the finish line?"

"They won't turn on the projection until the trials, but if you look right there," Father indicated a spot in the air above them, "that's where it ends."

"Why is it called Race to the Clouds if it goes *above* the clouds?"

"The title is a bit misleading." Father chuckled. It was the first time he'd genuinely laughed in her presence in a long time. When she looked over at him, he had a wistful expression on his face.

"What was it like racing here?" she asked.

"Exhilarating." Father let out a deep sigh.

"Why . . ." Urban hesitated then pushed through. "Why did you stop?"

Father's expression closed up. "Let's go. It's time to meet your team." He turned and walked away.

Urban watched him go. *What is he not telling me?*

17

THE TEAM

WHEN URBAN AND HER FATHER ARRIVED BACK at the house, five people stood waiting on the doorstep, three men and two women.

Trig stood among them, and Urban launched herself at him. "You're alright."

"Yes," Trig said in his deep, formal voice. "My recovery period is over, and I've returned to my duty by your side."

Urban grinned. "I'm glad." She already felt safer knowing her trusty guard was back.

Turning, she studied the four other people. One of the women had spiked black hair and sharp facial bones. Urban didn't need her retina display to tell her what she was. By the tech at the woman's side, she had to be an Inventor.

The man leaning against the wall next to her was fit enough to be a sports KOL, but Urban's retina display picked up Giver genetics.

The third figure wore a dark cloak with a hood obscuring most of his face. Urban still found it odd that Dr. Yukio would volunteer to join them.

The fourth woman was tall with a perfectly proportioned figure and wore a chic metallic pantsuit. It took Urban a moment to recognize her as none other than her old roommate and rival, Blossom. Urban stiffened.

"Excellent. You've all arrived." Father strode over and shook each of their hands. "Let's gather in the prep room and have a round of introductions."

He gestured the four newcomers inside the house and sent a guard in search of Ash and Lucas. Back in the prep room, the once-brilliant view of the mountains was now obscured by an overcast sky, the mirrored walls reflecting the gray outside.

Lucas and Ash joined them while the guests were served tea. Ash slid into a seat next to Urban, tucking his wings behind him.

Father stood and addressed the newcomers. "This is my daughter, Urban." He gestured at Lucas next. "That's my son, Lucas, an experienced Aqua. And finally, we have Ash, who will be our eyes in the air and help with the flight portion of the race."

He motioned at the newcomer in the hood. "Urban, I believe you've already met Dr. Yukio. He'll be your sports psychology mentor."

Dr. Yukio dipped his hooded head in acknowledgment.

Father moved on to the athletic Giver. "This is Cho Ivan. He's your strengthening coach."

Ivan gave a respectful nod.

"Coach?" Urban blurted. She wanted to protest that she didn't need one. She'd be riding her motorcycle, not running, after all. But she kept her mouth shut.

Lucas was less diplomatic. "Why does she need to work out?"

Ivan stared in disbelief. "Rookies." He let out an exasperated breath. "Most champions are highly competitive athletes. In their spare time they run marathons or set records in weight lifting. Otherwise, the extreme forces they experience while racing would shred their bodies."

Urban's stomach tightened. She was no athlete.

"Do you know what traveling up 3,000 meters in under fifteen minutes does to your body?" Ivan asked. "Of course, there's altitude to worry about, but that's the easy part. The point is, you need to be in top physical shape to prevent injuries."

Urban swallowed hard.

"Most racers train for years and are elite athletes before they even qualify for the RTC." To demonstrate his point, Ivan projected a vid of a man holding something in between his pinkie finger and thumb. "That's last year's champion in the Time Attack Division. He's holding a chestnut."

Urban watched as the champion smashed the chestnut as easily as if it were a piece of over-ripe dragon fruit.

"Is that what they mean by 'cracking a tough nut'?" Lucas chortled. "I've been doing it wrong this whole time!"

Ivan ignored him and eyed Urban. "That's the caliber of athleticism you'll be competing against. We'll start with strength training *today*."

A wave of exhaustion hit Urban at the mere thought. Even though she'd trained with the Dragons and on her own in the days following capture, this sounded far more intense.

"Continuing the introductions," Father motioned at Urban's former roommate. "I believe you know Li Blossom."

Blossom sat at the farthest end of the table, leaning back, arms crossed. Her straight black hair dropped around her sharply angled face, no different than the last time Urban had seen her back in the Western Federation. From behind thickly lined black eyes, Blossom surveyed Urban and the group with an expression verging on boredom.

"Yes, we know each other," Blossom said lazily. "It would seem there is much we have to catch up on." She straightened and her tone turned sharply business like. "I've received Urban's lab results from Dr. Watanabe. They were pretty standard and what I expected. But I'd like to conduct my own tests to assess her baseline capabilities as an Aqua."

Other than breathing underwater, Urban hadn't tested any of her new enhancements. She wasn't even sure how. But she was eager and anxious.

Only, it was Blossom who would be conducting them. Why did the person AiE send to work with her have to be Blossom? The one person who would probably take joy in sticking her with needles and other painful medical contraptions.

Urban sat rigid. "And if I decline your labs?"

"Then," stated Blossom, "we have a problem."

Father leaned forward. "Blossom, you mentioned that you had some physical tests? Maybe we could start with those."

Blossom's expression didn't change, but she nodded respectfully. "I'm sure AiE would be fine if we started there. For now."

"This is Ngo Poppy, our technical trainer," Father said hastily, attempting to override the palpable tension in the room. "Poppy will manage your helmet, suit, and any specialized training equipment, as well as anything obstacle related. It's an important job, and one I wouldn't trust to any other Inventor."

He gave Poppy a smile. "She was excellent back in the day when we worked together, and has gone on to work with five other RTC champions."

"I can't guarantee your success," Poppy picked up, "but I can get you close with all the best training tech and race day equipment. I was able to secure a fiber carbon shell helmet with direct access oxygen to help combat the altitude, as well as the latest g-suit for practice. Ivan and I will be working closely together on your training regimen."

"Now, the motorcycle division isn't something I've ever personally competed in," Father admitted. "Which is why I've brought along one other person."

"Sorry I'm late." Everest burst into the room.

Urban's mouth fell open.

"Perfect timing." Father clapped Everest on the back before gesturing at a chair for him to sit.

Urban's spirits lifted. Here was the boy who had taught her the thrill of racing. The one who'd shown her how to weave through the populated Outskirts and survive.

Everest had been her first coach. He was also an incredibly skilled racer. With him here, she felt like she finally had someone on her side. Someone who believed in her.

A spark of hope ignited in her chest.

He gave her a broad smile and took the open seat across from her.

"Everest will be helping with our security and also coaching Urban on her racing techniques," Father told the group. "Since I won't be able to help on that front."

"Not to be rude, or anything," Lucas piped up, "but Everest is a Natural."

Urban nearly gasped, but Poppy, Ivan, and Blossom seemed unfazed by the admission.

A ping arrived in Urban's retina display.

[Everest: Your team all signed confidentiality agreements to be here. They know everything. Well, almost everything . . .]

A winking emoji appeared in her retina display and Urban nearly laughed.

Lucas persisted. "How will he be able to help Urban figure out her genetic enhancements when it comes to racing?"

"That's why you're here. I think between the three of us"— Father gestured—"we should have all the bases covered. A winning mentality, motorcycle techniques, and optimizing Urban's Aqua enhancements."

Father flicked on a holo display of Mount Emei. The green mountain spun slowly before them. "This is the most dangerous race in the Asian Federation. For the motorcycle division, it's the most dangerous race in the *world.*"

His words sobered the room.

"The obstacles are one of the bigger dangers on the race course."

"Will I get to practice with them?" Urban inquired.

"Usually, during the practice run, you would. Due to the last-minute change in location, most likely not. The RTC team is still setting up all the obstacles. It's much more complicated than the obstacles housed in the arena. This takes time, planting each and every one within the mountain."

Urban's heart sank. The first time she'd be facing the obstacles would probably be on race day. That is, if she made it into the race at all.

I'll qualify. For my family, and for Everest's sake, I have to.

Images of the Western Federation disintegrating into civil war filled her mind.

"Road conditions are also a major concern," Father added. "Not only can the weather change drastically during the race, but wildlife may appear on the road. It's a completely unpredictable environment."

"What's the most dangerous part?" Urban asked.

"That would be the plethora of blind corners," Father explained. "One hundred and fifty-six to be exact. Unlike traditional racing, there aren't any turn warnings, guardrails, or markings."

"What do I need to do to win?"

"Work on your reflexes and get them as fast as you can, which Poppy will help with. You need to be in top physical condition. That's Ivan. And you need to be the best racer you can be." He nodded at Everest and Lucas. "That's where these two come in. But most importantly, you need to memorize every turn and bend of the course. Otherwise, if you think you're on a large bend in the road when really, you're at a hairpin curve, you're going off the edge. Not having the race course memorized could cost you race time, at best. At worst, it could cost your life."

Urban's voice was barely a whisper. "So, I have to be familiar with all 156 turns?"

"No." Father leveled his gaze at her. "You need to have all 156 turns perfectly memorized. That's the only way to win and stay alive."

Urban's insides tightened.

After Father finished going over team logistics, the group dispersed, leaving Urban alone. She pulled up a 3D holo of the race's map and studied it carefully as it spun before her.

It truly was a beautiful course. Thick green foliage draped around the road, sheer white rock cliffs caressed the sides, tendrils of white clouds snaked around the midpoint, and up above, the mountain glowed in radiant sunlight.

Despite Father's warnings, Urban couldn't wait to test it out. She'd only ever raced in concrete jungles. An actual forest looked like pure magic.

RTC, I'm coming for you.

18

无家

ORIENTATION

THE RTC APP BEEPED.

<Mandatory competitor's orientation meeting commences in one hour. All contestants make their way to the Mount Emei Convention Center.>

Urban couldn't believe two hours had passed during her first attempt to memorize the race course. Blinking out of her training program, she put on one of her most progressive outfits from Croix with bright colors and patterns. Then she unpacked her hair-and-makeup-bot and had it work on her appearance.

A couple of minutes later, a knock sounded on her door.

"Can I come in?"

Urban unlocked it from where she sat, and Everest stepped inside.

He came to stand beside her. Urban's hair was partially styled, half in disarray on top of her head. Her makeup was also in the middle of being done, with the foundation and contouring complete, but no color added.

Everest grinned. "Getting ready for something?"

"Orientation." Urban spoke out of the corner of her lips as the hoverbot tried to apply a pH extractor to them.

"I guess I'll do the talking," Everest quipped. He looked at her in the mirror. "Things are going to change, and I want to be sure about one thing. No more of the fake dating. No games."

The bot moved away from Urban's lips and raked a curling iron through her hair.

Urban met his eyes in the mirror and she smiled. "I agree." But then a new thought crept in. "Are you sure it's safe?" she asked. "I mean, with me being the hybrid, it's probably dangerous for you to be near me at all."

He bent down to her ear. "I would risk it all for you."

She tried to still her heart. "So, we make it XR official?"

Everest's brow creased. "XR official?"

"Isn't that what we were just talking about?" Urban asked.

"Why does it have to be in XR as long as we know we're dating?" He stood. "The whole world doesn't need to be in the know."

Urban considered this. "But I don't want to hide it anymore. Not to mention, the KOL gossip channels thrive on hidden relationships. It's better to come out with the truth than let rumors spread."

Everest exhaled. "I guess. I just hate having the whole world watching and commenting on everything we do."

"That's the life of a KOL. Always in the limelight." Urban smiled sympathetically.

"Alright." Everest ran a hand through his hair. "Fine."

Urban blinked back into augmented reality. "Changing my status . . . now."

"Done," Everest said.

Urban quickly blinked out of XR before her system exploded with messages. Everest was watching her with such intensity that she blushed.

"I'm glad for a third chance with you, Urban," he said quietly. He ran a finger down her cheek. "Third time's the charm."

Urban smiled at him, and he bent down to embrace her. The bot doing her hair let out a warning beep, and Everest leaned back with a laugh.

"Looks like I'm getting in the way." He straightened. "I don't want to make you late for your orientation. I should inspect the mods on your rev cycle anyway."

"See you soon, Everest." Urban watched him go, her heart filling with warmth.

She was grateful for his presence at RTC, and for his willingness to risk it all for her.

She had to race. And win.

As the bot completed the final touches to Urban's hair and makeup, another knock sounded on the door.

"Come in!" she called out, deactivating the lock.

Ash poked his head in. "Ready?"

Urban released her bot to its charging station. "Is it just us?"

"And the guards. Lucas is at a party, and the rest of your team is prepping your gear for training. I get to be one of your extra bodyguards." Ash unstrapped the polearm he kept lodged in his armored back and spun it until it glowed. "Being on the military Flyer path has it perks, I suppose."

Urban rolled her eyes. "Save the showing off until my sister gets here."

Ash instantly brightened. "Is Lillian here?"

"Come on." Urban dragged him out of the room.

Father approached as they were about to leave. "Stick around after orientation," he advised. "Meet some of the other racers. You never know when you'll need an ally on the road."

"I'll do my best," Urban said.

He nodded and turned away.

Outside, Urban's retina display showed even more invisible Camos tailing her. She and Ash, plus her security detail, climbed into several waiting armored vehicles, then took off.

She half expected AiE to insist she fly into orientation on the Gamelyon to draw attention. The offer stood to ride the creature, but with it being housed back in the New Beijing Zoo, Urban didn't have time. Though it would be fun to swoop in on its powerful dragon-scaled hide . . .

Twenty minutes later, they pulled into a parking lot next to a large building and made their way inside.

They entered a large room filled with the sound of chattering voices. A short stage and podium stood at the front decorated in the crimson red and forest green of the RTC colors. The race logo projected on either side of the stage, spinning slowly in a circle. Most of the seats were already full, but Urban managed to find two for her and Ash near the middle. Several heads turned to stare as they sat.

"Alright, let's begin," a familiar voice said.

To Urban's dismay, she looked up to find Orion standing on the stage.

"Welcome, racers, to the 2124 Race to the Clouds," Orion said over the voice enhancers. He was naturally charismatic, and his voice carried the weight of authority. "While relocating the race to Mount Emei has posed an interesting challenge, PKU and the race officials are partnering to make sure we have the needed obstacles."

PKU's arena had a huge storehouse of real animals, bots—anything and everything possible needed by the AI—underneath the stadium.

Mount Emei had hundreds—thousands, even—of hidden alcoves for race day obstacles. PKU and race officials certainly would be working overtime if they planned on bringing that same level of challenges to the mountain.

"This year," Orion continued, "it looks like we have a tough line-up of competitors and can expect a fabulous race. But before I get carried away, I wanted to take a moment to introduce the woman behind it all. Please join me in welcoming your Race Director, Clover Jensen."

Orion gestured toward the side of the raised platform where a woman watched. She looked to be in her early thirties, yet held herself like the Premier of a Federation.

"Clover is a four-time world champion of RTC," Orion announced. "She's set records in the Time Attack and Unlimited Divisions. She's the youngest racer to have ever qualified for the competition, at age fifteen, and still holds the record for the fastest ground-to-sky time. Let's give Clover Jensen a warm round of applause!" Orion stepped off the platform as clapping ensued.

Clover crossed the front of the stage and faced the crowd. "Like Orion mentioned, I'm the four-time world champion. But thankfully for you all, I'm retired now."

She flashed a cocky smile, revealing razor-sharp teeth. "Which means, I now run the orientation program, rookie training, technical inspection, and ultimately, report my findings to the RTC Board. I will make a recommendation on whether or not you are qualified to race."

Clover paused, letting her words, and their power, sink in.

Several of the racers shifted uncomfortably in their seats.

Urban noticed most of those around her were older and wore monochromatic suits. She glanced down at her own brightly patterned one and felt out of place.

"There are 207 racers total across all categories," Clover said. "Each of you have one qualification attempt. If you miss your time, get two red flags, or otherwise fail to abide by the rules, your attempt will be forfeited and you will be disqualified from competing. Am I clear?"

Urban nodded in compliance, along with everyone else in the room.

"Before your initial attempt, your vehicle will undergo a technical inspection. Only if it passes are you permitted to proceed to qualification. Please ensure your vehicle adheres to all of the rules in the technical handbook, which can be found in the RTC competitor's mode of the app."

Clover projected the app and where to find the technical handbook. "We on the RTC committee expect everyone to be professional. This is not street racing. Anyone caught in any sort of misconduct will be penalized, including but not limited to fines and exclusion from the competition."

The room fell completely silent.

"All competitors are expected to have protective helmets, smart suits, and gloves. If your protective gear does not meet our standards, you will be unable to race until wearing the proper gear. For the full regulatory guide, check section 6.7 in the handbook.

"Which brings me to another point. Everyone with a vehicle that has already been submitted and passed the inspection is registered in our system as a contender for qualifiers. As such, you can log in with your credentials to access helpful features such as compliance rules, racing schedules, line-up positions, and more. I recommend you take advantage of this.

"That's all for now. You are free to go." Clover waved her hands. "There are drinks and refreshments in the adjacent room. This is a time for you to meet the other competitors, if you so choose. If this is your first year racing, please stick around for Rookie Orientation."

Clover waited until the room emptied and only a smaller group remained seated. Most of the other rookie racers looked just as awkward and uncomfortable as Urban felt.

"Alright." Clover clapped her hands. "Let's get started. As I stated before, each of you will have one and only one qualification attempt. It begins the second your vehicle crosses the start line and will not end until you reach the finish line in the sky. This is separate from the actual race. In order to be eligible to compete you must first qualify.

"Each of you will have one designated practice session on each part of the race course. You have the next week to complete this going the speed limit. If you are caught going faster than this, you will receive one infringement. If you do this multiple times, you may be disqualified from racing. Is that clear?"

The rookies all nodded.

"Good," Clover said crisply. "Last thing. The Race Director, that's me, has the right to terminate the race at any time if unforeseen circumstances or an emergency arises. While highly unlikely, if this occurs, awards will be doled out based on positions when the race ended. Or awards will not be given out at all. It is at the discretion of the RTC committee.

"Should you have any questions about any of the rules discussed here or in the handbook, feel free to contact us via the app. You are dismissed."

Several of the racers made a beeline toward the drinks. Urban followed them slowly, her mind in a haze.

"You okay?" Ash asked.

Urban shook herself. "Oh, I'm fine."

Most of the refreshment room was crowded with people. She wanted nothing more than to leave Orion far behind, but Father's encouragement about meeting the other racers came to mind. Sighing, she resigned herself to socializing.

Urban examined the crowd. No sign of her enemy.

A table hovered at the center of the room with a cauldron labeled "oxygen-infused water." Another enlarged teapot labeled as spiked green oolong was filled to the brim with a steaming hot liquid. Urban watched as racers poured themselves drinks into delicate teacups.

She made her way toward the table and opted for the infused water. Taking a tentative sip, she made a face. It tasted just like normal water but worse.

"So, are you going to keep drinking water or meet some people?" Ash grinned.

"I thought that was my wingman's job," Urban retorted.

Ash scanned the mingling clusters of people. "That group looks less likely to bite."

He led the way toward two Flyers, a Super, and one Inventor. After a quick round of introductions, Urban learned the Inventor was the only one competing. His retina display had an electric blue rim around them, similar to Urban's own.

The Inventor was in the Time Attack Division, so she didn't need to worry about racing against him. After the conversation dwindled and they all linked, the group broke apart.

Urban was warily scouting out who to mingle with next, when her gaze snagged on a girl with a backward hat and high-top shoes shimmering into view.

Urban gasped.

Qing Coral.

Coral's eyes met Urban's. A deep sadness lurked in the shadows of the gold and black birdlike eyes.

She hadn't seen Coral since the underwater research lab. She barely restrained glancing at her wrist where her scars remained.

Coral looked the same as she always did. Urban could almost trick herself into believing nothing had changed between them. Still friends, still on the same team.

But then she noticed who stood next to her. Orion.

He draped an arm over Coral's shoulder and pulled her possessively close. Coral stiffened but then smiled. Too wide.

There was something odd about their exchange.

Urban thought back to Coral's parting words when she'd helped her escape the underwater prison: *"I can't afford friends."*

What did that mean?

"Let's go," Urban whispered to Ash.

Coral's eyes bored a hole in them as they left.

Urban walked faster. She was still pondering Coral's presence when a sudden realization stopped her.

She turned to face Ash. "Did you notice the color of Coral's retina display?"

"The color?" Ash frowned. "Um, goldish? I think they were lined in . . . blue." His eyes widened. "But why would she be racing too?"

Urban shrugged helplessly. "I don't pretend to understand her motivations anymore. But I do know she's a really, really good racer."

The last thing she needed was more competition. Especially from Qing Coral.

19

REV CYCLE

"IT'S TIME WE TAKE A LOOK AT THE REV CYCLE,"
Father declared to the team.

Poppy's face lit up with excitement. Disappearing into the
garage, she soon returned, pushing a slick motorcycle with
huge wheels.

Lucas raised his eyebrows in admiration. "What is that?"

"The fastest thing on the road." Poppy grinned. "Byronne
and I made a few tweaks to its software and hardware. The rev
cycle now goes even faster than the standard version."

Urban was thrilled. This was exactly why she was so glad
to have Father as her coach. Even if he was hiding something
from her, he was one of the best of the Inventors. She had no
doubt this bike was incredible.

"Most qualifying vehicles optimize for one thing, either
ground or air time," Father explained. "No vehicle is made
for both. If you're fast in the air with wings and jet engines,
you have more drag time on the road. If you're wind-resistant
on land, you won't have the heavy-duty equipment to propel
you faster into the air. This one is the closest you can get to
both. It is incredibly fast on the road, but it also has a really
quick transition. You will lose some time in the air, though,
since it's a bit slower on that front. Which means in order to

win, you have to be in the lead by the time you make it to the transition grounds."

"Win by the transition lot." Urban ran her fingers over the machine's surface. "Got it."

"It weighs just under one hundred kilos and uses its wheels as hydraulic actuators to fly." Poppy adjusted the controls and the wheels popped out from under the motorcycle to form four smaller wheels horizontal to the ground. They powered on, then thrust the motorcycle slowly up off the ground.

"That's what the standard model does," Poppy shouted above the roar of the engine. She adjusted the settings again, and it returned to its motorcycle form.

"Unlike most models, which require you to stop and wait for a couple of seconds for it to heat up, like you just saw, we made some pretty cool mods."

The motorcycle transformed again. Only this time, the front two wheels popped up and heated up before the back ones followed suit. "This allows you to transition from driving to airborne in less than three seconds and with zero stop time," Poppy explained. "We estimate this will save you fifteen seconds of time during the race."

Excitement tingled up Urban's spine. Never had she ridden any sort of conversion machine. Most were required to follow both ground and air traffic regulations, which made them complex to drive. Not to mention there were heavy regulations around such crafts.

A thought occurred to Urban. "Do I need a special license to drive—or, I mean, fly this?"

"Normally, yes. But since RTC is in the mountains, away from the city and heavy traffic, they've waived that rule. All you need is a standard motorcycle driving license and a proven track record with flying your machine. That's why they have all rookies run a few tests drives. Pass those, and you're good to go."

Urban's eyes went back to the machine. "Can I give it a try?"

"I just transferred over access to the controls," Poppy said as she powered down the vehicle and handed Urban a helmet. It was noticeably heavier than Urban's helmet back home. She had to keep her body straight to prevent adding strain to her neck. For a second, everything was silent and dark, and then her vision flickered to life. Red and blue notifications filled the corners of her view. A noise cancellation bubble immediately activated.

"Can you hear me?" Poppy's voice reverberated loudly inside.

When Urban nodded, the weight of the helmet nearly threw her off balance. The added burden would definitely take some getting used to.

"I connected your com link to our team channel," Poppy informed her. "That way, you can communicate directly with any of us during practice. During race day, that feature will be blocked, according to the RTC rules. But for now, we'll use it to coach you, especially during take-off and landing. That's the trickiest part."

Urban climbed onto the vehicle, eagerly exploring handholds and footholds, familiarizing herself with each. Then she turned the machine back on.

Sheer power rumbled beneath her, filling her with adrenaline.

"One more thing," Father shouted.

Urban winced. "I can hear you just fine through the com."

"Right." Father spoke at a normal volume again. "These roads can be dangerous due to the unpredictable wildlife. On a bike like yours, hitting one could be deadly. So I took the liberty to design an added layer of protection for you. If any sort of wildlife gets in your way, do not, I repeat, do *not* swerve to avoid them. At such high speeds, you'll lose control of the vehicle and wipe out. Instead, I've designed an automatic energy propulsion shield. It will blast away any animals on your path. It's like a proactive force field," Father added.

"Is this legal?" she asked. Visions of animals struck by the force field plagued Urban's mind. She wasn't sure she wanted to use this device.

"It's legal," Father responded firmly. "But I'm the only one who knows how to operate it."

"Stay on the back roads," her father advised. "If they catch you practicing on the main one before your designated time, you'll be disqualified."

Urban gave a thumbs-up before pulling out of the driveway and onto the empty path. Riding in a forest was not at all like driving in New Beijing. There were no smart lights to avoid or vehicles to swerve around. Just thick trees and undergrowth on all sides in a cocoon of green. It was quieter here too. Back home, even with her noise cancelling helmet, there were always the background sounds of blaring horns, music, and chatter.

The motorcycle was a little clunkier than she was used to, so she practiced taking the turns slowly, experimenting with each bend in the road.

"Are you ready to fly?" Poppy asked through the com link. "Just remember, don't activate the transition on a turn."

Urban did as she was told, waiting for a longer stretch of road before powering up the flying mechanisms. Despite Poppy's claims that the bike could handle it, Urban slowed her speed while the transition took place.

With a jolt to her stomach, the front wheel pulled upright like she was popping a wheelie. Visions of losing control, falling, and being crushed by the huge cycle filled her mind. But the vehicle held steady.

Hot air blasted her legs as the front wheel converted into two thrusters and pushed air out from under her. With a pop, the back wheel followed.

The craft hovered a moment, pressed her back into her seat, and then she was airborne.

"Pull up," Poppy instructed.

Urban shot into the sky. The weightlessness, the cool air brushing against her, the rugged mountains and forest below, all of it totally new and exhilarating. She'd ridden in pods back in the Asian Federation, but they were autonomous and kept you seated securely within.

They were nothing like this.

Here in the mountains, on this bike, Urban was in control.

Gradually, she increased her speed, until she was soaring through the sky. This was what she loved about bikes—the sense of freedom.

There was no safety belt, max speed limit, or path she was forced to follow. Urban could blaze her own trail. She wondered if this was what it felt like to be a Flyer.

She wondered if she could actually become one. She could be turned into an Aqua, so why not a Flyer too?

The thought of sprouting giant wings was unnerving. She doubted it was possible, anyway. Even if it somehow were, she had a feeling it would be an extremely painful procedure.

"You should turn around soon," Poppy advised. "You'll be approaching a town with a no fly zone over it."

Urban guided the bike gently back around then experimented a couple of times to see how quickly she could turn while maintaining a steady grip in the air.

"For the landing, it's the same process but in reverse," Poppy coached. "Just make sure to err on the side of being too far above the ground rather than too close. If you're too far above, you'll drop to the ground once your wheels convert back. If it's the other way around, the wheels won't be able to fully extend. You'll damage the vehicle and potentially wipe out."

"Got it." Urban guided the bike slowly back down to earth, watchful for the space between her and the ground. When the thrusters converted back to wheels, she fell the remaining distance with a heavy jolt. A high-pitched whine emanated as the bike wobbled, but then it straightened and shot forward.

She was soon pulling into the driveway, where everyone stood waiting. Her vehicle automatically decelerated, startling her.

Poppy guessed her confusion. "I can remotely control your vehicle to ensure your safety. Don't worry, during the race itself, the RTC app will disable that feature and you'll be on your own."

Urban wasn't sure how to feel about that. Of all the times when she wanted her team to be able to help, that would be the day.

Ash offered her a high five. "That was some very impressive flying."

Father was watching her with an unreadable expression.

"Great job," Everest said. "I noticed you taking that last curve a bit slow." His eyes twinkled. "Want to give it another go?"

Urban couldn't stop the grin spreading across her face as she nodded.

Revving the engine, she streaked away.

20

THE DEADLY FOURTH

"THERE'S OUR STAR!"

Urban blinked sleepily at her overly bright surroundings. She stood in Croix's private studio for her first KOL photo shoot. Rap music and warm air blasted her from all sides, banishing the early morning chill from outside.

An Artisan gestured Urban to follow. He led her into a large side room equipped with hoverstools and smart mirrors. A dozen stylists milled around, stopping mid-conversation as Urban entered.

The Artisan turned to Urban. "We're going to help you look your best and get a few shots for an upcoming Croix ad. Once you're done, the pre-game interviews are being held right across the hall in Ballroom B."

Urban nodded, trying to stifle a yawn.

Artisans flitted around, extracting her lips' pH levels, straightening and braiding her hair, and dabbing sponges over her face.

Urban zoned out of her immediate surroundings.

According to the RTC app, she had a full schedule today. First, there was her obligation to her sponsor. Then, her pre-race interview. Father had prepped her for it late the night before, but it sounded relatively easy.

The practice sessions on the road started after that. While Urban's designated slot wasn't for another few days, she was eager to scout out the competition.

After that, she had her performance evaluation of her new Aqua abilities. She wondered for the hundredth time what could be done with her new enhancements.

She was still thinking about all the different ways her genetics might have been altered when one of the stylists declared her finished.

Urban was handed clothes with the familiar Gamelyon symbol emblazoned on them. After changing, she was led away to an adjacent room with LED walls and hovering cameras that snapped her image.

Nearly an hour later, she was finally done. She didn't have far to go before arriving at the ballroom for her pre-race interview. Her security team surrounded her on all sides as she entered.

Urban scanned the ballroom. The competitors there all sat chatting or sipping drinks as they reclined on hovering couches. Urban was relieved to see Coral wasn't among them.

A guard stood next to a sectioned-off portion of the ballroom. Urban's name flashed on a display above it.

She walked over to him. "Lee Urban, here for my interview."

"Right this way." He led her to a back room sectioned off by sound-proof dividers. Lighting and camera bots hovered in the air ready to capture every angle.

Urban stood in front of another LED wall, this one with the RTC logo splashed against it.

"Remain here," the guard instructed and left.

Compared to the frenzied activity in the Croix studio, this felt like a tranquil bamboo forest.

"Lee Urban?" A bot hovered into the room.

Urban straightened. "That's me."

"Stand over there with your back to the wall and your feet aligned with the holo marker."

Urban stepped up to the glowing indigo marker.

The bot pointed at one of three vid recorders hovering nearby. "Look here during the recording. Please leave a few seconds of silence before answering each question. Are you ready, Lee Urban?"

She nodded.

There was a pause as the vid recorders turned red.

"First question, Lee Urban. You're one of several rookies competing in the most prestigious global race. What makes you think you'll be lucky enough have a shot at winning?"

Urban swallowed. That was the question that plagued her every day since signing up for the race.

The image of her father's winning racing helmet came to mind. She licked her lips. "I don't believe in luck. Winners make their own way."

The bot made no indicator it heard as it moved on to the next question. "It looks like your Father, Lee Byronne, was an extraordinary racer. He lost his favorite racing buddy, Phan Fox, who perished during the championship race. Why are you willing to take a similar risk?"

Urban's brain stuttered to a stop.

Phan Fox. Father's friend.

Why hadn't she seen it before?

Details clicked into place. Father's reluctance to teach her. Why he never competed again. His speech about sacrifice and danger.

Everything made sense now.

Urban realized she'd been silent too long. The vid recorders were waiting for her to answer.

She attempted to wrangle her wild thoughts. "We must take risks in order to accomplish greatness. And that's what I intend to do."

The vid recorder's blinking red light shifted to orange.

"That's all for now," the bot concluded. "Thank you for your time, Lee Urban."

Urban left the studio.

She considered this new information about her father. He had lost his closest friend in this race. Someone he cared about. It's why he didn't want her to compete.

Outside, fog hung ominously in the air, and a monkey screamed in the distance, making the hairs on the back of her neck stand on end.

She followed her team and guards as they wove through paths amid dense trees until they made it back onto the main road. There, they switched to one of the hover transport units that went up and down the mountain. Scenery zipped past them on the other side of the glass walls. Green foliage. White cliffs. Outcroppings of spectators, vendors, and pop-up food stations came and went.

The pod came to a smooth halt as they reached one of the upper portions of the racetrack, and Urban stepped out. This section of the road was alive with activity. A large hoverboard projected the names of the racers who were up next for their practice sessions. Pit crews raced around them in a flurry of activity.

Everest motioned toward several hovering platforms. Swiping his tatt, he opened the entrance. They all stepped onto a lift, which shot up into the sky before slowing at the top. Once off, Urban surveyed her surroundings.

The chaos was further removed at this height. Still, shouts, music, and the delicious scent of battered *youtiao, mantou, nanguabing*, and some of Urban's other favorite carb-laden snacks wafted toward them.

A familiar figure stepped up onto a podium. Clover flashed her toothy crocodile grin.

Urban's stomach tightened. Was Orion also nearby? She scanned for any signs of him and relaxed when she didn't see him.

"Attention racers!" Clover used a voice enhancer to address the crowd. "Once you have passed the technical inspection, you will be assigned a number. When your number is called, you may line up at the start line and have your practice run. Failure to show when your number is called means forfeiting your right to practice. The schedule is on the RTC app and cannot be altered. Each contender must practice within the division they are trying out for. Thank you and good luck."

Clover stepped off the podium and a robotic voice announced: "Practice session for racer number one commences in five minutes."

A contender sat on her bike at the holo start line, adjusting the controls. She looked young, almost the same age as Urban. She smiled and waved excitedly at a small group of people.

"Number one, you may begin in ten . . . nine . . ."

The countdown continued until the holo line changed from red to green. The racer shot forward and around the bend, out of sight. Jumbotrons followed her progress.

Using the RTC app, Urban pulled up the racer's stats. Her name was Melinda Rocks and she was from the Western Federation. Like Urban, she was a rookie this year.

The racer started out at a nice pace but quickly gained confidence and sped up the mountain, flawlessly executing each turn. Soon she was at the tunnel.

"She's going too fast," Father said tensely.

Urban's heart seized as she watched the racer shoot out of the tunnel.

Straight toward Reaper's Bend.

The girl slammed on the brakes but not soon enough.

Urban's hand flew to her face in horror.

The back of Melinda's bike fishtailed wildly as she skidded straight to the side of the mountain. There were no guard rails, and she wasn't slowing.

The crowd, now also realizing the mistake, held a collective breath.

All was silent as Melinda slid toward the edge of the sharp drop-off.

In what felt like slow motion, she sailed over the road and plummeted downward. The Jumbotrons showed her violent fall from multiple angles.

Urban felt sick to her stomach, yet was unable to turn away from the smoking heap of metal.

Protective suits could only do so much. Unless Melinda had some very special bone and organ enhancements, there was no way she had survived that fall. By the odd angles her limbs were bent, Urban doubted that was the case.

Medbots zoomed overhead toward the girl's location, the only sound in the eerie quiet.

Urban stood in shock, her brain unable to grasp what she was seeing. She'd watched people die in the vids and flicks, but this was different.

She's fine. She'll survive. Her mind rushed to assure her, even as another darker part whispered that nothing about this situation was fine. This *race* was not fine.

Urban's team stood completely still nearby, not saying a word but all thinking the same thing—that could have been Urban. It still could, if she wasn't careful.

Urban felt a sudden rush of tears.

That poor girl.

"A general reminder to all," a robotic voice said over the speakers. "As Emei Shan is a new race course for most, please remember to keep a steady speed during practice sessions. The purpose of these sessions is to familiarize yourself with the road. This is not the race. Thank you."

"One less competitor to worry about," someone joked loudly.

Urban glanced down, appalled. It was the next racer in line for a practice session. His fully armored rev cycle more closely resembled a machine of war than a bike. He had a cocky stance and spiky black hair but snapped his visor down before she could get a look at his face. A venomous yellow serpent entwined with a bloodied stinger, adorned his helmet.

"That's a member of the Deadly Five, Yokai Wraith, the Fourth," Everest said in a low voice. She felt him tense. "It looks like he's competing in your division."

21

AQUA EVAL

URBAN'S BLOOD RAN COLD. OF COURSE THAT was a member of the Deadly Five. Who else would be so blasé about the death of another racer?

Olive's warning echoed in the back of her mind. *Someone in your division will try and kill you.*

"Racer number two, you may begin your practice session in ten . . . nine . . ."

The Deadly Fourth crouched low on his bike.

When the holo line flashed green, he shot forward, much faster than the previous racer. At first Urban thought maybe he too would take a wrong turn and end up at the bottom of the mountain. She very quickly abandoned that idea. Wraith seemed to have all the turns memorized and timed every break and acceleration to perfection.

With the ease of a professional, the Deadly Fourth made navigating one of the trickiest roads look like child's play. His bike converted to a flying machine and streaked through the sky so fast he was barely more than a blur.

"His vehicle is optimized for flying," Father observed. "To beat him, you'll have to get ahead before reaching the sky."

"Racer number two, you have taken a green flag in practice," the robotic voice said. "You may now enroll in the qualifiers."

The Deadly Fourth swaggered off his bike. His pit crew surrounded him, and the Jumbotrons switched to show the next contender.

Urban watched several more racers practice until they switched to several of the Time Attack sessions.

"Come on, let's go," Everest said.

Urban followed her team to their vehicle to head to the training facility. All the while, images of Melinda crashing and the Deadly Fourth laughing, circled in her mind.

As their vehicle turned a bend in the road, they entered a stretch of less populated forest. Jagged mountains stretched majestically upward, and a building stood in the side of the cliff.

The structure was smooth, unlike the rocky crags around it, but was the same color as the stones, making it difficult to spot where the mountain ended and the center began. The words Elite Elevation glowed in silver lighting across its side.

According to Urban's retina display, it had a sosh of 90.

The training facility had tunnel-like layers that stacked upon each other, mostly gray slabs except for the ends which glinted in the sun from the plexiglass and neon light fixtures. One of the tunnels jutted out on another side of the building, hanging over a cliff. Magenta, fuchsia, and green lights flashed from within, making it look more like a club than a workout center.

The autonomous vehicle with Urban, Ash, and her guards slowed to a stop in front of an entrance where another vehicle sat idling.

The rest of the team joined Urban as she climbed up the steps toward the doorway.

A squad of ten Supers and five Inventors stopped them at the entrance. All held weapons ranging from stun pikes to poleaxes, each pulsing red at the ready. There were even two huge Enhanced guard dogs, both taller than Urban and with hackles raised, emitting low growls.

Urban was not expecting this level of security for a gym.

"Tatts," one of the Supers commanded, approaching the group.

Despite Ivan's assurances her banned status wouldn't matter here, she couldn't help but worry that she'd set off an alarm like she had at Infini-Fit.

The guard scanned each of them, then stepped aside. "You may enter."

The giant concrete door slid away.

Urban's shoulders relaxed as she and her trainers entered and the door shut behind them. The entryway was cool, dimly lit, and smelled of magnolia air freshener. A stark contrast to the loud, pumping music blasting them from all sides.

A Super bounced toward them. She had dirty blonde hair pulled up in a tight braid and a workout suit that accentuated the muscled planes of her arms and abs.

"Welcome to Elite Elevation, or E2, as the locals call it." She smiled warmly. "As a top KOL training location, we pride ourselves in security measures. It looks like your sponsor, Croix, has rented out our facilities for a private training session."

They did?

Glancing around, Urban noticed how empty the space was.

"Please let us know if there's anything you need, and we'd be happy to assist. Would you like a tour?"

Ivan stepped forward. "I've been here before, thanks."

The Super nodded and left.

Ivan led the way down a long hallway with charcoal-colored floors and cement walls backlit by florescent light. Windows lined sections of both walls and gave glimpses into the rooms beyond. All were dark and not in use, but Urban caught a glimpse of weighted racks, Flyer wind tunnels, sonar vision rooms, and all sorts of other equipment.

"It's going to be challenging to build up your strength in time for race day." Ivan stopped in front of a door leading to a room full of pools. "On hairpin turns, you'll be going from up to 225 kilometers per hour down to eight. The g-force required to stop and come out of that sort of turn can do serious damage to your internal organs."

Her mouth fell open. "Like what?"

"If your core isn't prepared, you could have severe internal bruising."

She wasn't sure she wanted to hear more.

"You also need to be used to extreme endurance," Ivan said. "You'll most likely maintain a heart rate of 140 bpm. If, at some point in the race, any part of your body gives out, it's over. If your neck muscles get tired of supporting your fiber carbon helmet, weighing five kilograms, you won't be able to hold your head up."

"Did—did you say five kilograms?" No wonder if felt heavy.

"It's for your own good. Trust me," Poppy chimed in.

Inventors and their tech.

"The point is," Ivan continued, "when a part of your body fatigues and you are in pain or cramping up, you are no longer devoting one hundred percent of your energy to the race. Your attention is divided, and you can't win that way."

"But don't worry," Poppy assured her. "With my tech, you'll be prepared in no time."

Urban had her doubts but didn't say anything.

They approached the pool. "But first, we will test your Aqua baseline abilities," Ivan said.

Dark water with streaks of indigo lapped at Urban's feet. Overhead, a sea of blinking stars stretched across a holo ceiling. The space was dimly lit, automatic foot lights flickering on as they walked.

Blossom tossed a swimsuit back at Urban. "Change into this."

Urban stepped past Poppy and Ivan as they set up testing equipment.

In the dark locker room, her feet met cold, smooth wood. Lights flicked on to reveal the wooden benches of a sauna.

After a couple of minutes, she was pulling on the suit's lightweight fabric.

Silky black material covered her from shoulder to thigh with spots of breathable mesh netting woven throughout. The professional training gear of Aquas fit perfectly. Looking in the mirror, for the first time, Urban thought she actually looked like an Aqua.

It was easy to forget, day in and day out, what had happened to her body, and that she had become Enhanced. But in moments like these, it came back in a heady rush. Excitement mixed with dread. Joy punctuated by loss. Too many emotions all at once.

Pushing it away, she reemerged to find Blossom adjusting several tools near the water. She tapped the edge of the pool. "Warm up with a couple of laps."

Urban gazed down at the water.

Soon I'll have answers about my Aqua abilities.

She waded into the lukewarm water. She'd never been a strong swimmer and felt self-conscious as she did laps. At least now she didn't have to deal with the awkwardness of lifting her head up to breathe every few strokes.

She marveled at the water's coolness in her lungs. She wasn't sure she'd ever get used to it.

How long do I have to do this?

Urban stopped in front of her team, water dripping down her face, looking up expectantly.

"Why did you stop?" Blossom demanded. "Keep going."

Urban held in a sigh and dove back under, swimming slower now. She was on her seventh lap and her arms were burning when a strange sound made her pause.

Lifting her head up, she searched for the source. Blossom sat close to the edge of the pool holding a device.

"It works," she said. "Your underwater hearing is enhanced." Her eyes unfocused as she made notes in QuanNao.

A moment later, her gaze went back to Urban. "Alright, let's try something else." Blossom waved her out of the pool. "Time to test your spatial awareness and S1."

Blossom walked to a darker and deeper pool. "Here." She threw a device in. It glowed a sunset orange as it sank to the bottom.

"Hope you like puzzles," Blossom said. "Give it your best shot."

Urban stared in bafflement at the orange device before jumping in after it.

"We'll need to work on your dive," Blossom muttered from above.

Urban swam down to the bottom of the pool and gingerly picked up the glowing orb. She twisted it in her hands, examining it.

A white light shot out from it and scanned her face.

"Lee Urban confirmed. Now initializing 3D spatial reasoning sequence." Urban found she could understand it perfectly, despite being underwater.

A sudden light projected onto the edge of the pool. Glowing shapes and patterns danced in the ripples of the water.

"Which should come next in the sequence?" the device asked, then projected four 3D options.

Urban cocked her head, studying the pattern then the options before her.

She selected one easily, not even sure how she had known which one came next. It was as if her subconscious knew what to do.

The device beeped green and moved onto a new problem. Several objects floated in the space around her, another puzzle.

Urban quickly solved this one as well.

More tests appeared, each increasingly harder, until Urban got one wrong and they stopped.

Four more new devices splashed into the water at opposite corners of the pool. They lit up, forming an underwater obstacle course. "You have three minutes to complete the course and its associated puzzles," a disembodied voice said. "Starting . . . now!"

Urban instantly began swimming through the course. She wasn't sure how much time she spent weaving through all the obstacles before the timer beeped and she was allowed to rest.

"Enough spatial dimensions testing," Blossom declared when Urban surfaced again.

Urban glanced up at her. Blossom's expression was maddeningly empty of any answers on how she was performing.

"Time to see about your lungs." Blossom placed a holo stopwatch on the ground. "Hold your breath for as long as you can. Go."

Urban inhaled a deep breath and held it, watching as the flashing neon numbers ticked up. A minute and a half flew by easily. That used to be her max.

The pressure in her lungs, the drive to breathe, increased at four minutes, and finally, became painful at the end of six. The holo had just reached seven minutes when Urban inhaled, gasping for air.

Lucas high-fived her. "Good job, sis."

"I didn't know Aquas could hold their breath longer on land too," Urban marveled.

"It's not just Aquas," Lucas explained. "All Enhanced lungs are strengthened and able to do what you just did."

The Enhanced truly are at an advantage in everything. What could someone like Everest do with these sorts of genetic alterations?

"Next, we'll test your Aqua voice enhancer," Blossom stated. "Go ahead, let out your best roar."

Urban's brow furrowed. Breathing underwater and solving the sequences had come naturally. Roaring, on the other hand, required concentration. And it wasn't something she'd ever attempted before.

Hesitating, Urban opened her mouth and let loose.

Definitely not a roar.

Blushing, she shut her mouth.

"Try again," Blossom said.

Urban inhaled a deep breath and pitched her voice lower this time. Now she just sounded like a strangled hippo.

Blossom tapped her foot impatiently.

"Here, let me try and help." Lucas stepped in. "Sometimes it's easier to start underwater." Fully clothed, he dove gracefully into the pool.

Urban climbed down the ladder after him.

Lucas spun in somersaults before her. "This should feel more natural. Roaring underwater. Watch." He opened his mouth, took a deep breath and then let out a thundering roar.

The water around them vibrated, and even the walls of the pool trembled. Urban had to cover her ears.

"Now you try," Lucas encouraged.

Urban sucked in a deep breath, opened her mouth and let loose her frustration and everything else into one long scream.

A stream of bubbles escaped.

Urban sighed. "Did you have to learn how to roar?" she asked Lucas.

"It was so long ago. . . I think it came naturally. Like walking." He looked at her thoughtfully. "If someone who'd been paralyzed their entire life suddenly gained the use of their legs, they'd have to learn how to walk. The mechanics wouldn't come all at once. With you becoming an Aqua later in life, there's probably a few Aqua skills that you'll have to figure out. Don't worry, it will come."

Despite his pep talk, her inability to roar weighed on Urban as she climbed out of the water.

The rest of the team departed in preparation for Urban's next test. Only Blossom remained behind with her. "It seems your S1 has improved."

"My what?"

"The primary somatosensory cortex."

Urban stared at Blossom.

"Didn't you pay any attention in school?" Blossom huffed. "It's the part of the brain that processes and controls all sensory and motor functions. It's critical for any racer to have heightened reflexes and precise movements. Your hands and feet have the most receptors in them. That's why Aquas make such good racers. Their primary somatosensory cortex, or S1, has been enhanced. This allows for enhanced reflexes and dexterity for more precise turns on the road."

Urban pursed her lips.

"It used to be that men had a higher S1 functionality," Blossom went on. "That's why all the best racers back in the day were primarily male. But now, with this enhancement given to females and males alike, women are as capable of dominating the RTC. Lucky for you."

Urban eyed Blossom. "Can I be frank?"

Blossom folded her arms. "I'd advise against it."

Urban made sure they were alone before speaking. "Why are you here? Clearly you don't want to be."

Blossom raised an eyebrow. "Do you think I have a choice?"

"You always have a choice."

"Says the girl who became AiE's local pawn."

"I'm not their pawn." Urban's face flushed. "And that was my choice."

"Yes, well. We all made choices that led us here."

"Then why do you hate—I mean, dislike me?" Urban amended. "What happened? We were friends once."

Blossom was silent a moment. "The Western Federation has rubbed off on you. You are too honest." With that, she turned and strutted away.

22

HYDRO COMBAT

LUCAS TOSSED URBAN A KNIFE. THEY STOOD AT the bottom of a pool, and she barely caught the hilt as it sank in a zig-zagging pattern.

"What is this?" The knife was cool to Urban's touch and had odd markers on its side that lit up in rose gold.

"It's a hydro blade. DNA activated. This is the best part of your eval. Aqua Arts." Lucas grinned. "It's underwater martial arts. Each gene pool has their own specialized version. But Hydro Combat is the coolest, in my opinion."

Urban regarded him in surprise. "I had no idea you knew how to fight."

"What can I say? I'm a man of mystery," Lucas said airily. "Now, let's see how good of an underwater fighter *you* are."

Lucas sliced his own green dagger through the water with lightning speed.

"If you squeeze the hilt twice, you'll activate underwater mode," he said. "The dagger is linked to your retina display. It senses the direction you're striking, traces the arc of the blade, and then adds a boost of power in that same direction. Thus, overcoming the water's resistance and making you super-fast."

He gestured. "Try it."

Urban squeezed her dagger twice. It flashed, but at first, the usual lag of water slowed her movement. Then it was as if all resistance disappeared. Her blade flew through the water.

"Pretty cool, huh?" Lucas grinned. "Works above ground too. But be careful if using it on land. You'll go too fast and could hurt yourself. It takes some getting used to."

Urban examined the blade with admiration.

"Now, sparring time!" Lucas began undulating.

Urban realized his movements were the equivalent of fight stance, but for underwater. She tried to imitate him but quickly gave up, feeling ridiculous.

"Come on," Lucas urged. "Don't be a scaredy-cat."

Urban charged, only it was a slow swim forward, and nothing like the fast-paced sparring she was used to at the gym.

Lucas somersaulted away with super speed.

"Hey!" Urban protested. "No fair."

Lucas laughed before zipping back toward her, air bubbles shooting out from his specialized boots.

"If you're underwater, you'll also want to keep a pair of these handy." Lucas tapped his shoes. "Learning to control your blade and body are the majority of what Hydro Combat teaches."

Lucas motioned her to approach. "Try again."

This time, Lucas didn't zip away. Urban activated her dagger and watched her hand sweep through the water of its own accord.

"Better. Let's test your reaction times." Lucas held up what looked like a kick shield, only it had a glowing fuchsia pink spot on the upper right corner. "Hit the target with your fist as fast as you can."

Urban did so. Her arm felt sluggish in the water after the super speed of the knife. Her knuckles struck the shield with little force, hitting something pliable and rubbery.

Instantly, the glowing target vanished, replaced by a different one, this time at the bottom left.

"Good. Again," Lucas instructed.

Urban tried to get into fight stance, but kept drifting off to the side. Finally, she got close enough to land a jab to the shield. The glowing target vanished again, changing to a different part.

They continued on like this until Urban's arms grew weary.

"That's enough. Good job," Lucas said. He began to put away the equipment.

Urban hadn't realized just how tired or hot she was until she was back in open air. Sweat mingled with pool water and slid down her skin as she gasped for breath. How odd that breathing underwater had actually required less effort.

I should train in the pool more often.

Urban sank onto a chair and gulped down air while the team regrouped.

When her breathing steadied, Poppy held out what looked like bungee cords and a helmet. "Now for the real training. Put this on."

Like the racer helmet, this one was heavier than Urban's regular one.

Poppy clipped the bungee cords to the helmet. "Give this a go."

The helmet lurched to the right. Urban had to crank her head in the opposite direction to keep from tipping over. "Ah! What was that?" Her voice sounded muffled inside the helmet.

"That's our new little game," Poppy said perkily. "Try and stay upright. If your neck starts to cramp up, let me know. We don't want you to get any pulled muscles."

When they were done, Urban's neck felt tighter than the bungee cord. She rubbed its sore muscles as Poppy packed up the equipment.

After that, she was allowed a brief break before more training began. Ivan had her run a mile, climb a rock wall, do sit ups and pushups. All while he made notes with either pleased or disgruntled sounds at each result.

Finally, he said, "Alright, that's it for your evaluation."

Poppy offered an encouraging smile. "Why don't you take it easy and head to the recovery room? They'll know what you need."

Urban didn't need to be told twice. Her guards followed, leaving her at the entrance.

The floors, walls, and high ceiling of the recovery spa were all a perfect, pristine white. A hovering desk backlit with an herbal green sat at the center of the space with a Natural and bot assistant behind it. Puffs of lemongrass filled the air.

The Natural who stepped out from behind the reception desk wore a simple white pantsuit with hair pulled back in a professional bun. "Hello, Miss."

She scanned Urban's tatt. "Lee Urban?" Without waiting for her to confirm, the Natural continued. "It looks like your trainer has ordered the complete recovery package. Let's get you started by changing."

The Natural handed Urban a soft, white robe and pointed her in the direction of a private room.

Stripping out of her swimwear, Urban wrapped the crisp robe around herself and returned to the front desk.

The bot attendant guided her to an overly bright and cold cryotherapy room. Urban stepped out of her robe and into the neck-high frosted glass casing.

Instantly, coldness seeped over her and into her bones.

Two long minutes ticked by until the door opened again. Urban stumbled out, numb limbs instantly alive and invigorated as warm air blew over her.

Donning her robe again, she followed the bot attendant past mirrored hallways to a softly lit room with a hovering bed. The Natural attendant stood by arranging acupuncture needles.

After Urban lay down, the attendant gently massaged Urban's scalp. Meanwhile, the bot targeted specific regions of her head for acupuncture.

The effect was instant relaxation.

It was over too soon. "The last part of your therapy is the ASMR room." The Natural led the way to a zen space with tranquil lighting.

The floor was covered in moss, which filled the room with

the aroma of damp earth. Flora grew on the walls. A large, bean-shaped object sat at the center of the room, soft light glowing out from its rippling casing.

"Miss Lee, you can cool down on this multi-sensory relaxation bed." The attendant motioned at the bean-shaped sleeping platform.

As Urban climbed on, it felt like balancing on top of water. Once she was on her back, trying not to roll off, the attendant activated several settings before leaving.

The bed vibrated and a strange sound permeated the air. It was like a boat paddling through water paired with the occasional gong and notes of a zither. An artificial wind blew over her.

The effect was surprisingly soothing, and Urban sank deeper into the bed.

After her workout, it was heavenly. As the knots in her body loosened, her mind drifted.

Breathing underwater. Improved sensory and motor skills. Underwater martial arts.

So much had changed.

Before she had time to dwell on it, she had fallen asleep.

23

UNDERWATER BASH

LATER THAT DAY, A VIRTUAL LOCATION REQUEST appeared in Urban's retina display. Glancing at the avatar ID, Urban inhaled a sharp breath and immediately accepted.

Mako materialized before her as she was transported into what looked like an office. "Hello, dear."

"Hello, Mako." It was her most professional tone.

"I'm sorry to disturb you, as I know your schedule is quite full, but there's one KOL bash exclusively for Aquas tonight. As the Croix representative, we'd like you attend. You'll be pleased to know we've limited the number of events to the bare minimum. This and a photoshoot are the only things we'll ask of you before the prelims."

Why is he still sponsoring me? "I'll be there."

"Excellent." Mako gave a nod. "I'll have my makeup artist come assist and bring your clothes for the evening."

Urban hesitated.

"Do you have any questions?" Mako asked.

"Yes, actually." Urban swallowed. "Are you aware of . . . uh, my . . . status?"

He regarded her a moment. "The banned list?"

Urban tensed but nodded.

"I am aware."

"And you still want to sponsor me?"

"Ah," Mako said knowingly. "Many people are shortsighted when it comes to these sorts of things. Me? I'm a true visionary. What other sponsors don't see is how one day, you'll be in the history vids as the first ever hybrid."

Urban inhaled a gasp.

"Yes, I know about that, as well." Mako leaned back. "You see, while short term we may not make any money off sponsoring you, one day, when you become a legend, you'll be wearing our brand. It will solidify us as the number-one brand in the future and will be quite profitable."

Urban regarded Mako. "So, it all makes financial sense for you?" Urban asked.

"Yes," Mako replied simply. "Croix is my passion and my world. I built it from the ground up. It's always about what makes sense for the business. And in this case, our goals are aligned."

Urban tried not to think about what would happen if their goals no longer aligned. "I'm glad."

"Me too, darling." Mako flashed a radiant smile. "Now, I'm sorry, but I have another meeting I need to attend to. I'm glad to see you doing well and look forward to great things from you."

Mako's avatar vanished, and Urban padded into the kitchen, thinking.

So Mako knew she was the hybrid and on the banned list. She wondered what else he knew. For right now, however, she had to focus on the upcoming bash.

Finding an Ivan-approved energy booster, Urban took a sip and gagged. It tasted like raw eggs, fizzy water, and pills. Wincing, she downed the rest of the concoction, then went into the prep room where the makeup artist would soon arrive.

She didn't have to wait long.

A diminutive woman arrived toting several giant hovering bags. Urban was surprised to find only one person instead of Croix's usual swarm of people.

"I'm Sage," the artist said, extending a hand for Urban to shake.

It took Urban a second to realize the artist was a Natural. Her colored retina displays and brand clothing had thrown her off for a second, but she was definitely a Natural.

Why would Mako, a leading KOL of the top brand in the Asian Federation, send me a Natural? Despite the cheaper price of hiring one, most Enhanced wanted an Artisan with steadier hands for their makeup or hair. Price was rarely an issue for them, and they wanted the best.

Is this an underhanded insult?

But Mako didn't seem like the type to play mind games. Especially when he had such a high sosh and no reason to insult Urban. Not to mention, he'd been pretty direct so far regarding her contract and standing.

Strange.

Sage led Urban to the preparation room and adjusted the room's settings so that warm, natural light flooded the space, despite the growing darkness outside. Two smart mirrors folded down from the ceiling and a seat hovered into the room and stopped before them. The artist gestured to the chair.

"I specialize in Aqua makeup." Sage pulled out a bag and began rifling through it. "Have you ever been to an underwater bash this big before?"

"I've never been to one at all," Urban confessed.

Sage's eyes widened.

Urban watched in the mirror as Sage transformed her image by putting on a special form of waterproof makeup.

Sage dusted Urban's skin lightly with a makeup brush. "You really haven't been to an underwater event?"

Urban shook her head. "Have you?" She immediately regretted the question.

Sage's laugh was unnaturally high-pitched. "For us Naturals, we don't have the luxury of going to any bashes. I'm lucky to have escaped the AI tech jobs and be here at all." She eyed

Urban critically. "I don't expect you to understand."

Urban felt like she'd been sucker punched by a Super. She wanted to tell Sage everything—that she did understand. That she had worked a manual tech job before. That she was just like her.

But was she?

Urban had never lived among Naturals in the Outskirts. She'd voluntarily taken an AI training job. She'd always had plenty of opportunities due to the wealth and influence of her parents and their standing in the Metropolis.

Even though she'd been a Natural for most of her life, had she ever really belonged among them? She'd spent so much of her time hiding from the Enhanced and pretending to be one of them, she'd always assumed she belonged among the Naturals.

And yet now she wasn't sure.

Could the hybrid claim to relate to Naturals when she had Aqua genetics?

Her chest tightened with an emotion she couldn't place.

Urban didn't have a chance to respond before Sage was gone.

Urban sat staring at her transformed image in the mirror. Her retina displays were cobalt-blue, her eyeliner a seafoam color, and a light dusting of silver and blue tinted her skin. How many different versions of Lee Urban were there? And which—if any—were the real one?

Who am I?

Her retina display beeped and drew her back out of her thoughts.

<Time to leave for the Underwater KOL Bash.>

Urban climbed out of the chair and changed into the outfit laid out for her. It was a rugged black athletic pantsuit made of a material used for quick dries. Holes riddled the pants and the ends of the sleeves were frayed, giving the entire piece a tough look. But the sheen of the expensive cloth balanced it out, speaking of quality tailoring and luxury.

After tugging on a pair of waterproof boots, she headed

downstairs. The house was empty, the rest of the team most likely winding down for the evening.

Urban envied them.

Instead, she headed outside, guards trailing close behind. She was approaching an armored vehicle to climb into when a shadow darkened the sky.

With a soft thump, the Gamelyon landed next to her, a man riding on its back. "You must be Urban."

Urban looked at the man in surprise. "That's me. And you are?"

The man smiled and hopped off the creature's back. "AiE sent me. I'm your Gamelyon's trainer and keeper. They wanted you to ride this to any meetings, bashes, or big events going forward."

"Uh . . . okay." Urban's brow furrowed. She'd ridden the Gamelyon twice before without incident, but those had both been spontaneous. She wasn't sure if she could just climb on and expect it to take her exactly where she wanted.

The man smiled as he helped Urban onto the Gamelyon's back. Once settled, she turned to Trig and the rest of her guards. "Meet you at the bash?"

Trig nodded and gestured to the other Flyer guard. "We will follow you in the sky."

"Alright then, let's go." Urban clucked her tongue, but the Gamelyon remained still. Then she squeezed the sides of its ribs with her legs, and it took off running. With a jolt, it leaped into the air and pumped its giant scaled wings.

Soon, they were soaring past the treetops. With the steady beating of wings and the scent of rosewood and the calm quiet, she found herself actually enjoying the flight.

All too soon, the horizon sparked with color, light, and sound. A street full of hover campers, night vendors, and RTC fans came into view.

The Gamelyon dropped down toward a small collection of buildings nestled within the side of the mountain. Swooping low to the ground it landed abruptly on the grass. Urban thought she might have arrived undetected, but then the creature let out an earth-shattering roar. Flames shot into the sky, and the surrounding Aquas gasped and ran away.

As Urban awkwardly slid off the creature, Trig landed next to her. The other guards and the trainer were not far behind, pulling up in vehicles. Aquas around her cowered from the Gamelyon, but some of the bolder ones hesitantly moved closer to get vids or snaps.

She wondered if their posts would be taken down. So far, it seemed mostly brands and news outlets paid attention to her banned status. That probably didn't apply to individuals. Maybe AiE knew what they were doing after all.

She hoped so, anyway.

Urban's gaze snagged on the huge, brightly lit event venue before her. The KOL bash was at a natural hot spring that had been expanded to include a huge indoor fish tank. Schools of Blackberry Silver Dollars, angelfish, and Asian redtail catfish swam around the Aquas clustered inside.

The tank was similar to the one her parents kept back home, only larger and with even more stunning decor. The similarities between the two struck Urban. How many times had she looked at that tank with loathing and fear? She'd always seen it as an extension of Lucas and his attempt to drown her.

Now, here she was, as an Aqua, joining in on the activities inside a tank like it.

There were two entrances. The entryway at the top had a high platform from where Aquas dove gracefully into the water. Urban was pretty sure she'd end up doing a belly flop and humiliating herself if she tried that way.

The other option was on the ground floor and involved a transition immersion room. She headed toward that entrance instead.

As she stepped inside, a glass door closed behind her and the one in front opened, flooding the room with tepid water. Urban gripped handholds on the walls until the water swirling around her slowed. Then she swam into the pool.

Several Aqua groups cast quick glances her way. Urban knew she should socialize with them but, feeling hopelessly out of place, started to the bar instead. She'd always wondered what it was like to drink something while underwater.

A waiterbot resembling an octopus attended her. "What can I get you?" A menu flashed on the counter under Urban's fingers. She pointed at a nonalcoholic champagne.

"I'd start with something else." Lucas took the seat next to her. "Trust me, anything bubbly doesn't settle well when you're swimming."

Urban looked at him. "What are you doing here?"

"This event is open to any Aqua, not just people competing in the RTC. And you know me, never one to pass up a good party." He wiggled his eyebrows mischievously.

The waiterbot came back with a sealed drink and offered Urban a straw.

"What happens if I drink without the tube?" Urban asked curiously.

"Then you inhale a bunch of water." Lucas grinned.

Urban glanced at the clusters of gathered Aquas and sighed. "I suppose you want us to socialize?"

Lucas shrugged. "We can. But I'm just here for you."

"Oh?" Urban looked at her brother in surprise. "Thanks."

They sat in companionable silence before Urban spoke up. "Do you ever wonder what happened to Father?"

Lucas shot her a glance. "Like why he's such a jerk?"

"I wasn't going to put it quite like that."

"I've been wondering that my whole life." Lucas snorted, but then his face changed. "I've done a lot of digging. Our parents were betrayed by someone within AiE and their sosh dropped big time, but I don't think that's it. From Dad's avatar's history, he was lowering his alcoholic threshold levels and was a grump even before that incident. Did you know he used to smile?"

Lucas didn't wait for her to reply as he stared wistfully into the distance. "I found some pictures in QuanNao where he looked truly happy. It was about ten years ago, somewhere around 2113. That's the last vid record I found on his public profile where he looks happy."

2113. Why did that year sound familiar?

Then it clicked.

"That was the year of his last race."

Lucas looked skeptical. "If racing made him happy, why did he give it up?"

Urban took a quick sip of her drink. "He lost one of his friends in a race. Maybe it has something to do with that?"

"An interesting theory," Lucas mused. "But I guess it doesn't really matter. Now that racing is out of his life, he'll never be happy. It's not like his family would ever be enough to bring that smile back." He barked a laugh. "Now, what do you say we stir up some trouble for those annoyingly pompous party goers?"

He pointed at a group of huddled Aquas with rainbow hair.

Urban groaned. "Please don't. I'm only here because I have duties for Croix to uphold."

Lucas let out a long sigh. "Let's go be boring, socially acceptable citizens then."

He led the way toward the Aquas and easily joined in the conversation. They all linked and chatted underwater. Urban found it odd having an entire conversation with a group of people while in a giant fish tank. There was a slight current in the water that had them drifting apart, and Urban kept paddling to keep from floating away.

"Are any of you doing the augmented-free challenge this week?" one of the Aquas asked. She had a blinking yellow light in the corner of her retina display. "I hear some of the biggest KOLs are doing it."

Goosebumps rippled over Urban's skin.

Another augmented-free campaign? That must mean AiE was trying to get some important news out, and by the looks of it, were shut down. Again.

Urban realized the Aqua was waiting for her to give an answer.

"Oh. No. Not this time." *I have more important things to worry about than a sosh boost.*

There was an awkward silence in which Urban realized she might have offended the girl.

But then Lucas came to the rescue. Ever the life of the party, he soon had the whole group laughing as he told stories of Urban's escapades. He talked her up so much that by the time they dispersed, they all held admiration in their eyes for her.

Urban turned gratefully to him. "Thank you, Lucas." She looked around. "I feel so out of my element here."

"Like a fish out of water?" Lucas asked innocently as Urban groaned.

"Come on!" She tugged at him. "Let's meet some more people so I don't lose Croix as my sponsor."

"I still don't see how you, the fashion rookie"—Lucas gave her a once over—"landed a sponsor like them. Nice jumper, by the way."

"They gave it to me," Urban admitted.

"Of course." Lucas said wryly.

After meeting nearly every Aqua in the tank and snapping with a handful of the most influential KOLs, Urban and Lucas were ready to leave.

A commotion at the other end of the pool caught Urban's eye. Several Aquas were shouting and gesticulating wildly.

"Are they drunk?" Urban indicated the group.

Lucas looked where she was pointing. "Aqua parties can get a little wild. Let's leave before things get out of hand."

Urban cast a final glance in the direction of the commotion and froze.

It wasn't an Aqua but a Natural girl younger than Urban. She looked as if she had fallen into the water and was now being pulled to the bottom of the pool by several of the drunken party goers. The Natural kicked and lashed out at the nearest Aqua, but he only laughed.

Anger burned in Urban. She knew exactly what it felt like to be trapped underwater. The nightmare of her own experience still haunted her.

"Come on," Lucas tried to direct Urban toward the exit but she slipped out of his grasp.

"We have to help!" She pointed at the girl.

Lucas swore. "I'll help her. You go."

"No." Urban withdrew her hydro blade and activated it. "I'm coming."

Lucas lowered his voice. "If anyone recognizes you—it's not safe."

"There's too many of them for you to fight alone," Urban protested. "She'll drown."

The Natural screamed, an odd warbling sound. Urban didn't wait another second. She activated her Aqua boot propellers, zipping through the pool toward the girl. Loud swearing followed not far behind.

"Who's this?" one of the Aquas asked the others, watching Urban.

"Release her," Urban demanded.

The Aqua ignored her command. "Hey, you're that influencer who's trying out for that race." His eyes gleamed. "I wonder how much my sosh would jump if I hurt you."

Urban started.

Would this Aqua really try and injure her just for a sosh boost? Infamy had boosted more than one person's sosh before. Then again, it had also tanked them.

Behind the Aqua, the Natural clawed at her throat, eyes widening in terror.

Abandoning diplomacy, Urban charged the Aqua. He was too wasted to put up a fight. One good kick to his midsection sent him floating away.

She reached for the Natural but something slammed into Urban from the side, sending her the opposite direction.

"Watch out!" Lucas shouted.

Urban managed to halt her spinning with her boot thrusters

and turned with blade at the ready.

An Aqua wielding a pulsing broad sword swam behind her. He whipped the blade toward her with lightning speed.

Squeezing her dagger twice, Urban parried just in time.

The force of the blow rattled her teeth. An odd sensation underwater, but not one Urban had time to dwell on as the Aqua charged again.

Urban squeezed her blade and her hand flew out on its own accord.

In the wrong direction.

Wrestling her blade into submission, Urban tried to redirect it, but instead lost her grip. She watched helplessly as the dagger shot away into a patch of coral reef.

Sensing movement, she activated her boots and twisted her body, barely managing to miss the broad sword that sliced past her chest.

Her back was pressed up against an underwater castle as her attacker closed in. His eyes held a look of triumph as he raised his sword again.

Can he kill me with that thing?

Urban didn't want to find out. She scanned her surroundings for something, anything she could use to protect herself.

Nothing.

But just then the Aqua jerked to the side, sword falling away. He froze and floated off. Lucas stood behind him with an underwater gun extended.

"Drunken fools," he muttered.

Behind him, the other Aquas, in a similar fashion, were immobilized and drifting across the pool. The Natural girl floated lifelessly in the water behind them.

"The girl!" Activating her boots, Urban reached for her and then shot toward the surface. With Lucas's help, she pushed the girl out of the water and onto the edge of the pool.

"She's not breathing!" Urban panicked.

Lucas's face was knit in concentration as he knelt down and

began CPR.

Urban watched helplessly. The Natural was so skinny and young. Probably only eleven or twelve. And yet, she wore a pink *qipao* like the other servants at the party. Was she already working a job?

Suddenly, the girl leaned to the side and retched.

She's going to be alright.

Tension flooded out of Urban's body.

Trig and the rest of Urban's security team had pushed the watching crowd aside and attempted to pull Urban away.

"She needs care," Urban insisted. "I'm not leaving her here."

Especially with these people.

Trig hesitated only a moment. "The girl comes with." He spoke into his com link. "Bring up the vehicles and activate the medbot."

One of Urban's Super guards lifted the girl effortlessly. Her wet silk dress clung to her frail body as she leaned against his massive armored chest.

Two Flyers beat their wings together, clearing a path. Drones buzzed loudly at anyone who got too close as they all went down the stairs, past the giant pool, and finally toward a SpideX.

Urban hadn't seen one of these massive vehicles since Lunar New Year. The extra space was a welcomed relief. A medbot waited for them inside and immediately began tending to the girl.

As soon as the doors closed behind them, Lucas berated Urban for her foolish decisions, but she didn't care.

Those Aquas would have let her die.

Urban's eyes went to the girl. She sat upright and, while white as sticky rice, appeared otherwise unharmed.

Lucas' lecture over, Urban made her way to where the medbot checked the girl's vitals and tended to her as she sat on the floor, swaying with each lurching step of the SpideX.

Urban offered her a smile. "How are you feeling?"

"Alright." The girl's voice was barely a whisper. Her eyes immediately darted downward, the way all Natural servants did.

"You can look at me."

The girl's cocoa eyes flashed upward at Urban in surprise. She gave Urban a once-over and shuddered.

A stab of pain shot through Urban. She knew exactly what the girl was thinking. She'd been taught the same thing, after all. Enhanced are dangerous.

"I probably don't have my job anymore," the girl squeaked out.

Urban's heart twisted.

She's thinking about her job? Not the fact that she almost just died?

"My parents both lost their AI training jobs," the girl seemed to trust Urban. "I dropped out of school to take a serving position to support my family. I don't want to go back to the pool to work." Her body began to tremble.

Urban wanted to reach out and give her a hug. She was so small and young. The legal working age was thirteen, but there was no way she was that old.

What if other drunken partygoers decided to turn her death into another sick game? The thought soured her stomach. Suddenly, Urban had an idea. "Would you want to work for me?"

Confusion showed in the girl's eyes, then disappeared as she masked her emotions.

This was familiar too. Hide all emotions to stay safe. She decided to take a different approach. "I'm Lee Urban. What's your name?"

The girl gazed at her a moment. Then her expression softened, giving her an even younger appearance. "My name is Yu Solstice."

Urban smiled. "I love that name."

"My parents named me after the change in seasons. They hope I will be the one to change our fortune."

"I know what that feels like."

The girl looked up quickly. "Really?"

Urban hesitated. Maybe it was because the girl had almost died. Or maybe it was because of her conversation earlier with Sage. Or maybe it was simply to see how a Natural would react to news of the hybrid. Regardless of the reason, Urban found herself saying: "Have you ever heard of the hybrid?"

The girl's brow furrowed. "I don't think so."

Urban explained what hybrid genetics meant for the world. When she finished, the girl's wide eyes stared at her. "So . . . you're a Natural who got enhancements?"

Urban nodded.

Solstice gazed at her in wonder. "That's amazing. I've never even heard of this before."

"The augmented-free challenges," Urban explained. "Every time we try and get the word out by hacking a network or getting some news coverage, the networks all shut down, blocking our message."

"But . . . why?"

Urban looked at the young face and spoke carefully. "Some people don't want things to change. They're afraid things will get dangerous."

Solstice wrapped her arms around herself, voice dropping to a whisper. "They already are."

"Not everyone sees it that way," she quickly assured the girl. "They don't want it to get worse."

The girl was silent a moment. "I want to help," she blurted. "I'll work for you. I have useful, employable skills." It sounded like a chant. "My parents say I make good—" she blushed. "I mean, decent, *jiaozi*."

"Uh oh. That's Urban's weakness," Lucas piped up. "Hire her now, sis, before she gets away."

Urban knelt down beside the girl. "Would you like to work as my personal chef?" she asked.

Once more, Solstice stared wide-eyed at her. "Really?"

"Really." Urban offered the girl a hand up. "In the meantime, how about a hot drink? This vehicle is equipped with a built-in latte maker."

That elicited a small smile, and Urban procured hot

matcha lattes for them. Sitting beside the girl, she made light conversation the rest of the trip.

After arriving back at the house, one of the guards led Solstice to a room, but Trig pulled Urban aside. "You cannot bring someone into the compound like that," he scolded. "I must conduct a background check to ensure she is not a security risk—"

"She was almost *killed*," Urban interrupted. "Besides, she's maybe eleven, and if that's not something you all can handle, then I question my safety."

Trig started to protest, but Urban stopped him. "Do what you must, but the girl stays."

There was a weighted silence between them. "It would be nice to have someone cook," Trig relented finally. "I must test every food delivery for poison, tracking devices, and other dangers."

Urban smiled at him. "See? I'm sure she'll save you time. And you can hire another chef while you're at it." Urban patted him on the back, then made her way into the living room.

Lucas sat, cleaning his weapon before returning it to a holster.

"What is that?" Urban eyed the device.

"An Aqua's best friend. It's called an AquaBolt pulse pistol." Lucas declared. "They only work underwater. Use it on dry land and it will short circuit and probably get you killed."

"Sounds"—Urban swallowed—"fun. How do I get one?"

"You talk to your underwater arms dealer. A.k.a. me." Lucas winked. "Just be careful. You have a magnetic attraction to trouble." He shook his head. "Why Mother and Father think *I'm* difficult, I'll never understand."

24

AQUA GENETICS

"WHAT KIND OF BREAKFAST IS THIS?" LUCAS YAWNED.

The table before Urban was ladened with eggs, cold cut meats, cheeses, and yogurts. After all the training the day before, she was ravenously hungry and scooped large portions of eggs and yogurt into her bowl.

Solstice entered the room carrying in another tray full of food. Urban watched as the Natural carefully set down a porcelain plate full of sausages. The girl had taken to her new position eagerly and with minimal supervision. She seemed happy.

Catching Urban's gaze, Solstice offered a tentative smile.

"Where's the *nanguabing* or *youtiao*?" Lucas complained.

Solstice darted out of the room like a frightened fish. Urban shot Lucas a glare, but he only blinked innocently.

"Those fried foods have way too many carbs in them," Ivan said. "I instructed the chefs to make foods that build Urban's muscle. Which is why we have mostly protein options. From now on, Urban will be on a very strict diet."

He looked at her. "I've just sent you a tracking app that will allow you to easily record everything you eat for my evaluation, as well as provide recommendations at each meal."

"But why do we all have to be on a diet with her?" Lucas muttered.

Father cleared his throat. "Let's go over yesterday's evaluation results." He nodded at Poppy and she began.

"We have analyzed Urban's physical and mental condition and mapped out a plan for going forward."

"Urban's biometrics look good," Ivan interjected. "She's not in peak physical performance yet, but she's not too far behind, either."

Good to know all those pushups and planks while I was trapped in a cell are finally paying off, Urban thought wryly.

"The next few weeks will be grueling in order to get Urban into top athletic shape," Ivan said. "But we're hopeful given her baseline it will be doable."

Father turned to Blossom. "What of your analysis?"

Blossom switched on a holo display of a DNA strand. "The team of bioinformaticians back at Dr. Watanabe's lab provided a report on the variants she displays. The findings are interesting, to say the least. That, combined with my own analysis and data from surveying her abilities, is enlightening."

Urban leaned forward with anticipation.

"How so?" Father inquired.

Blossom's face lit up. "For starters, her genome sequence is unlike anything in the global database. It's completely revolutionary. But of course, we already guessed that. Currently, we're mapping each of the variants' locations to see if we can replicate them on a test subject."

"So, are you done experimenting with me?" Urban asked hopefully.

Blossom regarded her. "I'd like to keep studying you, evaluating your abilities and limits, and collecting samples. I'm afraid without the microneedle patch, though, we'll be unable to test our theories. Until we have that tech, our work will all be theoretical. Reverse engineering will take finding the microneedle patch."

Urban thought back to her genetic engineering course her first semester at PKU. The probot had said there were three in existence worldwide. One was at some highly secure laboratory.

Urban knew exactly where the second microneedle patch was. At the bottom of the ocean. She tried not to think of the underwater research lab.

But where was the third patch?

She was pondering this when Poppy began her assessment.

"Urban shows all the standard enhancements for an Aqua." She projected over the table and graphs and charts appeared. "Ultra-fast reflexes, greater lung capacity, a lower resting heart rate, which will help cope with the adrenaline rush of the race, and improved VO2 max, which aids oxygen consumption in the muscles. She was missing the ability to roar, but that's not really relevant to the races. In summary, if she's a good driver, we can make this work.

"What's interesting about Urban's results is not her reaction time, but her precision. On the course, you need lightning-fast reflexes, but you also need exactly *precise* reflexes." She glanced curiously at Urban. "You already have excellent precision. Are you sure you don't have some sort of steadying enhancement?"

"No, but I have been training to be a painter for many years. I hope to be an Artisan," Urban confessed.

Poppy nodded. "Ah, makes sense."

"That's it. The way we're going to win." Father's smile grew broad as he faced Urban. "We found your edge."

25

TEST RUN

"MY WHAT?" URBAN SWALLOWED HER LAST bite of eggs.

"In order to win, you need an edge," Father said. "Over the years, the champions have always had that one thing in common—an edge. It only makes sense. Last year's winner had a vehicle able to transition from ground to sky faster than any other. The year before, an Aqua had inhumanly fast reflexes. A champion has to be better than everyone else at something.

"We'll sharpen and hone your edge, Urban," he continued. "Since this race is all about turns, it's the perfect strength to have. If you can precisely master each turn, that's your advantage."

After the team finished breakfast, they began preparations for the technical inspection.

They gathered outside, several vehicles among them. One was a giant translucent truck that had Urban's rev cycle inside. Neon blue lights shone on the bike, giving it an otherworldly appearance—almost like it was underwater. The rev cycle truly was beautiful. She couldn't wait to ride it again.

Urban climbed into one of the other vehicles along with Ash and Everest. They traveled through the dense forest until they reached a noisy and crowded street, roped off for the ongoing practice runs.

A nearby parking lot had a holo sign marking it as the Technical Inspection Site. A variety of motorcycles already crowded the space, racers eagerly chatting or examining each other's cycles. Poppy walked Urban's bike out from the truck and handed it off to Urban.

With Everest and her guards by her side, Urban pushed her way through to an open space marked out for her.

"All contenders must report for technical inspection before their practice session," said a robotic voice. "Failure to appear will result in automatic disqualification."

A few Inventors clad in the red and green RTC colors moved from bike to bike, examining them. They had almost reached Urban when she spotted a familiar backward hat in the crowd.

Coral.

Her gut clenched.

Just get through this race and be done with her.

"Urban Lee?" An Inventor with a Western accent and cobalt eyes approached her.

Urban resisted the urge to correct him. People in the Western Federation never understood that surnames came first.

"Is this the vehicle registered under your name for the race?" he asked.

"It is," Urban confirmed.

His eyes roamed over her cycle. "May I take a look?"

Urban nodded. While the Inventor began his inspection, she glanced back to Coral, just in time to watch as her entire bike shimmered out of sight.

She has an invisible bike.

Urban pursed her lips and turned her attention back to the Inventor. He projected the guidebook standard over the cycle's design and meticulously examined every centimeter of the bike.

He tapped the front of the motorcycle. "The wheels convert to the thrusters, then."

Urban wasn't sure if it was a question or a statement, so she remained silent.

"Very interesting," the Inventor mused.

A few minutes later, his blue eyes met hers. "You have passed the technical inspection. Your number is eight."

Urban hid her smile. Even though she didn't believe in luck, she knew her father would be pleased with the number. "Thank you," she said.

The Inventor began to leave, but she stopped him. "Excuse me, but will there be any obstacles on the trial run?"

"Race officials are still working to outfit the course with the necessary obstacles. But don't worry," he smiled reassuringly, "you can expect their work to be done by the time of the actual race."

As if that were a concern. What worried Urban was adding dangerous obstacles to an already deadly race without a chance to practice. But she kept her thoughts to herself.

After the inspector left, Urban turned to the RTC app for her schedule. She was due to practice on one of the lower portions of the race in an hour.

She found her team and spent the next hour double-checking equipment and staying hydrated. Poppy kept fiddling with the controls and settings of Urban's helmet and bike until even Father had enough and asked her to stop.

Finally, when her nerves felt nearly frayed enough to sever, it was time.

Urban and her team made their way toward the base of the mountain where a large crowd of spectators was already gathered.

"Contestant number seven, you are next up for a practice run," a robotic voice said. "Contestant number eight, please make your way down to the pre-start position."

Urban wove her way through the crowds and toward a designated spot behind the next racer.

"Contestant number seven, you may go in ten . . . nine . . . eight . . ."

The contestant sat on an elegant bike that blended aerodynamic design with high-powered tech. LED strips of colorful light wove across the frame in intricate pulsing patterns. He revved his engine and took off.

The crowd cheered and flashed holo signs displaying the number seven.

For a practice session, he seemed to be going really fast. Urban pulled up his stats. Number seven was a repeat contestant. He'd placed third in last year's race and was not a rookie like she was.

"Contestant number eight you may get into position now," the robotic voice said.

Urban walked her bike up to the start line.

"Remember, this is not a race," Father said through her helmet's com.

She acknowledged his words with a nod.

This part of the road was surrounded by boulders, ferns, and thick trees. Her team was on the sideline holding holo signs with her number. All except Lucas. Her brother waved an embarrassing sign that read: Long live Gasair Minnie!

Urban was too nervous to care.

"Contestant number eight, get ready," the robotic voice boomed.

Urban checked her settings one last time. This part of the road, she'd be keeping her vehicle in driving mode. No need to convert it to a flying machine.

"Contestant number eight, you may go in ten . . . nine . . . eight . . ."

Urban crouched further down in her seat, eyes focused on the road.

"Three . . . two . . . one. Go!"

The crowd cheered and Urban's adrenaline spiked. *This isn't a race,* she reminded herself. She twisted the throttle and rolled gently forward, slowly gaining momentum.

Her first turn was a sloping right curve. She navigated it easily.

As the crowd disappeared in the distance, she relaxed.

Next one is a sharper left. As she approached the bend in the road, Urban pulled on the brakes allowing herself plenty of time. Soon, she fell into a rhythm.

Turn twelve. Right hairpin curve. Slow down.

Turn thirteen. Left. Sloping. Keep the speed up.

As she passed through the mountain, her confidence grew. She hadn't forgotten a turn yet. This part of the course was different than the section by their rental home in the forest. The road was wider but more worn and less maintained. She'd read that these lanes were some of the worst to race on due to the constant freezes that occurred. It was certainly a bumpier ride than she'd expected.

Soon, she reached the end of her practice section and the roar of the waiting crowd. She slowed to a stop, took off her helmet, and wiped the sweat away.

Soon, her team caught up with her.

"Great work," Poppy praised, and the others echoed her sentiments. All but Father, that was. His set jaw and folded arms hurt more than she cared to admit.

The team waited together for Urban's next, and final, practice session on a different part of the course.

Five hours later, it was finally time for her next attempt. This time, Urban wanted to see if she could go a little faster.

She pulled back on the throttle, getting comfortable with the switchbacks and her new bike. By the end of her route, she was going full speed and maneuvering with grace.

There was only one moment where she blanked on the upcoming bend in the road. She had to slow quite a bit on that part in case it was a hairpin turn. It hadn't been, but safety was the priority at the moment.

Still, it had been a good run. Hope bloomed within her as she made her way off the course and toward her waiting team.

"How'd I do?" she asked, rejoining them.

They were all effusive in praise, but Father only nodded

gruffly. "You raced decently."

Lucas leaned in and whispered, "If that's not the best compliment I've heard all year, I don't know what is."

"You have taken a green flag in practice," the robotic voice announced, and a virtual flag flashed in the air above them. "You may now contend in the qualifiers."

Everest grinned at her and she beamed back. *One step closer to the Race to the Clouds.*

26

NATURAL RIGHTS

"WE SHOULD HAVE URBAN WORKING WITH the LED precision honor," commented Poppy.

The team was gathered in the dining hall, discussing strategy. They'd been arguing for the past thirty minutes. Given the limited time they had to train, opinions varied drastically.

Urban was pretty sure arguing was the least effective use of her time. She massaged her sore muscles and gazed out the window where the normally majestic mountains were obscured from view by an overcast sky. The weather really was fickle here.

"You saw her practice run," Everest said. "By my analysis, Urban could shave off an extra ten seconds on her time by perfecting each turn. What she needs is more time with her new bike. That's what's slowing her down. She's not comfortable with it yet."

Father held up a hand. "Let's pause the discussion for now. It looks like AiE is location-requesting everyone."

Urban noticed the ping in her retina display.

Ivan, Poppy, and Dr. Yukio left the room for a tea break while the others remained.

As soon as Urban accepted the invite, she was transported to a virtual rendition of AiE's boardroom. Several members were already there, seated.

Sato Winter gave no formalities and immediately began speaking. "It appears Supers Against Soups somehow knows of our plan for the races. It's no coincidence they've put forth the Deadly Fourth to compete. The only purpose it serves is to get one of their operatives close to Urban."

Close enough to kill me, is what she means, Urban thought with a shudder.

"It's possible they have connections within the racing organization. By the time it was public information that Urban was competing, SAS should have missed the registration window. The fact that they were able to get one of their operatives registered means they must have bribed someone within the racing organization."

"What does that change going forward?" Father wanted to know.

Sato Winter regarded him with her sea-foam eyes. "Nothing. We continue as planned, only with increased security measures in place."

"Surely we must pivot strategies if SAS suspects our plans," Father countered. "It's no longer safe."

"Too much is at stake for Urban *not* to compete." Sato Winter looked pointedly at Everest. "Care to update everyone on what your undercover operatives are seeing?"

Everest nodded. "The media isn't covering it, but my scouts report growing violence among Naturals and Enhanced in nearly every Metropolis across the Asian Federation."

Urban sat up straighter.

"Naturals have targeted the edges of many cities. They blew up a portion of the air filtration barrier, allowing toxic air to enter. Many of the Enhanced have been forced to wear filtration masks for the first time in their lives. Some have even been hospitalized by the sudden influx of pollution."

Urban thought back to her own experience entering into polluted areas. Since she and Lillian had grown up in the Outskirts before being adopted, their lungs were used to the bad air. But all her other Enhanced friends and family always had difficulty when crossing over.

"Those are the mild demonstrations," Everest continued to

report. "The more serious ones involve infiltration to the center of the Metropolis, where the rioting turns into vandalism and violence."

Father shot him a glance. "Are these Naturals affiliated with AiE?"

"Some."

Father frowned. "Why are they rioting now?"

Everest's face was grim. "A lot of Naturals are watching the Western Federation and realize that change is possible. But they think violence is the only way to get there."

Urban listened in dismay. The last thing she wanted was for her home to follow in the footsteps of the West.

"How are the Enhanced responding?" Father inquired.

"They're losing patience," Everest responded. "For those who have been injured or killed by these protests, they've retaliated. There've been over twenty reported murders of Naturals by the Enhanced. The news doesn't cover that, either."

Urban thought about Everest's family, Solstice, and all the Naturals who served in the city. She thought about Auntie and those living in the Hutongs. She thought about the Dragons, Ash, and her family—all of them pitted against each other.

Civil war.

The thought chilled her.

"Thank you, Everest." Sato Winter inclined her head. "That's why we must continue on our current trajectory. In the meantime, the first outing to publicly acknowledge Urban's hybrid status has arrived."

Urban was taken aback. While she'd been expecting this, it suddenly felt like it was happening too fast. She thought about Dr. Crane eyeing her in the lab like she was nothing more than a specimen. Orion's cold, calculating eyes. Everyone and anyone who'd wanted to use her DNA or saw her as a means to an end would suddenly view her as a threat or a savior.

I'm not ready.

"At the Dragon Boat Festival later this week," Sato Winter

said, "we have a prime opportunity to showcase Urban's presence. With sizable in-person audiences expected, a live interview would garner significant visibility.

"We have scheduled numerous live interviews at other key upcoming events. The imperative is to disseminate information about Urban's hybrid genetics and start spreading the word through any possible means. We'll have Jasmine send the talking points for tomorrow's speech."

Urban's stomach twisted at the thought of her first big public speech—and of sharing her hybrid status to the world. *So soon.*

"On a positive note," Winter continued, "we have made significant headway in getting the Natural Rights Act the traction it needs."

Urban glanced up quickly.

"In order to get the Natural Rights Act passed," Winter told them, "the first step is to get Naturals representation on the board. Which we've just succeed in doing, with our bill getting passed to allow for Natural representation."

"That's fantastic news," a Super with a buzz cut remarked.

"That was my initial assessment as well, Ray," Winter said. "However, it appears that someone inserted qualification language into the legislation that eluded our attention. A clause was included stating that in order for a Natural to secure election to the position, they must possess a sosh exceeding 75 and reside within the Metropolis city limits for at least three years."

Glacier ruffled his wings, the bags under his eyes prominent as ever. "Do any Naturals meet that requirement?"

Urban's heart sank, already suspecting the answer.

Winter shook her head.

But then Urban spoke up. "Would I qualify?"

Everyone looked at her in surprise.

Ray was the first to speak. "You?"

"I meet all the requirements, don't I? High enough sosh, and I've lived in the Metropolis for over ten years. I may not be a

Natural now, but I have my genomics records to prove that I was one while living here."

"That's quite the radical idea," Glacier mused. "But it's worth trying."

"Radical?" Ray blurted. "It's insane. First of all, she's not a Natural anymore—"

"There's no specific language about whether she still needs to be one," Glacier pointed out.

"Second," Ray paid no attention, "the youngest board member is forty. A high schooler will never qualify."

Urban glared. "I'm in uni."

Ray waved her away. "Practically the same. The point is, most of the board members have smart socks older than you."

Sato Winter shook her head. "I don't think we have any better ideas at this point."

Urban immediately jumped in. "What do I need to do to apply?"

"A meeting with the Capitol Prefects immediately," Glacier answered. "I can arrange that. Be back in New Beijing tomorrow at 0800. We'll have a high-ranking official accompany you into the meeting. That will help lend you more credibility, despite your age."

"Who would be willing to do that?"

"I have someone in mind," Sato Winter said. "Xi Mako."

"The head of Croix?" Urban blanched. "My sponsor?"

"He's also one of the highest-ranking Prefects."

"He's a part of AiE?"

"No. But he's in my *guanxi* debt and owes me a favor," Sato Winter replied. "Mako is well respected within the council. His presence will lend you support, and help to at least ensure a hearing. One of our stylists will also attempt some makeup magic before your meeting. Hopefully they can add a couple of years to your appearance."

Ray gave Urban a disapproving once-over. "*Tiana*, you look young."

27

CAPITOL PREFECTS

EARLY THE NEXT DAY, URBAN FOUND HERSELF in front of a smart mirror back in New Beijing.

Half a dozen stylists flitted around her. Her hair was pulled back in a tight bun and her makeup done as only her parents' generation did, with painted blue eyebrows and no color variations to her skin.

I look like Mother, Urban thought as she watched her image transform.

She wore a traditional pantsuit that made her cringe. But if AiE thought this would help, Urban would wear it.

A woman in stilettoes and short-cropped green hair stepped up. "I'm Yu Jasmine, your new media consultant. AiE sent me to help give you some pointers."

Jasmine was all business as she took a seat, her sharp green eyes flashing to Urban. There was a look of deep intelligence and understanding there, and her expression softened. "You're nervous, yes?"

"Yes," Urban admitted.

Jasmine nodded knowingly. "Most people are. They just hide it. All you have to do is conceal your fear. Which is what I'm here to help with."

Urban nodded her gratitude.

"Now," Jasmine said, "fifty-five percent of communication occurs through body language, and you need to exude confidence and age. Be sure to walk in slowly, with intention, and head held high."

Jasmine then proceeded to agonize over Urban's posture, facial expressions, even hand placement. Urban practiced the tips Jasmine gave her, feeling overwhelmed by it all.

"You're going to follow Mako and stride in with purpose," Jasmine instructed.

They'd already gone over the plan three times.

The stylist swatted at Jasmine. "The girl's got it. Leave us be so I can finish my work."

Yawning, Urban regretted not having slept on the ride over. She popped an energy pill and almost immediately felt the boost of her brain clicking back on. The crash later would be twice as hard, but that was a price she was willing to pay.

Finally, Urban had the sign-off from the head stylist and Jasmine.

Trig and her security followed close by, but today, there were additional measures in place. The AiE counsel had stressed how potentially dangerous this could be. Eight separate GX100s, each resembling a mini tank, awaited her outside. Urban felt like the Premier of the Asian Federation with how large her entourage of security had become.

Climbing into one of the GXes, she found herself heading toward downtown New Beijing.

The vehicle soon glided to a stop on the Zeolite-coated road as they got stuck in morning rush hour. Urban twisted a huge golden bracelet Mother had loaned her. Her augmented maps showed, due to the traffic, they would arrive right on time, rather than early, like she'd planned.

When they finally pulled to a smooth stop in front of a skyscraper, she had three minutes.

Scrambling out of the vehicle, Urban began to run before remembering her high heels.

She slowed to a safer, more sustainable pace, and walked through a grandiose lobby before stopping in front of a receptionist.

After checking Urban's credentials, the woman escorted her to a private set of elevators. Urban was given a one-time access code, and then she was shooting up so fast her ears popped.

Ding!

The doors opened, and they crossed a small room with a few couches and a floor-to-ceiling view of the Metropolis. Mako stood waiting on the other side.

He looked different than the last time Urban had seen him. Of course, that had been at the prison. Now, in place of his trendy distressed jeans and holo glasses, he wore a bright red tailored suit. His hair was styled in the latest fashion, half shaved and the other half slicked back.

His eyes sparked with the same fire, though, and the way he carried himself made Urban grateful for his presence. He looked like he belonged here.

Mako raised a brow as Urban approached. "That's an . . . interesting look on you."

Urban glanced down at her attire. "It's meant to make me look older," she confessed.

The corner of Mako's lip twitched. "I see." Without another word, he flashed his tatt at the guards and motioned Urban to follow.

They stepped forward and the golden door slid aside.

Urban's breath caught as they stepped inside.

The room was cavernous and bled red. Everything from the marble floors to the plush seats, even the ceiling above, was crimson with accents of gold. The circular space was filled with numerous government officials seated in rows around an open area at its center. There, the biggest virtual flag Urban had ever seen hovered, with the golden hammer and sickle glowing bright against the dimly lit interior. A long table with the Head Prefects and Capitol Speaker sat beneath it.

Red pillars supported a second-floor balcony where there were even more people watching. Underneath, between each pillar, eight blue holo displays spun—one for each gene pool. Their respective GP representatives sat in the spaces between.

Urban glanced up at the Aqua holo of a tall man with flowing black locks of hair rippling in virtual water behind him. The sea-blue eyes watched her.

Urban realized she wasn't sure where she was supposed to sit. She scanned the space for designated seats for Naturals. It seemed the Prefects didn't anticipate any Naturals actually joining them, as there were none.

Thankfully, Mako led the way, and Urban followed. Several hundred people watched them in the silence that followed their arrival.

Most of the Prefects looked to be in their fifties, sixties, and seventies. Urban was grateful for the extra makeup and clothing she wore. It would have probably helped if she looked about thirty years older.

Urban took her seat next to Mako and breathed a sigh of relief. At least she hadn't tripped in her heels.

"Next on the agenda, we have Xi Mako with a proposed representative for the Natural Rights Act." The House Speaker, an elderly Flyer, glanced down at Urban and frowned.

Murmuring rose among the Prefects.

Mako stood. "Esteemed Prefects, as you know, Naturals with a sosh of 75 and Metropolis residency are now eligible for representation in our beloved Federation. Which is why I am pleased to announce I have with me the first Natural delegate I'd like to bring forward as a potential candidate."

"What is the meaning of this?" One of the Capitol Prefects at the center table peered at Urban. "According to Miss Lee's avatar, she is an Aqua. Not a Natural."

"Not anymore." Mako paused until he had the whole house's attention. "She was a Natural until recently."

Mako motioned Urban to stand, and she did so. "I present to you Miss Lee. The hybrid."

Urban could have heard a grain of rice drop in the following silence. She tensed as all eyes scrutinized her.

"The—the hybrid?" the Capitol Prefect at the head of the room asked uncertainly.

"Let us see proof of her genetics," another Capitol Prefect demanded.

Urban's genome records transferred to the center of the room on display for all to see. She squirmed. This was almost worse than when she was experimented on at the underwater research lab. She'd been on display there too, nothing more than a specimen to observe.

It took everything in her to remain standing.

"Aqua genetics recently activated in her. Prior to that, Miss Lee didn't have a single enhancement. Not one. She was a Natural," Mako said as the members continued studying her genomics records.

A new set of data flashed before them, and Mako continued. "That was her DNA three months ago. As you can see, Miss Lee was a Natural."

The room erupted.

Some of the Prefects zoned out in QuanNao, no doubt spreading the news.

Maybe the word will get out without having to win RTC.

Urban's hope was short-lived as people began shouting. Some of the Prefects eyed Urban suspiciously, scanning her with their retina displays and snapping images of her.

A Capitol Prefect at the center table leaned over and spoke to the House Speaker, who nodded. It took him several attempts before regaining control of the room. When it grew silent again, he spoke. "While this development is certainly interesting, Miss Lee cannot qualify for a Natural, due to the fact that she currently has Aqua genetics."

"There is no language in the Natural Rights Act specifying that," Mako asserted calmly. "The bill states that a representative must be a Natural who resided in the Metropolis for three years and has a sosh of 75. Miss Lee meets both of those criteria."

"That's absurd!" someone shouted. "She's Enhanced now. That's what matters."

Uproar broke out again.

"Silence!" the House Speaker demanded. "Silence!"

He finally managed to regain control of the Prefects again. "This is unprecedented, and we have no clear course of action. As such, we'll take a vote on the matter."

"All who believe Miss Lee—" he gestured to Urban— "should qualify as a Natural, indicate your decision now in your retina display."

A holo projection appeared at the center of the room with a virtual number. It started at zero, then a one appeared, then two, then the numbers changed so fast they became a blur. At 120, it slowed and became visible again. It ticked up a few more times as the last few Prefects cast their vote.

"Anyone else?" the Speaker asked.

When the number remained the same, he nodded. "Very well. We have 124 votes in favor of allowing Miss Lee representation as the first Natural. Now, all who believe Miss Lee does not meet the criteria, indicate your decision."

The holo flickered back to zero and the count flurry begin again. It became readable once more at 180, and Urban's heart sank. Slowly it ticked up, ending on a final count of 201.

"The vote is 124 to 201. Miss Lee does not meet the criteria to be elected as a Natural representative," the Speaker concluded.

Mako stood to leave, but an idea struck Urban.

If she didn't qualify as a Natural, maybe that meant she did qualify as something else. Mustering all her courage, she spoke up. "Do I qualify to register as an Aqua?"

Mako blinked in surprise, and even the Head Prefects stared at her a moment before one of them responded.

"I'm sorry Miss Lee, but your DNA isn't, strictly speaking, Aqua. You're something . . . other."

Other.

The word was like a stun pike to Urban's stomach.

Mako tried to nudge her out of the room, but she didn't move.

"I don't qualify for either one?" Pain and bewilderment brought the words out of Urban's mouth less diplomatically than she'd intended. "Surely I belong—qualify for something."

The speaker projected the agenda, already moving on to the next topic. He glanced briefly at Urban. "I'm very sorry." His words were final, dismissive.

Urban wanted to use her Aqua voice to roar in frustration, but she couldn't do even that. Maybe the council was right. She didn't belong among the Aquas.

Turning, she followed Mako, trying to tune out the whispers around her.

I don't belong. Not among the Naturals. Not among the Enhanced. Not anywhere.

BELONGING

THE NEXT MORNING, EVEREST RAN THROUGH A list of settings, checking gears and gauges, before he nodded at Urban to climb on her bike.

Urban did so numbly. She'd spent the trip back to New Chengdu playing the past few hours over and over again in her head. *What could I have done differently? Why won't they accept me?*

It felt strange, diving straight back into her training routine with the team. As if nothing had happened.

All Urban wanted was to sit alone and gain a foothold on her constantly shifting reality. That, or sleep. Sleep would be nice.

Urban had already survived a grueling workout session with Ivan earlier that morning. Now, it was time to practice with Everest.

"Let's get you more comfortable with your new bike." Everest straddled his own rev cycle, a slim black one. "You're a great racer. All you need is more confidence."

Urban pulled on her helmet and, side by side, they glided though the hushed forest. The familiarity of riding with Everest brought her comfort. It reminded Urban of when they first started dating. The thrill of Everest teaching her how to navigate quick turns and jumps felt like ages ago.

So much had changed since then.

Urban focused on a tricky section of the road. Her new cycle still felt bulky and slow but more familiar with each ride. She was finally breaking it in.

She picked up the pace, pulling ahead, and Everest matched her speed.

The wind rushed through her like she wasn't there, giving her the feeling of flying and the freedom that she loved. They took a few more turns and arrived at a scenic outlook. Everest slowed, then stopped.

"How do you feel?" he asked, dismounting.

The adrenaline coursing through Urban had loosened some of her tension. "More comfortable with my bike, I think."

Everest nodded approvingly before coming over to her cycle. "I'll make a few tweaks. I noticed you're still dragging a little on some of the corners."

He sat leaning against a boulder. Urban took a seat next to him, dirt and rocks making an uncomfortable seat beneath her.

She gazed out at the stunning panorama before them. Lush trees decorated the surrounding black crags and peaks stretching for kilometers in all directions. The sun dipped behind a billowing cloud, and the temperature dropped.

Urban let out a sigh and Everest cocked his head. "What's going on?"

"It's nothing." Urban shook herself. But her mind kept going back to her meeting with the Prefects.

Everest arched a brow, not convinced.

Suddenly, she blurted, "I can't believe the Prefects rejected me as a Natural."

Her throat burned. Before she could stop herself, the maelstrom of emotions and words came pouring out. "My whole life, I've known I didn't belong among the Enhanced. But I always thought I at least belonged to the Naturals. But the Prefects determined I'm not a Natural. They said I can't qualify for an Aqua, either. I don't belong anywhere."

Everest was silent, pondering her words.

"Why does it matter where you belong?" he finally asked.

Urban gaped at him. "What?"

"Where you belong," Everest repeated. "Why does it matter?"

"B-because it's important," Urban stammered.

"If you base that on who accepts you, you'll never belong anywhere. Only you can decide where you belong. No one can do that for you."

Urban stared at Everest in surprise. His words did have a distant ring of truth to them. "But how does that work if even I don't know where I belong anymore?"

Everest took her hand gently in his firm grip. "You will."

Urban's retina display sent her a reminder ping.

<AiE requests Lee Urban's presence to prepare for the Dragon Boat Festival.>

Her heart skittered. She'd almost forgotten about it.

"I've got to go catch a helix back to New Beijing," Urban said as they both stood. She looked up at Everest. "See you at the festival?"

He smiled down at her. "I wouldn't miss it."

29

DRAGON BOAT FESTIVAL

THE DRAGON BOAT FESTIVAL UNFOLDED LIKE A kaleidoscope of vivid color, movement, and people around Urban. Each twist and turn of her armored vehicle displayed new sights.

After an hour of hair and makeup, followed by another two with Jasmine and a PR consultant, Urban had finally been deemed ready for her first big speech.

She felt anything but.

At least she had talking points in her retina display, should her mind go blank. She clung to that small bit of comfort as her door opened into the festival.

Taking a deep breath, she stepped out into flashing lights. Urban had expected some fanfare when AiE said they'd informed the event coordinators concerning the celebration of her presence. But she hadn't been prepared for this.

Crowds pressed up against her. Supers, Flyers—every gene pool tried snapping or linking.

Urban's breath came quick and sharp. She furtively checked her surroundings for potential attackers, weapons, exits—anything and everything. The sense of being trapped overwhelmed her senses and logic.

"Move!" Ash and her guards cleared a path, and Urban

followed close behind inside a building.

The door shut behind her. Blissful silence filled the space. Her fear of being attacked subsided but was quickly replaced by a new one. In a few minutes, she would be speaking in front of several thousand people. Her palms grew clammy at the thought.

Urban followed her guards up a set of stairs, down a corridor, then onto a large balcony overlooking the festival. The space was opulent and rich, as if it were typically used for KOL bashes. Currently, the only people inside were Jasmine, stylists, and more guards. One of the Artisans touched up Urban's makeup then ushered her toward a plush seat to wait.

Urban took in the view below.

Hundreds of tourists and festival-goers strolled by. Booths filled with piping hot street food and souvenirs lined the road. Steam billowed out from the stalls. Wicker chairs and tables clustered beside them, and stacks of triangle rice dumplings wrapped in bamboo leaves towered in the air.

Urban searched the crowd for Everest. He'd sent her a ping explaining he was running late. She hoped he'd arrive soon. Dragon Boat Festival was his favorite holiday, and she'd been looking forward to finally being able to bring him into this slice of her world.

She slid into one of the fancy chairs next to a table piled high with steaming *zongzi*. A clear force field blocked off the large balcony window but still gave her a clear view of the festivities below. Her guards and Ash formed a protective circle. Trig and several more of the Camos only appeared on her retina display. Still, she felt a sense of unease sitting in such a public place— even if it had top security measures.

Her fingers itched to touch her hidden stun shield and AquaBolt pulse pistol.

Where's Lucas? He was supposed to meet me here.

Urban checked her pings, but there was nothing from her brother.

She reached for one of the *zongzi* off a gold platter. Heat warmed her face as she untied the red and white cord wrapping it and peeled back the leaves. Soft and sticky rice, red bean paste, jujubes, and raisins sang in her mouth.

Urban took a few more bites before returning it to the platter.

Jasmine glided over and sat down. "Now, remember everything we talked about. Head up, shoulders back. Slow your words, speak with confidence, and try to avoid fillers like 'um'."

Urban nodded absently, gaze following the flow of the crowds below toward an algae-coated lake. They pinched off bits of their *zongzi* and threw them into the water for good luck.

Urban doubted throwing rice into a lake would help improve her situation. She threw her *zongzi* remains in the trash.

"All Dragon Boat racers to the front line," a voice announced.

Jasmine stood. "I'll leave you be. You'll do great on your speech." She smiled in encouragement and then left.

Several of the brightly colored long racing boats were already lined up, and team members stretched or warmed up in preparation for the race. Urban scanned them for her brother. He was competing this year on Shanghai Ocean University's team, but she didn't see him there, either.

Her gaze snagged on the middle of the lake, where a small island held the victory cup and an instant sosh boost. The prize was surrounded by festive paper lanterns decorated in green, red, black, white, and yellow. Several Artisans ran around adding final touches.

"Hey," Ash leaned over. "Have you seen Lillian? She was supposed to meet me here, but she's not answering my pings."

"I haven't seen her."

The announcer began to speak again, and Urban's attention returned to the lake.

"As our racers get ready, we have a special message as a part of today's festivities. We have our very own KOL, Lee Urban, here to kick off the day!"

The audience clapped enthusiastically. A spotlight illuminated Urban, and hoverdrones swarmed toward the balcony, ready to display her image on the jumbotron.

Urban rubbed sweaty hands against her jumpsuit and made her way toward the front of the balcony.

This was it.

She looked out over the drones, booths, crowds, and water. So many people. Hundreds. Thousands. She spotted Everest in the crowd near the front, and her breath came a little easier. He gave her a nod of support.

Everyone was waiting for her to say something.

Urban moistened her lips.

Her brain raced, trying to remember her speech. Then with relief, she recalled her note cards and pulled them up in her retina display.

"Welcome, Festival-Goers, to the 2124 Dragon Boat Festival!"

No response.

Urban glanced at her team near the back of the balcony. Jasmine made a motion for her to stand closer to the voice enhancer.

Urban did so and tried again.

This time, the crowd clapped and cheered.

Relieved, Urban continued. "Some of you all know me as the girl who crashed PKU's AI Games. Others of you know me as the victor from the Games."

Her words were coming out too fast. In her mind, she heard Jasmine telling her to slow down and add more emotion.

On a whim, she dismissed the note cards and faced the crowd. "But few of you know the real me. Some of you may have heard rumors of a supposed hybrid. Someone with the DNA malleable enough to allow for enhancements after birth." Urban paused, sucking in a deep breath. "Well, it's true. The hybrid does exist. I am the—"

Her mic cut out.

"Enough boring speeches," a vacillating voice said. A modulator had been used to disguise it. "Time to make this party a little more . . . interesting."

Several people in the crowd gasped.

Dread spread through Urban's veins. Jasmine and the rest of her PR team erupted into frantic activity to get the voice enhancer fixed.

On the island, a flurry of movement caught Urban's attention. A masked woman stepped out from the forest.

"Many years ago," the woman said, "May used to be called the poison month, due to the increased sickness and widespread illness during that time. It was the month of the five deadly poisons."

This isn't part of the show.

The narrator motioned, and a brightly cloaked individual stepped out from the forest.

"Centipedes."

A Super Flyer extended a weapon that unfurled in his hand like the tiny feet of a centipede. Two sharp, wing-shaped objects appeared. The points of his weapon gleamed blood red as he spun his laser hand ax so fast it blurred.

His size and wings indicated he was both a Super and Flyer—someone rare enough to have two main gene pool enhancements. If he was from the Asian Federation, he must have acquired additional illegal enhancements. The Super Flyer wore an identity scrambler displaying a red spider and concealing his true identity.

Something about him looked familiar . . .

"Scorpions," the announcer continued.

The biggest Super Urban had ever seen crawled out of the forest. He had a tail like that of a scorpion and giant muscled arms with metal pinchers.

"Spiders."

A huge Inventor, cloaked in black, scuttled forward on eight retractable legs stemming from her back.

"Snakes," the announcer gestured at a man with the fangs

of a snake emblazoned on his faceless mask. He slithered back and forth through the shadows.

"And," the announcer concluded, "poisonous toads." She gestured at herself.

Realization dawned. Urban was looking at the Deadly Five. Her blood ran cold.

But if that were the case, the Deadly Fifth had formerly been Dawn's dad, the man with toad-like eyes and poisonous skin. The same man who had tried to kill Urban after the Games in the Western Fed. But who was this? Could this woman possibly be his daughter?

Urban's eyes darted to Deadly Fifth's slender build. She couldn't be sure, but she looked similar to her former teammate: Dawn.

A collective hush fell over the crowd.

Inside the balcony, Urban's team worked frantically, but she barely noticed.

Why are the Deadly Five here?

The Dragon Boat Festival was their origin story, but why make themselves public now?

As if in answer, the snake-like man, Yokai Wraith, stepped forward and jerked his head at the trees. The Spider Inventor crept forward on her eight spindly legs. Using her extra arms, she withdrew four bound and gagged people and tossed them onto the sandy beach.

Each figure wore an identity scrambler, and their faces were programmed to look like blank slates—no facial features, just an eerily bare swath of skin. There was something familiar about the one closest to the water.

The Deadly Fifth—Urban was sure it was Dawn—spoke up, drawing her attention. "Ancient lore has it, the Dragon Boat Festival originates from poet Qu Yuan," her disguised voice vacillated. "Upon his land being captured, Qu Yuan committed suicide by throwing himself into the middle of the lake and drowning. The citizens tried to rescue him by racing to save him on dragon boats. The beating of the drums was to scare away the fish from eating his body."

Urban's skin crawled.

"A heart-warming story if I ever heard one. So, since there are four teams, we have four challenges today."

The crowd shifted restlessly. Urban's throat tightened. *Where are the Jingcha?*

"But first, I present an opportunity to end the fun. Lee Urban, want to come down here?"

Urban gasped.

"Oh, Lee Urban?" Dawn said in a singsong voice. "No need to stay in your ivory tower. We just want to have a friendly chat."

Next to her, Ash stiffened, and her guards shifted protectively closer. But Urban's eyes were glued to the Deadly Five.

"Here's my proposition for you, Urban. Come join us on this island, and that will be the end of today's show. Or, remain where you are, and we'll have a little fun."

"Urban, this is all a mind game," Jasmine warned. "We have to get you out of here." She tried to pull her away, but Urban remained rooted.

"You have one minute to make your way onto this island," Dawn said. "Starting now."

She gestured toward the bound prisoners. "In case you were wondering whose lives are at stake, should you not accept our offer . . ." Dawn stooped and ripped the identity scramblers off.

Urban's blood drained from her face, and she stumbled back into Ash.

Mother, Father, Lillian, and Lucas. Lucas's face was swollen and had an unnatural hue to it, his eyes closed. Mother remained stoic as ever, Father's eyes flashed with anger, and Lillian kept a tight lid on her emotions.

Urban's brain short-circuited.

This had to be a bad dream. This couldn't be happening.

"You can run, Urban, but your friends and family can't." The threat from her attacker in the Hutongs came back to her.

Urban watched in numb shock as Dawn spoke again.

"Meanwhile, my friend here will be administering a poison that will result in short-term paralysis."

The man with the spinning red weapon stepped toward the four bodies lying on the beach. He touched each of them with his poisoned laser hand ax. *No. No!*

This can't be happening!

Dawn nodded at the Inventor. Using her mechanical legs, the Spider picked up each limp body and held them dangling in the air.

Urban burst into movement toward the edge of the balcony and ran straight into the force field. One of her bodyguards pulled her away.

"No! Stop!" Urban cried.

"Urban," Ash caught up to her. The color had drained from his face and his voice quavered. "We have to get you out of here."

"I'm not leaving my family!" Urban struggled wildly.

"I know," Ash said firmly. "But you stay here. We'll go."

"Time's up Lee Urban," the Deadly Fifth announced.

Urban looked at the island in horror. Bile rose in her throat as the Inventor launched the lifeless bodies of her family into the lake. A holo image of a venomous yellow serpent entwined with a bloodied stinger, the mark of the Deadly Five, highlighted the spot where each one hit the water.

Urban screamed.

Pandemonium broke loose.

The force field around the balcony disappeared, and several of her protectors and Ash launched into the air. They flew toward the quickly sinking bodies, but crashed into an invisible barrier at the water's edge.

"No cheating," Dawn's mechanical voice chided. "The only way to save them is by boat or Urban gracing us with her presence. Nothing else can get through my force field."

Three of the dragon boats glided forward, each rower

working quickly to slide the boat through the water. The fourth boat remained docked as its members argued and scrambled to get into position.

A prioritized ping appeared in Urban's retina display. She was about to blink it away when she caught the name of the sender.

Trembling, she opened it. Text scrolled across the corner of her vision.

[Unknown sender: Hello, Urban. There is only one guaranteed way to save your family's lives.]

Urban inhaled a sharp breath.

[Join us on this island. Open the attachment in this message for the way.]

At the end of the message, a sickly yellow box pulsed.

On the island, the Inventor began drumming with her eight legs a haunting melody, the normally festive beat turned somber.

Dun! Dun! Dada! Dun!

Urban's family had slipped beneath the lake's glassy surface. All that remained were the ghostly glowing markers of the Deadly Five.

The drum's deadly rhythm hammered in time with Urban's pounding heart.

She stood frozen, unable to think or move into action.

Sirens pierced the air as the *Jingcha* pulled up. Supers and bots, clad in gold and black with the hammer and sickle emblazoned on their armored uniforms, poured onto the scene. Several of them fired at the force field but to no avail. The Deadly Five's tech held strong.

"By order of Asian Federation law, you are ordered to release this force field," the lead *Jingcha* said over a voice enhancer.

The Deadly Five ignored the warnings.

"If you'd like to place bets on which participants will live or die, enter the *heiwang*," the Deadly First announced.

"They're the only family you've got," Uncle's words from what felt like a lifetime ago came back to Urban.

There was no other choice.

Jaw tight, Urban quickly opened the attachment from the Deadly Fifth. Instantly, her ear piece buzzed.

"Wise choice," a warped and distorted, new voice said.

Urban glanced around to see if anyone had heard. Her team was consumed with running around speaking to security, pulling up conference calls, and readying weapons.

A map overlaid on reality, a putrid yellow arrow, guided Urban.

"This will lead you to a secret doorway onto the island," the voice informed her. "Once you arrive, we'll release the force field and allow your family to be rescued by law enforcement."

Urban glanced anxiously at the water.

The voice spoke again. "I suggest you close your eyes and cover your ears in three . . . two . . . one."

Urban did as she was instructed.

Blinding light and a sharp crack blasted the air.

When she opened her eyes again, the crowd was blinded, disoriented.

"Run," the voice commanded.

Urban broke free from her guards and sprinted away.

"Stop!" Footsteps pounded behind her, but Urban increased her speed.

Out of the building. Into the crowd. Past the stalls.

Shoving, darting, scrambling.

Faster!

Each second that passed was one closer to her family's death. Her lungs burned, but the pain only reminded her of what they must be facing at the bottom of the lake. Gasping, she pushed herself harder.

A shock of black hair flashed in her peripheral vision.

Everest.

He ran after her, trying to close in, but Urban didn't slow.

The pulsing arrows pointed toward what looked like another *zongzi* stall. Urban slid to a stop in front of it. A painting on its

side caught her eye. A yellow serpent twisted around a stinger—
the Deadly Five's symbol.

Bending down, she touched the side, jerking back in surprise
as it slid away. A set of stairs appeared and descended into
darkness.

"Urban! Wait!" Everest yelled, nearly catching up to her.

Urban didn't wait as she withdrew her stun shield.

Then she plunged into darkness.

30

BLACK MIST

URBAN TRIPPED ON THE LAST STAIR DOWN, landing hard on the ground. Something was cold and wet, but it was too dark to see.

Activating her tatt, she used the golden light to illuminate a natural cave of sorts. Mold permeated the air. Water dripped from the ceiling into puddles on the ground. The cave tunneled a few more meters then forked into two different directions.

The path to the right projected a yellow arrow.

She hesitated, and suddenly, Everest was beside her, panting. At the sight of him, the darkness retreated a little. As much as she wanted him there, she was afraid he would try to stop her. "Everest," she began.

"Which way?" he interrupted in between gasps for breath.

Her spirits rose. "This way!" Urban pointed, and they sprinted toward the yellow arrow.

She tried to gauge their current location to the island. They should be close.

To her relief, she spotted another set of stairs that led upward. She took them two at a time, but Everest's legs were longer, and he reached the door first.

Flinging it open, they barged into a room. It was a small, circular space with large windows. They were underwater, at the bottom of the lake.

Urban sucked in a breath. She searched for her family. Though she spotted Lillian's bound form, the water was too murky to find the others.

The door closed behind Urban and Everest with a soft click. Her retina display flashed a warning.

<Entering purple zone. DANGER!>

It's a trap.

Urban's eyes went back to Lillian. Her sister was thrashing and trying to break free of her bonds.

A voice in Urban's ear piece spoke again. "Did you know that purple zones were my invention? They started off as a way for Enhanced to protect themselves during the Genetic Revolution. But now, only my closest allies have the codes to access them—"

"I did what you asked!" Urban was beside herself. "Let my family go!"

Everest's eyes widened, then flashed at her outburst, and he bent his head closer, trying to listen.

"And ruin the fun? You're too easy, Urban. After that Natural woman nearly drowned at the underwater bash, we saw your true colors. You have a soft spot for drowning people. An admirable weakness, but a weakness nonetheless."

Urban froze.

"We knew the same trick would work again in getting you here. But this time, I'll let your heroics shine. You'll get to sacrifice yourself for your family."

"Why?" Urban demanded, nearly choking. "Why are you doing this?"

When the voice spoke again, it came from above the doorway, no longer in her ear piece. The modulator was also gone.

It took Urban a second to place the speech, but then she gasped. She turned, but only saw walls trapping her.

The last time she'd heard this voice had been at the PKU bash. And it belonged to Lennox, the head of the Games for

Peking University.

"Do you know why my daughter has special needs?"

Everest spun around, withdrawing his Magtouch, and positioned himself between Urban and the door.

A vision of Odonata's horrible form rose in her mind.

"Odonata is our only child. She was born during the Genetic Revolution. Naturals were jealous of her enhancements and attempted to drown her. She was six." Lennox's tone hardened to stone. "She fell into a coma and has never been the same since."

"I'm sorry." Urban tried to keep the desperation out of her voice at the time passing by. "But we weren't the ones responsible. Why are you doing this?"

"I know what you are, Urban. Your life is a ticking time bomb that will end our world. It comes down to this: your life or my family's. I would do anything for family."

"Well, you have me. Please. Let my family go!"

"If I let them survive, it will be obvious what I'm working to accomplish. When you all perish together, the media will frame it as another hate act by the Deadly Five against those harboring a former Natural."

Urban's knees buckled in the following silence.

Everest was already looking for a way out. There were no other doors, tools, or anything helpful.

Funeral black mist crept toward them out of pores in the wall. A small tendril of it brushed up against Urban's skin, and she jerked back in pain. The mist eroded her skin where it had touched.

"It's not over yet, Urban." Everest looked her in the eyes. "Take a breath."

Urban stood and took several as black tendrils of deadly mist filled half of the room, obscuring the windows. Only the doorway and part of the walls remained untouched.

Everest pressed closer to the exit, away from the danger, and withdrew a shiny metallic ball.

The lock hacker, Urban realized.

He slapped the device on the door and adjusted the settings. Then he stood back and waited.

Nothing happened.

Everest grew rigid. "Lennox has Inventor tech blocking the hacking frequencies."

Muffled voices came from the other side of the door. "Urban? Are you in there?"

"Ash!"

"Sorry it took us so long to find you," he called. "We took the other tunnel, which we think leads up to the island, before realizing you weren't there—"

"Ash!" Urban interrupted him. "Get us out!"

"The door's jammed," came the reply.

The black mist crept closer.

Urban's eyes skirted to the water. She could no longer see Lillian, causing her panic to grow.

Urban unstrapped her Aquabolt Pistol. "We have to get out of here *now!*"

"What are you doing?" Everest grabbed her arm and she hesitated.

Lucas had been very clear about *not* using the weapon on dry ground. Firing it in an enclosed circular room might very well kill them both.

But they were out of options.

"It's our last chance," she insisted.

Everest's jaw flexed, but he released her.

She aimed at the door and fired. Blue light sizzled and sparked. She dropped to the ground, covering her head. Everest crouched over her, shielding her.

A blast ricocheted off the door, to the window, then back onto the wall again before dissipating.

Urban tried to steady her breathing. Black burn marks lined the exit, but the door remained intact.

"I'm hoping that short-circuited whatever security measures

were in place." She gestured to Everest's device. "Try again."

Everest reattached his hacking device, and a moment later, the door clicked open. She could have cried in relief.

Ash and Trig stood on the other side, but Urban pushed past them and began to run. "We need to hurry!"

They retraced their steps down to the fork in the tunnel and took a left this time. She tried not to think about how much time had passed, only slowing as the tunnel came to a dead end.

Urban felt the walls for a hidden lever or door. Something that might lead her up to the island and to her family.

"I think the way out is up." Trig stood with head tilted back, studying the ceiling with the dim lighting of his tatt.

He reached up and ran his fingers along the top, then pulled down, and an opening appeared, allowing sunlight to filter in. A ladder slid toward them.

Everest pushed forward. "I'll go up first and provide cover. Urban, you go last, in case the Deadly Five are still up there."

Urban was about to protest, but Everest was already climbing up quickly, followed by Ash and an invisible Trig.

Urban crested the opening. Light blinded her, and there was a huge *boom* as an explosion shook the ground.

The island was in chaos—a blur of movement, harsh sounds, and light. The Deadly Third, an Inventor, used four of her robotic legs to hold a cannon. The other four legs braced against the recoil, each blast pushing her further into the sand.

Up above, Ash dove and spun out of the way.

A Super Flyer chased after him, his body partially visible where he'd been wounded. He wielded a glowing laser hand ax, blood red wings pumping furiously. Vance.

Somehow, the Scorpion's captain with multiple enhancements, who tried and nearly succeeded in killing Urban twice, had found her again. But when had he joined forces with the Deadly Five?

Urban didn't have time to dwell on it, as the Deadly Second rumbled past, chitin-like limbs chasing after something. He spun in a circle, robotic pinchers clicking furiously. An invisible force sliced through one of his metallic limbs, cutting it clean off and leaving a sparking mess of wires and metal.

Trig.

Urban spotted Everest crouched behind a tree. Using his Magtouch, he fired off a round of quick succession shots. The Inventor was forced to withdraw a giant webbing shield and play defense, giving Ash cover.

From out of dense overgrowth, Wraith barreled into Everest. The two rolled away into a thicket.

"By order of law, I command you to release this force field," a *Jingcha* ordered over a voice enhancer. They were still on the other side of the lake. Which meant . . .

Urban surveyed the island for the last of the Deadly Five.

Dawn was missing.

Hopefully, gone. She seemed the least deadly of them all. Her enhancement was a Giver and, like her father, she had a poisonous touch. But only if applied to Naturals. Hopefully, Urban didn't have to worry about that anymore.

Urban sprinted toward the lake.

The dragon boat in the lead neared the first marker and dipped below the surface. Their boat and its crew of Aquas disappeared entirely.

Urban was almost to the shore when a whistling sound had her instinctively drop onto the damp, sandy beach. She was about to roll to her feet when she saw Dawn advancing not far behind, a neon metal chain and mace in hand.

Urban balked at the weapon and her former teammate.

I might have slightly underestimated her.

Dawn flung her weapon again, the chain and ball slicing down toward Urban's head. She dodged out of the way just in time.

The mace struck the sand, sending it shooting into the air and leaving char marks on the ground.

"Our world teeters on the brink of civil war—over you," Dawn nearly spat at Urban. Then her expression changed. "Let's tip the scales, shall we?"

Urban glanced sideways at the water.

One of the dragon boats popped up to the surface. The crew cradled Mother in their arms. She wasn't moving, and they immediately began to perform CPR. A moment later, she was leaning over the boat heaving.

Urban's heart squeezed.

Mother was safe. But what about the others?

Several more of the dragon boats glided silently across the water toward them. Urban wasn't sure they'd make it. So much time had passed.

I can't lose them!

Urban tried backing away toward the water, but the ground rumbled as Vance crash-landed next to Dawn. They both converged on Urban at the same time.

Vance was even bigger than Urban remembered. His laser hand ax spun in deft fingers, glowing.

Crouching into a fighting stance, Urban withdrew her stun shield.

Catching movement in the lake, she saw the surface of water break. The next dragon boat popped up with Lillian on board. Her sister gasped for air.

Urban went weak with relief. All that were left were Father and Lucas, who was an Aqua, so he should be fine in the water. She wondered why the Deadly Five had bothered throwing him into the water at all.

Blasts skimmed the air nearby.

Everest sprinted out of the forest, Magtouch aimed at Vance and then Dawn. His shots had been enough to redirect the attention of Urban's attackers.

"I'll take this pathetic Natural," Dawn growled. "Finish her."

Everest tried to cut around Dawn to get to Urban, but Dawn arced her mace overhead and brought it down.

Everest dodged then went on the offensive.

Urban's heart lurched in her chest. All it would take was one touch from Dawn and he'd be poisoned.

Vance stepped closer, blocking her view. But Everest was a good fighter, he'd handle himself. Urban, on the other hand . . .

She looked up at Vance. And up and up.

Tiana.

She'd forgotten just how huge Vance was up close. She recalled his enhancements. Super. Flyer. Inventor. Aqua. Camo. Basically everything. A walking lethal weapon.

Vance lunged toward her, and all thoughts fled as instincts kicked in, and she swiftly raised her stun shield.

Not a moment too soon. His laser hand ax hurled toward her.

She deflected, but the impact to her shield was jarring.

As a Natural, she had managed to defeat Vance once before by outsmarting him. But that tech glitch wouldn't work again. All she had was her jiujitsu training and her weapons.

In hand-to-hand combat, Vance had the advantage with his longer arms, and Urban would be stuck playing defense unless she got in close.

Withdrawing her hydro blade, Urban dodged Vance's next grab and advanced.

He tried to step back, but Urban mirrored his movements, sticking with him. Squeezing her hydro blade twice, her hand jerked forward at lightning speed.

But the aim was off and she only grazed his ribs.

Urban let out a hiss of frustration.

She understood now what Lucas had meant about fighting above ground being difficult with underwater weapons.

Before she could try again, a knee connected with her midsection.

Urban gasped and keeled over, only vaguely remembering to move, barely avoiding a death blow from Vance's ax. Out of her periphery, she saw the Deadly First run at them, cannon blaster hoisted on her back.

As the Inventor reached Urban, a partially visible Trig darted forward. Behind him, the Deadly Second lay unmoving, his giant stinger a mess of smoking ruins.

Trig leaped onto the Inventor, knocking the cannon blaster out of reach. She flipped onto her back, spider-like arms clawing and curling around him. He fought back, caught in a tangle of thrashing mechanical limbs, arms, and wings.

Ash dove from the sky, and his polearm sliced through one of the Inventor's spindly legs.

At the chaos, Everest freed himself from Dawn. He launched himself at Vance, taking him down from behind.

Urban seized the opportunity and went after Vance with her weapon.

Vance grunted and, with violent strength, swung at Urban with his hand ax.

She tried to step back but wasn't fast enough. Everything was slow motion as Everest wrapped his arms around her to spin her away, placing himself between her and the weapon. As the blade struck him, he shuddered and fell to the sandy beach, both ends of the hand ax impaled deep within his chest.

Time stopped as Urban stared, uncomprehending.

There was a deadly weapon protruding from Everest's chest. It wasn't possible.

The world came rushing back, and she cried out, falling to her knees beside Everest.

But Vance was there in no time, knocking her down.

Before he could use his body weight against her, she trapped him in Spider guard, creating distance and keeping him off balance.

Blasts rang out somewhere above them.

Vance's eyes darted upward, and Urban used the distraction. She grappled to get into a better position. But huge hands encased her neck. Urban sputtered.

Too tight. Too strong.

She bucked and fought wildly.

Crushing. Choking.

Breath—no air.

Spots blurred the edge of her sight.

Numbness slowly wrapping her in its sticky webbing.

Urban's head listed to the side, sandy beach filling her vision. The individual grains of sand seemed large this close up. Everest lay unmoving several centimeters away. Her hand dropped between them.

Movement beyond cast shadows and lights in her fading vision, but it took too much effort to concentrate.

She could see Everest beside her.

But his eyes didn't meet hers. They stared up, glazed over. Blood soaked the sand between them.

Too much blood.

We'll die together.

Somewhere in the distance, there was more yelling, more blasts. But she was consumed in a coffin of silence and darkness which was swallowing her whole.

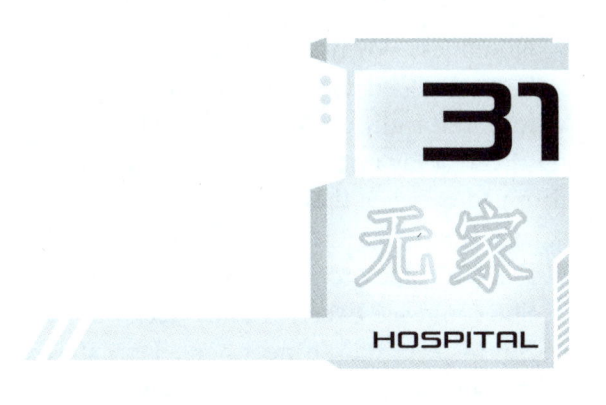

31

HOSPITAL

A LOW-PITCHED WHINE FILLED THE AIR, GROWING louder and louder.

There was a shattering boom, and a brilliant electric light illuminated the sky.

The pressure around Urban's neck fell away.

Urban heaved in gulps of air and coughed. When her vision slowly returned, the force field was gone. *Jingcha* were storming the island, along with medbots and Givers administering aid.

The Deadly Second lay in a heap of charred wreckage. The Inventor tried to crawl away toward the forest with her remaining mechanical legs but was quickly taken down by two officers. Dawn, Wraith, and Vance were nowhere to be seen.

Urban found her thoughts groggy.

A woman in a crisp medical uniform leaned over her.

"Are you alright, dear?" The woman's voice was honey-smooth, and it had an instant calming effect. "We'll get you the help you need."

Urban found herself believing the words.

"I'm going to have you examined by a medbot, alright?"

Urban nodded, and her neck hurt. Her throat felt dry. There was a patch of red on the white sand.

That was odd.

So much red on the sand. Like smashed red paper lanterns. Or shredded red *hongbaos*. Or . . .

Blood.

Urban struggled to sit.

"Everest!" She tried to shout Everest's name, but her voice was raspy.

He was gone.

Urban got to her feet, an aluminum blanket slipping to the side. "Everest!" she rasped again. Fear drove her. Lightheaded, she listed to the side into the returning medic.

The Giver caught her. "Slow down. Everything will be fine." The woman motioned at several medbots. "We're going to examine you to make sure you're alright."

"Please, I have to see him!"

Urban squirmed frantically, but two medbots held her in place while a third one scanned her.

"Does this feel tender?" the bot asked with maddening calm.

"This will only take one minute." The Giver wrapped the blanket back around Urban's shoulders.

Urban shivered. Why was it so cold?

"The patient has sustained minor injuries, including bruising to the throat, and is currently experiencing shock," the medbot informed the Giver. "We recommend she be kept warm and hydrated while transported to the hospital for further evaluation."

"Officer Xin here will escort you to the hospital." The Giver motioned at a Super clad in a gold and red uniform. "He has some questions for you."

Urban numbly followed the Super into a heavily guarded hovercraft. She was vaguely aware that several of her own security Flyers and bots trailed them. They must have finally made it onto the island.

"Please. Is my family okay? My friends?" Urban begged.

"I believe I'm doing the questioning here." The Super's voice softened. "Your family members were all rescued."

"My friend Everest was injured. He was right by me."

"I believe I met a fellow named Ash helping with the medbots. He's fine. I don't know about anyone else." The *Jingcha* climbed into the waiting vehicle and Urban followed him.

The ride to the hospital was a blur. Urban forced down hydrating liquids. She knew she answered questions but couldn't remember what any of them were. Her mind only had one focus.

Everest.

When Urban was released, she found her guards waiting outside of her hospital room. She sent her family members a quick ping, ensuring they were safe, before hurrying to the main lobby. A bot concierge regarded her and her retinue of guards expressionlessly.

"Where is Chong Everest?" Urban burst out.

The bot blinked its eyes slowly, scanning her. "Lee Urban? I see you are on the authorized list of visitation personnel and I am released to share PPI regulatory information with you. Chong Everest is in the OR."

"The operating room? Where's that?"

"I have transferred access to the viewing room," the bot said.

A map of the hospital, along with directions, appeared in Urban's retina display.

She arrived at the thirteenth floor in front of a white door with a blinking marker above it that identified it as room forty-four.

She swallowed.

The entryway slid open with a swipe of her tatt. A gush of cool air carried the scent of overpowering antiseptic.

The dimly illuminated room was absent of decor. A silent holo display projected the latest news above a few chairs. The events on the island unfolded again, but Urban didn't watch. She had already lived it. Her focus was on a large viewing glass with an intensive medbay beyond.

Surgicbots and Medbots hovered around Everest in the operating theater. A smart sheet covered him from his abdomen down, and machines monitored his vital signs. The hovering table he rested on was elevated, and it was difficult to see what the bots were doing. A metal limb from the bed locked onto Everest's collar bone, keeping him immobile for surgery.

He was motionless, deathly white.

Urban's heart clenched.

He looked so fragile. Her strong, fierce Everest.

Suddenly weak. Vulnerable.

One of the medbots hovered out of the room.

Urban stopped it. "What's wrong with him?"

"The patient has had organ failure and hypovolemic shock. He's been given a blood transfusion and is currently undergoing an emergency lung transplant until we can find a match for his second lung."

Urban paled. "A lung transplant?"

"A lung transplant is the process by which a patient—"

"I know what a transplant is," Urban interrupted. "Why does he need one?"

"Both of his lungs received critical damage. One lung is completely nonfunctional. The other lung is only partially functional. He needs both replaced."

No. *Everest.* She felt faint. "Will he survive?" she asked weakly.

"The probability of that outcome is currently unknown."

She couldn't bear not knowing. "Unknown or you won't tell me?"

The gears in the side of the medbot's head whirred faster and turned orange, as if this question required greater computing power. It eventually hovered away without answering.

Urban watched it go, a sinking in her stomach. Then she turned back to the operating room.

With fingers pressed against the viewport, she wished desperately she could be on the other side, next to Everest.

"Oh, Everest. It should have been me."

She leaned her forehead against the viewport and her shoulders shook as tears streamed down her face.

Urban wasn't sure how much time had passed when the surgicbots stopped their work. Several heavier looking machines transported Everest into a transparent tube full of blue liquid, lowering him gently. He sank slowly, like falling through jelly. The top of the tube sealed shut over him.

Everest's parents rushed through the door, hurrying to the viewport. His mother uttered a cry and collapsed into her stricken husband's arms.

Urban quietly left, tears filling her eyes again. She opened her pings in search of her family. They were all released and at dinner in the private KOL section of the hospital. She went in search of them.

Several minutes later, she arrived at a doorway, flanked by a swarm of security guards. Three Supers. Five Inventors. Ten bots. Urban stopped counting and extended her tatt for one of them to scan.

The guards stepped aside and the entry slid open. Urban blinked.

A man-made brook flowed down a pebbled channel through the room and into a small pond on the other side. Artfully placed patches of grass and flowers grew interspersed throughout the room. Crickets chirping, along with whispering wind, permeated the sound system. The floor was made entirely of sand and the heat lights beating down from above made it feel like she was at the beach rather than in a hospital.

Then she saw the four individuals gathered around the pond, sitting in lounge chairs.

Relief flooded over her.

Lillian was the first to spot her. "Urban!" She leaped out of her chair and ran toward her, engulfing her in her arms.

Urban hung onto her. "I'm so glad you're safe." She pulled back and looked Lillian in the eye, tears brimming.

Lillian's complexion was paler than usual, her makeup smudged and her hair pulled up in a rough messy bun, but she seemed uninjured.

Soon, Urban was hugging Mother and greeting her father, but she stopped short at Lucas.

Her brother wore a wrinkled jumpsuit, his normally stylish hair plastered to his face, reminding her of a wet dog. Bloodshot eyes looked up from under the tangled mess of hair. His face had an unnatural sheen of sweat and paleness to it.

"Lucas? What happened?" she asked. "You look like death."

Lucas cracked a smile, though he grimaced with the effort. "That does tend to happen when you're poisoned."

Urban's eyes rounded. "Poisoned?"

He pulled at an unraveling strand on his jumpsuit. "Useless hospital wardrobe," he muttered. He looked back to Urban. "Apparently, since I can breathe underwater, those lunatics poisoned me with some neurotoxin, making me as vulnerable as you all. That way, I could drown too."

Urban gaped at him. "How did you survive?"

"Thankfully, the last dragon boat rescued me. Looks like the afterlife doesn't want me crashing their bash yet."

Mother, in a rare display of physical affection, raked her fingers gently through Lucas's hair.

Father cleared his throat and then gave Lucas an awkward pat on his back, but looked at Urban. "We're all glad you're alright. That we all are."

"I bet. You would have been hard-pressed to explain how your Aqua son drowned." Lucas's eyes took on a dreamy expression. "Trolling you even from the grave, I like it."

"Life isn't all about pranks," Father said sternly. "Having nearly died, I'd think you would have learned that by now."

"Or maybe life is too short to take too seriously," Lucas countered, and they were back to their usual arguing.

Mother let out an exasperated sigh. But Lucas seemed less desperate to be seen and Father less cutting in his remarks. Urban smiled.

Mother turned to her. "How's Everest?"

Urban's smile vanished.

"The *Jingcha* told us everything." Mother's voice was laced with concern. "His injury sounds serious."

"Yes." Urban choked out the word.

Lillian put a reassuring arm around Urban. "He's going to be okay, and they have the best critical care units in the federation here. He's in good hands."

Urban nodded, unable to say more. She was acutely aware of the dozens of body guards and security detail at a distance, surrounding them on all sides, pretending not to watch the interaction. Why could she never be alone anymore?

Right on cue, a visitor ping appeared in Urban's retina display. She reluctantly accepted. Soon, the sharp click of high heels drew toward them.

"I'm sorry for the ordeal you all have been through," Jasmine said by way of greeting. She didn't wait for a response. "The press is already having a heyday after today's events."

Her sharp green eyes took in the Lees' haggard appearances. "I can see that now is not the time to discuss these things at length. I'll make this brief."

Jasmine took a seat, legs crossing delicately. "As Urban's PR and media advisor, my advice to you, and the entire family, would be to avoid the media for now."

Exhaustion hit Urban at the thought of anything media related. Were they really having this conversation?

"My team of PR specialists is working to craft talking points that will ensure a sosh boost and paint this all in a positive light," Jasmine went on, "Most importantly, they will ensure your safety going forward and prevent against future attacks."

As if talking points will keep us safe. All the same, Urban realized she was grudgingly grateful for Jasmine's help.

"Until then, I suggest you get some rest and stay away from the press." Jasmine stood.

"Thank you," Mother said, and Urban nodded.

Jasmine gave a head nod in return and left.

Urban looked at her family. "Could we go?"

"I've eaten about as much stale *mantou* as I can stomach," Lucas declared. "Let's head out."

"Yes," Mother said. "Let's go home."

Home.

It seemed a strange word at a time like this.

Is home safe? Is anywhere?

The image of Everest's mother weeping in his father's arms flashed through her mind.

Would Everest be going home?

32

MUTANT ZOO

URBAN'S FINGERS TIGHTENED ON THE ARMREST as the vehicle zipped through New Beijing's Metropolis. Chintzy lights, K-pop, and perfume from the luxury stores sneaked its way into their vehicle; familiar and foreign all at once.

How could the city go on as it always had, boasting bashes and shopping as if that were all that mattered?

Life just went on.

The vehicle rounded a corner and Urban's jaw dropped.

As they reached the entrance to their apartment, guards swarmed the streets and the air—even the side of the building had Camos clinging to it like lizards.

Are we entering a high-security military base or going home?

With everything that had happened, Urban appreciated the extra security. And yet, it made the one place she was hoping their presence wouldn't be so invasive feel unfamiliar.

Urban made her way past the security detail lining the entryway, up the elevator, into her house, and straight to her room.

She just needed to be alone.

Once in bed, Urban wiggled under a thick comforter. Her body was shivering. The warmth from her bed didn't stop it. She curled up, trying not think about the day's events. Eventually, she fell asleep.

The next morning, she awoke, still in her clothes, to nearly a thousand missed pings. Blinking them away, Urban ordered her AI to run a search through the pings for any update on Everest.

Nothing.

Heart sinking, she got out of bed, cleaned herself up quickly, and changed.

Downstairs, her family was gathered in the dining hall for a late breakfast. Urban served herself some egg and scallion crepes, then pushed them around her plate, unable to eat.

"We'll be leaving this afternoon to return to Chengdu," Father said.

Urban glanced up quickly in surprise.

"I know it feels soon." Father actually looked sympathetic. "But the qualifiers are only a few weeks away, and you must keep up your training regimen."

RTC was the last thing on Urban's mind. It was like nothing had changed. She wished she could escape the race. Her life.

How was she supposed to focus on competing when Everest may not live?

"I'm going on a drive," Urban stood.

"Have you lost your senses?" Father looked at her askance.

"I have half the Asian Federation's security force tailing me. No one in their right mind will try to attack again."

"No one in their right mind would have thrown us to the bottom of a lake just to spice up the Dragon Boat Festival," Lucas pointed out. "I'm with Dad on this one."

But Urban needed time to think. Away from the guards, AiE, training, her responsibilities—everything.

"I have to go," she blurted.

Father's lips thinned. Mother and Lillian exchanged glances.

"I'm coming with you," Lillian said.

"I need to be alone," Urban emphasized.

"And you will be," Lillian told her. "I'll just be following at a distance to make sure you stay out of trouble."

"Good luck," Lucas coughed under his breath.

"How about you stay here and I use a disguise instead?"

Urban went up to her room and returned pulling on a bucket hat and tucking her hair inside. Then she slipped into a hoodie.

Lucas snorted. "Now you look like you have no sense of fashion. Which is pretty normal for you, I suppose."

Realizing the hat wouldn't fit under her bike helmet anyway, Urban tossed the disguise aside.

"I'm coming." The tone of Lillian's voice left no room for argument.

Urban sighed. She took an apple off the table and pocketed it, then headed to the parking garage, Lillian and a swarm of guards surrounding her. She felt claustrophobic.

Her old bike rest against the wall where she'd last left it in the chilly and damp space. She touched its familiar slick black gears and knobs.

Memories of time she'd spent with Everest, riding side by side on their bikes, flooded her mind.

Fighting against the lump rising in her throat, she climbed onto the cool leather seat. The bike rumbled to life, purple light shone from under her, and illuminated the control panel. Everything felt different compared to the giant rev cycle she was training with for the Race to the Clouds. But both had one thing in common. Urban switched the settings to manual mode and breathed a sigh of relief.

There was something about riding without auto control that made her feel free—even if it was an illusion.

Her protectors and Lillian followed her out of the garage on bikes or vehicles of their own, but Urban paid them no mind as she shot onto the street.

Weaving through traffic and accelerating around a smart light, she noted with satisfaction her security guards struggling to trail her. The Flyers and drones had no problem, but those on bikes were falling behind. It probably didn't help that she had no clear destination and was wandering the streets in an unpredictable pattern.

An idea struck her.

It was sure to be the last place anyone would think to look for her. A place she hadn't been since she was small. She would be safe there. Alone.

Urban accelerated and didn't slow until she reached the edge of the Metropolis. The traffic died down, and she skidded to a stop in front of a large holo sign that read: New Beijing's Enhanced Zoo.

It was one of her favorite places growing up. Maybe because she'd always envied the animals and their genetics, wishing she too were Enhanced.

Now, she'd give anything *not* to be Enhanced. Not to have this burden of being the hybrid.

Urban scanned her tatt at the entrance, watching as it subtracted crypto points, then walked into an open space.

Since it was in the middle of the week, it wasn't crowded, just a few families happily enjoying the sights. Heads turned at her giant security team. Urban walked faster.

Vendors selling *tanghulu* on bamboo skewers filled the air with the sweet aroma of hawthorn berry and caramelized sugar. Resisting the tantalizing scents, Urban followed her maps, passing the aviary, aquarium, and heading into the pits.

Several sleeping Enhanced wolves lounged on rocks in their cages. Larger than normal size, each had a unique color of fur, ranging from chili pepper red to shades of matcha green. At the next set of cages, a miniature elephant chomped on bananas. Nearby, monkeys swung from branches, their screeching similar to that of songbirds.

At the other end of the zoo, Urban stopped in front of a heavily patrolled structure. A Super blocked the way and scanned her tatt before allowing her to pass.

Urban stepped through a reinforced door and into a large circular space designed to look like a jungle, with leafy trees and thick underbrush.

The scent of petrichor and manure reached her nostrils as

she tread gingerly across the damp earth.

A roar shook the branches on the trees, halting her progression.

Before she could second-guess her decision, a giant creature bounded out of the foliage. Right before it reached her, the Gamelyon slid to a stop, spraying Urban with dirt.

She forced herself to stay her ground.

The creature nuzzled her shoulder gently, eyeing her with its large golden eyes.

Nerves still tingling, Urban slowly extended a hand and ran her fingers through its thick, tangled mane.

The creature let out a low growl, and Urban froze.

But it wasn't a growl. It was deep and throaty. The Gamelyon leaned into Urban's touch. It was purring.

Gaining confidence, Urban continued stroking the creature, scratching behind its ears and down its muscled neck.

Her security team hung back near the entrance. Even Lillian gave them a wide berth.

Finally, Urban could be alone. Stepping further into the enclosure, she used the thick plants to hide from prying eyes.

She reached into her pocket for the apple and extended it to the Gamelyon. The creature sniffed it, then snorted and turned its head away.

"I don't have an appetite either," she said.

Why am I talking to an animal?

Reality returned.

What am I doing here?

She should be training for the RTC. Or practicing Jasmine's public speaking tips. Or doing one of a million things required of her by AiE, Croix, or her RTC team. Her responsibilities piled up longer than the Great Wall of the Ancient Federation. But Urban couldn't force herself to do any of them.

She just wanted to be alone. To rest. To sit in silence.

Flashes of the past twenty-four hours plagued her mind.

Lennox. His sickly daughter. The Deadly Five. Her family at the bottom of the lake. Everest taking the blow for her. Waking up alone and cold on the beach. Everest sinking to the bottom of the blue solution at the hospital.

Urban's chest constricted.

It was too much.

She leaned her head against the Gamelyon, still stroking its coarse mane. "How am I supposed to go on?" she whispered. "I can't race without Everest. And I'm not the person to change the world for better. Hybrid or not."

She wanted to cry but was too tired.

The Gamelyon nuzzled her gently. It licked her face, and Urban jerked her head back.

A small laugh bubbled out of her as she wiped off slobber.

Urban gazed at those round, gold eyes. Come to think of it, she knew very little about the animal. Conducting a quick search in QuanNao, she read some of the results.

<Gamelyon is a mythical hybrid creature.>

She returned her gaze to the beast. Its lion snout and heavy mane slowly transformed into the hard scales of a dragon, its cruel talons, heavy tail, and wings so different from the rest of its body.

The Gamelyon was a mix of lion and dragon. Exhibiting traits from both, but not fully belonging to either.

How similar we are.

She continued reading.

<Only one Gamelyon has ever been created by the Western Federation, after many years of experimentation and revolutionary research in gene splicing. This first and only Gamelyon was used by game wardens in the 2124 AI Games. This freak of nature . . . >

Tears pricked Urban's eyes, and she let them fall, burying her wet face in the creature's mane.

The memory of her meeting with the Asian Federation Prefects resurfaced. They had determined Urban didn't qualify as a Natural or an Aqua.

She was a freak of nature.

We're both trapped in the cage of in-between.

She stood there, staring off into space, the side of her head pressed against the Gamelyon, when an urgent ping demanded her attention. Reluctantly, she opened it.

[Lee Byronne: Why aren't you back yet? We need to leave within the hour. We must go on. We must continue training. We must win.]

Blinking back tears, Urban grit her teeth.

While she wanted nothing more than to hide in the enclosure and never reemerge, he was right. Too much depended upon her.

[Lee Byronne: Also, your designated practice session is today. If you miss it, you will be disqualified from racing.]

"*Tiana!*" Urban gave the Gamelyon one last pat and hurried away.

33

SHADOW BAN

THE TRIP BACK TO NEW CHENGDU WAS ONE long, grueling practice session, thanks to Father. Urban's memory kept slipping to Everest, and she got many of the turns wrong.

"You're not learning fast enough," Father frowned as the helix touched down.

Urban felt listless. "I'm doing my best."

"I know." Father's expression softened for an instant, but then he became stern again. "But you have to do better."

Urban tried not to let hopelessness grow as she stepped out onto the helix pad. It was foggy, warm, and humid, and her smart suit stuck to her skin.

A short drive later, she was standing at her designated practice section, where a small crowd had already gathered to watch.

Her bike and team were also there. Everyone but Everest.

Oh, Everest.

His missing presence weighed on Urban like the heavy fog. But she forced those thoughts away. Otherwise, she'd lose all motivation, or worse, focus. And driving up this mountain without focus was a sure way to get herself killed.

The RTC app flashed her a reminder that the official practice time would commence in ten minutes.

To distract herself while she waited, Urban explored the app's other features. There was an interesting variety of game play options, and a message appeared at the corner of her retina display.

<Would you like to enable shadow ban mode?>

Urban selected it and a console of options appeared.

<Please choose who you would like to race against: your previous time or another racer.>

Curiosity sparked Urban and she selected another racer. Since this was her first time practicing on this portion of the course, there would be no way to compare it against her time anyway.

<Would you like to compete against a champion or select someone else?>

Urban opted for a previous year's winner and scrolled back until the right date. Sure enough, there his name was, flashing in gold: Champion Lee Byronne.

Immediately, a holo figure appeared on her left.

Turning to get a better view, a younger version of her father came into focus. He sat within a slick vehicle waiting for the signal to go. A shiny blue helmet with a lotus flower on it—the Lee family's emblem—covered his head. Urban recognized it from Auntie's room of trophies.

She looked back up at her team. Could they also see what she was looking at? She shook herself. Of course not. The image was coming from the RTC app. Her father's holo wasn't really there.

The retina display beeped.

<Lee Urban, your practice time will commence in one minute. Please make your way to the start line.>

A virtual line appeared a few meters in front of her on the Zeolite-coated road. Urban made her way toward it.

Ash soared into the air, ready to follow her from above and film her movements. Poppy tweaked a few settings in Urban's controls. Lucas gave her a thumbs up.

<Ten seconds.>

Urban snapped her helmet down and focused on the road—and the virtual racer beside her.

<Three . . . two . . . one . . . You may now begin your practice session.>

Urban's bike shot forward, keeping pace with the racer next to her.

They both took the upcoming curve in the road smoothly. The crowd of people was left behind as she entered the silence of the forest with no one but the racer beside her.

Urban and the holo wove from one side of the lane to the other, depending on where the upcoming turn was.

Occasionally, a few parked hovercrafts and spectators dotted the side of the road. But Urban zoomed past and into the next curve before she had a chance to really look at them.

Suddenly, a blur of fur streaked in front of her.

Instincts had Urban slamming on the brakes and starting to jerk the handle bars away from the animal before Father's words came back to her.

Gritting her teeth, she maintained her course.

Sure enough, her propulsion shield activated with a flash of electric purple. With a howl, the monkey launched backward and out of her path.

Urban cringed. Just in time, her bike shot past where it had been. The monkey rolled to its side as she passed it.

Alive.

She would have felt awful otherwise.

Father's holo had gained some ground on her because of it, though, and Urban increased her speed. She fell into a familiar rhythm, nailing the turns perfectly and catching back up to him.

It was cathartic to be on the road again. With her utmost attention needed on her immediate surroundings, Urban felt grounded. Present without the weighted burden of her thoughts and emotions dragging her down.

Her spirits lifted as she raced up the course. All too soon, the finish line came into sight.

<Approaching final section. Maintain current speed to tie with Lee Byronne.>

Exhilaration filled Urban. She was actually racing against a previous year's champion, her father no less, and keeping up.

Her bike converted into flying mode, and she shot into the air for the final portion of the race.

Then she was passed the finish line.

Turning her bike back around, she landed on an airstrip on the tower. Her team rushed forward. By the excitement on their faces, Urban had done well.

A moment later, the RTC app confirmed it.

<Lee Urban your time against Lee Byronne was faster by fifteen seconds. Great job on setting a new personal record!>

Her mind drifted back to the underground race she'd competed in to boost her sosh. If her bike hadn't been hacked, she would have done well. And that was before she had been Enhanced with faster reflexes.

Racing was something she'd naturally been good at. And Everest had always known.

She smiled.

After grueling physical training with Ivan and Poppy, Urban was finally released for the last session of the day. She trudged toward the house's art studio in utter exhaustion.

The scent of fresh, living plants from the biophilic design elements helped her relax. Bright, natural lighting filled the work space. Noise-proof walls carpeted the room in deep silence, the only sound the soft scraping of marble as Dr. Yukio mixed together a poultice.

His holo projection was turned off and Urban wondered if

he was planning on a silent work session.

When she joined him at the table, he handed her a marble bowl of her own, along with a grinder. Urban took them wordlessly, and began mashing the gold into a fine powder.

She wasn't sure how much time had passed when Dr. Yukio's projection clicked on, halfway engulfing her, causing her to startle.

"How are you today?" the holo asked, looking at Urban, even as Dr. Yukio's hooded face remained focused downward on his poultice.

"I'm . . . fine."

Dr. Yukio's hood shifted. "What is on your mind?"

The attack at Dragon Boat Festival. Her family. RTC. Croix. Being on the banned list. AiE. Discovering her new Aqua abilities. Her inability to roar. Belonging to neither the Naturals nor Enhanced. Belonging anywhere. The Deadly Five.

Everest.

She swallowed.

Urban decided there was probably only one safe topic. "I'm an Aqua but I can't roar."

"And?" Dr. Yukio prompted.

"And Aquas don't see me as one of their own."

Dr. Yukio was silent a moment. "I am blind and deaf—a living, walking holo projection. Like you, I have experienced society's judgment for things out of my control. Birth, DNA, status—none of that is of consequence. What matters is how you choose to live with what you've been given."

"I never wanted to be an Aqua. I don't feel like a real one if I can't roar," she confessed.

"Sometimes the gifts we've been given take time to cultivate," Dr. Yukio responded. "We are always given what we need to endure, no more, no less."

Urban's throat constricted.

Her mind drifted back to her first semester of uni. Her mother had read her the rule book, as they called it back then.

All the things Urban needed to do to stay safe.

Only, the rule book hadn't kept her safe and had proven a poor road map for life.

Now, Urban felt as if she was left without any sort of playbook. Everyone around her knew what they were doing except her.

Maybe my mentor's right, maybe it just takes time.

Unfortunately, time was the one thing she didn't have.

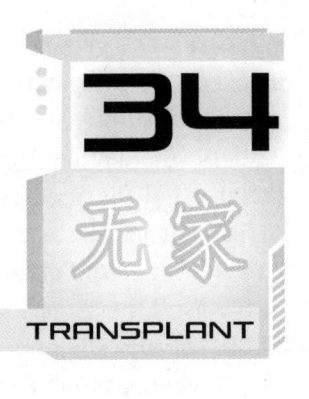

34

TRANSPLANT

THE DAYS LEADING UP TO THE QUALIFIERS FELL into a routine. In the morning, Urban endured exhaustive training with Poppy and Ivan. Despite their extensive biometric monitoring and personalized recovery plans with cryo therapy and massage, Urban always left the gym feeling like boba jellies.

Next came a healthy lunch of some awful combination that should never have been made. Ivan insisted it was exactly the right portion of proteins and healthy fats Urban needed. Century egg with durian and *doufu* had been the worst offender. The house smelled of rotten eggs and fruit for days. Even Ivan had struggled to choke that meal down. Urban caught the rest of the team sneaking in *chaomian* later.

Afternoons were reserved for practice on her bike, followed by mind crunching memorization tasks with Father.

After another disgustingly healthy meal, Urban was back at Elite Elevation, this time in the pool practicing her Aqua abilities with Lucas and Blossom.

That was always the worst part of the day.

Urban still wasn't able to roar, and Blossom's increasing disapproval wasn't helping.

The last part of the day was either a mentoring session with Dr. Yukio at the house's private studio, or more motorcycle practice.

There was a gaping hole in her heart for where Everest should have been training her.

Urban hadn't heard from him in two weeks and was growing restless. She'd attempted to visit him multiple times, but Father had insisted she needed every spare minute to train.

So instead, she was stuck in New Chengdu with a virtual coach from an old biker friend of Father's.

It wasn't the same.

But she was still on the banned list, and all the good coaches didn't want to touch her.

Public outings were always the worst. Urban tried to keep a low profile.

Every news outlet had taken it upon themselves to cover the Dragon Boat Festival story. It was nearly impossible for Urban to go anywhere without reminders of her worst nightmare.

She went to extra efforts to try and stay out of sight, or at least paste on a semi-happy smile while in public. Still, blurred photos had been captured of her looking angry or confused, with ridiculous captions attached, and rumors spread wildly throughout XR.

One of them had even gone viral.

An unflattering, and completely fabricated, AI generated image of Urban fist-fighting an old lady. She'd been horrified upon discovering it on the home page of her news feed one day.

Do people really think I'd bully on old lady? Surely they know it's a deep fake. Then again, people believe all kinds of things these days.

The thought sickened and enraged her.

She had tried to remind herself that this was the price to pay for being AiE's figurehead, but that did nothing to make her feel better.

Thankfully, Croix had come to her rescue and threatened to sue the media outlets if they didn't remove the photo. The image disappeared shortly after, and a public apology had been issued.

It paid to have a good sponsor.

Urban worried Croix would cancel her contract after all the bad PR she was attracting. But Mako had assured Urban this sort of thing was quite common among KOLs. Which was a relief, because they were days away from the qualifiers, and Urban couldn't afford to lose them.

Sometimes, Urban felt her life was as precarious as a paper lantern in a gale storm. She was one strong gust of wind away from disaster.

All too soon, it was nearly time for the qualifiers. Urban spent the day before with Father, reviewing turns at the house.

"You're doing better," he said.

Urban had managed to pass the simulation without getting a single turn wrong. She beamed. "Does that mean we're done?"

"For today." Father stood. "The rest of your workouts are cancelled as well. You need to rest before your big day tomorrow."

"About that," Urban hesitated. "Since I have the afternoon free, I'd like to return to New Beijing."

Father frowned. "New Beijing?"

"To see Everest."

"Ah." Father scratched his stubble. "You're supposed to be resting today—"

"I'll rest," Urban broke in. "I'll take a nap on the way over and back."

Father regarded her for a moment.

Could he sense her heart banging wildly within her chest? "I need to see him," she pleaded.

Father let out a resigned grunt. "Be quick about it."

Urban nearly hugged him. "Thank you! I will!"

She sprinted away, ordering a helix pod as she ran. Ash,

Trig, and her retinue of guards scurried to keep up with her.

Urban tried to sleep on the short trip over, but the thought of seeing Everest had her energy spiking. Soon, the pod touched back down in the bustling Metropolis of New Beijing.

One short hover trip later and she was standing in front of the hospital. Urban tried to calm her jittery nerves as she made her way to Everest's wing.

She had a moment of panic when she scanned her tatt at his door. What if she'd been removed from the authorized list of guests? What if they'd relocated him?

But then the door hissed and slid away, and she was inside, leaving her guards behind.

The dim interior of the room carried the sharp scent of antiseptic and there was something playing on the holo display. She immediately gravitated to the viewport.

Everest floated in a clear tube surrounded in blue solution. His bare chest disappeared into an enclosed portion of the casing, obscuring the rest of his body from sight.

Urban tried not to dwell on just how fragile he looked.

An elderly man in a lab coat was in the room with Everest. Her retina display picked up his identity as an Inventor named Dr. Song.

After a moment, the doctor emerged into the viewing room.

"How is he?" Urban asked, consciously aware she was ignoring all formalities.

"Hello." The doctor blinked, as if surprised to see her. He studied her a moment. "I see you have been granted PPI privileges and I am allowed to share with you his update. We were able to find a match for his second lung and the surgery was a success. Though, we are seeing abnormalities in his white blood cell count."

Urban's heart pounded. "What does that mean?"

"Nothing, yet." Dr. Song paused. "But it could indicate the body's rejection reaction for one of the lung transplants received. We're closely monitoring the situation. But if the trend were to continue, we'd be looking at another lung transplant."

"And if his body rejects that one?"

The doctor's face shadowed. "Then we'd be looking at a less than five percent chance of survival."

Urban gaped.

"I'm sorry."

Five percent survival rate. Urban's thoughts spiraled.

"Do you want to talk to him?" Dr. Song asked.

Numbly, Urban nodded.

"He's about to wake up." The doctor motioned at the blue liquid encasing his body draining away.

Urban stepped into a cleaning chamber that sprayed her with disinfectant before crossing over into Everest's room. The liquid was gone, along with the tube, and he lay upon a bare metal bed, a sheet draped across him.

Too-bright fluorescent lighting cast a blueish hue to his body. Or maybe that was just how he looked after all the blood loss.

"Everest?" Urban's voice came out hoarse. She wasn't aware of moving, but suddenly she was by his side.

Everest blinked, disoriented. He tried to sit up and let out a low groan.

"Don't move," Dr. Song ordered him.

Everest's gaze moved from the doctor to Urban. A ghost of a smile flitted across his face. "Is that my *meinu*?"

"And please try to limit your talking," the doctor advised. He gave Urban a reprimanding look before leaving them alone.

"Everest." So many thoughts and emotions filled that one word.

His raven black eyes gazed at her. Urban kneeled on the floor so she was eye level with him.

She couldn't breathe—couldn't move. Too afraid that if she did, the moment would shatter.

Everest's eyes shifted, and he looked like he wanted to say something. He stared up, a question plaguing his expression.

"I'll tell you everything once you're better," Urban reassured him.

Because you will get better.

Words weren't needed as they faced each other. Her thumb traced his firm jawline and she tried to freeze this moment—to memorize every part of him.

Everest's fingers gently caressed her arm, but the movement was slow and glitchy, like a bot at the end of its life cycle.

He's strong. He's fine. He'll pull through, Urban told herself.

And yet, where her fingers met his skin, he was cold, the gelatin-like solution they'd kept him in sticking to her. Frigid hospital air blew down on them, adding to the dampness seeping into her limbs.

His smiling eyes blinked sleepily and then slowly drifted closed.

Urban fought the panic welling up with in her. Those eyes. Those beautiful, strong, black eyes. What if this was the last time she would ever see them opened?

He's strong. He's fine. He'll pull through. Why wasn't the mantra working?

Five percent survival rate.

All she wanted was some guarantee that Everest would be okay. That he'd survive. That the person who knew her better than anyone else—who she loved—would live long enough to love her back.

Love.

She realized it now; the truth was obvious. She had always loved him. Even during their breakup. She had been so foolish.

I don't want to look back on this moment and regret it.

Urban moved closer to him. "I love you," she whispered.

Everest didn't move or react.

She wasn't sure if he was awake anymore, but it didn't matter. She had to say it.

Otherwise, she might not get another chance.

35

无家

HOT POT

NESTLED WITHIN EMEI'S MOUNTAINS, A NEON-lit alleyway sparked to life. Bustling with people, delivery drones, and smart pop-up tents, the street exuded a vibrant energy. Rich traditional architecture clashed with cheap temporary shelters hastily constructed for the qualifiers.

Urban's team had already finished assembling their prep tent and were meeting for dinner. It seemed pointless to eat when Everest was stuck in a hospital in critical condition, but Croix and AiE had insisted Urban make a public appearance.

Something about helping the cause.

She hadn't really been listening. In fact, Urban had been in an off-kilter haze ever since visiting Everest. Nothing felt real anymore.

Why am I here? I'm wasting time that could be spent with Everest.

An image of his pale body flashed in her mind.

What if he doesn't make it?

The thought that had plagued her all day popped up again. The mere possibility of a life without Everest was incomprehensible.

Urban tightened her fist until her fingernails bit into her palms. *He'll make it.*

Her vehicle lurched to a stop. Sucking in a breath, she tamped down all thoughts of Everest into a tightly locked box.

Think about him later.

Ash and her guards led the way toward a restaurant. A crowd of spectators had already secured the best race day spots and were lined up on the sidewalk and street. Urban's gut churned at the thought of all the people who would be viewing the qualifying race tomorrow.

Hopefully, they would witness her making it into the finals and not dying.

She locked those thoughts in the box as well, then pushed her way into the crowded restaurant.

Warm air blasted her as she stepped inside. The scent of spices, garlic, and chili pepper oil wafted up from each of the steaming pots placed at the center of the tables. Lo-fi beats played but were nearly drowned out by raucous laughter and the sound of an XR projector above the bar spouting the latest news.

The team was already gathered around a large square wooden table, with an empty pot in front of them.

Urban took off her jacket and slid into a seat next to Lucas. "Where's Father?"

At the exchanged glances, her heart sank. She glanced toward the bar. Sure enough, Father was sitting alone, three glasses in at 1800.

He can handle himself. Three glasses is nothing for him, Urban reasoned with herself.

Turning to her team, she forced a smile. "I heard I get to carb load tonight?"

"Finally! This awful diet we've been on has been affecting my looks." Lucas patted his perfectly styled black hair.

Urban perused the menu in the following heavy silence. Despite her lack of appetite, she ordered a few of her favorites: quail eggs, potatoes, and lotus roots. She doubted she could stomach anything but had to try.

While she waited for the others to add to the order, she got up to join Father.

"Hey." Urban sat on a hovering bar stool next to him.

Father kept his eyes on the broadcast instead.

Urban considered trying to manage some sort of civil conversation but gave up after one look at his glassy expression. "Why don't you want me to compete?" she asked flatly.

Father took a long sip of his drink.

When he still didn't speak, Urban whispered, "I need your help."

Father still refused to look at her. "I don't want you to get hurt."

Urban jerked upright in surprise.

She was temporarily speechless. Finally, she managed, "But you competed."

He slowly set his glass down. "I paid a steep price for that victory. A sacrifice that, if I could go back in time, I would take back." He considered her. "I wonder what price you will have to pay. You cannot emerge a victor from this race unscathed."

He abruptly downed his drink and turned back toward the vids.

Urban returned to her table, shaken.

The giant pot of broth had arrived, with its scent of garlic and chili peppers, and the team surrounded the condiments bar. Urban added toasted sesame paste, soy sauce, garlic, rice vinegar, and scallions to her porcelain bowl.

Back at the table, it felt empty. With both of her coaches missing—Father and Everest—it was as if Urban only had half her support system.

All she wanted was to get on the next helix and fly back to Everest's side.

The torrent of emotions rose up within, threatening to overwhelm her again. She bit her lip.

A bot hovered toward them pushing a cart full of the raw meats and vegetables. The team began unloading them onto the table, dumping some of them immediately into the boiling pot.

A few seconds later, Urban scooped up one of the lotus roots, inspecting it to see if it was cooked.

Ash leaned close to her. "How are you feeling?"

Urban glanced toward the bar where her father still sat alone with his growing companion of empty glasses. "Okay."

Ash followed her gaze. "Is he . . . drunk?"

"Not yet."

Ash's brow knit together in concern.

Urban reached for the serving spoon, dipping into the pot, but Ivan swiftly intervened. "That's your side." He redirected her away from the steaming red stew, toward the other half of the pot where a creamy broth bubbled placidly. "No spice. We want you to have a happy gut tomorrow."

And so you brought me to a hot pot restaurant in New Sichuan?

"This year's Race to the Clouds qualifiers are about to kick off," an announcer said. Urban's gaze went to the holo display above the bar.

"That's right, Sandy," another commentator agreed. "Qualifiers start tomorrow, and we have quite the line-up of hopeful racers. By the end of the day, we'll have our list of competitors. What's interesting is that the race day obstacles still haven't been finalized. These racers will be practicing without the obstacles traditional racers face in the tryouts. For anyone who qualifies, the first time they go up against the obstacles will be on the actual race day."

"How lucky, or unlucky, for them," Sandy commented. "Now, let's take a look at the weather forecast."

Urban's team fell silent. Even Father, slumped at the bar, straightened to get a better view.

"We've had a storm moving in this evening and temperatures are dropping," the announcer said. "There was a chance of a southern breeze blowing that storm away, but at this point, it doesn't look like that will be happening. A serious thunderstorm will be arriving tomorrow. Back to you, Sandy."

The brunette reappeared looking grim. "Not what contestants of Race to the Clouds want to hear, folks. The weather determines everything in this highly dangerous race . . ."

Urban turned away from the broadcast. Conversation at the table resumed, though she had the feeling it was more for her benefit than anything else.

When the last of the food had been plucked from the hot pot and only the spiciest of broth remained, the group collected their jackets and made their way out.

Urban took one last glance at the bar.

Father still sat alone, nursing another drink. His words came back to her. *I wonder what price you will have to pay?*

36

QUALIFIERS

URBAN'S EYES FLASHED OPEN. GOLD SHONE from her tatt, illuminating the dark and silent room. Something had woken her.

Was a person in her room?

She fumbled for her hydro blade until she realized what the sound was. Her alarm.

Then she remembered why her alarm was going off at 0300. Nervous adrenaline kicked in and propelled her out of bed.

Today is the qualifiers.

Urban tried not to think about it as she quickly hopped into the shower. Using her retina display, she adjusted the water's temperature to a steamy hot. The warm stream beating against her skin relaxed her tense muscles but did nothing to alleviate the churning in her stomach.

Everest should be here.

Needing distraction, Urban selected a pump-up music playlist and blasted it through the shower's speaker system. She emerged, and after drying off, pulled on her black g-suit and opened up the RTC app. It informed her she'd been assigned the fourth racing slot of the day.

Four.

An unlucky number.

Not that she believed in luck. All the same . . .

She brushed off the sense of trepidation and tugged on a hoody and a pair of waterproof boots. Scooping up the breakfast Ivan had prepared for her, she joined Ash and her guards outside.

Darkness cloaked her surroundings, and a chilly wind nipped at the exposed areas of her skin. Urban pulled her hood down lower and shoved her hands into her pockets. Tall dark trees surrounded her on all sides, but that was all she could see. Lightning flashed and illuminated the path before her in a haunting streak before everything plunged back into darkness.

Father had warned about storms. They were the worst type of weather to compete in. Urban waited for the following boom of thunder, but it never came.

Maybe it's too far away.

Urban and her guards rode up the mist-shrouded mountain until they reached the neon-lit alleyway, its colors now subdued in the early morning light.

The vehicle went as far as it could before the road was barricaded off. They continued on foot, weaving through people clogging the street preparing for the race.

Despite the early hour, the rest of the team was already gathered in her tent. The space was full of Ivan and Poppy's training equipment and viewing feeds.

An expensive bottle of champagne sat in a fancy cooler—a sign of her team's belief in her. Urban hoped it wasn't misplaced.

"There's the sleepyhead," Lucas quipped at her arrival. "We've been up for hours but decided to let you sleep in."

Ivan inspected Urban's biometrics and measured out a hydration drink before handing it to her. Lucas and Ash talked animatedly while watching replays of practice sessions. Poppy checked and rechecked the vehicle. The air thrummed with nervous anticipation.

But Urban's energy quickly evaporated at the sight of a figure passed out on the couch.

Father.

"There you are," Poppy said by way of greeting.

Urban ignored her trainer. Striding to the couch, she poked Father's prone figure.

He grunted but remained asleep.

Not today. I can't do this. Tears burned her eyes. Bad weather. Dangerous competitors. Everest gone.

Now Father.

Her coach, her own father, could not bother enough to be sober on the day of the qualifiers.

A sudden weariness overtook her.

Poppy tried again. "Urban, let's get you into your gear."

Something snapped within Urban.

She reached for the bottle of champagne. Lucas appeared by Urban's side, trying to stop her. "Whoa. Slow down. That's for after—"

Urban popped open the bottle, aiming it. A fire hydrant of spray and foaming bubbles smacked Father in the face.

He jerked awake, spluttering and coughing.

Urban tossed the bottle down and pushed past her team and climbed onto a warm up machine.

Only Lucas dared approach her. "Sis, Dad has a lot of issues, but he's not doing this on purpose—"

"If Father wants to defend himself let him do it."

Lucas stood for a moment, then left her alone.

Urban knew she shouldn't be lashing out, but she was so angry she could hardly think straight. Without Father, no one knew how to run the energy propulsion shield. She'd be racing without the protection she needed.

Urban finished her warmup just as Father came wobbling toward her. She tried to pass him, but he gripped her arm.

"Don't go."

"I have to get ready," Urban snapped. She tried to yank her arm away, but his grip was too strong.

"Don't race." Father's bloodshot eyes tried to focus on her. "It's too dangerous."

"Dangerous?" Urban's voice rose. She yanked at her arm again. "Yeah, it is. Especially now that you're wasted out of your mind so there's no one to run the shield."

Father just shook his head. "Not again. I won't lose anyone else."

"This is about Phan Fox, isn't it?" She checked the RTC app. She only had a few minutes before she needed to be at the start line. "You should be helping me stay safe. Not putting me in greater danger by being hungover."

Father said nothing, just kept shaking his head.

"I have to go." Clenching her jaw, Urban left to change into the rest of her game day uniform. She had just drained the nasty drink concoction Ivan had given her when Ash appeared by her side.

"Hey, I think we found someone to help with the propulsion shield."

"Who?" Urban asked skeptically. "It's proprietary tech. Literally no one knows how to run it except my father."

"And me!"

Urban spun around. "Lillian?"

Her sister grinned. Urban felt like she was going to cry.

"What are you doing here?" she finally managed.

"Lucas pinged me last night and told me Dad was spiraling. He suggested you needed a back-up to run the shield, so I got here as soon as I could."

Lucas, her carefree brother who seemed to pay more attention to parties, pranks, and pretty girls. Urban looked up to see him standing by them.

"I tried to tell you earlier," he said.

And she had been too angry to pay attention. "Thank you, Lucas," Urban choked out, suddenly overwhelmed. She turned back to Lillian. "So, how do we run this tech?"

"Dad showed me when he was first building it." Her sister's face brightened. "The shield is pretty simple, really. You finish getting ready. I've taken care of it."

Urban exhaled. For the first time in a while, she felt . . . hope.

37

UNLIMITED DIVISION

URBAN'S NERVES TINGLED AS SHE LINED UP behind the other racers. A light drizzle made it difficult to see.

"It could clear up by the time it's your turn," Lillian said.

Urban nodded, too nervous to speak. Her sister was right. It could clear up by that time.

Then again, it could get worse.

Judging by the RTC weather forecaster, that's exactly what would happen.

Her bike was optimized for ground speed, and rain affected that part of the race the most. Urban and any other racers who'd placed their bets on getting ahead via their ground time were going to be at a disadvantage.

There was nothing she could do about it now.

Despite the dreary and cold weather, spectators were out in full force. The crowd had swelled and were now choking out every part of the road not roped off for the racers.

Around Urban, a small reprieve of space existed; just enough to fit her team. Poppy went over every set of instructions at least twice, and Lucas took it upon himself to quiz Urban on the turns in the absence of Father and Everest.

"Ladies and gentlemen, are you ready for the qualifiers?" A familiar voice blasted the air. Urban's stomach soured.

On the announcer stage, Orion sat at a metallic table with Clover. Seeing her former Dragons teammate, Urban was reminded of Coral and Dawn. Were they here too, somewhere?

She hoped not.

"Contender number one, you may commence," Clover announced.

A woman with pink-tinted skin crouched low to her sleek purple bike. Urban pulled up the woman's stats and found her name was Jamie Bloom. She was from the EuroAsian Federation, and this was her second time competing. Last year, she hadn't placed at all.

Jamie sped up as she approached the holo start line. Then she passed it and shot off around a corner, disappearing from sight. Urban followed the woman via the RTC app, pretending it was her racing. There were two curves Urban drew a blank on and would have had to slow down for. Otherwise, she remembered every bend in the road.

Jamie finished and slid to a stop in the transition lot. Her vehicle began to convert into a flying device. The process took nearly thirty seconds, too long by Urban's calculations. Then Jamie was thrust skyward at an impressive speed. She made up for lost time in the air and finished the race with a total time of 9:01.18.

"Contender number two to the start line," Clover said.

The rain was pouring by the time the contender finished. He had to slow his pace considerably to stay safe.

Please let the rain stop.

"The good news is, you won't get electrocuted," Poppy said, in an attempt to cheer Urban up. "One of the mods I made will protect you from that. So at least you'll be safe."

Nothing about this race was safe.

Even with Poppy's supposed modifications. Lightning may not kill her, but slick road conditions were just as dangerous. Especially ones involving cliffs and no guardrails.

By the time the third contender finished, lightning streaked across the black sky. The following boom of thunder wasn't far behind.

Ivan swore.

"You'll do fine." Lillian placed a reassuring hand on Urban's shoulder.

Urban nodded again, unable to speak, mouth dry.

"You can do it," Lucas encouraged.

"Contender number four to the start line," Clover said.

Urban's heart pounded as she walked her bike over. She pulled her helmet on and disabled her map settings.

Taking a couple of deep breaths, she attempted to calm her jittery nerves.

"Stay safe," Lillian whispered.

"*Jiayou!*" Lucas said, and the rest of the team echoed his cheer.

From up on the platform, Orion's eyes seemed to follow Urban as she climbed onto her bike.

The crowd swelled around her. She forced herself to ignore them—and Orion—zeroing in on the road. Everything else was just noise. A blur. Unimportant.

With complete concentration, she waited for the signal to start—every muscle taut.

The speaker crackled. "Go!"

Urban accelerated. Adrenaline, and the very real prospect of death, pulsed through her veins.

She relied on memory as she sped toward the first turn. It was gradual and she slowed only as much as was necessary due to the rain, then accelerated through the rest of it.

Turn number two. Hairpin right.

Her bike started to hydroplane, but she regained control. She swallowed, reaching the next bend in the road.

Turn three. Sloping left. Go fast.

Despite knowing she should take the turn full speed, she recalculated for the road conditions and eased off the throttle.

Turn four. Right. Maintain speed.

Rain splattered noisily against her helmet. White light flashed around her, followed by a deafening boom.

Gritting her teeth, Urban hyper-focused on the race course.

A few more cautious turns and the landscape around her became lighter.

The rain lightened and Urban gradually increased her speed. *Turn forty-five. Right. Go fast.*

She had to slow down on two turns due to the slick roads, but otherwise maintained an impressive speed.

As she neared the last portion of the road, the rain stopped. A few turns later and she was above the cloud line. Sunlight broke through and the road was dry.

Reaching the tunnel portion of the race, she slowed. She curved around Reaper's Bend with a nice, manageable speed.

Then she accelerated, making up for lost time. So far, she'd managed to remember every turn perfectly.

As the transition lot came into view, Urban started activating the thrusters. The engine rumbled and grew warm beneath her as the front two wheels lifted up off the ground. The back two quickly followed.

By the time she reached the lot, she was flying. Urban yanked on the thrusters and shot skyward. The mountain slipped away out from under her as she soared, past the tree tops and the watching tower. The holo finish line pulsed up ahead. A crowd watched from either side on a hover platform.

Urban focused on nothing but the finish line, willing her machine faster.

Then she was past it.

Her retina display beeped, clocking her time.

8:49.07.

Nearly nine minutes. Her heart sank. Checking the score board, she found that currently she qualified, but there were still around two hundred racers left. All it would take was ten of them beating her time and she would be out.

Letting out a breath, she flew back down to the other side of the mountain where her team was already waiting.

"You did good," Lillian told her.

"Not good enough," Urban countered.

Lillian caught her eye. "You did the best you could with the weather."

"Let's just get out of this rain." Urban was trying desperately to will away the burning in her eyes.

The team went through the crowds and back to the house.

Inside, there was no sign of Father. Urban changed into slippers and peeled off layers of wet clothes so as not to track water and mud into the house.

She plopped onto a seat in the main dining hall next to a fogged-up window. Solstice entered the room and poured her a cup of hot green tea.

"Thank you," Urban said.

The girl nodded politely before turning to serve the others.

Urban wrapped her hands around her cup, trying to warm herself. She realized she was shivering, though not from the cold. Remnants of adrenaline were only just starting to wear off.

Ivan turned on a holo display of the race, and everyone watched in tense silence.

No one said anything as Solstice and another maid came back with steaming plates of stir fry dishes. Urban was too nervous to eat lunch and kept drawing the numbers 8:49 with her fingers on the fogged-up glass.

So far one racer had already beat her time, and they were only through twenty-one racers. However, the thunderstorm grew worse, and the next forty racers went by without beating Urban's time. Hope sparked inside her. The others began to lean forward, eyes fixed on the holo display.

Then the rain stopped.

The next two racers beat Urban's time, and following one was contender sixty-four.

One-hundred and thirty-six more racers to go. It takes only seven more.

The rest of the afternoon stretched on agonizingly slowly.

Sometimes a long streak of contenders would go by with none of them beating her time, and Urban and her team would grow hopeful. Then one would have a faster time, pushing her lower down on the score board, and the table would grow tense again.

They were down to the last five racers. Eight contenders had already beat Urban's time. The odds grew higher that she would qualify, but she tried not to get her hopes up.

The next racer didn't beat her time. Then the second, third, and fourth competitors were also slower. With each contender that went, the tension around the table loosened a little.

Only three left to go.

Urban noticed the next contestant leaning up against his bike. Something about his spiky hair seemed familiar. Her blood chilled.

It was Yokai Wraith.

Why were the Race Officials allowing him to compete? Surely they knew he was one of the attackers from the Dragon Boat Festival. *He must have some powerful attorneys.*

The Deadly Fourth started by weaving his way up the mountain with smooth precision. Each turn was flawless.

When he finished and stepped off onto the air pad, he waved with the confidence of someone who had life handed to him on a silver platter.

"And it looks like Wraith has just set a new personal record!" Clover exclaimed in breathless amazement. A moment later, his name appeared first on the scoreboard.

Urban's heart fell.

Even though she knew it was futile, she was really hoping Wraith wouldn't make it into the race.

Two racers left to go. If either one beat her score, Urban would be disqualified. Her whole body strained as she watched the second to last racer get ready.

After a moment, it appeared the racer had technical difficulties and was therefore disqualified.

Urban gripped the table tighter. She held her breath as the

last racer lined up at the start line.

The whole team was on their feet with eyes glued to the projection.

"Next up, we have our final contender for the qualifiers," Clover was saying. "He'll need a time of just under nine minutes. Let's see how he does."

The start line turned green and the racer shot forward. He took every turn with effortless ease. But, despite his smooth driving, his time lagged slightly behind Urban's.

Then he reached the transition lot. It took his car almost twenty seconds to convert, but once it was in the air, it propelled upward so fast, it blew over the small trees nearby.

"This contender has optimized for air travel, and it shows," Clover commented.

The racer shot through the sky impossibly fast. Then he was through the finish line.

Urban held her breath, intensely watching the score board.

This was it.

The holo display was dark for a split second. Then it lit up.

38

SCOREBOARD

NUMBERS FLICKERED ON THE SCREEN.

8:46.00.

Urban blinked at the holo display, trying to process the rider's score.

His time was three seconds faster than hers. Her stomach twisted in realization.

I didn't make it.

She stared at the holo, mind still unable to believe what her eyes were seeing. Defeat crept in like a slow, numbing poison, infecting the whole room. No one said anything for a moment.

"At least you're alive," Lucas remarked.

Urban tried to be grateful, but she couldn't stop the tide of disappointment. She'd let everyone down. She'd failed. What would they do now?

Without a word, the team began packing up.

It felt wrong.

The loss, stillness of the house, their sudden packing—all of it surreal.

All along, Urban had known failure was a very real possibility. But she hadn't imagined it would actually happen. That it would look like this.

Shame colored her face crimson as they boarded several

private helix-pods. Her team and family seemed to sense her need for space.

Once seated, Urban flicked on a holo of the news to try and distract herself, but her mind still wandered. She replayed the race over and over again in her mind. She wasn't sure what she could have done differently.

But that didn't matter. The divide between Enhanced and Naturals would remain.

I failed.

Tears stung her eyes.

A ping from AiE arrived, wanting to debrief once she was back in New Beijing at some point.

Urban's stomach curled.

What would they do now that she hadn't made it into the race?

"This just in." An announcer on the holo caught Urban's attention. "Unrest between Naturals and Enhanced spreads to New Sichuan, where the Race to the Clouds qualifiers just concluded."

The news showed an image of a crowd wearing face shields, black bandanas, and weapons storming forward.

Urban's eyes went wide.

It was the very road she'd just been competing on. The mob had signs that read: "Get rid of enhancements at birth" and "Stop enhancement corruption" and "We want equality."

Didn't they fear retaliation or arrest?

As if in answer, *Jingcha* arrived on the scene, a swarm of hoverdrones in their wake.

A flash bomb detonated. Blinding light bloomed and turned everything white.

As it faded, many in the crowd could be seen holding their ears or kneeling on the ground. The *Jingcha* rounded them up, using stun pikes and nano cords to bind them.

Urban wondered what would happen to those arrested for rioting. A sosh infringement? Prison?

Who were these people, and why were they rioting now?

Was it possible Urban's declaration about being the hybrid among the Capitol Prefects was finally spreading? Or maybe it was possible that, despite being cut short at Dragon Boat Festival, people had figured out what she was trying to say?

So many questions.

Should we resort to violence to capture the media's attention? Would change be faster that way? Would a little brutality now save us from civil war later?

She thought about the smoked outlines of the Western cities burning from the revolution and the Hutongs exploding. No. Violence wasn't the answer.

Maybe it's not up to me anymore.

Blossom and the genetics team would continue their study of Urban's DNA, but otherwise, she would be free.

The thought only brought a wave of guilt. Try as she might, Urban couldn't shake the feeling that her role in all of this wasn't over yet.

Only one thing was clear.

They were running out of time.

39

THIRD WHEELING

"UP! UP! UP!" A VOICE ORDERED.

"Wha–" Urban jerked up in bed. She lifted a hand to shield against the sudden brightness flooding her room. The blinds retreated upward into the ceiling of their own accord.

She rubbed her eyes.

Lillian leaned against the wall. "Listen sis, I know you have a lot going on right now, but you can't just keep sleeping. It's been two days."

"What are you doing?" Urban muttered.

"What you would do for me. Now get up and put these on." Lillian tossed a pair of workout clothes onto the bed.

Urban groaned and pulled her blanket over her head.

Instantly, the covers were ripped off, and, in one swift movement, her sister had her trapped in an arm bar.

"Let me go!" Urban tapped out.

"Promise you'll train with me. It's not like you have anything better to do."

"You're the worst." Urban yelped as Lillian pulled harder.

"Promise." Lillian's voice had the obnoxious tone only older sisters could master. "Thirty minutes. That's it."

"Fine," Urban breathed.

Lillian immediately released her hold and Urban rubbed at

her arm and glared at her. "You do know there are other ways to convince people to do things other than wrestling, right?"

"But why use them when jiujitsu is so effective?" Lillian grinned.

"Effective *wo di pi*," Urban grumbled. All the same, she shooed Lillian out of the room so she could change and get ready.

Twenty minutes later, Urban found herself at a gym Lillian claimed was one of her favorites. Urban was just grateful it was mostly empty and her banned status didn't stop them from entering.

They made their way to a large open mat where Ash stood waiting for them.

Urban immediately turned to her sister. "I didn't invite him this time, I swear."

"I know," Lillian said simply.

Urban looked at her sister more closely. "Did you invite him?"

"He's part of your security team." Lillian's pace increased. "He probably just decided to join on his own."

As she reached the mat, Ash beamed at Urban.

"Ash! It's good to see you again—"

"It's *Master* Ding now," Ash corrected, grin still on his face.

Urban arched an eyebrow as Ash withdrew a sharp, wing-shaped blade and swung it in an arc at his side. "I passed my exams. You're now looking at a Master of crane-bot. This is my hard-earned laser hand ax." He stopped and brushed off an invisible speck of dust with a flourish, drawing attention to his new red and gold combat uniform.

Urban gave him a mock salute.

She turned back to Lillian. Her sister was staring at Ash with a strange expression.

"Lillian?"

Lillian jolted into awareness. Her cheeks tinged pink. "Jiujitsu starts now!" she barked.

Urban hid her amusement as they started working on inverting and guard recovery while Ash stood by watching. Occasionally,

Lillian would use him to demonstrate a technique.

"Did you know I've started learning underwater martial arts?"

"Hydro Combat?" Lillian momentarily stopped practice. "Lucas is teaching you?"

Urban nodded. "He's pretty advanced."

"I doubt that." Lilian snorted. "Not to mention, that's the easiest martial art to learn." She side-eyed Ash. "After crane-bot, that is."

"What?" Ash feigned outrage. "Let's see you try to dodge and weave while *flying*! Crane-bot is the most prestigious, most—"

"Useless," Lillian interrupted. "Why would you need to spar mid-air? Seventy percent of fights get taken to the ground. Jiujitsu is the most practical."

Urban smiled as her sister and Ash continued to argue which martial art was superior. But as she watched, an ever-present ache in her chest intensified.

Her throat thickened. She wanted badly to go check on Everest. She just wasn't sure she could face him after not making the qualifiers. He had risked his life for her, and she had lost.

She forced all thoughts of Everest and the race far, far away. Somewhere they wouldn't threaten to rear up and crush her.

She threw all her effort into the next round of drills. But, for some reason, she felt oddly wobbly and lightheaded.

Lillian was at her side in an instant, concern in her eyes. "What's wrong?"

"I'm just—feeling a little lightheaded." And dizzy. She tried to stand straight.

Lillian's expression grew serious. "Sit. Transfer your biometrics to me."

Urban obeyed, and Lillian's eyes glazed over as she read through them in her retina display. Her lips tightened. "You're dehydrated and have low blood sugar. Have you eaten anything in the last forty-eight hours?"

She actually wasn't sure.

Lillian rummaged in her bag once more, returning with a small packet. "Put this in your water. Extra electrolytes."

Urban took it and emptied the packet into her water bottle before taking a drink.

Lillian watched her with sharp eyes. "Drink all of it." Her tone left no room for debate.

Urban did as directed, and slowly, she started feeling better.

"You need to take better care of yourself," Lillian's admonishment was firm but gentle.

"Why?" Urban loosely waved her hand. "Why does any of this matter anymore?"

"It matters because you matter," her sister said.

Urban could feel the tears coming again.

Lillian looked her in the eyes. "Losing a race doesn't change that."

In the following silence, Urban waged war against her emotions. *I will not cry.*

She managed a wobbly smile. "So, are we done with torture for the day?"

"Excuse you," Ash interjected. "It's not every day a Master of crane-bot graces you with his presence." He huffed. "Done with torture, she says."

Urban smiled for real this time. "No one cares about your title, Ash. Except my sister."

"Hey," Lillian protested. "Martial arts are extremely challenging to gain mastery over, and involve a lot of brain use too. Take jiujitsu, for example. Did you know that one of the founders, Helio Gracie, adapted judo moves to work for smaller people? It emphasizes technique and leverage over brute force and is one of the few martial arts that allows smaller practitioners not to be disadvantaged. Tell me that's not brilliant."

Only Lillian would find such facts fascinating. Though, by the look on Ash's face, she wasn't the only one.

I miss Everest.

"I have to go." Urban began collecting her things.

Lillian looked at her sharply. "Where are you going?"

Urban hesitated. "To the hospital."

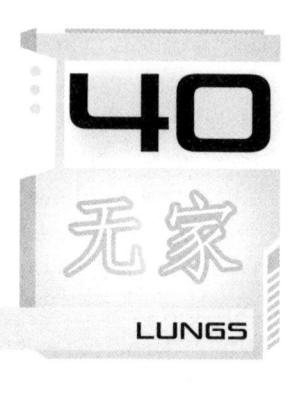

40

无家

LUNGS

URBAN'S EYES GRADUALLY ADJUSTED TO THE darkness of the hospital room.

Everest was still beyond the viewport, suspended in blue liquid. Without his usual strength, kind smile, and daring streak, he suddenly looked old. Like someone who'd survived the genetic revolution and emerged alive, but barely.

He looked so . . . lifeless.

It was surreal seeing him like this. As if this was just one long nightmare she would be waking up from at any moment.

As a KOL, Urban had learned there were a great number of things she had power to control.

Everest's life, however, was not one of those things.

Helplessness welled up within her as she watched him. *There has to be something I can do.*

An Inventor in a white lab coat appeared, and she flagged the man down.

"Dr. Song!"

"Hello there . . ." The doctor paused. "Urban."

Urban skipped the formalities. "How is Everest?"

Dr. Song looked grave. "His white blood cell count is rising."

Five percent survival rate. "Will he need another transplant?"

"Possibly. We've already started him on immunosuppressant

medications. Hopefully that will help with the body's rejection reaction and allow the transplant to take. Give it another week. In the meantime, we are keeping him in an oxygen rich environment to keep him stable."

Urban glanced back at Everest's limp form floating in blue liquid again. "Is there anything else that can be done?"

"I assure you, we're doing everything we can," Dr. Song said kindly.

"Can I visit him?"

"You may." The doctor nodded with a smile, then left.

Taking a deep breath, Urban entered Everest's room. The space was cool and cloaked in silence, except for the gentle beeping from the monitoring machines.

Apart from his neck and face, the rest of Everest's body was hidden in the casing. Eyes closed peacefully, he could have been asleep, except for the unnatural tint to his skin.

No matter how many times Urban saw him like this, she'd never get used to the horror of it.

She stood there for several moments.

All at once, she couldn't bear it. She needed to see his eyes open. She needed to not feel so alone in this dark room.

Urban entered augmented reality and pulled up her recorded memories. Her RET-Anti-Hack flashed an update at her.

<Lee Urban, now you can view memories not just using facial recognition. You can correlate them with moments of increased heart rate or elevated blood pressure. Would you like to give it a try?>

She would be able to view memories with Everest in them when she'd had her adrenaline pumping. Urban selected the option, and a curated montage unfolded before her, overlaid on reality above Everest's lifeless form.

There was Everest whooping and hollering as he sped in front of Urban on his motorcycle as they raced through the Outskirts.

It had been one of her first times on a motorcycle, and her

heart had been pounding wildly at the danger of going so fast without any sort of regulations or safety belts.

The image faded and a new one appeared.

She and Everest stood at the entry to Auntie Lee's grand ballroom. Red paper lanterns hung overhead, and happy, upbeat New Year's tunes filled the air. Urban had been so nervous at introducing Everest to her extended family over the holidays. And she had to do it while hiding both of their Natural genetics and fake dating.

The absurdity of it made her smile.

As Everest took her hand, Urban looked down.

The holo was so life like, every scar exactly as she remembered it. She squeezed, fingers brushing empty air, and . . . his hand faded into nothingness as the next memory started.

Everest stood with hair slicked back in a Metropolis style and gold eyes shining. Urban took a second to place the moment. A tatt temple came into view, and she shuddered.

Then there was Everest at her jiujitsu gym as they trained together. Everest at Mooncake Festival with his parents. Everest giving her a necklace for her birthday. Eating noodles with him in the Hutongs on one of their first dates.

Kind, gentle, tough Everest, who took it upon himself to keep the Outskirts safe. Everest who made her heart beat wildly. Who believed in her. Who could always pick up on her mood and somehow knew the right thing to say. Everest who knew ginger bubble tea was her favorite drink.

Who knew her better than anyone.

Urban's vision grew blurry.

She stopped the images and closed her eyes.

It seemed unreal that Everest was holding on by a thread. That he might not make it. That she might have to go on continuing the fight without him—

Urban opened her eyes back to the dimly lit hospital room where Everest lay motionless. Her carefully guarded box of emotions burst, and she sank to the cold hard floor.

Tears streaming down her face, she leaned up against the casing trapping his body, no longer able to look at him.

She wasn't sure how long she sat there when another memory, not from her retina display, surfaced.

It was at the Dragon Boat Festival. She was on the ground after being trapped in the purple zone about to die. She had given up and collapsed to the floor then too.

Everest had encouraged her not to give up.

Using RET-Anti-Hack, she accessed the memory and froze it the moment Everest looked her in the eye.

The intensity in his expression seized her heart. Black locks of hair hung down in his eyes as he waited for her to breathe.

Everest always fought for me.

She unpaused it, and the memory of Everest spoke, gentle but firm. "It's not over yet."

Urban stared into his holo eyes willing his words to be true.

Then she wiped her face and forced herself to stand.

It's my turn to fight.

"It's not over yet." She repeated the words first as a whisper to herself. Then, turning to Everest, as a promise. "It's not over."

FUTURE STRAND

URBAN SAT IN A WHITE LEATHER ARMCHAIR overlooking a stunning view of New Beijing. Colorful Flyers and shiny new delivery drones hovered past the large windows.

Around her, the AiE board was already assembled, along with her parents. By their rigid postures, Urban had a feeling this debrief meeting was to discuss her failure.

A knot formed in her stomach. She spoke up. "I'm sorry I didn't make it into the qualifiers."

Sato Winter waved her off. "No need to apologize. It's an extremely competitive race and, like I initially said, the odds of you winning were slim to none."

Her words stung.

"In the meantime, the rest of our organization will assist in enabling the social standing of several Naturals to reach 75 and then facilitate their application for Metropolis residency. Everest being our leading candidate should he . . . recover."

She means not die. Oh, Everest.

"However," Sato Winter continued, "the process will most likely be within a one- to three-year timeframe."

Urban breathed in sharply.

"One year?" Ray growled. "We'll have a civil war on our hands before then."

"I'm afraid that's the earliest."

Violet's Inceptor eyes fastened on Sato Winter. "There have to be some Naturals who meet the criteria."

There was only silence.

Urban's mind was reeling—searching to come up with a solution. It was hopeless.

Mother cleared her throat. "I will represent the Naturals."

Urban's eyes opened wide. *What?*

"I meet the requirements," Mother stated, head held high. "I am a Natural."

Urban's thoughts stuttered to a standstill.

Sato Winter narrowed her eyes. "Mrs. Zhou, what is the meaning of this?" she demanded.

"I am a Natural. I have a sosh over 75. I have residency within the Metropolis," Mother explained calmly.

"Do you mean to suggest," Sato Winter said slowly, voice edged, "that you're a Natural and have been masquerading as an Enhanced this entire time?"

"Yes."

Urban gasped.

Little details that had never quite added up all began clicking into place. Why Father wouldn't let Urban take her mother's DNA for PKU's genetic scanners. Why, at the tatt temple, the memory of Mother as a child had been removed.

All along the Lees had been harboring *two* Naturals.

It also explained why Mother had always pushed Urban the hardest out of her children. Urban had been forced to study more, tamp down her emotions, follow the rule book, keep her head raised, get a high sosh—all because Mother knew exactly what it would take for her to pass as an Enhanced.

But why didn't she tell me?

As if sensing her thoughts, Mother's eyes met Urban's. They were as unreadable as ever.

The AiE council members began intensely discussing what this revelation meant for their strategy. How they could play it to their advantage and what it would take to get Mother officially on the voting council. But Urban's thoughts went round and round.

Mother is a Natural. Like me.

As soon as the meeting ended, Urban stood. She needed air. She'd only made it a few steps when the harsh click of heels followed.

"Urban! Wait," Mother called after her.

Urban slowly turned.

Mother eyed the hallway. "Perhaps we can talk somewhere else?"

Urban became aware of the guards watching them.

One hoverstop and a silent, awkward walk later, they were in front of a shiny ticket booth with a sign that read: "Future Strand Showcase: Unraveling the Threads of Tomorrow's Genetics."

An enhancement fashion show seemed an odd place to have a private conversation, but Urban wasn't surprised by anything anymore.

Mother extended her tatt and paid the entrance fee. Then they were inside a luxuriously grand lobby with holo projections of humans and various genetic enhancements. Small clusters of people holding glasses of wine gathered around the displays. Compared to their silk ball gowns and suits, Urban was extremely underdressed.

Mother is a Natural. The thought repeated endlessly as they made their way past clusters of people and hallways lined with exquisite artwork.

One particular piece of art jumped out at Urban and she slowed her pace to get a closer look.

It was a painting of a skinny boy grinning up at a night sky illuminated by fireworks. The signature at the bottom right was the character *Zhou*—Mother's maiden name.

Urban didn't have time to dwell on it, as she raced to catch up.

Mother led them up a set of staircases and to a private booth overlooking a long runway surrounded by people.

"Next up, we have a bio-luminescence enhancement," an

announcer boomed as a girl strutted down the runway. The room darkened until all that could be seen was the glowing blue girl.

Several *oohs* and *ahhs* emanated from the crowd.

"This enhancement is perfect for the late-night partier and one you'll definitely want for your little bambino to help boost their sosh. Currently, only ten are slated for Asian Federation this upcoming year, making this enhancement extremely rare."

The lighting came back up, and Urban and her mother took seats in one of four plush couches in the booth.

Most of the people attending the event were young couples. They wore the latest luxury brands and were draped in more diamonds and gold than the emperors and empresses of old.

"I have the bio-luminescence enhancement starting at one million points." The auctioneer's rapid-fire words opened the bidding. "Who wants to place the first bid on this rare enhancement?"

A holo sign flashed above one of the couples.

"Over there, yes!" the auctioneer gesticulated.

The whole event sickened Urban, and she turned away. "This is more private?"

"I never said it was." Mother smoothed her dress. "But I have an art show in one of the adjacent rooms below in thirty minutes." She pulled her hair out of its meticulous bun, letting it fall loose around her shoulders.

Urban had only ever seen this look a few times her entire life. Her mother almost appeared to be a different person.

Mother now looked at her steadily. "I've wanted to tell you the truth, Urban. I always have."

"Then why didn't you?" Urban blurted. "Why did you let me risk my life volunteering as the first Natural Prefect when you could have done it?"

"I'm sorry," Mother said quietly. "I never wanted to risk your life. Father and I debated and discussed it at length. We came to the conclusion it was safer for our family for you to volunteer. Your Natural genetics were going to be revealed soon anyway. But mine . . ." She paused, then went on.

"Mine were never meant to be public. It is too dangerous to have two Naturals in one family." She shook her head. "We are sure to be at increased risk now. But it's a calculated risk we have decided to take."

"But why didn't you ever tell me?" Urban asked.

Mother's eyes drifted to the fashion show below.

A muscular woman wearing a sequin leotard swaggered down the catwalk. Light blazed from her eyes.

"And here we have the latest enhanced synesthetic perception," the announcer went on. "With the ability to dial up or down any sensory experience. Too much body odor at the gym? Turn down the olfactory senses, and poof!" The announcer made a motion with his hands. "Gone! Want to fully appreciate that expensive glass of wine? Heighten your sense of taste and sense every floral and earthy note. Your child will thank you later."

"Did you know I've met one of the Deadly Five in person?" Mother said into the air.

Urban blinked, then thought back to one of the memories she'd seen at the tatt temple. It was of her mother as a little girl. She had watched as the Deadly Fifth killed someone right before her. Urban swallowed.

"I saw the memory from grandma's lens."

Mother rubbed her arms. "That memory scarred me for a long time. I was frightened by the Deadly Five." She looked at Urban. "It's why I've always been so protective of you, making sure you were never discovered as a Natural. Making sure I was never discovered, either."

Mother glanced at the fashion show, then back to Urban. "Do you know why that memory you saw was deleted?" She didn't wait for an answer. "When I was in middle school, my parents shipped me off to the Eastern Federation, where there used to be a program designed to equip Naturals to enter the world of Enhanced.

"In that program, they made every Natural swear an oath that they would only ever tell one person about the program and that they were a Natural. Otherwise, the program, and all of us linked to it, would easily be exposed. For me, that one person was your father."

"But what about Naturals? Do you care about them?" Urban thought of times with her family. She went on boldly. "It seems you have yourself so well disguised you've forgotten you are one."

"Did you see my painting downstairs?"

Surprised, Urban nodded.

"It's not of the latest skinny genetics. It's of a Natural. All my paintings are."

That one time I snuck into Mother's studio her artwork changed to display other images. Now, it makes sense.

"I create so that my painting reflects one way, but if you look closely, in every single piece, there are Naturals. The same goes for my poetry—it applies more to Naturals than Enhanced." She looked straight into Urban's eyes. "I care deeply about Naturals."

Urban couldn't think of what to say. She was still trying to take it all in.

Her mother placed a hand on her arm and looked at her questioningly. Her many diamond and topaz rings caught the dim lights, sparkling. Urban had always found Mother's rings, her perfection, everything about her—to be annoyingly fake.

But haven't I been doing the same for most of my life? Just putting on a mask to fool everyone in order to keep those closest to me safe?

How drastically she had underestimated Mother. Zhou Flora wasn't the person Urban had made her out to be at all.

Neither was Lucas.

I feel like I'm only just discovering who my family really is for the first time. How many other people have I misjudged?

Urban thought about Ash, her first real Enhanced friend. Then she remembered Coral.

Her true colors could have shown themselves earlier.

"My art show is about to start," Mother said, breaking into her thoughts.

"I—I should probably head home anyway," Urban stammered.

They both stood, hesitated, then Mother took Urban in her embrace. When she leaned back, she searched Urban's face. "I love you, daughter."

"I love you too," Urban whispered back, and she found that she truly meant it.

42

HELIX

AN UNSEEN FORCE CRASHED INTO URBAN AS she returned home. A moment later, Baozi shimmered into view. His flaming purple spots glowed as he purred and rubbed against her leg.

"It's good to see you again too." Urban smiled as she stroked her giant house cat.

Protective drones, Supers, and Inventors littered the house, making it feel less like a private residence and more of a public gathering. Urban wanted nothing more than silence and to be alone. And yet, after the past few days, she also had a greater appreciation for security.

Making her way into the main parlor, she found Lucas lounging on the couch playing a virtual game. Lillian and Father battled it out in a game of strategy. There was the sound of jade against cedar as her sister made a move. Lillian waved at Urban. Father looked up and regarded her for a long moment, then returned to the match. Urban noticed the fountain at the center of the room was still dried up, as if the Lees didn't plan to be at the house for long.

Urban sat on the couch next to Lucas.

"Don't distract me." Lucas' eyes stayed focused on his game in QuanNao. "I'm about to beat this boss. If I die now, I'll kill you."

Urban rolled her eyes, then watched her brother.

"Stop looking at me," Lucas said without turning. "It's distracting."

She was about to voice a reply when a ping marked as urgent appeared.

[Ding Ash: I have some info you and your family will want to hear. You free?]

"Ash has some news for us," Urban turned to the others. "I'm going to live request him."

Lucas groaned then blinked out of virtual reality. "You made me lose!" But he was only being dramatic as he leaned back in defeat.

A moment later, a holo of Ash's T-rex avatar appeared at the center of the dining room.

"Ash." Urban smiled.

"I'm so glad you all are safe." Ash scanned the room, eyes landing on Lillian, and she shifted uncomfortably.

"I'm so sorry to interrupt this family gathering," he went on, "but there's important news. An update on the Race to the Clouds."

"Does it matter? I didn't qualify," Urban reminded him.

Ash waved the question away with his tiny arms. "That's just it . . . you did."

The room went still.

Urban found her voice. "*What?*" It sounded like a squeak.

"You qualified." Ash grinned. "You get to compete."

She stared at him, disbelieving. "But how's that possible?"

"One of the other contenders received two red flags during a practice session. They're disqualified. The handbook states that in the event of a contender disqualifying, their replacement is the next person in line. That's you!"

Urban drew in a quick breath. "Really?"

"Yes! That's what I've been trying to tell you! You're going to compete in the Race to the Clouds *tomorrow*. Pack your bags, it's time for a flight back to New Chengdu."

Ash winked at Lillian before vanishing from the room, leaving them all in stunned silence.

Father sat rigid in his chair, and Lillian cast a worried glance in his direction. Something passed between them, a silent conversation of sorts.

Urban tried not to read into the exchange, but she tempered her elation. "Well, that's good news. I guess."

"Yes . . . good news," Father echoed staring off into the distance.

"Congrats, sis," Lucas piped up. "Seems you get your death wish after all."

Lillian stiffened.

"I'll take an atomic sake," Father ordered from one of their maids.

Lillian offered Urban her trademark encouraging smile. The one that meant she had zero faith any of this was going to end well, but she was rooting for her nonetheless.

"I'd better get ready," Urban said.

Back in her room, Urban let out a breath. She made a cup of oolong tea then sat cross-legged on her fluffy white rug, trying not to think about her family's response to what lay ahead.

Instead, she turned on some pump-up music and began packing. Her sound system resumed her playlist from the last time she'd been home. The TingBings blasted over her room's full-immersion sound system. Everest's favorite band.

The thought of him brought a sharp pain.

I have to fight. For him.

RTC was the only way.

Urban was grateful for this second chance to race but also very wary. Two people had died, and the real race hadn't even started yet. RTC was upholding its reputation as the world's most dangerous competition and she, more than anyone, had reason to cut corners when it came to her own safety in order to win.

Not to mention, there would be other racers on the road

with her this time, making it much more deadly. Like Wraith—who wanted her dead.

Also the never seen before obstacles.

No big deal.

Urban closed her eyes.

Her more immediate worry was Father. Now that he was away from the stress of the races, he'd grown sober, but that didn't change the fact that Urban was still without a coach.

If only I had made the top five in the qualifiers. Then I'd have more of a shot at winning, and I'd still have him as a coach.

Instead, she was on her own.

Father had already taught her a lot, and she had her team supporting her, but Urban felt lost without him.

Not having Everest only made it worse.

Are the immunosuppressants working for him?

Her thoughts spiraled. A gentle knock sounded on the door, jolting her out of them.

"Come in!"

Father opened the door and stood uncertainly at the entrance to her room. He was surprisingly sober. "Packing?"

"Yes."

He cleared his throat. "Would you mind if I came?"

Urban's mouth dropped open. "You want to come?"

"I know what I said earlier about not being your coach if you didn't make it into the top five qualifiers, but I've changed my mind. I wasn't exactly the most professional coach. You deserve better. If you'll still have me, I want to come."

Indecision warred in her chest.

Can I trust him?

Her mother wasn't the person she once thought she was. Maybe Father deserved a second chance too. Besides, she needed a coach.

Urban smiled hesitantly. "I'd like you there."

Father's face struggled to stay impassive. He inclined his head. "I'll do my best to be there for you this time."

"Thank you, Father," she said quietly. She shifted, feeling awkward. "Well, the pod is about to arrive. You'll want to be ready soon."

He gave a firm nod, then left.

Urban watched him go, baffled. Father was a piece of her family she would never understand. Right now, she needed to focus on the race.

She surveyed her packing.

"I think that's everything," she said to Baozi. Her cat blinked sleepily up at her before arching his back and stretching.

She took up her suitcase handle.

New Chengdu, here we come.

43

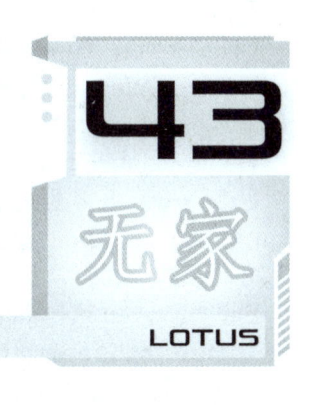

无家

LOTUS

HEAT RIPPLED THROUGH THE AIR AS URBAN set foot back in New Chengdu. The muggy weather had her XR suit humming to keep her cool. Despite the short trip, Urban's team were all gathered when she arrived at the house.

Everyone but Everest.

Poppy and Ivan were all wide smiles and energy as they greeted her and motioned her inside. Urban couldn't seem to match their enthusiasm.

"Hello, Urban," a gravelly voice said.

"Dr. Yukio," Urban said in surprise. "What are you still doing here?"

"Waiting for you," he said. "It seems we have just enough time for one final lesson. Come."

Art lessons were the last thing on Urban's mind.

"Today is a day to prepare yourself mentally." Father nodded at Urban. "Go."

Urban hesitated before following Dr. Yukio.

He guided her to the art studio. The room, warm and filled with the scent of paint and tar, exuded a minimalist beauty. It was sparsely furnished, with each item having a clear purpose and place. The openness and whitespace directed the eye, focusing attention precisely where it was intended.

The broken teaware sat in pieces on a table. Dr. Yukio arranged supplies of rabbit hair brushes, bamboo tweezers, and a small pot of powdered gold. "We'll start where we left off."

He gently sanded down the final parts of his pot.

Urban took a seat at the table and ran a finger over her own creation. She marveled at its smoothness, despite the cracks and fissures in it. Reaching for her pot of powdered gold, she carefully applied some with her brush.

"Why kintsugi?" Dr. Yukio asked. "Why do we preserve this ancient art form?"

"I don't know," Urban confessed.

Dr. Yukio's mechanical eye darted at odd angles before focusing on her.

"The art of kintsugi is about drawing out beauty from the ashes, joy from the tears, wholeness from the broken."

He continued slowly, methodically working. "It's also about patience."

Urban pondered his words as she added the finishing touch of dust, then stood back and admired her work. The teapot was different now. Even though it had the same shape and coloring, what was once a rather plain black tea-pot had taken on new life. The cracks and fissures snaking up its sides were covered in glittering gold. It was unique. It had been restored. It was both broken and whole at once.

And.

Urban contemplated the word. Two things at once connected by the word "and." *Is it possible that I am an "and" too?"*

She thought about her Natural roots. Her Enhanced life. She'd always seen them as two separate identities. If she was doing well fitting in as an Enhanced, she felt like a fraud. But in the Outskirts, she also felt like a fake. If she was doing well at embracing one, she felt a tug of neglect at the other end.

She was always hiding a piece of herself.

But what if, like the teaware, she didn't need to hide the broken pieces of her identity? What if piecing them together and putting them on full display made her even more beautiful than she ever could have been before?

What if I can be Enhanced and Natural?

The thought gave her goosebumps.

She'd always straddled two worlds. Now she could connect them, glue them back together into something beautiful.

As the hybrid, I am both.

Urban awoke the next day to darkness. She was disoriented for a moment, until she remembered she was back in New Chengdu, and not in her own bed back home.

Sitting upright, she drank some water and set a timer for fifteen minutes to hydrate again. All the travel had left her exhausted, but she would control what she could.

Downstairs in the kitchen, she ate prepackaged egg snacks. The latte machine sent phantom whiffs of caffeine her way, but she resisted its siren song.

She was about to leave, when footsteps creaked down the wooden staircase. A moment later, Father entered the room.

"*Zao,*" he said.

"Good morning to you too."

He took a seat at the island on the opposite side of Urban.

"Weather's looking tense," he noted.

"Yes."

"You should probably get changed soon. Croix left your gear over there." Father pointed at a mesh bag with wrapped parcels.

Urban finished her last few bites, then picked it up and went to her room.

There, she put on her silky smooth under armor. Next, she placed the smart exterior layer with the Gamelyon logo on it. Black plates conformed perfectly to her body.

Urban hoped she wouldn't need the smart armor. The memory

of the rider who'd slid off the mountain during practice flashed in her mind's eye. The suit could only do so much.

Taking a steadying breath, she donned her gloves and leg guards—each made of what looked like solid gold.

Urban spun in a slow circle in front of the mirror, admiring the Croix logo glowing on her back. She looked like a real racer. *I wish Everest was here.*

Outside, her guards escorted her to the race track, pushing their way through the crowd and clearing a path for her.

She was grateful there was a roped-off section designated exclusively for contenders and their pit crew. Heavy security patrolled the area, not allowing anyone else in.

"I wanted to give you something." Father handed Urban a large object wrapped in smart silk.

Tentatively, Urban took it and was surprised by its weight. The silk fell to the ground and she stared, stunned.

She held a helmet made of reinforced blue gears and shiny attach points outlined in gold. The visor was multi-colored with a purple hue. At the back, all the gears and parts tapered so that it looked like it had small fins streaking behind it. The helmet's visor had etched into it a single lotus flower and their family's motto: Winners make their own luck.

It was her father's legendary racing helmet. The one he'd won with so many years ago.

"I know winners make their own luck but . . . I thought you could use a little extra today."

Urban reverently held the priceless family artifact. "Thank you."

"I made some adjustments so it should be your size."

Urban donned the helmet, which fit snugly.

Father studied it, then nodded his approval. "Remember. Stay near the back of the heat as long as you can."

"Got it."

He turned to leave, but then turned back. "Urban!"

She looked up at him.

"I believe in you, daughter."

44

无家

RACE ON

THE CRISP MOUNTAIN AIR FILLED URBAN'S lungs as she inhaled deeply, the subtle scent of tea leaves calming her nerves. Around her, Inventors fine-tuned vehicles and race teams prepped for the big day. The air buzzed with excitement. Dressed in distinct styles, people from every Federation roamed about, their languages a clash of dialects and accents. Some pointed at Urban.

Her guards quickly steered her away.

<Race to the Clouds contestants, please head to the start line. The competition will begin in thirty minutes.>

Urban's guards carved a path through the clamor. Throngs of shouting fans and media drones from every Federation surged and pushed at race officials who were attempting to keep them at bay.

The scent of bean paste and fermented snacks tinged the air from vendor stalls. Beyond them, the road gave way to lush bamboo forest and rocky cliffs and rugged mountains. Somewhere along its craggy sides waited tigers, dragons, or whatever death-defying obstacles the race officials had chosen to inflict.

Urban tried not to think about the giant alligators from the PKU kick-off bash.

She climbed onto her bike and made her way to the back of the heat. Holo lines marked out ten spots, one for each competitor, Urban's spot being at the very back.

Urban eyed the other motorcycles. All were sleek but weightier than the average bike due to the extra machinery needed for flight. Colors ranging from fluorescent pink to luminous green pulsed with the undercurrents of light.

A pristine white, fully armored rev machine, stood in the lead position. The rider swiped at a holo display panel, adjusting settings. His seat had a full back that was almost concealed behind the wind-resisters that rose up above his head. A familiar venomous yellow serpent entwined with a bloodied stinger adorned his helmet.

Urban quietly turned away from Wraith.

This race is for you, Everest.

She ran a hand over her own motorcycle. The air was damp with humidity, and her fingers came back slick with condensation.

Urban studied her surroundings. Sure enough, wetness clung to everything—the green shoots of bamboo, the vendor stalls, and, worst of all, the road.

She'd have to be extra careful not to hydroplane.

"Five minutes until the Race to the Clouds will begin," a robotic voice intoned.

Some of the riders around her spoke into their com links. Others drummed frantic beats with their fingers. Knees bounced. Engines hummed to life. The air crackled with energy and excitement.

Urban stilled as a gradual prickling sensation crept up her spine. Twisting, she caught sight of a rider staring at her. A darkened helmet obscured the face, but Urban recognized the bike. Coral sat astride a familiar neon green vehicle watching her.

Orion stood near the sideline with arms crossed over his broad chest. His piercing blue eyes mocked her.

Urban tried to shake off the uneasiness coiling within her. She turned her focus to the road and was surprised when a ping arrived from Coral.

What mind game is she playing at now?

Urban blinked the ping away. Whatever the game was, she wasn't going to play.

Up ahead, the race official motioned the contenders forward. A holo counter above the start line flashed one minute until starting time.

This was it.

She snapped her visor closed and switched off augmented reality. Her bike rumbled to life beneath her with a low, powerful hum, its sturdy metal providing a steadying force against the frantic pounding of her heart.

"The race will commence in ten seconds," the announcer boomed. "Nine . . ."

The crowd joined in as the holo counted down.

"Eight."

Engines revved.

"Seven."

Slowly, the bikes inched forward toward the start line. Urban's fingers itched to yank on the throttle.

"Six."

Her muscles tensed.

"Five."

"Four."

Glowing red orbs clicked to life one by one on either side of the road, illuminating the way.

"Three!"

"Two!"

I have to win.

"One!"

Or die trying.

A surreal moment of calm—a collective pause—swept over the racers. The split instant between the countdown ending and the race beginning seemed to expand and stretch. Then it snapped.

Red orbs blazed green.

"Go!"

Urban smashed the throttle, bike jumping forward.

Too fast. She nearly crashed into the rider ahead. The way forward clogged with other contenders gaining speed as they wound their way up the mountain.

She concentrated on the racer in front of her. On the next turn, she accelerated past him.

The brakes engaged as she neared a bend in the road, then she streaked forward, closing in on the next two racers. Coral wasn't among them. Then again, she could be anywhere, with Camo-mode enabled.

Around Urban, bamboo forests turned into interspersed broadleaf trees. The sky above grew darker, and the air became cold and heavy. Crowds dotting the sidelines wore smart jackets and beanies pulled low over their eyes, their breath swirling and white.

Something in her periphery caught her attention.

The mountain . . . moved.

No. Not the mountain.

She was looking at a giant monster. The artificial creature was huge, nearly the size of the cliff from which it emerged.

The bike in second place skidded to avoid running into it, clipping the side of the mountain and spinning out of control. Urban and the other racers swerved as they passed the downed contestant.

The giant monster swung low, swiping at the remaining contenders.

Urban hugged her bike. Giant, razored claws swept above her, a gust of air brushing her neck.

Maybe Father was right. Urban zoomed past the creature and around the next bend to safety. *The back is the safest place to be. For now.*

Fortunately, the monster didn't pursue her, but she remained alert.

Urban didn't have to wait long for the next obstacle.

An odd buzzing sound permeated her helmet. At first it was so faint, Urban thought her com link had somehow been activated.

Another round in the bend, and the hiss intensified—a collective hum like a thousand XR suits clicking to life. A dark cloud moved forward.

The racers who had shields activated them. Urban's own propulsion shield activated as she reached the cloud.

Something shot through her defense, however, and splattered against her helmet. It was a huge fluorescent bug.

She knew exactly what this was. A tarantula hawk wasp. They had the most painful sting out of any insect. Given this one's enhanced size and coloring, Urban wondered if its sting had been modified.

She swiped at it to clear her visibility, but bug guts left a trail of slime across her visor.

Urban focused on the road again and jerked in surprise as another wasp smacked against her.

How were they getting through her shield? Then two more flew past, barely missing her neck and thigh.

They must be too small for the propulsion shield to pick up. Though small didn't seem the right word.

The last wasp crawled up her arm.

Urban violently shook it off, nearly losing control in the process.

The rider ahead also was having difficulty. Only, he wasn't so fortunate and, with a loud cry, skidded toward the edge of the mountain. Urban's heart stopped. The rider screeched to a halt centimeters before the drop-off.

Urban released her breath in relief as she zipped past the racer.

More of the tarantula hawk wasps struck Urban's suit. By

the random cries around her, they were finding ways to sting, despite the heavy smart suits. Her wrists and a small sliver of neck were the only exposed part of her skin. Surely the wasps wouldn't be able to reach those while they were going so fast.

And yet, that's exactly what they seemed determined to do. Had the wasps been programmed to target skin? As more of them careened into her, the ones that didn't die immediately picked themselves up and crawled toward her neckline or down her arm.

Urban did her best to shake them free while focusing on the road—and also trying to remember which turn she was at.

Turn sixty. Hairpin turn right.

She slowed and navigated the curve with caution.

Pain pierced her neck, startling her. Urban's grip on the bike wavered.

What just happened?

Stunned but gritting her teeth against the pain, she forced herself to focus and regained control of her vehicle. Had she been electrocuted?

Urban glanced down and uttered a scream.

Her suit was covered in a writhing black mass of pain-inducing insects. She frantically swatted at them.

She was now in seventh place.

The cloud of wasps thinned and Urban regained her speed. Ignoring the burning in her neck, she concentrated on the road.

For a few turns, there were no obstacles. Other than the death-defying switchbacks, someone who wanted to kill her, and the ominously fickle weather. And the kamikaze monkeys, of course.

But none of the wildlife interfered, and it was fairly peaceful on the race course. That is, until Urban reached a flat expanse.

Shifting, wispy objects poured over the mountain toward the racers.

The approaching obstacles struck the rider in the lead first. They engulfed him harmlessly before passing over and drifting toward the next rider.

They were holo projections. Nothing more.

But then the rider in the lead wobbled. Another racer slammed to a stop as more of the holo projections poured out. Urban barely avoided crashing into him.

That's when she saw the faces.

She recognized the fake ghost closest to her as *Popo*.

Her grandmother's kind eyes were framed in smile lines and her hair was pulled back. Only, that's where the similarities between them ended. The face was rotting, with sharp cheekbones protruding from under peeling skin.

They programmed the holos based off of our connections in QuanNao.

Her stomach soured.

The next ghost was Urban's grandpa. Then a classmate who had died in grade school. The next face had Urban's bike wavering.

Everest.

There were a couple of screams from the racers in front of her but she hardly noticed, eyes glued to the approaching ghost.

They were Everest's eyes, there was no doubting that. Seeing them open when he might not live . . .

He's not dead.

It's just another part of the race. An obstacle to overcome.

She firmed her jaw and accelerated, and Everest's holo passed over her. With it, came a sense she would never see him again.

Blinking away tears, she pressed on the throttle until her surroundings blurred with speed, passing one of the other contenders.

She was going too fast, but she was desperate to outrace the image now haunting her.

As she approached the next curve in the mountain, Urban tried to remember where she had been in her count of turns.

Berating herself for getting distracted, she slowed her pace.

Thankfully, she wasn't the only one.

The road up ahead was bottle-necked with racers taking it slow.

Which was just as well, because it turned out to be a hairpin curve. Urban recognized it. This was turn seventy-six. The next one, seventy-seven, was a gradual slope right leading past a waterfall and into the tunnel.

Encouraged by this knowledge, she accelerated again.

Only, as she drew nearer to where the waterfall should be, it wasn't there. Had she miscalculated? Turn seventy-seven had a waterfall next to it, didn't it? But where was it, and where was the tunnel?

Then her jaw dropped.

The waterfall had moved.

Instead of cascading down the side of the race course, it now engulfed the entire road. Racers up ahead slammed on their brakes to make their way into the tunnel behind the waterfall.

Maybe it was another trick of the eye. A holo.

The racer in front of her hydroplaned and crashed into the side of the mountain.

Fourth place.

Cold water sprayed Urban as she approached. This was real.

She braced herself for its full force, but she passed underneath, mostly dry. Water thundered down around her on all sides, the sound ricocheting as if she were in an enclosed space. Her force field had encapsulated her in an umbrella of protection and dryness.

Now, she was in a musty, dark tunnel.

Her eyes took a moment to adjust. Fluorescent light from the bikes ahead illuminated the tunnel in neon blues, reds, and greens. Steady lights blinked on the ceiling where the vid recorders observed their progress.

Urban was halfway through the tunnel when the blinking lights went away.

Strange.

She caught up to the next racer, hugging the side of his vehicle closely in an attempt to pass. Every time she tried, he'd swerve and cut her off.

Urban was on her next attempt when a strange sound punctured the air.

Another obstacle?

As her eyes focused, she saw Wraith stop at the other side of the tunnel, bike blocking the exit, aiming a device at Urban.

What is he doing?

The device glowed amber in the darkness. A sense of dread filled her. Her com link crackled.

"It's been fun playing games with you, Urban." Wraith's voice.

How was he accessing her helmet's com link? Unless . . . he had hacked it.

Her eyes latched on the unblinking vid recorders. *Had he hacked these as well?*

"But as all games must, our time together has come to an end."

The device was spinning and glowing red hot.

"Goodbye, Urban."

Light and sound exploded in the tunnel as a fireball shot straight at her.

45

BLACK OUT

RIGHT AS THE BLAST WAS ABOUT TO HIT URBAN, it struck an invisible force just meters in front of her.

A neon bike blinked into the empty space. Light and energy zipped through the vehicle, lighting it up in blue, then powering down.

In shock, she watched as Coral shimmered into view.

The blast struck her bike instead of me.

Coral cried out in pain and clutched at her leg, but she was alive. She activated her flamethrowers.

Wraith attempted to fire at Urban with a click. Nothing happened. He threw the weapon to the ground and peeled out.

Coral tried to shoot flames at Wraith, but her bike clattered onto the slick pavement. It slid, catching the tire of another racer. The momentum carried both racers out of the dark tunnel and into the light.

Straight toward Reaper's Bend.

The other racer jumped off his bike and clutched at the crags of a rock. But Coral was going too fast.

Urban raced out of the tunnel toward her but couldn't gain enough speed. Coral's bike hit the sharp curve and slid off.

Urban watched helplessly in horror.

She slowed her vehicle, and another competitor rammed

into her and she nearly lost control.

Coral.

Urban peered in her rearview mirror. Medbots and hovercrafts zoomed down the mountain after her.

She risked her life to save me. But Coral was so much more than this one moment. All the little things that made her who she was that Urban had taken for granted. And now, they were gone.

The thought of leaving felt wrong. She couldn't leave Coral alone.

In Urban's place.

She did this to save me so I could win.

I have to keep going.

Pledging a silent promise to Coral, Urban pushed her bike faster. She zeroed in on the road ahead, putting all her energy into the race.

Urban studied Wraith's huge white rev cycle as she drew nearer. His bike was optimized for flying. If Urban didn't pass him soon, she would lose.

Crouching lower to her bike, she squeezed the throttle. Wind pushed back, a tangible and powerful force.

She pulled up behind Wraith—the only one standing between her and victory.

Turn 126. Sloping right. A good one to pass on.

Urban leaned into it, leg extended. Bending her knee, she shifted her body weight so that she was nearly touching the ground.

She attempted to take the inside.

Wraith wouldn't let her have it. They were so close, Urban's arm brushed up against Wraith's leg. Accelerating out of the turn, Wraith kept his lead.

Urban reviewed a mental map of the course. The next two turns were too tight to attempt passing. But the third one, 129, was her next opportunity.

It was also her last.

After that, it was all switchbacks until the transition lot. No chance of passing.

Urban kept on Wraith's tail, waiting for her opening.

Turn 127. Turn 128. Here we go.

Heart pounding, she pulled into a straight portion of the road. Her surroundings blurred with speed.

Both she and Wraith drifted across the road to the other side, getting into position. Urban eased off the throttle and leaned to her left, cutting in beside Wraith.

Her bike wobbled.

She was a fraction of a second away from losing control, straddling a thin line between daring and danger. Her bike resisted giving into gravity due to her precarious balancing act, and she closed the gap between those last few centimeters that separated her from wiping out.

With precision and control, every fiber of Urban's body in tune to her bike, she held her position. She remained on the inside of the turn, gaining ground on Wraith. Then she was pulling out of it, this time in the lead.

A sense of relief filled her. *The race isn't over,* she reminded herself. *Focus.*

As she wound her way to the top of the mountain, she directed her attention on nailing each turn perfectly. Wraith fell further behind, but was it enough?

At the next turn, she reached the transition lot.

Urban activated the jet engines, the front two wheels picking up from the ground. A few seconds later, the back two lifted off and she was flying.

Yanking on the thrusters, her bike rocketed toward the blinking holo finish line above.

Wraith reappeared below. And quickly gained speed.

Every muscle in Urban's body tensed as she willed her bike faster.

Still, Wraith caught up.

Then he was pulling up alongside her. Electric blue eyes

stared back through a dimmed black visor. He grinned as he drifted closer.

Urban tried to accelerate but was already at max thrust, the g-forces crushing against her. Above, crowds of people gathered in the watch tower and on nearby hover platforms observing the end of the race.

Come on! Urban gritted her teeth.

Wraith's vehicle inched forward.

They were within eight hundred meters of the finish line.

I'm so close.

Wraith slowly pulled ahead. His voice cracked in her com link. "So long, little mutant. We'll find you later."

Mutant.

The word brought a shard of pain to Urban's chest. Then anger.

A vision of the kintsugi teapot flashed in her mind. Broken. Once an ordinary teapot, now something beautiful and unique.

Four hundred meters until the end of the race.

Urban glanced ahead at Wraith.

He roared. An earth-shattering sound that shook Urban to the core.

Wraith jerked away in surprise and fumbled his vehicle.

Wait. The roar wasn't coming from him. It was coming from . . . her.

Urban blinked, stunned. A spiderweb of cracks crept across her helmet. She quickly shut her mouth.

Too late.

A hissing sound filled her ears as air rushed in.

Shooting upward, the oxygen leaked from her cracked visor and she grew short of breath and lightheaded.

The glowing holo line above grew blurry.

Almost there.

She willed her eyes to stay open and sensed Wraith close, even as the edges of her vision blackened. Urban stayed focused on the glowing finish line as the crowds faded to black. The mountains below, black. Wraith–black.

Her fingers tingled and pressure built in her temples.

So close.

And then the finish line itself faded.

Black.

46

CHAMPION

A HEADACHE POUNDED AGAINST URBAN'S temples. Her whole body ached. Groaning, she looked up. Florescent white light burned down, and she immediately squeezed her eyes shut.

"You're awake," a familiar voice said.

"Father?" Urban croaked.

Feet pattered. "Urban." It was a statement of relief.

"What am I doing here?" Urban opened her eyes again, squinting at her surroundings. *Where am I?*

"The race!" She bolted upright. "What happened?"

"You blacked out," Father said. "Right after that, you passed the finished line and we regained access to your vehicle. We were able to guide you to a safe touch down."

"Yes, but—" She hesitated. "Did I win?"

There was a glint in Father's eyes. "You won."

Urban sank back into bed in shock. A sense of elation washed over her like the evening tide.

I did it.

It was as if one of the broken pieces in her had settled into place—made whole again. Then her brow furrowed as she glanced around the room. "Where is everyone?"

"The medical staff only let one of us in here, and the team

decided it should be me." Father searched her face. "How are you feeling?"

"Awful. But definitely alive."

"We were quite worried about you. When the vids went off and you were in that tunnel . . . we had no idea what was going on."

So the vids *had* been hacked.

"Wraith attacked me," Urban said. "He almost killed me but . . ." She uttered a small sound and sat up straight. "Where's Coral?"

"The girl who fell off the cliff? She's . . . recovering." Something about the way he said this made Urban uneasy.

"What do you mean *recovering*?" At least she was alive. That alone was a miracle.

Father avoided Urban's eye.

A knock sounded on the door, and Lucas poked his head in. "The media wants an interview with you, Urban. How long do you need to be ready?"

"Now. I'll do it now." Excited, Urban started to climb out of bed.

"Slow down. They're not going anywhere," Father told her. "Take a few minutes to get more fluids in you. And now that you're awake, the team can come visit. They've been waiting to see you."

My team. We won!

Urban agreed, and Father left to go get the others. A medbot entered with several hydration packs.

Urban's brain replayed the race. The Deadly Fifth's attack, Coral's sacrifice, the roar, and now . . . her victory.

I can't believe it. I actually won.

She'd done the impossible.

Urban didn't have time to dwell on it any longer as the door burst open. The rest of her family came rushing in and engulfed her in a giant, collective hug.

"You did it!" Lillian screamed.

Urban grinned.

Jasmine entered, stilettos clipping across the floor, cutting the joyful moment short. A host of makeup artists trailed in her wake. "Let's get you ready for your big moment."

Urban inwardly groaned.

Her family gave her some space, and Jasmine pounced on the opportunity. "The first few questions will all be easy and simple," she said, pulling a chair close to the bed. "Toward the end of the interview is when you'll drop the big news."

Stylists raced around Urban reapplying makeup. It all seemed to be happening to someone else—an out of body experience.

"The host will say: 'You are an Aqua, but you weren't genetically engineered for this race. How were you able to win?' And that's your opening." Jasmine looked at Urban critically. "And how will you respond?"

Urban recited her lines but inwardly kept thinking.

This is really happening. Everything we've fought so hard for. This chance to change the world.

Given instructions to change, the room emptied so Urban could get back into her now-cleaned race day silks and reinforced plates. She wore everything but her helmet as she left the room.

Accompanied by her guards, Jasmine, race crew, and family, she approached the building where her interview would be conducted.

Nervousness spiked through her. It all came down to this moment of her being in front of the media. Winning the race was only a means to an end. What she said in this upcoming interview would reach millions with the news of the hybrid.

It would determine everything.

Urban entered a darkened room. A mini amphitheater packed with people milling about surrounded a small set with bright lights. The stage was empty except for two sofa chairs and a glass table.

"Welcome, Miss Lee," an attendant warmly greeted her. "We have reserved seating for your family and any other key individuals." The woman motioned at a roped-off section on the front row.

Ash and the guards made their way toward the seating while Urban's family gathered around her for the last time.

Urban let out a shaky breath. "I guess this it."

"You'll be great." Lillian gave her an encouraging smile, but her eyes were wide and round. She looked almost as afraid as Urban felt.

"You're a Lee." Mother straightened Urban's ensemble. "Hold your head high."

Urban nodded, too nervous to speak.

"Yeah, try not to embarrass us in front of millions of people," Lucas chimed in.

"Lucas!" Lillian swatted at her brother.

"Urban." Father's tone was serious. "Since you first arrived on our doorstep, you've been making your own way. Now, make a way for others."

"It's time," the attendant stepped in.

Father moved away, Mother and Lillian following.

Lucas waited until the others left. "No matter how this goes down, we've got your back," he whispered. "Oh, and should things get dicey, I smuggled in several ink bombs, a voice enhancer, two hydro blades, an identity scrambler—"

The attendant cleared her throat.

"Just in case," Lucas finished, and then he too was gone.

"This way, please," the attendant said.

Urban was led up several steps to a brightly lit stage. She sat stiffly in one of the chairs while the media crew touched up her makeup, making sure not a wisp of hair was out of place.

"Are you ready?" the attendant asked.

Urban was convinced she would never be ready to speak in front of several million people but nodded anyway.

"We're sorry to inform you that our host has fallen ill," the attendant said. "But don't worry, we have a backup prepared for just such an occasion."

Right at that moment, the new host walked onto the stage and took a seat across from her.

Her heart stopped. She gripped her chair to keep from keeling over.

The new host was none other than Orion.

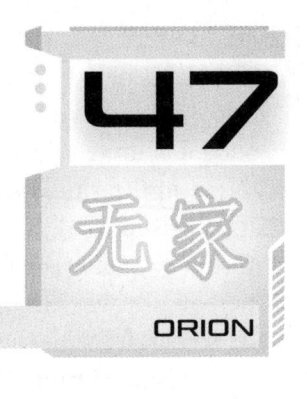

47

ORION

"HELLO, URBAN." ORION FLASHED A SMILE that made Urban's insides curdle. "Let me know when you're ready to start."

An attendant placed two glasses of water before them and then rushed off set.

Why is Orion here? What does he want? Is he going to try and capture me again? Urban's thoughts spun wildly.

"Just remember, this is all live," Orion said. "Whatever is said will go down in history."

There was something ominous in his tone.

He knows.

Urban glanced out to amphitheater toward her family, but blinding light prevented her from seeing anything. Did they realize what had happened? Only Lillian would recognize Orion. But what could her sister do?

"Quiet on set!" a woman yelled.

Everything stilled.

Why was her mouth suddenly so dry? Urban took a quick sip of water and folded her hands on her lap to try and keep them from trembling.

"We're live in three . . . two . . . one!" The woman pointed at the stage and the beeping yellow lights of the vid recorders shifted to red.

Orion turned to face one of the hovering vid recorders. "Welcome, ladies and gentlemen, to the 2124 Race to the Clouds Unlimited Division Championship Interview. I have with me in the studio, none other than Lee Urban, the rookie that surprised us all by winning this year's race."

Orion's mannerisms were relaxed, playful even. The switch in personality was jarring and reminded Urban of why she had to be so careful with Inceptors.

"Welcome." Orion turned to face her.

"Thank you for having me here." Urban managed to sound calm despite the havoc in her mind.

"Now, before we talk about the race, tell us a little bit about yourself, Urban. You've certainly made a splash in the news, from crashing PKU's AI to racing. Do you think competing in the AI games is a transferable skillset to racing?"

"No, I don't," Urban answered. "However, I do have experience as a racer in addition to my training in the AI games."

"Really?" Orion asked. "This isn't your first race? Why haven't I seen anything in QuanNao about any of your other races?"

Urban bit her lip. Jasmine hadn't rehearsed her on this.

Orion was trying to get her to admit to attempting a sosh boost, making her appear shallow. Which, in hindsight, she had been.

Urban had to show a different angle, one of bravery and adventure.

"The other races weren't, how should I put it . . ." Urban thought quickly, "*allowed*, if you know what I mean." She flashed a smile she hoped looked daring and didn't reveal the fear now pulsing through her veins.

"Sneaky! Staying off the radar by playing more dangerous games. We love it!" Orion threw back his head and laughed.

How is he such a different person?

The crowd followed Orion's example and laughter rippled

through the room. Urban glanced out over the stage, but again, the hot lights blinded her.

Just as quickly as the laughing started, it stopped and Orion turned serious. "Tell us Urban, what made you get into racing in the first place?"

Everest. Being in the Outskirts. The sense of freedom it brought her as a Natural trapped in the Metropolis.

But she couldn't say any of that.

"I guess I'm just an adrenaline junkie."

"I don't doubt it." Orion grinned jovially, and Urban found herself a little less jarred by this new version of him. "Now, let's talk about today's race."

They were getting closer to the moment when she'd drop the biggest news ever to break. Her palms grew clammy in anticipation.

Urban's answers came on autopilot. The tension in her chest at having to sit so close to Orion began to ease. So far, he hadn't been too bad of a host.

Urban shook herself.

Orion is using his Inceptor abilities. Don't let your guard down.

Her mind was only partially focused on the interview, the other part sorting out Orion's motives and anticipating arriving at the question. The one that was an open door for her to share how she was the hybrid.

"Well, we wish you the best of luck on future races and thank you for your time," Orion pronounced.

All the breath left her.

How is the interview already coming to an end? Panic gripped her.

He hasn't asked the question yet. This isn't supposed to happen.

Her fists tightened.

This is why Orion is conducting the interview.

Orion turned to face the crowd. "And that concludes our interview today."

No. I won't let him stop me.

"Wait!" Urban blurted loudly.

Orion turned slowly.

"I have one more thing I'd like to add," Urban interposed. "If I may." She offered up a smile, one she hoped appeared innocent.

Orion studied her a moment, expression calculating. His lips curved, but his cold blue eyes could cut through Zeolite.

"I'm so sorry, but we're out of time." Orion's voice was commanding and final, leaving no room for disagreement.

Urban scrambled to find another opening. This was chess in real time, and she was playing against an Inceptor.

A hundred ideas zipping through her mind in an instant. Only one seemed remotely plausible.

Orion was motioning to the camera crew to shut the vids down.

"I have a secret!" Urban nearly yelled. It sounded so silly, but it was all she had.

The vid recorders kept blinking. They were still live.

For now.

"It's a secret I've been saving just for tonight," Urban rushed to explain. "One I think you all will want to hear."

"Share it!" someone in the crowd yelled. It sounded like Lucas. He shouted it again in a sing song voice.

Another person joined in—Lillian. Then Ash.

Then a blaring, off-key voice. Lucas' voice enhancer. If Urban hadn't been so terrified, she might have laughed.

"Share it! Share it!" The chant rose up, swelling and gaining momentum.

Orion observed the crowd as the chorus swept over the audience. Too late to go back.

His smile was still firmly in place, but a muscle ticked in his jaw. He quieted the crowd with a gesture and faced Urban again.

To the public, he was still the jovial host. Up close, there was something dangerous in his expression.

He bent toward Urban so that only she could hear his next words. "I hope what you're about to say was worth Coral's life."

A wave of nausea overwhelmed Urban.

Her mind reeled as Orion leaned back, a wicked grin on his lips. He was playing mind games.

And yet . . . it was hard to tear her mind away from his words. What did he know of Coral's accident? Surely she wasn't dead. Was she?

Orion was motioning at the cameras again, and Urban realized the lapse in time.

He's just trying to distract me.

Fury bloomed in her chest.

I won't let him win.

Urban forced thoughts of Coral aside. Instead, she focused on her family. Even though she couldn't see them, knowing they were close brought her renewed strength.

The Lees weren't perfect, but she wouldn't have made it this far without them. Father as her coach. Lillian helping with AiE for many years and running the propulsion shield when Urban needed it most. Lucas saving her from her underwater prison and proving a supportive brother despite his jokes and pranks. And above all Mother, who all along had been a Natural teaching Urban how to hide in plain sight. Who even now risked her life to be the first Natural representative on the council.

All of them fighting together for a cause bigger than themselves. And now it was Urban's moment alone.

To fight.

The Enhanced used to intimidate Urban. But now, as both a Natural and Enhanced, she had a power uniquely hers. She could fight for both worlds to coexist.

Urban corralled her thoughts, and squared her shoulders. She looked straight into the closest vid recorder. "I know I may have caused one of the biggest upsets, as a rookie winning the Unlimited Division. But when you know my full story, it really shouldn't come as a surprise."

Orion's gaze bore darkly into her, but she wouldn't back down now.

"Some of you have heard rumors of the hybrid. Someone with genetics that allow for enhancements to be added later in life. I'm here to confirm those rumors. The hybrid exists."

A murmur rippled thought the crowd.

"I am the hybrid."

48

无家

FALL OUT

ORION MADE A SLASHING MOTION AT THE CAMERA woman, and this time, the vids blinked off.

No one moved.

Then the exclamations and whispering began. Orion's glare sharpened and his hands twitched.

Urban stood.

Without waiting for dismissal, she began to walk offstage, trying to remain calm and composed. Or at least appear that way.

In an instant, her guards and family surrounded her, ushering Urban toward a back door. Lillian's drones took flight and hovered protectively above.

The crowd grew louder.

Violent.

A man launched himself at Urban, but Lillian's drones took him down. Another woman smiled at Urban and tried to get her to snap. An angry-looking teen rushed menacingly at Urban.

Lucas swept out his hydro blades and blocked the way.

The teen faltered.

Then the whole amphitheater ignited in chaos.

"Run!" Trig ordered.

Urban and her family pushed their way past people and to a

back door. Then they were running through the hallway, down stairs, and out onto the road.

There were several waiting armored vehicles at the ready. The Lees piled in, and they immediately zipped through the New Chengdu Metropolis to a transport hub.

Lucas cocked a grin. "Well, that was fun."

Lillian shook her head.

Urban tensed, waiting to hear from her parents. They shared a look, and Mother turned to Urban, red rimming her eyes. "We're so proud of you."

"You crushed it!" Lucas extolled.

Lillian looked at her sister with affection. "Not only did you survive an impossible race, you stood up to Orion." Her voice, which once held such admiration for their jiujitsu instructor, now was filled with contempt.

Urban could hardly take it all in. She sat there numbly, nodding along as if they were all talking about someone else. Someone other than her.

Yet, despite her victory, despite her family being there, something was missing. There was a hole in her heart without Everest.

How was he recovering? She hadn't received any updates and was hoping no news was good news.

Urban tried not to think about it. Soon enough she'd find out.

New Beijing's Metropolis brightened the horizon as their pod zipped closer. The sun faded and the lights from within the skyrises blazed out.

Remembering something, Urban turned to Father and said quietly, "You never told me Phan Fox from your race was also your friend."

Father stiffened. It was a moment before he spoke. "He was my best friend. We were neighbors, and when my parents divorced, his family took me in."

Urban knew her grandparents had been divorced, but no one ever talked about it. The event brought too much shame.

Urban had never thought about what it must have been like for her father growing up.

"Mooncake Festival, Lunar New Year, Dragon Boat Festival—I spent most holidays with the Phans. They were like family. Growing up, Fox and I always talked about racing. It was our dream. Fox was an Aqua, and with me, an Inventor, we both had the genetics for it, even if we weren't specifically designed for the races.

"We trained together. Years later, when we both qualified for the races, we were ecstatic. And naïve. During our race, despite being the two rookies, Fox was in the lead and I was right behind him. As we neared one of the last turns, I accidentally clipped his vehicle. He lost control and wasn't able to make it. He—he fell off the cliff."

Father blinked rapidly.

Urban had never seen a display of emotion like this from him. She wasn't sure how to respond.

Mother put a comforting hand on his knee.

"I saw the vid," Urban said softly. "It wasn't your fault."

Father shook his head. "I knew I shouldn't have followed that close. I was just so competitive." He closed his eyes. "Because of that, I killed him."

He opened his now clouded eyes. "The Phans haven't spoken to me since. The only family that ever felt like home."

Urban and her brother and sister kept a respectful silence. Mother murmured something to Father.

Then Lucas shifted. "You know you have us, don't you, Dad? We're your family."

Father looked at his son a moment, then his gaze flickered over the rest of the family, one by one, and his face softened. A waking awareness came to his eyes.

He started to reply when an urgent location request appeared in all of their retina displays.

It was AiE.

49

HYBRID

FATHER ACCEPTED FOR THEM ALL, AND THE projected form of Sato Winter and the rest of the AiE board members appeared at the center of their pod.

Winter's silver was hair pulled back, giving her a more youthful appearance. "Congratulations, Urban, on a successful mission." Her sea-foam blue eyes glittered.

Urban couldn't tell if the woman was pleased or disappointed— it was so hard to tell with her.

"Another augmented-free campaign has begun," Sato Winter continued, "but I think it's too late for news of the hybrid to be stopped. You're now the world's top trending KOL with a sosh higher than even the Premier of the Asian Federation."

Urban's mouth fell open.

She quickly checked her sosh. Sure enough, it had jumped to a whopping 99.

"The pressure it puts on our political allies and opponents is in our favor. Already several of the Prefects have converted to our side."

"That's great news," Father declared. "We're headed back to New Beijing and will await the results there."

"I'm afraid that won't be possible." Sato Winter's expression changed. "Someone leaked your apartment's location on the *heiwang*."

Urban gasped. "The dark web? Why?"

In answer, Winter sent them a live vid. It was of the lobby to their apartment complex. The space was packed with so many people it was hardly recognizable. There were some cheers, but most were involved in launching squid bombs in the air or producing graffiti on the walls. The *Jingcha* tried to get control, but there were so many people, they spilled out into the road, blocking traffic.

Mother's hand covered her mouth.

"That isn't the worst news," Winter's commanding voice cut into her thoughts.

What now? Urban was feeling faint.

"It's about the the Natural Rights Act. It was in our favor by one vote in the preliminary polls. But last night, one of our supporters died in her sleep. And we don't think it was of natural causes."

Father watched Sato Winter. "You think she was murdered?"

"Yes." Winter gave a single nod. "We've already opened a report with the *Jingcha*, and the primary suspect is one of the Deadly Five."

Mother gasped.

Father swore.

"We're doing everything we can to find one more Prefect to convert to our side, but so far, we're out of luck. Unless we can come up with something, it's going to be a tie. Which means, it will come down to the Head Prefects' vote and they won't pass it."

Everything she'd worked so hard for was slipping away. Everest's sacrifice. Coral's. Everything. Gone.

Urban wanted to cry. To roar. To disappear and never come back. The pain was too much.

"Is there anything that can be done?" Father's face was pale.

"We're two days away from the vote. So far, we haven't been able to come up with any ideas."

"Are there no more Prefects we can convert to our side?" asked Mother.

"None," Ray said bluntly. "We've tried every last one of them."

Urban hesitantly leaned forward. "Would getting me back on the news help at all?"

"Doubtful." Glacier ruffled his crimson wings. "You've already done as much as you can. More media coverage won't change anything."

Everyone fell into a heavy silence.

We can't give up.

An idea bloomed in Urban's mind. It was insane, but it could work.

She looked up to face the council. "I have a proposition."

"Yes?"

Urban hesitated. "I'd rather not say it now. Just in case it were to be leaked ahead of time."

Sato Winter raised an eyebrow at this. Several AiE members frowned, but Ray nodded approvingly.

"And how will we know if this idea has any merit?" Winter inquired.

"You won't," Urban stated firmly. "You'll just have to trust me. But it will require getting me back to the Prefects before the vote goes up."

The council was silent again.

Sato Winter was the first to move. She let a long breath. "This is rather bold."

"None of what I've done will matter if we can't sway the vote," Urban pointed out. "This may be our last chance."

Council members exchanged quick glances.

"You can trust me," Urban said. "Haven't I already proved that in the Race to the Clouds? Give me one more shot."

"We are out of time and options," Sato Winter said. "I'll see if I can get you on the agenda tomorrow."

"Have my topic listed as: Genetic Trait Standardization and Compliance Protocols," Urban said.

Ray's eyebrows shot up. "That sounds like it has nothing to do with the Natural Rights Act."

Urban smiled knowingly. "Exactly."

50

PREFECT

URBAN SAT AMONG THE PREFECTS. SO FAR, NO one had paid her much attention. She was grateful, for once, at how vast the room was.

The cavernous red space was still divided into eight sections by gene pool, but this time, there was also a small, newly carved out section reserved for Naturals. Mother was the only one sitting there. She caught Urban's eye and gave her a subtle nod.

Urban expelled a breath.

This will work. It has to.

She glanced toward the center of the circular room where the Head Prefects sat on a raised dais at their long table. Beneath the enormous virtual flag stood the Capitol Speaker, wings tucked neatly behind him. He addressed the issue of foreign species imported to enhance crops.

Urban tried to follow along but was too nervous and kept checking the agenda instead.

After this topic, it was time.

She rubbed her damp palms against her smart suit. Unlike the last time, when she'd looked like a phony version of an adult in a pantsuit, she'd dressed in her favorite clothes and done her makeup the usual way. No more pretending.

"It's a two-thirds majority on the Grafting Invasive Species

Act," the Speaker concluded. "The bill is passed."

Urban sat straighter in her seat.

"Next on the agenda is Genetic Trait Standardization and Compliance Protocols."

Urban scanned the members in attendance. The ones loyal to AiE were obvious. They sat forward in their seats, rapt with attention.

The rest seemed less interested. The one next to her yawned, while another sipped tea with a sigh. Several made their way toward the break rooms.

"As you all know, compliance protocols have been a long-standing regulatory requirement," a Prefect began.

Sato Winter couldn't have picked a better person for the job. A few minutes in, even Urban, knowing what was coming, found her eyes glazing over.

". . . and in fact, we have someone here who'd like to provide further insight on the topic."

Energy zapped through Urban's legs and arms. She wasn't even sure when she had stood up, but she was suddenly aware of all eyes on her.

"What's she doing here?" someone angrily protested, and there was a chorus of disgruntled agreements.

Urban steadied herself. "I have a simple question. Is it possible for me to join the Prefects and to vote as a Natural?"

"What does this have to do with genetic trait standardization?" someone demanded.

"Everything," Urban replied.

The Capitol Speaker at the head table looked at her closely. "We already discussed the matter. The vote was decidedly a *no*."

Urban straightened, heart beat quickening. "How about as an Enhanced?"

"I'm very sorry, but that's not possible either."

"I belong to neither?" Urban confirmed.

The Capitol Speaker frowned. "I don't see why this is relevant—"

"Answer the question," Urban interrupted. "Please," she amended.

The Speaker eyed her. "I'm sorry, but no, you don't qualify for either voting class."

Urban's heart was now racing erratically. This was it. The moment that would determine everything.

"And yet," she began, "Precinct 488 states that every resident of the Asian Federation has a right to vote. If I belong to neither Naturals nor Enhanced, that means I belong to my own class. A class of not neither-nor, but of *both*. I am both Natural and Enhanced. One that currently has no representation. A class of hybrids, of which I would like to be the first representative."

Silence.

It stretched on.

Sweat trickled down Urban's neck. Many of the board members zoned out as they pulled up Precinct 488 to double check Urban's statement.

"This cannot be," someone said.

A low rumble swept over the house. Several of the board members began to argue, while those gone on tea breaks raced back into the room.

"This is not allowed!" a Prefect shouted his displeasure and others echoed his cry.

The Capitol Prefects at the raised table gathered together bowed low, intensely discussing. After a few minutes, the commotion died down.

One of them, a Super, stood. "She's right." Murmurs rippled across the room and he held up his hand to silence them. "As such, I have no other choice than to award Lee Urban the first ever position as the Hybrid Seat of High Council. She will acquire all the rights of a Prefect, including, but not limited to, voting, starting now."

Urban sat in disbelieving triumph, utterly stunned.

She'd done it.

51

无家

BIOLUMINESCENT

GLOWING ICE-BLUE LIGHT DRIFTED AROUND
Urban in the cool, dark reservoir, setting the water ablaze.

Bioluminescent.

That's what Father had called it when they'd arrived.

Since Urban had cast her vote on the upcoming bill, she had
been whisked away into hiding at one of Father's underwater
luxury apartments. The results hadn't been announced yet, but
Urban's vote should have swung it.

At least, that's what AiE said.

Urban remained wary. She'd had too many surprises over
the last few weeks to believe it until she saw it.

She still couldn't believe she'd started her own gene pool
representation as a hybrid.

Despite being on the banned list, news of her genetics had
spread. Everyone, it seemed, knew about her and what her
DNA meant for enhancements going forward.

As a result, unrest had grown worse in some places. But in
the Asian Federation, everyone seemed to hold a collective
breath—waiting to see the results of the upcoming bill.

It all came down to Urban's vote.

The verdict would be announced that evening. Each minute
leading up to it passed with agonizing slowness.

Electric blue orbs swirled around Urban, a canopy of underwater stars hidden within a lake. The scent of mossy freshwater greeted her. She breathed in and out, still marveling at her ability to do so.

So much had changed.

Her brain could hardly process it all.

Everest's recovery was tenuous and slow, but his body hadn't rejected the new lung transplant. The immunosuppressants had worked. The doctor said they were past the worst of it, but Urban still hadn't been able to see him.

She checked to see if there was any news from him. Her heart skipped several beats upon spotting a ping.

[Everest: I'm officially on the mend. I know you need to take extra precautions right now, but I'm dying to see you. Pun intended.]

Urban made a strangled choking sound halfway between a sob and a laugh.

He's okay. He's going to be okay.

The thought, once a blind grasping in the dark to a fool's hope, was now solid and real. She wanted to cry. To celebrate. To find him immediately and feel his strong arms wrap around her. To never ever let go of him again.

There were so many things they'd left unsaid amidst the chaos of the race and that awful moment when he'd sacrificed everything for her.

She sent a ping back and was about to close out, when an older one caught her attention. It was the message Coral had sent right before the start of the race.

After the lack of interaction with her over the past few months, Urban's AI had deprioritized it, and she had completely forgotten about it.

Hesitating, she opened the ping.

[Coral: Urban, I know you don't trust me, and you're wise not to do so. I once told you that I couldn't afford friends. I still can't. But I wanted to explain.

I have a sister. She was my only true friend, and Orion and the division of WEO they work for took her as a hostage. They used her against me and made me do unspeakable things. Everything I've done was to protect her. My goal has always been to free my sister.

I didn't want more friends. I was afraid they would end up as liabilities like my sister. But despite my best efforts, you've become just that. A friend. Which is why I couldn't let them keep you in the research lab. Why I had to free you. I will never forgive myself for turning you in to them. But I wanted to say I'm sorry.

My sister is almost free. Which means I will be too. Free to disappear and never follow a command to hurt someone—especially you. I just have this last race to compete in. I left you a special present in my old locker back on campus at PKU. Attached is the access code to it. Inside, you'll find what you're looking for. The microneedle patch.

I'm sorry things ended between us the way they did.

Thanks for being my friend, however brief it was. I'll never forget it.

Stay safe. Win.

Goodbye.]

Urban was frozen, staring at the screen.

I should have read the ping.

Tears began to flow down her cheeks, and soon she was weeping with unexpected agony of grief. Memories flooded her. Memories from their first meeting to the sudden appearance of her intervening mercy floated through Urban's mind.

The true Coral. In the end, a real friend.

Father had said she was alive but recovering.

Urban scoured QuanNao for an answer and found a news article.

Opening it, she scanned past the details of the race and stopped at a picture of Coral being airlifted away. Her body was crumpled beyond recognition. Urban's stomach turned at the sight.

Coral's injury list was long, grotesque, and Urban wasn't even familiar with half the words. Another section caught her eye.

"...paralyzed from the neck down and has been in a coma..."

Urban blinked hard to read the blurry words.

An updated story revealed Coral's parents planned to try one last treatment before sending her to a purple zone in a hospital to end her coma. And her existence.

Urban started to shake.

Coral.

Coral jumping through the window of their dorm room back at PKU and scaring her other roommates. Coral studying with Urban at a burger joint and explaining the meaning of her *weiji* tattoo. Coral shimmering into view in class with her backward hat and ridiculous high-top shoes. Coral introducing Urban to the Western Federation and teaching her how to two-step. Coral competing in the underground races to help protect her, and then again for Everest.

Urban couldn't stop crying.

I wish I could have said goodbye.

52

EVEREST

THE OUTPATIENT WING OF THE HOSPITAL WAS warm and welcoming. A stark contrast to the cold, dim surgical unit where Everest had been housed for all those weeks.

Urban passed medbots and doctors until she reached his room. Nervous anticipation tingled through her. She stepped inside.

The room was small, with only a bed, table, and two chairs in it. Oddly enough, there was a decoration on the table beside it. A painting of two goldfish chasing each other's tails. It was the one she'd given him ages ago.

Then Everest moved, and Urban had eyes only for him.

"Everest." The word was barely a whisper.

She was at his side in seconds.

Everest was still pale, but his skin had more color to it. Stubble lined his firm jawline, and his shock of black hair refused to be tamed, sticking up wildly. He blinked sleepily up at her, a slow smile spreading across his face.

Urban found it suddenly hard to breath.

"You're alright." She tried desperately to keep from crying.

"Urban," Everest murmured, voice low and throaty.

There was so much Urban wanted to say that she didn't know where to start. "You're looking better."

Everest reached for her hand. "Come. Sit."

Urban sat next to him on the tiny hospital bed.

"You're alright," she said again. The words sounded in her head over and over as if she were trying to convince herself this was real. For a moment, she wondered if it was a dream and she would wake and find him lifeless.

"Hey," Everest squeezed her hand lightly. "It's okay. I'm here."

Urban bent and lay her head on his shoulder, breathing in deeply his scent. He smelled different. More like a sharp sterilizing agent. His familiar jasmine and smoke only a faint memory.

This is real. He's real.

Tears pricked at her eyes.

"It's okay to cry," Everest gently whispered in her ear.

Urban sat up and clutched his hand, laughing through the tightness in her throat, a strangled, high-pitched sound. "I've done enough crying for a lifetime. I want to enjoy this. I only dreamed of seeing you again—" Her voice broke.

"Hey."

She looked into his raven eyes. "I don't want to get all weepy again." Urban tried to smile through her tears.

Everest kissed her hand, and they looked at each other for a long moment. "Tell me what happened after I went down. I know some, but I want to hear it from you. I want all the details of everything that happened."

Everest remained motionless as she went on to update him on everything that had happened. "It's almost unbelievable. Like there was something outside of you guiding the way."

Urban smiled. "I had a pretty good coach."

Everest smiled briefly back. "You did beyond what any coaching could do." He looked thoughtful.

She almost started crying all over again.

"What about reverse-engineering your DNA? Is there any development on that front?"

Urban realized she'd left out that part. "Oh! Coral left me a clue to finding the last microneedle patch," she told him. "We thought it was possibly another trap, but AiE sent an operative to investigate. Turns out, she was telling the truth. She had the third microneedle patch all along. It's in AiE's possession now. They'll actually be able to complete the work on the hybrid genetics."

Everest's eyes lit up. "That's terrific. It will be the basis for changing so many things and providing long-awaited freedom."

"But first, we need to get the Natural Rights Act passed," Urban said. "The results are released tonight."

"I still can't believe how you tricked them in their own game by playing the hybrid card." Everest grinned. "That's brilliant."

Urban's cheeks warmed.

"I'm honored to be in the presence of the world's first Hybrid Prefect."

For some reason, they both burst out laughing.

Suddenly, Everest's expression turned serious. "What about the Deadly Five?"

"Three of them were caught at Dragon Boat Festival. Dawn and Wraith escaped but were captured after the Race to the Clouds."

Everest's eyes flashed. "How?"

"Wraith thought he'd deactivated all the vids in the tunnel when he tried to kill me. And he had." She tapped her temples. "But it turns out when I installed RET-Anti-Hack forever ago, it had redundant security measures in place and recorded everything. Wraith was arrested and is now awaiting his trial. He's expected to plead guilty. Dawn was also implicated. Oh, and Lennox has resigned from PKU. Only Orion seems to have gotten off the hook, but he's been in hiding. Apparently, he's made a lot of Natural enemies over the years, and now they're catching up to him."

"Finally," Everest said grimly. He touched her cheek. "Finally, you'll be safe."

Urban inhaled a shaky breath.

"I tried to protect you—" He closed his eyes. "But I couldn't."
Urban stared at him. "Everest," she protested. "You did.
You sacrificed your life for me."

"All I wanted was your safety." His charcoal eyes opened and
deepened. "I'll never sacrifice you for a special cause again."

Urban had once asked Everest if he had to choose between
her and his mission which he would pick.

He had chosen the cause. His goal would always be to fight
for Naturals. But he had risked his entire mission—and very
life—for Urban.

She would never doubt him again.

Urban found him gazing at her.

"Did you mean what you said to me the last time you visited?"

Urban's brow furrowed.

"What you whispered." Everest pinned her with a look.

Urban's breath caught. Her face reddened.

Everest leaned closer.

"Urban." His black eyes a swirling vortex of stars against a
backdrop of deep space. "I love you, too."

Everest brought her head toward him and pressed his lips
gently against hers. Then his arms pulled her in tight.

Urban's heart danced and time became irrelevant.

Finally, Everest pulled away and pushed up into a seated
position, a smile playing at the edge of his lips. "Want to break
me out of this prison—I mean place?"

"Are you sure you're up for that?" Urban eyed him doubtfully.

"Absolutely. The hormonal and probiotic regimen they've
had me on has really turbo-charged my recovery." Everest flung
off his thin hospital blanket. Underneath, he wore a full-body
vital monitoring suit. "Besides, if one more medbot accesses
my biometrics, I'm going to go crazy."

"There isn't anything for you to change into," Urban
pointed out.

Everest waved her comment away. "Ah, but Ash smuggled
some streetwear in." He motioned under the bed. "I've been

waiting for the right moment to make my getaway." He grinned.

She grinned back at him and then left him alone to change.

When she returned, Everest was pale but fully clothed and standing. He walked with halting steps but refused Urban's help as they left the room.

"We could use the hoverchair," she suggested, seeing one lying abandoned in the hall.

"Definitely not," Everest said firmly. "I'll save that for when we're eighty and you've gotten yourself into more trouble and need someone to push you around." He looked at her and winked.

They shuffled into the hospital lobby, where the windows displayed a bright and sunny day outside. One full of life and possibilities.

Everest took her hand, and together, they set foot outside.

53

AUGMENTED

URBAN STOOD IN A LARGE PENTHOUSE ballroom next to Everest. She shifted her weight from one high heel to the other and smoothed her XR dress for the tenth time.

AiE insisted on launching a KOL watch party that night as the results of the Natural Rights Act were aired. Urban would have rather been alone with Everest, instead of among a sea of people. Some watched the news announcer projected at the center of the room, others exchanged nervous whispering. There were many quick looks in her direction.

She tried to ignore them.

The scent of soy sauce and ginger from fried *jiaozi* tinged the air. She glanced over and spotted its source. A snack table ladened with street foods and dishes stood in a corner, untouched.

Beyond it, windows wrapped around all sides of the room. Flyers and delivery drones zipped past in the fading evening rays. New Beijing sparkled in dazzling pomegranate red and terracotta orange.

At the center of the bustling Metropolis sat a small patch of flat land. A dome surrounded it, and inside, the air was hazy from wood burning. Tourists roamed its historical land, while vendors hawked their wares and trained pigeons flew in circles in synchronized harmony.

A section of space near the middle lay in ruins under blackened bricks and caved in buildings. It was roped off for construction.

Urban found her mind drifting to Auntie and the other Naturals who had perished in the explosion. She swallowed hard. After today, she hoped the gap between Naturals and Enhanced would shrink. And those who lived in the Hutongs could dwell in safety.

"Next up, we have breaking news on the genetic engineering front," an announcer declared.

Urban completely stilled, eyes riveted on the holo projection.

"There's a new law that went to vote that could change everything about the way future generations think about enhancements. We'll be back after this short commercial break."

The feed switched to an ad for Croix.

A virtual Mako smiled broadly out from the holo with his firecracker eyes. "Today is a revolutionary day for our Federation. As a company that stands for the rebels, the rule benders, and the brave, I wanted to take a moment to say a very special thank you to the person who has fought harder than anyone else to make that a reality today."

With a start, Urban's eyes widened. Everest's hand closed around hers.

The holo image shifted to reveal a lone motorcycle zipping along a tiny road up the mountain. It zoomed in to reveal Urban on her bike. The image changed to display Urban flying in the Race to the Clouds, and finally ended with Urban riding victoriously on her Gamelyon.

"Lee Urban, thank you for everything you've fought for," virtual Mako said.

A lump rose in her throat.

"Many of you know her as the girl who broke PKU's AI," Mako continued, "or the girl to have won the games against the Scorpions. Or the rookie to win the Race to the Clouds Unlimited Division. And more recently, as the world's first hybrid. What most of you don't know, is Urban is one of the most daring and brave souls I know. That's why we're honored to have her at the top of those we sponsor.

"We at the Croix family couldn't be prouder of you, Urban." The holo smiled. "As a result, I wanted to make everyone aware of a new program. For the next month, we will be matching funds and helping open up the first ever Augmented School for Naturals caught halfway between dreams and reality." Urban gasped and Everest squeezed her hand. "A school where Naturals can augment their education and become world-class artists. Applicants who are accepted will be trained and mentored by elite Artisans. Starting now, any purchase of our athleisure attire will go toward the cause."

Mouth agape, Urban's gaze went from virtual Mako to the real one standing off in a corner. He caught her eye and raised a drink in salute.

Still stunned, she looked at Everest. "How did he know about my dream?"

Everest's mouth twitched. "It seems someone must have told him."

Urban's eyes rounded. "You?"

Everest waved his hand. "Well, it took some convincing, but Mako eventually agreed."

Tears pricked at her eyes. "I don't know what to say. I can't believe everything that's happening."

Everest put an arm around her. "I'm proud of you," he said. "We all are."

The newscast returned. "And now we're back with the exciting update. Today is a day for the history books. A new law just went up for vote that could change everything about genetic enhancements."

The quiet in the room grew thick. Urban sucked in a breath.

"Since the era of genetic enhancements, parents have been paying for the best ones they can afford for their children. Each Federation has their own system of regulating enhancements, but they all have one thing in common: after birth, children are stuck with their enhancements, or lack thereof.

"That is, until today. Earlier this morning, the vote was cast for the Natural Rights Act, which would allow for genetic enhancements after birth. Instead of being given enhancements in vitro, all embryos would be given a new genetic material that allows for enhancements to be given at a later date in the child's development.

"This means all children would be given the potential to be enhanced before they are full-grown. Instead of parents with the most money purchasing the best enhancements for their children, it will be a combination of aptitude- and purchase-based. Meaning, a standardized set of testing would allow children to show what natural gifts they have and receive an enhancement based on that gifting. Children who displayed promise could earn genetic enhancements on their own, regardless of their parents' wealth."

The image shifted to another newscaster. "That's right. And just hours ago that bill went to the Capitol Prefects. It was a tight race and nearly a tie, but in an unprecedented move, Lee Urban, the world's first ever hybrid, took a seat in the house and was able to swing the vote. As of today, the Natural Rights Act is now in effect."

The room erupted into cheers and applause.

Urban's legs trembled. Virtual confetti rained down around her, as she felt an almost out-of-body sensation in it all.

Then Everest was hugging her and she heard Lillian call her name. In seconds, her sister had taken Everest's place, and they held each other, laughing with joy.

At the center of the room, Lucas was throwing real confetti and rice into the air. Father approached him with sharp, clipped steps, then smiled. A genuine, real smile. Scooping some of the rice off the floor, he joined Lucas in launching it skyward.

In front of Urban, a line of people formed, wanting to offer up their congratulations. Everest stayed at her side. There was

Mako with a tip of his trendy glasses, Ash with a slap on her back, Yukio with a silent whir and dip of his hooded head, Sato Winter with her frosty eyes shimmering with unusual lightness. Poppy and Ivan. Then too many to keep track of—a blur of faces and words.

Urban's cheeks grew sore from smiling. Her heels cut off the blood circulation in her toes. But she didn't care.

Only a year ago, she was working an AI tech job in the Outskirts, about to go off to uni for her first semester of school. Her biggest worry was her sosh and keeping her Natural genetics a secret.

Now, the whole world knew her genetics. Her DNA was being reverse-engineered and would soon be distributed to the entire Asian Federation. She was a KOL. AiE's figurehead. An Aqua. The hybrid. But more than any of that, she was completely herself.

Around her, Naturals and Enhanced hugged and celebrated. There were AiE members and Croix. House representatives and PKU students. Her family, Naturals, KOLs, and more she didn't recognize—all here to celebrate this pivotal moment in history.

I truly belong.

She glanced at Everest, and he winked at her.

She corrected herself. *We all belong.*

EPILOGUE

THREE YEARS LATER . . .

URBAN HELD UP A GIANT PAIR OF SCISSORS AND cut through a projected red ribbon.

Clip.

Lights flashed from newscasters as people cheered and clapped for the XR domes which had once been used for AI training jobs.

Now that most companies built on AI had outgrown the need for human interaction, the building had been abandoned and cheap to purchase. And since it resided halfway between the Metropolis and Outskirts, it was the perfect location for both Naturals and Enhanced.

Urban stepped forward to address the crowd and they fell silent.

Looking out, Urban saw many familiar faces. Mother and Father stood on the front row. Despite the plethora of drinks being served, Father stood empty-handed. He'd been going to sobriety meetings for almost three years and had only relapsed once.

Mother held a look of pride as she stood close to her husband. Her hair was down from its usual uptight bun, framing her face and giving it a soft expression as she smiled up at Urban.

Mother had been the first to volunteer as an art mentor for the new school. Urban's own mentor, Dr. Yukio, had been the second. He stood now with his hood back and mechanical eye glowing.

Solstice stood next to him. Back when they'd started as a small group meeting in Urban's apartment, Solstice had been one of the school's first to attend. She had a beautiful voice and was well on her way to becoming their most promising student. Her Natural family gathered around her and waved up at Urban.

Urban's gaze roved over Lillian, Lucas, Ash, and Trig, who were near the middle of the crowd. Ash had his arms wrapped around Lillian and leaned in to whisper something into her ear. She blushed and playfully jabbed him in the ribs. Ash looked up, catching Urban's gaze, and grinned.

Ash had surprised Urban by volunteering to teach. He'd once told her his dream job was to be an irrelevant professor who would make learning fun. But the thought hadn't even crossed her mind to ask him to join the school.

His parents had fought him on the decision. But Ash had won. Now, he taught the improv classes and was quickly becoming a student favorite. Then again, maybe that was simply because he gave inside tips on how to outsmart probots and shared wild stories about how he had kidnapped one.

Urban's searching eyes found Everest near the front. He smiled widely at her. He had made a full recovery and even led one of the deadliest missions to expose the rogue division of WEO and their illegal research. After successfully shutting the underwater lab down, AiE had awarded him the Valor Service Medal for his work.

His parents stood proudly beside him and were surrounded by some of the AiE members from the Outskirts.

Blossom was alone near the back. After shutting down the World Enhancement Organization's illegal lab, AiE had partnered with the respectful half of WEO on their research.

Between their combined resources, Blossom and her team were making significant headwinds in reverse-engineering the hybrid genetics.

Urban's eyes shifted to Mako who stood stoically, accompanied by several Croix executives. He had been the third to volunteer at the school, and Urban had appointed him head of PR.

It was revealed he had always been secretly supportive of Naturals. He'd already secured several partnerships and opened up a whole new division within Croix specifically with the intent of employing Naturals someday.

"Thank you to everyone who has made this dream a reality," Urban said. "This school wouldn't have been possible without your support. Our first order of business is to get an air filtration dome over our school so that we can have a safe and healthy zone for all our Natural students."

Cheering erupted at this.

"With each AI factory that closes, we plan to open up another school. We will keep opening schools and building bridges between the Enhanced and Naturals until there is no gap. And now, it's time to reveal the school's name. It's being named in honor of a friend."

A pang of sadness hit Urban. A friend who had been willing to give the ultimate sacrifice. A better friend to Urban than she had ever known.

Catching Everest's eye in the crowd, they shared a look. He understood the loss, the sacrifice, and the meaning behind her choice.

I wouldn't be standing here if not for her.

So many had made sacrifices to achieve this day.

Urban opened her mouth to continue, when a figure in a wheelchair caught her eye.

She had to be imagining it.

Then Urban noticed the backward hat.

Coral.

She's out of her coma. She's here. She's here!

Coral looked pale and worn, but there was something free in those golden and black eyes now turned up to her.

The girl standing behind Coral's wheelchair could have been her twin, only the girl looked younger. Was this her sister?

The crowd was growing restless waiting for Urban to go on with her speech. But Urban only felt her heart swell, and looking straight at Coral, she continued. "In honor of this individual, the school is named Qing's Augmented School."

Coral's mouth opened in surprise. Her sister leaned excitedly over the wheelchair to say something. Coral inclined her head to Urban and smiled a smile as free as her eyes.

"Thank you," Urban remembered to say to the applause.

She stepped down, eyes searching.

Dance music started up. People crowded around Urban, but she excused herself and wove her way to where Coral had been.

She was gone.

Urban spun around searching, but Coral had simply vanished. She stood motionless a moment, disappointment welling up within her. But then it came to her.

Only Coral would have a wheelchair that can disappear.

The thought made her smile, and she found she couldn't stop. She made her way toward a garden and away from the celebration. She needed a moment of quiet.

Taking a seat next to a stone fountain, she slipped out of her heels, watching as turquoise water splashed down into the pool. Around her, cherry blossom trees bloomed, their tantalizing, sweet aroma filling the cool, spring air.

"Great job up there."

Urban turned as Everest sat next to her.

"I couldn't have done any of this without you."

Everest gazed at her with a smile. She still got the butterflies every time he looked at her like that.

"I have a proposition for you."

Urban went completely still. "Yes?"

Everest's starry night eyes searched hers intently before he stood and withdrew something from his pocket—a delicate gold and jade band.

He got down on one knee. "Urban, I loved you when you were a Natural, I loved you as an Enhanced. I love you as the hybrid. No matter your genetics, I will always love you. You have a way of bringing beauty out of the darkest of times. Over the past three years, we've been busy trying to get this school opened, but now we've finally done it."

Urban's breath caught.

"I know things going forward will still be hard for us," Everest slowed his words, "but I couldn't imagine doing hard things with anyone other than my one-of-a-kind *meinu*. So, Lee Urban, will you marry me?"

Urban sat stunned, heart stuttering. "Yes." Her voice was barely audible. She cleared her throat. "Yes, Everest, yes!"

Everest's face broke into a wide smile and he slipped the delicate band around her finger. He stood and pulled her to her feet. With the tip of his thumb, he lifted her chin, his touch gentle and yet secure.

Her body thrummed with happiness.

How many times she'd doubted this moment would ever be possible. The last fragment of her kintsugi teaware pieced together.

Leaning down, he met her lips with his own, and she melted into his embrace.

Everest took a seat on the bench and drew her to him. As he wrapped an arm around her, warmth seeped into her. She rested her head against his sturdy chest and breathed in his familiar scent of jasmine and smoke.

They sat watching as the sun sank low over the horizon, casting the Metropolis of New Beijing in a shimming haze. There was nowhere in the world she'd rather be than in this garden, in the Outskirts, with Everest.

For the longest time, the Outskirts were a painful reminder of how she didn't belong among the Naturals. How she didn't belong anywhere. She'd never felt Enhanced enough or Natural enough.

But now she understood it wasn't *this* or *that*. It was an *and*.

Urban was Enhanced *and* Natural, a bridge between the two parts of society. The first in the history of the Asian Federation.

Natural born, Enhanced by sacrifice. Designed by something beyond herself.

She nestled into Everest's arms and looked upon her new world.

DEAR READER,

I CAN'T BELIEVE THE MOMENT HAS ARRIVED.
There were moments I doubted I'd ever type these two words,
but here we are . . .

The end.

Or, in other words, goodbye.

Before we part ways, I want to take a quick moment to thank
you. Yes, YOU. Thank you for hanging with me through The
Hybrid Series!

Thank you for being patient as I wrote it and for the encouragement along the way. Please don't be a stranger! I love con-
necting with readers on Instagram: @candace_kade_author.
Or you can stick around by signing up for my newsletter on my
website: candacekade.com.

Thank you SO much for reading my debut series. I wrote
it for anyone who's ever had a foot in two different worlds. I
hope The Hybrid Series has helped you feel seen. There are
others who straddle worlds and cultures, home and belonging.
You are not alone. You matter.

Keep reading and adventuring, friend!

—CANDACE

ACKNOWLEDGMENTS

BEFORE I STEP AWAY FROM THIS SERIES, I wanted to say a couple of thank-yous. Starting with writing friends around the world! You all have made this journey so much more fun than when I started out alone in Beijing with just my laptop.

A big thank you is in order to my BMB gals, ORWG, OCFW, SCBWI, and any other unnaturally long acronyms I've forgotten. Thanks to all my incredible beta readers for reading horrible early drafts. Special shout out to Janine, Callie, Caleb, Rachel, and Hilary. Critique partners too! Thank you Katie, Ellen, Nova, Becky, and Rebecca. Your feedback has greatly improved this book and taught me so much.

Thanks to the Starbucks near my house for fueling my caffeine addiction and letting me stay far too long and even occasionally giving me free coffee. Barista work is no joke and you all keep the world running.

Thanks to Murph and everyone at Run Lab for brainstorming the science behind my plot while simultaneously getting me stronger. Thanks Dr. Robinson, for putting on your medical hat and helping me come up with science stuff.

Thank you launch community! You all do so much to get these books off the ground. Publishing is hard and it means the world to me that so many of you have joined in spreading the word about The Hybrid Series. You all rock.

Thank you Enclave and Oasis Media for publishing The Hybrid Series. You all have been the best possible home for this story. When I first started writing *Enhanced*, I never would have dreamed it would end up with you all. And I couldn't have been more grateful that it did. From gorgeous covers, to letting me put Easter eggs in the chapter headers, amazing edits, and fantastic communication, you all have helped turn this dream into a reality. For that, you will forever have this author's gratitude. A special thank you to Lisa, Steve, Avily, and Julie for your fantastic edits! Your story eye and attention to detail has greatly enhanced this book!

Thanks to my *yingxiong* and hero, aka my husband. Going through pregnancy and post-partum with our two sons all while on deadline for this trilogy has been a wild adventure. One that would have ended with me crashing and burning if not for your steady presence.

Thanks for the countless times you took the boys so I could write and edit and edit some more. I absolutely couldn't have finished this series without you. I could write an entire novel about how I'm the luckiest girl alive, but I'll stop before I embarrass you too much. ;) Thank you!

Finally, thank you to the author of life. You were broken for us. Only you can pick up the shattered pieces of our lives and make them something beautiful.

LEE URBAN'S SEARCH FOR TRUTH COULD DESTROY EVERYTHING

THE HYBRID SERIES

Enhanced

Hybrid

Augmented

www.enclavepublishing.com

IF YOU ENJOY

THE HYBRID SERIES

YOU MIGHT LIKE THESE NOVELS:

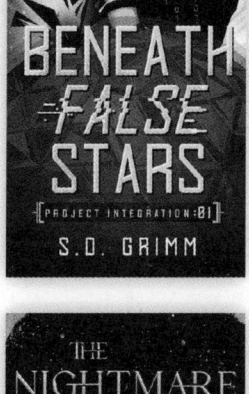
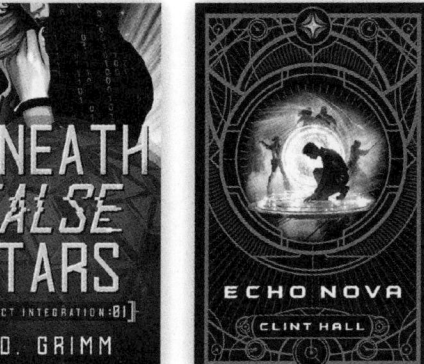

www.enclavepublishing.com